THORNS

OF

FROST

KRISTA STREET'S SUPERNATURAL WORLD

Fae of Snow & Ice
Court of Winter
Thorns of Frost
Wings of Snow
Crowns of Ice

Supernatural Curse
Wolf of Fire
Bound of Blood
Cursed of Moon
Forged of Bone

Supernatural Institute
Fated by Starlight
Born by Moonlight
Hunted by Firelight
Kissed by Shadowlight

Supernatural Community
Magic in Light
Power in Darkness
Dragons in Fire
Angel in Embers

Supernatural Standalones
Beast of Shadows

Links to all of Krista's books may be found on her website:
www.kristastreet.com

Thorns of Frost

fae fantasy romance

FAE OF SNOW & ICE
BOOK 2

KRISTA STREET

WELCOME TO THE FAE LANDS

Thorns of Frost is book two in the four-book *Fae of Snow & Ice* series, which is a slow-burn, enemies-to-lovers, fae fantasy romance.

This book takes place in the fae lands of Krista Street's *Supernatural World*. Although Krista's other paranormal romance books also features the fae lands, the *Fae of Snow & Ice* series is entirely separate so may be read before or after her previous series.

Brashier Sea

Ice Caves
Pentlebim

Kroravee

Isalee

Solisarium

Prinavee

Gielis

Floating Meadows

Highsteer Castle

Osaravee

Murlands

Duval

Harrivee

Guxbee

Bay of Korl

Barvilum

Tala Sea

Glassen Barrier Islands

GLOSSARY

Territories of the Solis Continent

Harrivee – the middle southern territory, coastal cities often fighting with the Lochen fae. Territory color is yellow.

Isalee – the northernmost territory, Cliffs of Sarum on its northern peak. Territory color is white.

Kroravee – the northwestern territory, most reclusive territory, very unwelcoming even to other Solis fae. Territory color is purple.

Mervalee – the easternmost territory, richly blessed with *orem,* borders the Nolus continent. Territory color is green.

Osaravee – the southwestern territory, coastal cities often fighting with the Lochen fae. Territory color is red.

Prinavee – the central territory, where Solisarium, the capital of the Solis continent, resides. Territory color is the royal palate: blue, black, and silver.

❄

Seas of the fae lands

Adriastic Sea – the ocean to the west of the Nolus continent.

Brashier Sea – the most northern sea in the fae lands, large icebergs often present.

Tala Sea – the ocean to the south of the Solis continent.

Terms

Affinity – the magical ability that each Solis fae develops at maturing age. Maturing age happens around thirteen years of age in the hundreds-year-long life span of a Solis fairy. A Solis fairy's affinity can be common or quite rare, weak or very strong. Most Solis fae only have one affinity. Very powerful Solis fae have more than one.

Archon – a fairy that holds power over a village, city, territory, or land. There are tiers of archons, and the more land that an archon manages, the more politically powerful that archon is. The most powerful archon on the Solis continent is King Novakin.

Blessed Mother – a magical life force of the fae lands that nurtures growth and life among the fae. The Blessed Mother is not a goddess but a force from nature that is similar in strength and power to the gods. The Blessed Mother is believed to reside deep within the land at the heart of the planet. This belief is unique to the Solis fae.

Defective – a Solis fae who is magicless and never develops an affinity.

Full season – the equivalent of one year.

Millee – the Solis fae unit of measurement, the equivalent of one mile.

Orem – the magic that infuses the Solis continent, allowing plants and crops to grow in freezing temperatures. *Orem* is replenished by celestial events and comes from the gods.

Solls – a term Solis fae use when they clink glasses to celebrate, like Cheers.

Fae races

Solis fae – the Solis fae reside on the icy, most northern continent of the fae lands planet. Solis fae have silvery white hair, crystalline blue eyes, and wings. They typically live for thousands of years.

Nolus fae – the Nolus fae reside on the central continent. They often have various shades of colorful hair, pointy teeth, glowing skin, and otherworldly strength. They typically live three hundred years, but royal Nolus fae live for thousands of years.

Lochen fae – the Lochen fae reside on a southern continent, islands, and in the seas throughout the fae lands. They can morph into fish-like creatures, similar to mermaids, but they can also walk on two legs and live on land. There are subspecies of Lochen fae that live in fresh-water rivers, lakes, and ponds. The Lochen fae typically have green eyes and varying skin shades and hair colors.

Silten fae – the Silten fae reside on a separate continent across the Adriastic Sea, west of the Nolus continent. They have animalistic features: horns, scales, hooves, and tails, and they are the most varied in how they appear. Most live in underground dens, hollow logs, or wooded forests, but Silten fae with more human-like bodies reside in cities.

Fae plants and food

Acorlis – a root vegetable, sweet flavor with an orange skin, similar to a sweet potato.

Cottonum – a plant similar to cotton.

Leminai – a bright-green alcoholic drink common throughout the fae lands.

Salopas – a fairy version of a bar with no serving staff. There are magically enchanted trays that serve patrons.

Fae animals

Colantha – a large cat that resides in jungles.

Domal – an animal similar to a horse but more intelligent.

Ice bear – a large bear with a naturally white furry coat and six-inch claws, which stands eight feet tall on two legs. An ice bear's coat can change color to match its surroundings.

Snowgum – the most feared ice creature whose magical ability allows it to become invisible for short spans. Snowgums resemble a large feline.

Trisilee – a tiny bird with wings that flap hundreds of miles per hour, like a hummingbird.

PRONUNCIATION GUIDE

Names

Ilara Seary – Ill-are-uh Seer-ee

Norivun Achul – Nor-ih-vun Ah-cool

Cailis – Kay-liss

Krisil – Kris-ill

Evis – Eve-iss

Sandus – Sand-us

Balbus – Bell-bus

Patrice – Pah-treese

Haisley – Hay-slee

Nuwin – New-win

Daiseeum – Day-zee-um

Novakin – Naw-vah-kin

Lissandra – Li-sahn-druh

Drachu – Draw-koo

Michas – My-kiss

Sirus – Seer-us

Meegana – Mee-gah-nuh

Georgyanna – George-ee-ah-nuh
Matron Olsander – May-trun Ole-sand-err

Fae Races & Territories
Solis – Saw-liss
Nolus – Naw-luss
Lochen – Lock-uhn
Silten – Sill-tun
Mervalee – Merr-vuh-lee
Isalee – Iss-ah-lee
Prinavee – Prin-uh-vee
Harrivee – Hair-uh-vee
Osaravee – Oh-sar-uh-vee
Kroravee – Quor-uh-vee

CHAPTER 1

"You're serious? I could be your *wife*?" My eyes widened even more as I gazed up at Prince Norivun Deema Melustral Achul, first son of the king, Bringer of Darkness, Death Master of the continent, son of Prinavee Territory, and crown prince and heir to the Winter Court's throne.

The prince growled low in his throat as his sapphire irises burned brightly. Artful silver strands of hair flowed to his shoulders, and massive wings tipped with talons rose from his back. Those wings looked as lethal as the crown prince.

"That's correct," he said.

My sister, Cailis, threw up her hands and stormed across the room.

"Please go," I whispered. "All of you."

Behind the prince, his four guards waited—Haxil, Ryder, Nish, and Sandus. Instead of heeding my request, they all looked to their prince for direction.

"Very well." The prince straightened from my bed, his aura

pounding from him in waves, before he strode from the Exorbiant Chamber with his guards, Murl, and Daiseeum following.

"I shall have refreshments delivered shortly. I'm sure you're famished," Daiseeum called from the door before bobbing her head and dipping into a curtsy.

"Thank you, Daiseeum," I replied automatically.

Once they all left, Cailis fumed. "This is absurd. Honestly, it's the most ridiculous thing I've ever heard. You have to join the Rising Queen Trial to be his potential *wife*?"

I gripped the bedsheets tighter as my stomach flipped. "So I'm not dreaming?"

"I wish this was a dream. I've been worried sick since he took you last month, despite your letters, but *this*—" She shook her head. "I never imagined anything like that."

"That makes two of us."

I flopped back onto my pillows. Sunlight shone through my bed chambers' glass doors. Outside, my beautiful garden glowed vibrantly in my private courtyard. The thriving *orem* in its soil meant our normal winter landscape didn't affect it.

I closed my eyes as I remembered what else I needed to do. "There's more than just the Trial, Cailis. There's so much more that's gone on during the past month."

She scowled. "What else has happened?"

I opened my mouth to reply, but a knock came on my door, and then Daiseeum entered, carrying a tray of food. My stomach growled, and I sat up when she placed it beside me.

"Enjoy, m'lady." She curtsied, her gaze darting between me and Cailis before she departed.

My sister's eyes bulged. "So much food."

"There always is."

❄

THE EMPTY TRAY sat between us as I leaned back, sipping my tea as I finished telling my sister everything that had happened since the prince had whisked me away from our village in Mervalee Territory over a month ago.

Her baffled expression grew, getting a frown out of me. "Did they censor all of this from my letters?" I asked.

She nodded. "I knew you were alive, but everything you just told me was blacked out." Nibbling her lip, she said, "So, let me get this straight . . . Prince Norivun is demanding that you save our continent by using your new affinity to make the crops grow again?"

I nodded.

A slow smile spread across Cailis's face until it turned into a wide grin. She laughed in delight. "Ilara . . . you have an affinity! *Multiple* affinities. You're not a defective anymore! And you have a fire affinity, just like mother and Tormesh did. Oh, Ilara, this is joyous news!" She grabbed my hands, then pulled me into a hug.

The anxiety that had been pulsing through me halted. A soft laugh escaped me too when she squealed. Air, fire, and the ability to create life pulsed inside me. I had actual affinities now, like most Solis fae. I wasn't a defective any longer. I'd simply bloomed late.

Yeah, like ten winters late.

"I still can't believe it," I whispered.

She pulled back, her smile still in place, until she said in a slightly scolding tone, "But, you also agreed to replenish all of our crops in a sealed bargain?"

I cringed, knowing her disapproval was coming next.

Sure enough, she let out a frustrated sigh. "Although I'm happy that you've finally bloomed, that was a very foolish decision, Ilara. How could anyone possibly fulfill that? It's one thing to revive a small garden but another thing entirely to replenish a continent's land mass."

"I know." I shook my head, still feeling sluggish from the unconsciousness I'd awoken from. "I did it in hopes that he'd be forced to let me go and leave me to live in peace."

"Yet, it still requires you fulfilling the bargain in order for that to occur."

I winced. "Right, well . . . in my defense, I was drunk when I did it."

Her jaw dropped, and I wanted to smack a pillow over my head.

"If it's any consolation," I added in a rush, "the prince is convinced I'm capable of replenishing the continent's *orem*, even though I've spent the past week trying to revive a field in Harrivee with nothing to show for it."

"And if he's wrong and you *can't*, you're bound to him indefinitely."

This time, I did smack a pillow over my face.

"So, not only did he kill Tormesh for speaking the truth last season about the dying crops, and then our parents when they came to the court to ask what became of him, but now Prince Norivun is demanding that *you* fix our continent's dying crops after finally admitting there *is* a problem?" She let out a disgusted sound. "What a load of hypocritical domal dung."

I pulled the pillow from my face to see Cailis scowling. And witnessing her righteous anger stirred the flame inside me, the fire that had raged so hotly when I'd first met the crown prince of the Court of Winter over a month ago. I'd forgotten . . . no, not forgotten . . . I'd temporarily dismissed what he'd done to our family, letting him charm me over the past week, but he was a murderer.

How did I forget that?

"I'm an imbecile," I said with a groan.

Cailis's expression softened. "I suppose what's done is done. We'll have to deal with it now." She patted my hand. "Enough of all of that, though. How are you feeling? You scared the daylights out of me last night when they brought you back to this room unconscious."

"I'm okay. I guess." I laid a hand on my stomach where that ever-present sensation rumbled. And to think all along what I'd been feeling were my affinities, not indigestion. "It's a lot to take in, though. I'm still coming to terms with it."

So much had happened since the prince's Betrothed Ball last evening. I still couldn't believe that I'd shared a scorching encounter with the murderer of my family on the throne room's balcony, only to then be attacked by Vorl and be entered into the Rising Queen Trial.

I shivered when I recalled how my village's archon had nearly choked the life from me.

Tilting my neck, I ran a finger against my skin.

Cailis frowned. "Does your throat still hurt?"

"It's tender, which I suppose shouldn't be surprising considering Vorl nearly crushed my windpipe."

"Bastard." She seethed. "At least he's been arrested. That's the only good thing that's come out of this."

"Agreed."

"Now, we just need to get you out of that Trial."

Another knock came on the door, and then Sandus, the prince's personal guard who he'd assigned to me, peeked in.

He wore traditional colored clothing—blue, black, and silver. As always, two swords peeked out from beneath his wings, one on either side of him in a crisscross pattern, and his beard looked freshly trimmed.

"There's someone here to see you, love."

My spine stiffened. I could only imagine it would be Prince Norivun striding into the room.

Sandus opened the door wider, and my heart thumped painfully, but it was Sir Featherton, the Rising Queen Trial archon, who sauntered into my chambers.

Sir Featherton had introduced the other three females in the Trial just last night—Lady Meegana Ockson, Lady Georgyanna Endalaver, and Lady Beatrice Leafton.

He hadn't introduced me yet, though. My admittance was still too new.

Bringing a fist to his chest in traditional Solis greeting, he bowed. "Lady Ilara Seary, daughter of Mervalee Territory, it is a pleasure to officially meet you. I'm the Rising Queen Trial archon, Sir Edmund Featherton."

Sir Featherton was tall, thin, and he held his chin high when he straightened. Navy slacks covered his legs. A crisp white top covered his upper half, and wings of a soft black draped down his back.

I gave a tight smile and wished I was properly dressed and not still in my nightclothes. I figured either my sister or Daiseeum had changed me into them when I'd been unconscious. At least they were modest, a full top and pants.

Regardless, I mimicked his movements, bringing a fist to my chest. "It's nice to meet you, Sir Featherton."

I pulled the covers higher, but Sir Featherton was either oblivious to my embarrassment, or he didn't care, because he clasped his hands behind his back beneath his wings and faced me squarely.

His gaze flickered briefly to my black hair. The crown prince's illusion spell, which had concealed its true color, had shattered last night after my affinities had manifested. But I wasn't the only Solis fairy with black hair. Queen Lissandra also bore that feature. Only, most Solis fae didn't know that since the queen's illusion affinity kept it hidden.

"What can we do for you, Sir Featherton?" Cailis asked briskly.

He gave her a cursory glance. "The king has sent me to explain the rules of the Trial to Lady Seary. Normally, the Trial's tests would have taken place next month, but since Lady Seary's affinities have only just manifested, the king has prolonged the Trial. You've been granted three months to train before the first test. During that time, you shall also be placed in the Trial's courtship, which has also been extended to three months."

Cailis scowled as blood pounded through my ears.

"Tests?" I murmured. "Courtship?"

"Indeed." Sir Featherton gave a slight bow. "There shall be three tests at the end of your three months of training. You will be required to compete with the other females in the tests. During the three-month Trial period, you will also date Prince Norivun. This is so you may become better acquainted with him should you end up his wife. However, despite any affections you may develop, at the end of the Trial, the winner will ultimately be chosen as his bride."

My gut churned, and not from my magic.

Cailis's scowl grew, but then the last bit of Sir Featherton's explanation seeped into my brain.

I sat up straighter. "So if I lose the Trial, I won't marry Prince Norivun, and I'll be free of any obligations to him?" A huge rush of relief swept through me. That seemed easy enough. I would simply make sure I lost the Trial.

Cailis exhaled, and we both shared a side-eye.

Sir Featherton's lips thinned. "No, my lady. If you lose, you shall marry another of the king's choosing. Throughout the Trial, other naturally blessed nobles will also be courting you."

My jaw felt as though it dropped to the floor.

Cailis's eyebrows rose as her wings flexed. "So you're saying that Ilara will be forced into an arranged marriage *no matter what*?"

Sir Featherton gave a curt nod. "Correct. It's the king's orders."

"But why?" I asked, trying to keep the panic from my voice. "Why must I marry someone the king chooses?"

Sir Featherton arched an eyebrow. "The king has resurrected an ancient tradition among the Solis in order to further advance our race. He's decided it's in the best interest of our continent to enact the Olirum Accords."

"Olirum Accords?" The only Olirum reference I knew of was a celestial event. "Is it related to the Eve of Olirum, the annual celestial event when the northernmost star shines its brightest?"

Sir Featherton canted his head. "Indeed, *but* if you paid

attention during your history studies in secondary school, that eve also used to be a time when the territories' elite were engaged. It was a time of great celebration. The most powerful children of each territory were married to fae of a neighboring territory to spread the Solis magic and further advance our race's power. It was a time of very strategic matchmaking and led to the great Solis nation we are today."

I shook my head, racking my brain for what I could remember of our history. "But that tradition ended over a thousand winters ago when it was deemed archaic and barbaric, right?"

The Trial archon's nostrils flared. "Only some viewed it that way. Others saw it as weakness on Lord Nifilim's part— Prince Norivun's grandfather, who ruled Prinavee Territory nearly twelve hundred winters ago. He only banished the tradition since he was trying to appease the masses who were rebelling against such control."

My heart pounded as I tried to recall more of our continent's history. I knew some of it from primary school, but my education had been stunted as a field laborer, and I'd never taken an interest in the court.

Until coming to Solisarium over a month ago, I hadn't really cared about royal politics or history. It'd been so far removed from my life in Mervalee Territory that it hadn't affected me.

But now those courtly politics were dictating my life.

Trying to calm my breathing, I said, "But what purpose could the Olirum Accords possibly serve now? That tradition was practiced during a time when the territories weren't united. Now they are. We have one king and one rule. What advantage could they possibly have?"

"True, King Novakin united us all, but that doesn't mean our race still can't advance." Sir Featherton inclined his head toward the courtyard—the courtyard that *I* had restored to life. "The king wants to ensure the Solis are the superior fae race in our realm. Breeding powerful fae will help grant that."

I scowled, but I didn't know why I was so shocked. None of this should have been surprising, given what I'd learned of the king. He'd forced Queen Lissandra to marry him because she held five affinities—something I'd never heard of any female possessing. And the son they'd birthed together, the crown prince, held six affinities. Prince Norivun was the most powerful fairy on the continent.

Now, the king apparently wanted to replicate that power. With dozens of fae as strong as Prince Norivun, our race would be unstoppable. Not even the powerful Nolus—the fae race residing on the continent south of us—would be able to stop us if war broke out.

I leaned back into my pillows as a million thoughts raced through my mind. Just last night, Michas Crimsonale, Lord Crimsonale's oldest son, had told me that there'd been hushed talk of invading the Nolus continent. Their climate was warmer and would ensure we were all fed since they didn't need magic to grow their crops, not like we did on our frozen continent that depended upon the celestial events to replenish our land's *orem*—something that they'd failed to do as of late. Entire territory's crops had died out.

Frowning, I wondered if that had anything to do with this old tradition being reborn. Perhaps the king wanted to birth and control powerful Solis fae so he could use them for his bidding in acts of war. Or maybe the two were mutually exclusive.

Because Michas had spoken of invasion as though it were outside of the king, as though it was coming from elsewhere, so perhaps the king wanted to build his army to deter other fae from thinking they could control the destiny of our race. Perhaps the king was doing this to *prevent* a war with the Nolus. But that would only work if he could control the powerful fae who were born and if war wasn't imminent.

I brought a hand to my head. A headache brewed. I didn't know what the motivations were behind any of this, and suddenly, I didn't want to know. I didn't want to be a part of this. I wasn't cut out for cunning court politics or games of power play. I was just a farm girl from Mervalee who, until a month ago, had been magicless, wingless, and lacked any desirable Solis strengths. But even though I was still wingless, the king apparently thought I was worthy of holding onto.

Ock.

Cailis glared at Sir Featherton. "Is there anything else my sister needs to know?"

"There are a few more details that I'll need to ensure she's aware of before the tests, but I can return later to explain." He bowed again, then did a one-eighty and strode from the room.

The second we were alone, I collapsed my head into my hands. "This is insane. First the prince takes me from our village, locks me up for a month, and then I have three affinities manifest, only to be told that not only will I have to save our continent from starvation, but I'll also have to marry a male of the king's choosing so I can produce powerful Solis children for some unknown purpose?"

My skin crawled just thinking about it. Whatever I'd hoped to achieve in my lifetime, *that* had never been it.

Cailis wrapped an arm around my shoulders and squeezed, then flared one of her wings protectively around my bare back.

"We could run away," she said quietly. "We could flee to another territory or seek shelter on another continent. Other Solis fae have done it. Why can't we?"

"Run away?" The thought had never occurred to me. I'd always been too guarded in the castle to escape, and the Exorbiant Chamber had proven impenetrable.

But part of the bargain that the prince and I had struck guaranteed I would never be locked within these chambers, or any chambers, ever again by him. Which meant escape was actually a possibility now.

I clasped her free hand and squeezed. "The gods would surely unleash either hideous magic or a curse upon me for failing to fulfill my bargain with the prince."

Cailis pulled her bottom lip into her mouth. "I know, but there must be a way out of this. Because there's no way in this realm or the next that I'm letting them do to you what Sir Featherton just demanded."

Frowning, I tried to think of an escape, and my breath caught when I remembered something the Lochen fae king, Drachu, had told me the night the prince had flown us to the Glassen Barrier Islands. The Lochen ruler had sensed power in me and had been intrigued.

Should you tire of the death warlord, my shores are open to you.

My chest rose faster. That could be a way out of this. There was no guarantee the Nolus fae or Silten fae would welcome us, but the Lochen surely would. Or perhaps Drachu would demand something of me too. I could just be trading one captor for another. Regardless, it didn't stop the fact that I would be running from our bargain.

I took a deep breath, knowing that we shouldn't do anything rash. If I truly was to escape the fate the king demanded of me, Cailis and I needed to work out a solid plan before acting.

But before I could even contemplate any further treasonous thoughts, another knock came on the door.

This time, Sandus didn't open it.

My heart seized when the crown prince strode into the room, not waiting for my approval to enter.

His aura pounded into me, his look dark and intense. Storm clouds raged in his eyes that were as dark as his all-black attire. Wind flew around him from his air elemental affinity, and the air felt as though it was sucked from my lungs.

Despite trying to stop myself, my gaze crawled over his muscular thighs, toned waist, slabbed chest, and broad shoulders. My stomach coiled, as something buried deep within my soul seemed to awaken in his presence even though he looked every bit the Death Master of the continent as he blazed a trail directly for me.

No, no, no. Damn this attraction to him, and damn my body for responding.

The prince stopped before me and eyed the empty tray. "Lady Seary, I trust you are ready now to begin the day."

His husky tone rolled through me, lapping at my insides

and threatening to suck me out to the sea that was Prince Norivun's masterful aura. I latched onto the memories of what he'd done. *Tormesh. Mother. Father. Tormesh. Mother. Father.*

I recited those names over and over and over. Again and again.

I would *not* be attracted to the murderer of my family. I would *not* respond to him as I just had. And I certainly would *not* envision the kiss we'd shared last night.

Gripping the sheets to my lap, I fought against my ridiculous innate urges. For whatever reason, my body wanted him, but my mind did not, so I would *not* show wanton longing or be weak or allow myself to feel any of the tumbling emotions that were spiraling through me at this very second.

This male was my enemy.

The only emotion I would allow myself to feel for him was hatred.

Images of my brother and parents suffering, then dying in the throne room pierced my mind. Pain threatened to engulf me, but I latched onto those mental pictures, and slowly, any heightened sense of longing for the prince faded.

"Back to fetch me already?" I said coolly.

His eyes narrowed, and he cast my sister a side-eye. "Leave us."

My hand shot out to cover Cailis's before she could rise from the bed. "No. She stays."

The prince's power vibrated the room, making the stones beneath my bed shiver. "I said she was to *leave us*."

"And I said she was *to stay*."

Cailis's hand trembled. I could only imagine the vivid fears running through her mind. She had no idea that I commonly challenged the prince.

"I see your insolence hasn't changed in the slightest despite the fact that you may be my wife." A flash of wildness shone in his eyes, but in a blink, it was gone.

I frowned. "I won't be your wife."

"What makes you think that?"

"Because I'd have to win the Trial to be your wife, and I don't know how to control any of my affinities or wield magic, so how could I possibly win?"

"You'll win because you're going to train. Speaking of that, you'll begin training with your tutor today. Your studies will start in earnest this afternoon, and since she's the best tutor on the continent, I have no doubt you'll succeed in three months when the tests commence."

I eyed him warily, not for the first time sensing he wished me to be the victor. "It sounds like you . . . *want* me to win."

His eyes shuttered, then flicked down to my neck. To where bruises lay from Vorl's attack. The crown prince's hands pumped into fists, and his aura flared hotter.

My brow furrowed, and my heart thrummed faster, just like it did every time I thought of my village archon.

"Where is Vorl anyway?" I asked, changing the subject.

"The castle dungeon. Still alive. I haven't decided what I'm going to do with him yet, but I have no doubt it will include some kind of torture."

Cailis recoiled, a small sound of disgust parting her lips as I choked out, "You're going to torture him?"

Prince Norivun smiled darkly. "At the very least. He touched you. *Hurt* you. For that he will pay."

The air seemed to thin between us again, and the tension rolling from the crown prince was so thick I could have drowned in it. He was going to hurt Vorl. For me.

"What if I don't want that?"

His eyebrows rose. "You don't want him punished for what he did to you?"

"Of course, I want him punished, but torture is—" Nausea roiled my stomach.

The crown prince's twisted smile grew. "I won't make you witness it if you're squeamish. I shall be the one who enjoys that pleasure."

"Do you hate him that much?"

A low growl tore from his throat, and Cailis jumped.

"He purposefully hurt you. He was trying to *kill* you. I saw enough to know that. When you stopped me from—" His jaw clenched so hard that his teeth made a grinding noise. "From ending him then and there, it allowed me enough time to realize you gave me a gift. Now, I shall be able to take my time with him." A perverse light shone in his eyes.

Cailis made another sound, a gurgle between disbelief and horror.

I squeezed her hand. "You're not helping to dispel the preconceived notion my sister has of you being a complete monster."

"Pity. I apologize." The prince bowed mockingly, and I realized he was still so caught up in his fantasies of what he wanted to do to Vorl that he probably didn't even realize how visceral he looked at the moment. He was like a dark demon coming to collect one's soul, and he was savoring every bit of it.

And to think I'd *wanted* the prince only last night. This convoluted male of a fae.

But I'd seen other sides of him too, kinder sides. Softer sides. But looking at him now, I wondered if I'd been a fool. A fool indeed since my fluttering attraction to him still burned my insides.

A flash of Prince Norivun's mouth on mine, his powerful body caught between my thighs, and my fingers threaded through his hair kissed my thoughts. I'd more than wanted him last night. I'd nearly begged him to take me.

Mother Below! I lurched from the bed and strode away from him. I had to. I didn't trust myself around him.

"Why are you here?" I called over my shoulder. "Isn't there some innocent family you should be murdering?"

Prince Norivun's aura pounded into my back as he followed me, and I could only imagine what my sister was thinking as she sat mutely on the bed. With a start, I realized it was the first time I'd ever seen Cailis at a loss for words.

I rounded the turn near the wardrobe and entered the bathing chamber, but the prince followed, not even slowing when I tried to slam the door on his face.

His hand clamped around my wrist and whirled me to him.

My breath sucked in when my body slammed against his as my breasts flattened against his chest. His arm curled around my waist, and he dipped his head—his eyes like pools of stars, so bright and dazzling that they threatened to suck my soul into their powerful galaxy.

"Is that how you treat your crown prince?"

I struggled in his hold. "Let me go."

His grip tightened as his gaze narrowed. "You responded to

me last night. I felt and scented how much you wanted me. Why the sudden change now?"

"I did not want—" My head snapped back. "Wait. What? *Scented?*"

His lips curved, and my jaw dropped.

"You have a sensory affinity too? You can smell things other fae can't?"

He shrugged. "It's not my fault if I can detect how much you desire me."

My pulse pounded like a wild beast as I frantically thought back to all of the times I'd been aroused by him, and to think he might have known it. No, he *had* known. *Blessed Mother.* Heat rose in my cheeks.

"What does that affinity allow you to detect?"

"In addition to an overall heightened sense of smell? I can also scent emotions."

Fuck me. So the prince had his death affinity, his illusion affinity, an air elemental affinity, and a sensory affinity. But that still left two more that I didn't know about.

"What are your other two affinities, my prince? I know you have six total, but I only know of four."

His lips twitched.

I fumed and had the strongest urge to slap him. "You're not going to tell me, are you?"

"It would be more fun to let you figure it out. But as I was saying, why the sudden change from last night? You wanted me then. Are you truly going to act like you don't want me now? That you don't wish to be my wife?"

I tried to shove him away, but he didn't budge. "Why would

you want me to be your wife? Why would you want a female who despises you to be married to you?"

"But you don't despise me."

"I do."

His lips kicked up in the most arrogant smile. "You don't. I haven't scented true hatred from you in over a week, and you certainly didn't despise me last night, even though it seems you're trying to forget our little encounter on the balcony."

My insides tightened, and a flush of desire swept through me that was as raging as the northern winds. His smile grew. *Bastard.* I swatted at his arm, but he didn't budge. Not even an inch.

"I was drunk. I always get a bit excitable when I'm drinking."

"Is that so?" He ran the tip of his nose along the column of my throat. "You weren't drunk, and don't even try to deny it. I can scent your lie."

Blessed Mother! I could hide nothing from this male.

He continued that embarrassingly pleasurable movement along my skin.

I gritted my teeth. *Tormesh. Mother. Father. Tormesh. Mother. Father.*

I needed to reclaim the absolute hatred I'd once felt so easily for this male. Because he was right. As much as I didn't want to admit it, I didn't hate him as much as I had when we first met. The other sides I'd seen—the tender, caring, and empathetic sides—were clouding my thoughts.

Truthfully, he wasn't all dark. Just . . . mostly dark. Him relishing the thought of torturing Vorl reaffirmed that.

But the thought of what Cailis would think of me if I fell for him . . .

My hands tightened into fists. "I could never truly desire you, and I certainly can't marry the male who killed my family."

He stilled and lifted his head. A moment of silence passed between us, and then another. Searching my gaze, he finally said, "Do you trust me, Lara?"

I frowned. "Trust you? Of course not. How could I possibly trust someone who wants to *torture* another?"

His arm around my waist tightened. "Can I trust you?"

My frown deepened. "What in the realm are you going on about now? What does trust have to do with anything?"

His jaw clenched, and something flashed in his eyes before he veiled it. He gripped the sink behind me, caging me in as he leaned down.

My entire body grew rigid, even more so when his nose brushed lightly against my neck again, then his tongue darted out for a taste.

I shivered, and a sound of satisfaction rumbled from his throat. "Even though you fight me, your body doesn't. You're primed for me."

I shoved against him, *hard. Tormesh. Mother. Father. Tormesh. Mother. Father.* "Let. Me. Go."

His jaw clenched until the muscle in the corner looked so sharp it could cut through glass. With a rough inhale, he finally released me.

I jerked my chin up as my heart hammered. Every fiber of my body was coiled. Ready. My magic hummed with a vengeance in my gut even though I had no idea how to use it, while my core ached with desire for him. I wanted to stab myself.

But even though I had no rational explanation for my body's fiery response to him, I did know one thing. I was the maker of my destiny, even if the king and the crown prince were trying to rule my fate. I would find a way out of this— Trial or no.

I crossed my arms and concentrated on controlling my breathing. "Again, why are you here?"

Nostrils flaring, he replied, "I'm here to take you to Harrivee Territory. There's something you need to see."

CHAPTER 2

C ailis sat wide-eyed on the bed when the prince and
    I returned to the living area.

"I need to get dressed," I said briskly to Prince
Norivun.

He leaned against the wall and hooked a foot around his
ankle. "Don't let me stop you."

I glared at him. "Why don't you keep Sandus company in
the hallway, and I'll let you know when I'm ready?"

"Do you need me to ring for Daiseeum?"

I rolled my eyes. "Do you really not know how to put on a
tunic and a pair of pants without someone's help?"

His lips curved. "Five minutes. Then I'm coming back in."
With that, he strolled to the door and let himself out.

The second the prince was out of the room, Cailis leaped
from the bed. "Blessed Mother Above and Below, what in the
realm was *that*?" she screeched. "Do you want to get yourself
killed?"

I rummaged through the wardrobe, searching for the lilac-colored tunic the castle tailor had made for me. "Prince Norivun won't kill me."

"He's a murderer, Ilara. He's the *Death Master* of the continent. Of course, he will kill you!"

"You're wrong. He won't because I'm too valuable."

Her forehead scrunched up as I shimmied out of my nightclothes, then pulled on my underthings. Smoothing her forehead, she did a once-over on me. "You've gained weight."

I shrugged. "And you will too. They have far too much food in this castle while everyone else on the continent is starving."

She looked down at her thin limbs and hollow stomach, then seemed to remember what we'd been discussing and snapped her head up. "And what was with that weird argument between you two? What happened on a balcony?"

"You heard that?"

"It was kind of hard not to. You two were practically shouting at each other."

A flush worked up my neck as I slipped the tunic over my head. It didn't fit quite as snuggly as it had before, which told me Daiseeum had made good on her promise to have the tailor return and let out my clothes now that I wasn't skin and bones. I smoothed the fabric over my waist and hips. It fit perfectly.

"Well? What happened?"

"I don't know," I finally said when Cailis began to tap her foot.

"Yes, you do."

I spun away from her and grabbed a pair of black leggings. "He's insane. That's all you need to know."

"Well, obviously he's demented, but you don't actually want to win this ridiculous Trial. Right?"

I hated the hint of doubt that crept into her tone. I hated that she truly thought I was capable of having feelings for a male who'd done what he had to not only our family but to countless others. But then something the prince had once told me flashed through my mind, about how he didn't enjoy killing fae but did what was necessary.

But is that even true? He certainly looked delighted at the thought of murdering Vorl.

I finished dressing—pulling on a pair of supple leather boots before grabbing the fur-lined purple gloves the prince had purchased for me in Pentlebim's market.

I snuck a peek at my sister before mumbling, "For what it's worth, he may be horrible, but he's not quite as evil as we both thought he was."

Her eyebrows shot up. "What does that mean?"

"I'm just saying that he's not purely evil, not as we always assumed. I have seen some good in him. He won't hurt me *or* you. I'm sure of that." I cringed. "In all honesty, I have found myself enjoying his company on occasion."

A flash of betrayal pierced her eyes.

"Cailis, I'm sorry." I quickly grabbed her hands and squeezed. "I know what he did. It's atrocious that I don't despise him even more now that I've met him, but—" I didn't know how to explain it. There was something about the prince, something I'd seen hints of that told me there was more to his story than I was aware of. He wasn't purely evil. Capable of doing evil things, yes, but I didn't think he enjoyed it. Well, maybe he would enjoy it with Vorl . . .

❄ 24 ❄

Cailis's lips thinned as she ripped her hands free and gripped my shoulders. "He just talked about *torturing* a male, Ilara. Have you lost your mind?"

"You don't even want to know how many times I've asked myself that very same question."

She shook her head. "What's gotten into you? Have they influenced you? Poisoned you? Blessed Mother, have they cast a love spell on you?"

"A love spell?" I snorted. "Are you serious? I don't love him. I'm just saying he's not as horrible as we thought." I waved my hand at the Exorbiant Chamber. "He's not keeping me in the dungeons, is he? And he let me write to you. Don't you see what I'm saying? He's not purely evil."

She crossed her arms, then arched an eyebrow. "He murdered our parents, Lara. He murdered Tormesh. Why do I need to remind you of that?" Disgust rolled across her features, and for the first time in our lives, something else did too. Disappointment.

Burning shame swept through me like crashing waves on the Tala Sea. I lowered my gaze to my toes. "I know. Honestly, I know. Don't worry. I would never forget that."

"You better not."

My stomach clenched. "Anyway, I need to get going. The prince and I have been working on a field in Harrivee Territory. He's taking me there again today."

"Can I come with you?"

She asked the question too quickly, and the look in her eyes told me why she really wanted to join us.

She didn't trust me.

My sister truly felt I was falling under some ridiculous spell the prince was weaving over me, and she probably saw it as her duty to free me from it.

"I'll be fine, Cailis."

Her lips pursed, reminding me of Daiseeum, my lady's servant. "See to it that you are, Ilara Seary."

Her meaning smacked me in the face. She'd just addressed me as our mother had when we roamed too late in the fields or were getting into mischief with Birnee and Finley.

Keep your distance from the prince. Don't fall any further for him. Don't betray me.

Her unspoken words made an ache form in my gut, but Cailis was right. Even if I had reluctant feelings for the prince, I wouldn't act on them.

I slipped my hands into my gloves, my thoughts finally aligning with hers. "You need to stop worrying. I won't do anything stupid with the prince, and you're right about what you said earlier. We should find a way to escape. But we have to be smart about it. We'll have to plan wisely."

"Do you mean that?" A look of such intense relief washed over her features that guilt again burned in me. My sister was what mattered. Not the prince. Not the court.

"I do." But then my thoughts flew to the Solis continent and the millions of fae who called our frozen land home. To the bargain I'd made with the prince to restore our continent's *orem*. If Cailis and I left, they would all starve.

The headache I'd been battling when Sir Featherton had been prattling on threatened to rise again.

"I'll see you when I get back." I kissed Cailis on the cheek, then strode from the room and out into the hall where the prince waited.

I tried to ignore the knowing smirk Sandus wore. I figured the guard was aware of the prince and my proclivities last night. Either that or he'd heard our heated arguing in the bathing chamber.

But seeing Sandus's amusement together with the disgust from my sister reaffirmed how easily I'd fallen under the prince's charm. I couldn't allow it to continue.

Cailis. Cailis. Cailis.

My sister was what mattered the most now.

It was best that I remembered that.

THE PRINCE MISTPHASED us to just outside of Barvilum, the small seaside town on the southern edge of Harrivee Territory.

Waves crashed against the shore, and the sun shone brightly when the realm formed again after we'd been ripped through mist and shadows, air and wind.

Familiar ground covered in snow appeared beneath my feet, and the faint call of birds cawed in the sky.

Nothing but the sea, sun, and snow surrounded us. Farther out in the ocean, the Glassen Barrier Islands were visible, along with huge icebergs floating in the waves.

Prince Norivun stood just behind me, and his aura—while not quite as pounding as it'd been when he'd spoken of Vorl— was still strong.

I tried to stop the shiver that danced down my spine. Once again, his nearness reminded me of the kiss we'd shared last night. It felt as if he'd touched my soul in that kiss, which was crazy.

It was just a kiss, Ilara.

"Well?" I said, putting more distance between us. "What did you want to show me?"

He cocked an eyebrow up. "You better tame that sharp tongue of yours lest I find something more useful for it to do."

My cheeks reddened. "And you best tame that perverted mind of yours lest you find my fist connected with your face."

He laughed. "Have you developed a new violent side?"

"Perhaps you're rubbing off on me."

He waggled his eyebrows. "Oooh, I might like that."

A thrill ran through me, but I schooled my expression. *Cailis. Cailis. Cailis.* I forced an annoyed tone. "Again, what did you want to show me?"

His eyes narrowed. "Come. It's over here."

He trudged across the snow, his wings lifting so they wouldn't drag through the white powder. To this day, he had the tallest wings I'd ever seen, yet he walked around with them as though they weighed nothing.

When he reached the middle of the field, he crouched down and parted the snow. "Look here."

I peered over his shoulder and gasped at the buds of wheat rising from the black soil. Vivid colors of gold, magenta, and emerald green shone from the small shoots. My heart suddenly felt like the surf pounding against the shore, and I dropped to my knees and laid my palm against the ground in the same breath.

An immediate faint hum of *orem* pulsed against my skin. My jaw dropped. "But . . . how? This wasn't here two days ago."

The prince gave a triumphant smile. "I told you that you could do it."

"When did this happen?" All week I'd been trying to restore life to this field, doing what I always did when I worked crops. I had thought it wasn't working since nothing had come of it. Until now.

"The life must have been forming since you started, and the plants have only just appeared now."

"Does anyone else know?"

"At the moment, no, just you and me. But in a few weeks, when these stalks appear above the snow, the entire town will be aware. There'll be much rejoicing here."

I sat back on my haunches. "Rejoicing? From a few plants?" When his smile grew, my eyes widened. "Are there *more?*"

He moved several feet away and pushed a pile of snow from the ground. Tiny wheat stalks appeared beneath, plants in the beginning stages of growth.

The prince stood, then grabbed my hand and pulled me up with him.

My insides clenched when his tantalizing scent of cedar and snow surrounded me. And his broad chest was only inches from my face. Every line of his was hard, unyielding. The male truly was a work of art.

My gaze fell to our joined hands. His palm was so warm. So large. It swallowed mine.

Pulse quickening, I ripped my hand free and smoothed my hair.

He paused, his eyebrows drawing together as his huge wings flexed.

"Come," he said tersely before stalking toward other areas of the field, areas I hadn't even concentrated on prior.

I followed, keeping my distance, but I couldn't stop my gasp when he revealed what grew beneath the snow. Small signs of life dotted the land everywhere we went.

"How far has it spread?" I asked in amazement. Had I done this? *Actually done this?*

"The entire field."

"All of it?"

"Yes, all of it. I think your work here is done."

Heart pounding, I concentrated on keeping my excitement at bay. "But I didn't really do anything, and there's no way I created *orem*. Only the gods can do that."

He grunted. "Then, like you said, perhaps your affinity creates life. Whatever it does when you're tending to fields is what our continent needs to thrive again."

"So what do I do now?"

"Now, I'll begin taking you throughout the continent each morning, to—"

"You?" I interrupted. "Must it be you?"

His jaw snapped together when he scowled. "Yes, it must be me." Grinding his teeth, he continued, "I know it's vast, but if you spend your mornings doing this, the *orem* will be fixed, and you'll still have your afternoons free to train for the Trial."

I rolled my eyes. "Right. The Trial in which I'll be forced to marry you or some other male I despise. Don't remind me."

The prince's eyes narrowed. "Marry another? What are you talking about?"

I crossed my arms. "Are you telling me that you didn't know Sir Edmund Featherton paid me a visit this morning, courtesy of your father? He wanted to inform me of the upcoming Trial and the rebirth of the Olirum Accords. Apparently, your father is resurrecting the ancient tradition of arranged marriages among powerful fae to expand the strength of our race, and I'm now one of the females he has his eyes on. If I don't marry you, I'm to marry another noble of the king's choosing."

The prince's gaze darkened. "You're *not* to marry another."

My heart thundered. For a moment, I couldn't reply. The prince looked downright vengeful.

Working a swallow, I finally got out, "I'm sure you would be fine with one of the other females. They're all beautiful and extraordinarily strong. I also hear you're to court them."

His nostrils flared. "A requirement of the Trial."

"And the other male suitors are to court me."

"*What?*" A flurry of his power rocked the ground beneath us as his irises blazed. "I shall speak with my father. Having others court you and possibly marry you is preposterous."

"Exactly." I sighed in relief. Perhaps the prince could stop my arranged marriage, and then Cailis and I wouldn't have to run away. Instead, I could finish the stupid Trial, lose so I didn't have to marry him or anyone else, and then concentrate on understanding my affinities and healing our land.

But once again, the prince's visceral response made me pause.

I eyed him suspiciously. "Why are you like this with me? Why are you so . . . protective?" I wanted to say *possessive*, but I couldn't bring myself to say that word again, even though I had last night.

The prince shifted closer, his inherent scent of cedar and

snow wafting around him. "If I'm protective, it's because you need to be protected." His nostrils flared, and he looked at the sky, toward the sun. "It's midday. We need to head back to the castle. Your first lesson with Matron Olsander begins at noon."

CHAPTER 3

The prince mistphased us back to the castle, and we landed in a corridor bustling with servants.

The unfamiliar wing was an area of the castle I'd never visited before. A large stone walkway, at least fifteen feet wide, cut a path through the castle in a straight line. A tall ceiling, rimmed with frosted glass windows, soared above. Servants carrying baskets of linens and cleaning charms gave us a wide berth when they passed, and the scents in the air let me know that wherever we were, it was near the kitchens.

"This way," the prince said, striding forward.

"Where are we?"

"The south wing. It's where most of the servants' quarters are, along with the kitchens and laundry facilities. It's also where the training rooms were built. When our affinities began to manifest, Nuwin and I did our schooling here."

"You did?" I followed after him, having to pick up a jog since his strides were so long. "I just assumed you went to the Academy of Solisarium. Isn't that where all rich fae go?"

"We did go there after our initial training ended here."

The prince led me into a room through a set of massive double doors. The second my feet crossed the threshold, a thickly layered ward washed over my skin. On the other side, my eyes popped wide open.

I gaped. "This is where you learned to control your affinities?"

The room before me, if it could even be called a room, reminded me of a cavern with its hundred-foot-tall ceiling. The training quarters were made of gray stone, the rock thick and dense. Near the ceiling, huge windows let sunlight stream in, and I had a feeling they were made of unbreakable glass if the iron-infused wards I'd just stepped through were any indication of how impenetrable this room was.

On the far wall, rows of weapons waited. I gaped at the broadswords, shields, spears, knives, throwing stars, blades of every size, axes, crossbows . . . The list went on. Beside the rows of weapons lay numerous bookshelves with hundreds of texts that I could only assume contained knowledge of affinities and learning.

The prince clasped his hands beneath his great wings. "All of those weapons are either enchanted or ancient enough to contain magic of their own. Do not touch them unless you're instructed to."

"Weapons?" I made a face. "Why in the realm would I need to learn how to use those?"

The prince's eyes darkened. "Some fae feel threatened when they encounter a fairy of greater magic-holding. Learning to use weapons is imperative, as is learning how to defend yourself."

I swallowed. "You're saying that my affinities alone can put me at risk? But once I learn to control my magic, isn't that enough? Surely having fire and wind elements mean that I could protect myself."

"Yes, you would likely be able to, unless your affinities were suppressed." His eyes shuttered. "If that were to happen, you'd be left with nothing but your skills to protect yourself. Weapons are a must."

My heartbeat picked up when I recalled how the prince had battled the fairy blessed with an ice bear affinity in High Liss. Initially, he hadn't used magic, only his hands and swords.

I was about to ask another question when a bang came from a corner door, then the shuffle of feet.

A female barked out, "You're late, Prince Norivun! Lady Seary's classes begin daily at noon on the dot. Now, you know what happens when a pupil is tardy. Off you go. Now!"

My mouth dropped at the absolute ire of the female and the unflinching way she'd just spoken to the Bringer of Darkness. Her wide black wings, rotund figure, and narrowed eyes gave her an intimidating air, and I had to make myself not take a step back when she approached.

But the prince just raised his fist to his chest in traditional greeting and dipped his head. "Apologies, Matron Olsander. It shall not happen again."

He strolled to the corner of the room where a chin-up bar waited. He leaped from the ground to grab it, then dangled. With a bend of his knees, he let all of his weight hang from his hands, and my jaw dropped even more as he began to lift himself.

Up, then down, up, then down. The crown prince was doing *chin-ups*.

"Snap that lid closed, my dear!" Matron Olsander swatted at my mouth, and I instantly closed it and stood straighter. Granted, it'd been a while since I'd gone to school, but I couldn't recall any teachers being this strict or terrorizing. Mother Below, Matron Olsander scared the sprites out of me, and I absolutely detested sprites.

"Over here. Sit." She bustled to a mat near the windows, her thick, black wings flexing slightly when she pointed toward the floor. "Prince Norivun tells me your magic has only recently manifested, and to date, you have three known affinities—the ability to create life, perhaps even *orem*, and two elemental abilities, fire and air."

She didn't even flinch when speaking of my multiple affinities, but I supposed if she was the reason the prince was so powerful, then perhaps three was something to scoff at.

"Yes, Matron Olsander. That's correct."

She plucked her hands on her hips. "Well, of course, it's correct. Did you think I was looking for you to affirm something I already knew?" Her heavy brow pinched together.

I clamped my lips closed. "No?"

She scowled and pointed to the mat. "On your rump. Now."

I fell to the floor, and she sat beside me. "Close your eyes. You'll feel your magic better that way when you initially begin to learn it." She sighed. "We have much to catch up on. Three months isn't long to master three affinities, so we'll work nearly every day. One day off each week, that's it. And during that day you're to eat and sleep. That's all. It'll be the only way to fully replenish your magic and keep it charged for all that I have planned. Understood?"

"Yes?"

"Do you always answer questions with a question?"

I was about to say, *no?*, but then I firmly replied, "No, Matron Olsander. Apologies."

"Good. Now, as I was saying, we have much to do to prepare you for the Trial." She sighed. "As it is, you're like a newborn fairy without an inkling of how to control your abilities." She looked at my wingless back and clucked her tongue. "Strange. Very strange indeed, but not unheard of. Queen Lissandra's affinities also bloomed late, and she also has black hair, but she does have wings."

"You know the queen has black hair?" I blurted, and then, unable to help my curious question despite her stern expression, asked, "Did you train the queen too?"

"Indeed I did! I've trained most of the royals. Now, enough questions from you and no more jibber jabbering. It's time we got to work."

Matron Olsander instructed me to sit cross-legged and close my eyes. "Feel for your magic. All fae are different. Some feel it in their minds, others in their heart, some in their guts, and some in their limbs. Where do you feel it pulsing?"

"My gut."

"Good, very good. Identifying your magic and where it resides is the first step. Now, I'm going to run you through a series of tests to determine your strength and ability to connect with your magic. Learning one's magic and mastering it are vital for powerful fae. Without true control, you're a threat to everyone around you should your magic become so powerful that you're unable to control it."

I snuck a glance over my shoulder to where the prince was still doing chin-ups. My mouth grew dry. He'd removed his tunic. Muscles, beaded with sweat, bunched and moved every time he lifted himself. *Blessed Mother*. Not an inch of fat was on the male. With each flex of his arms, sinewy tendons rippled, transfixing me.

A smack to the back of my head jolted me forward.

"Enough of that salivating, Lady Seary. We are here to work!"

My cheeks flamed, even more so when the prince cast a knowing look over his shoulder. Embarrassment tumbled through me. *Bastard*. He'd probably removed his shirt just because he knew it would catch my attention.

Clenching my jaw, I firmly ignored him and concentrated on what Matron Olsander was telling me.

She sat straighter, her no-nonsense aura piercing. "Now, as I was saying, we'll start with a series of tests."

My new tutor spent the next hour going through a multitude of magical assessments that I neither understood nor could explain, but from what I could deduce, my tutor's affinity was an unusual one. Every time Matron Olsander began a new test, I felt something foreign probing inside me, and after working up the courage to ask her what it was she was doing, she finally told me I was feeling *her* affinity.

Apparently, her affinity was a mental one and lay in her

ability to sense, stoke, and call out others' magic while helping them learn to master it. It was what made her such an excellent tutor.

When she finally finished, she sat back and rubbed her chin. "You're strong, very strong indeed, but I sense other things in you. Slumbering abilities perhaps that haven't fully manifested."

"What does that mean?"

"It means that I don't believe you're fully manifested yet, Lady Seary. I believe there's more to come."

My hands fluttered. "Are you serious?"

"Do I look like the joking type?"

"No, I mean, it's just that—" I stumbled with what to say. To have more affinities manifest, as *crazy* as that would be, meant that the king could take an even stronger interest in me. *Not good.*

Matron Olsander shook her head. "You're an unusual one, Ilara Seary, daughter of Mervalee Territory. Your magic feels unique. I can't say I've encountered another like you before, but something feels deeper in you. Perhaps yet untouched, or maybe not. I could be wrong."

Please be wrong. "What about the queen? Isn't she like me?"

"She's also an unusual one, although she's unique in her own way. You and she may share the same hair color, but your magic . . ." She shook her head. "While comparable in strength, your affinities are too different to be considered similar."

I could sense the prince's interest from across the room. He'd stopped doing chin-ups a while ago and now stood by the wall, watching and waiting. But since he hadn't put his shirt back on, I'd refused to look at him again.

KRISTA STREET

But now, after Matron Olsander had revealed what she had, his aura strengthened, brushing around us, demanding my attention. I shivered, trying to dispel the feelings he so easily provoked in me.

The matron cut him a sharp look. "Prince Norivun, if you insist on observing us, I am going to request that you either suppress your Outlets or go elsewhere to expel them."

The prince dipped his head. "Apologies, Matron Olsander."

I frowned. "Outlets?"

The matron sighed. "Blessed, I forget how new you are to all of this. Outlets are a learned control of one's magic, something you shall have to master as well, lest you suffer the consequences. When a fairy is as powerful as the prince and *you*, magic can begin to build up in one's system. It's imperative that you let steady streams of it out, otherwise it can fester, building inside and resulting in harm to oneself or those around you."

"Oh." I sat back, stunned and embarrassed that I literally knew nothing about magic. Since I'd never formed an affinity during maturing age, I'd been labeled a defective, which meant I'd bypassed that part of secondary school. Instead of learning about my magical affinity and how to control it, I'd been sent to the fields to learn about the crops several winters before the other village children.

"Tell me," my tutor continued, ignoring my blush. "Have you been experiencing any unusual symptoms lately? Perhaps intense aches, electrical jolts, severe stomach cramps, or moments of amnesia?"

I frowned, then thought about the strange reactions I'd had last night at the Betrothed Ball when the king and crown prince had been speaking of me. Several times, it'd felt as though lightning coursed through my veins, and then while dancing with Nuwin, I'd experienced something similar.

"Perhaps the electric one?" I explained in more detail what had occurred last night.

"Oh my." Matron Olsander shook her head. "You're already in need of learning Outlets. What you're describing is your magic building and having nowhere else to go, so it's attacking your essence and creating electrical responses beyond your control. Very well, we shall start there and then progress as needed as you learn to call forth each of your affinities individually and in tandem. On your feet. Now."

I scrambled to a stand, and for the first time, realized I didn't feel the prince's aura. Frowning, I wondered if he'd left the room, but when I glanced his way, he still stood by the wall, his arms crossed and his bare chest on display.

He winked, and I hurriedly looked away.

"Is that why I usually feel the prince's aura so strongly?" I asked my tutor quietly. "Because he lets his magic out through his Outlets?"

"Indeed." The matron led me toward the corner of the large room, an area that was padded with mats and swimming in strong wards. "It's why all of us feel his aura so acutely. Prince Norivun's power is so great that he must let frequent and steady streams of his magic out. If he didn't—" She shuddered. "May the Mother help us all."

I SPENT the next few hours working with the matron in the padded area. She had me continually call forth my magic to let small puffs of it waft from my skin.

At first, I didn't think it was possible. All I knew of my magic was that it resided in my gut, pulsing and throbbing within me. I didn't know how to call it forth, control it, or manipulate it to my will, but with the matron's insightful instruction, I was finally able to dispel those electrical feelings of shock if I concentrated on picturing my magic as though it were a stream blocked by a dam.

Matron Olsander informed me that visual learning was a common tutelage that helped young fae as they learned their affinities—that if I could connect my magic with a picture in my mind, that my brain would siphon those visual images to physical manifestations, which really meant that I spent several hours visualizing a dammed river being opened and closed. Opened and closed.

It was long, boring, and mentally exhausting, but it seemed to work because for the first time since my life-creating affinity had manifested, I felt lighter. And that pulsing sensation in my gut no longer bothered me and even vanished completely a few times before returning.

Matron Olsander nodded after I let another stream of magic out.

"Very good, Ilara. Now, remember that the key is learning to allow enough excess magic out while also retaining your power so it's always on hand should you call it forth. You don't want to open your Outlets so much that you run dry and need to rest and recharge to build your magic once more. Instead, you want to let out just enough that it doesn't overwhelm your system."

"Will it always be like this?" I asked. "Will I forever need to be visualizing dams and rivers to keep my magic from festering?"

She smiled, the first smile I'd seen on her. "No. This is merely a beginner's course on Outlets. As you grow and learn the intricacies of your magic, letting streams of it out through your Outlets will become second nature, like breathing. Eventually, you won't need to visualize or concentrate at all. Your body will naturally do it as needed, requiring little to no attention from you. Now!" She rapped her knuckles sharply against the floor. "Again. No more jibber jabbering! We shall next learn about Shields, another imperative magical practice that will provide defense against others' offensive magic."

I was panting when she finally declared I was finished working with my Outlets and Shields. It amazed me that something as simple as mental imaging could cause me to feel so tired.

"Are we done for the day?" I asked hopefully.

"Done?" Matron Olsander *tsked*. "We're only half through! Have you forgotten about the Trial? We only have three months to master your affinities! And the prince has also informed me that you're needed by him each morning to complete other tasks, so our time is even more limited than what I would like. Now, we shall next—"

The door to the training room banged open, and a spiel of

giggles followed. The three females the king had assigned to the Rising Queen Trial poured into the room, all of them wearing day dresses of varying shades.

Prince Nuwin followed just behind them, along with Michas Crimsonale, his brother Sirus, and a dozen other males I didn't recognize.

Prince Norivun pushed away from the wall just as one of the females, Lady Georgyanna Endalaver, daughter of Kroravee Territory—the one who'd worn the purple gown last night, had a lithe figure, slight and delicate features, yet reminded me of Vorl with her predatory gaze—sauntered seductively toward him.

"My prince," she said, her voice low and sultry as she dipped into a curtsy, her dress's bodice daringly low as it hugged her small breasts. "What a lovely surprise to see you again."

She practically devoured him in her hungry gaze, her greedy eyes traveling over his bare pecs and abs.

Prince Norivun dipped his head, not seeming the least bit self-conscious in his half-naked state. "Lady Endalaver."

My heart thumped harder when she straightened and boldly trailed a finger along his forearm.

"Would you care to train with me, my prince? We've been encouraged by Sir Featherton to practice within these training rooms in preparation for the first test. Since it's been postponed,"—she cast a scathing glance my way—"I thought it might be fun to pass the time sparring with one another, and I've never trained with a male as powerful as you. It would be most rewarding if you tested me using your skills."

A flash of fire raced through my veins, zapping everything

in its path when her finger trailed lower, along his stomach and toward his—

"Lady Seary!" Matron Olsander barked. "Control your affinities. Open your Outlets this instant!"

Georgyanna cast me a disdainful glare before she turned back to the prince.

"Is she the new one?" Georgyanna pouted prettily even though her scathing glance only a second ago told me she knew *exactly* who I was. "Such a pity that she has no wings. Are you sure she's not a defective? I heard she was considered that for many winters."

The prince raised an eyebrow. "She's not a defective, and I suggest you concentrate on your own training and not those of others, Lady Endalaver."

"Oh, my prince." She swatted his arm playfully. "Please call me Georgyanna. No need for such formality, especially during our courtship. Wouldn't you agree?"

She took another step closer to him and stood only inches away, her meaning clear as she glanced up at him through her lashes while running her finger along him again. Her movements were knowing and practiced, as though she were a true courtesan and had an affinity in seduction.

Blessed Mother, did such an affinity exist? Surely not.

But I didn't fully understand the complexities of affinities, and if I remembered correctly, one of Georgyanna's affinities was manipulation, which she seemed actively practicing at this very second given the slight trace of oily magic swimming in the air. That hadn't been there before she arrived.

Shuddering, I forced my attention away from her. The other two females, Meegana and Beatrice, still stood near the door. They shot the prince and Georgyanna curious glances before Nuwin waved toward the wall.

"Shall we, ladies?" The other males followed the young prince as he led the females across the stone floor. Everyone ignored me except for Michas.

The young lord gave me a mischievous glance when he passed, then dipped his head in acknowledgment.

I returned the gesture, but my cheeks flamed when all of them began casting their magic and showing off their affinities as they laughed and teased one another, making their "training" session look more like a courtship ball filled with bursting egos.

Lady Beatrice Leafton was the tallest of the three females and had the most athletic build. She seemed very practiced within her affinities. She spun around the room, weaving her hands through the air as objects lifted and flew under her telekinetic command, and every time her wings flexed, I thought she would take flight, but instead, the stones levitated her in a combination of telekinetic and elemental power.

Lady Meegana Ockson, while not as quick to show off her skills as Lady Leafton, didn't seem any less capable. She conjured water from the air, pulling the particles together to form at her command, then gave playful splashes to those around her. And under Nuwin's insistence, she shifted into her colantha form, the large jungle cat in complete contradiction to the sweet, shy side she'd exuded earlier.

The males laughed and showed off their skills as well, all of the elements at play between them along with various tactile, sensory, and emotional affinities. One of them must have had a seduction affinity. Such a thing *had* to exist because something hot washed over my skin, and then my nether regions were warming and craving.

"Blessed Mother Above and Below," I whispered. *How in the realm do I compete with this kind of power?* I cut a glance toward the crown prince, but Lady Endalaver had sunk her manipulative claws into him so deeply that she still had him cornered in the room.

A rush of lust and rage shot through me simultaneously when someone's seduction affinity hit me again.

Matron Olsander gave a frustrated sigh. "Lady Seary, you shall need to concentrate despite this interruption." She again smacked me upside the head, the pain briefly releasing me from whichever male held the seduction affinity, before she barked sharply, "Pay no attention to them as we begin your next lesson. You're falling prey to their affinities since you have no Shield in place." She clucked her tongue. "You have much to learn."

I rubbed my head, my cheeks warming *again*, but I tried to heed her warning as I valiantly attempted to ignore the triumphant glances from Georgyanna and the fluttering giggles from the other two.

But my lack of control and juvenile attempts at learning my affinities were on full display during my next lesson, which had my neck flushing and me wishing I could sink through the floor.

"How in the realm is she going to pass any of the tests?" Lady Meegana Ockson whispered. She was the smallest of the three, with short hair that curled at the ends. She'd shed her colantha form and had since returned to her fairy body, but I didn't bristle under her comment since her question sounded genuinely curious versus scornful.

Lady Beatrice Leafton shrugged and held her hand out for

one of the spears. It floated toward her. "I haven't the faintest idea, Meegana, but if she doesn't learn the basics by the time the tests start, she's bound to come in last."

Shame burned through me again. It was such an old, unwelcome friend, but a companion who'd been at my side my entire life.

And to think I'd felt nothing but joy and confidence this morning when the prince had showed me the field in Harrivee. For that brief moment, I'd felt special. Powerful. But it soon became apparent to me and everyone else in this room that I was the weakest of them all despite what Prince Norivun claimed I would be.

And that only meant one thing—there was no way in this realm or the next that I could ever win the Rising Queen Trial, which meant I was destined for marriage with whoever the king chose for me unless the prince was able to stop him, or Cailis and I escaped.

CHAPTER 4

By the time evening rolled around, I was so exhausted I could barely stand. But after seven hours under Matron Olsander's tutelage, despite my embarrassing failures and inability to control my affinities, I'd at least learned how to find my magic inside me, bring it forward, and utilize my Outlets while forming a weak Shield. Granted, I hadn't mastered the amazing skills I'd witnessed in the others, but I could see why Matron Olsander was the royal's tutor. The female knew her stuff, and her affinity made her unparalleled in her ability to teach a fairy.

I stumbled toward the training room's door, my legs wobbling since at one point, Matron Olsander had made me stand on a balance beam twenty feet in the air. It was only fear of dying every time she pushed me that had called my air elemental affinity to the rescue, completely baffling me as to how it happened.

But she said that was to be expected. After she quizzed me on what I knew of my magic, it hadn't been that shocking to finally understand why it had manifested during Vorl's attack. Apparently, when a fairy feared for their life, affinities came running. In other words, as much as I hated my village's archon, it was actually Vorl that had been the catalyst to my manifesting.

As for why it'd taken so long for them to show at all and why Vorl's previous attacks hadn't initiated them earlier, I didn't know, but Matron Olsander thought it was related to my black hair. For some reason, that neither she nor the queen knew, our affinities bloomed late because of our unusual genetics.

Maybe someday, after this idiotic Trial was over and the continent's crops were thriving again, I could dig into the history books to try to understand why I looked the way I did. But until then . . .

I refused to look toward Prince Norivun when I exited the training room. Lady Endalaver had spent the entire afternoon with him, and even though I repeatedly told myself that I didn't care and that it was for the best if she wove her manipulative spell around him, I couldn't stop the ache in my chest.

So stupid, Ilara. Just forget that kiss and your ridiculous attraction to him. He's the crown prince, and you're merely a pawn in the court's arsenal.

I forced my chin up and stepped into the wide stone walkway. Scents of food being prepared in the kitchens filled the air. My stomach growled in appreciation. Down the hall, Sandus waited next to a huge statue of the God Xerious. The guard had his hands on his hips, a pleasant smile on his face.

I was about to join him when a soft female voice said from

behind me, "You looked like you made progress today, Lady Seary."

I turned to see Lady Meegana Ockson. Since she was an inch shorter than me, I gazed slightly down at her soft smile and curious eyes. A genuine feeling of warmth radiated from her.

Some of the tension in my shoulders eased. Even though I didn't know her, there was something about Lady Ockson that reminded me of Birnee from back home, even though my village friend had wings so delicate it was a miracle they could carry her. Meegana's wings looked strong and sturdy despite her small form.

I shrugged. "Maybe, but I'm nothing like the rest of you, Lady Ockson." I waved sheepishly toward the training room, where shouts of fun and peals of laughter were still coming from the others.

She took a step closer to me, and a waft of either her perfume or her natural scent hit me. She smelled citrusy. It was a scent that reminded me of my mother.

Smiling, she said, "Please, call me Meegana. I always feel like I should be looking for my mother whenever I hear Lady Ockson."

"Okay, Meegana." I smiled tentatively in return. "In that case, please call me Ilara or Lara, whatever you prefer."

"Lara it is." Meegana's lips curved more. "Is it true the prince found you while you were working in a Mervalee field last month?"

"It's true."

"And I was told that your affinities only just manifested in the past few weeks, and that with your—" She blushed when she glanced toward my black hair and wingless back. "I'm so sorry. I'm being nosey and curious, but I mean no disrespect. Truly."

The stiffness that had been creeping between my shoulder blades abated, since her apology sounded sincere, but I still wished that Cailis was waiting with Sandus. Since my sister's affinity was truth, she'd be able to tell me in a heartbeat if Meegana was being genuine.

"It's all right," I finally settled with. "My entire life, everyone's been curious about me." I waved toward my hair and bare back. "But I suppose I'd rather have my affinities manifest late than continue having none at all."

Meegana laid a hand on my arm. "You would have been worthy either way." She squeezed my arm lightly before giving me another small smile and returning to the training room.

I watched her until she rounded the corner, my brow furrowing, because for the briefest moment, I'd felt that she'd actually meant that statement. That Lady Ockson truly felt all fae, even defectives, were worthy of love.

SANDUS and I strolled outside as we walked back to my chambers. Three moons shone in the sky, and the evening air swirled around us. I'd asked him if we could take the long way back to my chambers since I needed a moment to clear my head.

I'd seen and done so much today, but apart from my brief trip to the Harrivee field that morning, I'd been inside all day. Since I typically worked in the fields, staying inside wasn't something I was used to and definitely wasn't what I preferred.

"You did well this afternoon," Sandus said, nudging me.

I inhaled the crisp air and shrugged. "I'm not sure if I agree with you. The other females and the males are all so powerful. I can tell that all of them have more than one affinity."

"That's why they're in the Trial and are being considered as husbands for you all."

I stopped and faced him. "Wait . . . *those* males with Nuwin are who the king's considering we be married off to?"

"They are."

"How do you know that?"

He gave me a cocky smile, the corner of his mouth lifting, making his beard appear fuzzy. "Royal fae often forget when guards are near. They tend to loosen their tongues and speak freely."

"What did you hear?"

He cocked his head. "During a break this afternoon, the prince had words with his father. He's not happy that you're to also date other males in the Trial."

My heart rate ticked up. "And? Was he able to put a stop to it? Will I no longer have to marry another if I lose?"

"He was not. You're to be courted by all of the males in the Trial, and you're still to marry who the king chooses for you at the end."

My breaths came faster. "So it's decided then? There's no way out of this?"

Sandus's eyes softened. "I'm sorry, Ilara. The Olirum Accords stand unless the king changes his mind."

My breath stuttered out of me, puttering and dying until it felt as if all of the air had been ripped from my lungs. Even the crown prince hadn't been able to stop the will of the king. So it was official. There was no deviation from my fate. I'd have to escape with Cailis unless I wanted to fall prey to an arranged marriage.

Sandus patted my shoulder good-naturedly, oblivious to the cataclysmic response that was taking place inside me. "Look on the bright side, love. You could be Nori's wife one day."

"*That's* the bright side?"

"Indeed."

"How is that the bright side? And why do you look so happy at that possibility?"

"Have you learned weapons yet?" Sandus raised an eyebrow, bypassing my question entirely.

I huffed. "Weapons? No. I was warned not to touch the weapons. The prince told me that all of the weapons in that room contain their own magic, and I'm not to hold them without proper instruction. Instead, I learned how to find my magic today. That's it."

"Well, have no fear. The prince has instructed me to begin your physical training, and with time, I shall also teach you weapons."

My jaw dropped. "What?"

"I'm to train you in combat. Prince's orders."

My eyebrows rose, and for the first time a flutter of something positive, something tangible, flowed through me. To be able to defend myself without magic meant that I would never be vulnerable again to someone such as Vorl. In all likelihood, it could be the only blessing that came out of the next three months of pain and misery.

"You'll truly help me learn to fight even if I can't master my affinities?"

Sandus grinned. "Of course. The prince felt it was only fitting since I'm to be your personal guard for the foreseeable future. And even though Matron Olsander may be the best tutor in the entire continent, when it comes to fighting and weapons, myself, and the prince's guards are the true masters."

Cailis and I were sitting on my bed an hour later, several trays of food between the two of us as I told her everything that had happened at training while stuffing my mouth. I was inhaling the food. Roasted duck, citrus-marinated hen, buttered squash with nuts and cranberries, herbed potatoes, sautéed vegetables of every variety, bite-sized cheese and fruit kabobs, and flaky pastries that melted in one's mouth were only a few of the items. I was starving. And exhausted. But mostly starving after the rigorous mental and physical day I'd had. Matron Olsander hadn't been kidding. Food was needed to replenish one's magic quickly—a *lot* of food.

When I finally finished, ending the meal with a thick slab of chocolate cake covered with berry ganache and whipped cream, I lay back and placed a hand over my belly.

Cailis sighed and did the same, flopping down on the mattress beside me. "You're right. They really do have far too much sustenance in this castle. I can see why you've gained weight."

I smiled guiltily. "It's extravagance to the extreme, isn't it?" Nobody from our village ever got to eat like this.

"I'm not complaining."

Somehow, I managed to maneuver upright again so I could

pick up the trays and take them off the bed. A part of me wanted to return them to the kitchen myself, but I'd learned better.

Even after a month of being waited on, I still wasn't used to it, so when I'd tried to return my trays the other day, after I was finally allowed to leave my chambers freely, Balbus had nearly bitten my head off.

I shuffled to the door and awkwardly opened it. The hallway outside of my chambers held my nighttime guard. Jovin took the trays from me and set them on the ground, then resumed his watch.

Because I wasn't allowed to roam the castle without one of the prince's personal guards, I hadn't yet ventured outside of the Exorbiant Chamber after Sandus's shifts. Apparently, if I wanted to do that, one of the prince's guards would need to be awoken, and demanding that of them was the last thing I wanted to do.

"Have there been any further attacks or missing fae of late, Jovin?" I asked the nighttime guard. A cold chill ran through me every time I thought of the dangerous and mysterious activities that had taken place in the castle as of late.

Jovin shook his head. "None in the past week, my lady."

I breathed a sigh of relief, bid him goodnight, and then joined Cailis on the bed again.

It was just the two of us in my chambers, with only the crackling fire for company. I sat beside her and crossed my legs. "I need your help."

She propped herself up on an elbow, her wings splayed out behind her. "With what?"

"I don't know who I can trust in this castle. I don't know who's genuine and who wishes to see me fail or harm me."

My sister nodded. "It sounds like Michas Crimsonale and Meegana Ockson are two I need to check out. I'm not sure if you need me to assess Georgyanna Endalaver or not." She made a face. "It sounds like even you can tell she's a rotten one."

My stomach clenched when I recalled how Georgyanna had run her fingers along the crown prince's arms and torso all afternoon. I hadn't seen him since I'd left the training room and probably wouldn't again until he collected me tomorrow for more work on the dead fields. For all I knew, he was still with the sly female.

A rush of fire coursed through my veins, but I immediately tried to suppress it. Maybe it was for the best if Georgyanna sank her claws into him. It wasn't like I stood a chance of winning the Trial. And it wasn't like I wanted to.

Reminding myself of that, I added, "And we need to figure out how to escape."

I peered at my inner wrist, to where that leaf had embedded itself into my skin before disappearing when the prince and I had made our bargain. I had no idea what curse the gods would place upon me for running from our bargain, but I would *not* be a pawn in the court's games, although the thought of leaving our fae to perish made something inside me wither.

Cailis sat up straighter, a covert smile splitting her lips. "Now *that's* something I'd be more than happy to help us with."

"I have no idea how we're going to do it. We'll need to find a way to travel." I frowned and glanced at my wingless back. "Since I can't fly, and you're not strong enough to carry me, I'm not sure what we're going to do or where we'll go or how we'll survive."

Cailis placed her hand on mine. "We'll figure this out." She nibbled on her lip. "You said the prince is paying you now, right?"

"He is."

"So maybe we should keep letting him pay you for a while, let that amount build. If we start pulling out small amounts, pretending that we're going to go shopping, nobody will notice, but instead we can save it and hide it somewhere here, in your chambers."

"And when we have enough to survive on for at least, what? Six months? A full season? Then we escape?"

Cailis cocked her head. "The wisest decision would probably be to have enough to support both of us for a full season, but the Mother knows we're used to living frugally, so it shouldn't take that long to save up. How much do you have right now?"

"A thousand rulibs."

Her eyes bugged out. "That's what we're both paid for six months' work."

"I know, but the prince also said he'd back paid me, so that's really for a month of my time here."

She nodded, and from the way her face scrunched up and the calculating light in her eyes, I knew she was running through the numbers. "So we already nearly have enough. In one more month we definitely will, but your magic—" She frowned. "It would truly be best if you learned to control your affinities from your new tutor before we left. The more magically inclined both of us are, the better off we'll be, so what if we stay here for your three months of training, then we escape?"

My stomach fell. "So I stay and complete the Trial's tests?"

"Either that or we escape just before them." She frowned, tapping her chin. "Although, it might be better if you complete the tests. You're going to be watched heavily between now and then, but after the Trial finishes . . ." She let her words hang.

My lips parted in understanding. "I won't be watched as closely."

"Exactly, *and* you'll hopefully have mastered your affinities enough by then to know how to effectively use them."

"That plan will work as long as the king doesn't immediately marry me off the second the Trial's done."

She shrugged. "Even if he did, there's no reason we can't still escape and leave your new husband behind, especially if your new husband is the crown prince." She sneered.

"Do you think we should go to the Lochen or Nolus continent? A part of me thinks we should flee to the Lochen. Drachu did say I was welcome on their shores." I quickly explained who Drachu was and the encounter I'd had with him. "I don't think we'd be turned away from the Lochen, but the Nolus—" I shrugged. "It would be a gamble with them."

"The safest bet is probably the best bet." Cailis squeezed my hand. "Don't worry. We'll figure it out when the time comes. We have three months to prepare. For now, just concentrate on mastering your affinities as much as possible. The more powerful you are when we need to flee, the better off we'll be."

CHAPTER 5

The faint sound of the chime timer I'd set the previous night roused me from sleep. I opened my eyes, staring bleary-eyed at the clock ticking on the wall before remembering *why* I'd set the timer. I lifted the covers and hurried to turn it off as a beat of excitement ran through me.

Once my teeth were clean and I was dressed, I crept to the door.

In the hall, Sandus looked freshly bathed with his beard recently trimmed. "Why, good morning, love. You're right on time. Eager to start learning?"

"Very much so."

"In that case, let's get to it. Should we go to the training room?"

I made a face. I had no idea what the other females' schedules were, but the last thing I needed was more watchful eyes and snickering comments while I floundered with yet another new skill.

"I was actually hoping to train in my chambers, perhaps in

the courtyard? It's big enough to move freely and it's also warm because of the *orem*, not to mention the air is fresh, and the juniper blossoms smell divine, and—"

Grinning, Sandus held up a hand. "No need to convince me further. You had me at *warm*."

I laughed. "Just keep quiet while we go through the bedroom. Cailis is still sleeping."

I HADN'T KNOWN what to expect under Sandus's tutelage, but not using weapons and working on maintaining my balance while standing on one leg in various positions hadn't been it.

"You do have a natural advantage," Sandus said as he circled me.

I'd been holding my current position for over five minutes with one bare foot on the ground while my other leg was bent at the knee with my free foot tucked behind my standing leg at the thigh.

"Oh? What's that?" I panted lightly. In the last two minutes, Sandus had made me lift weights over my head, one weight in each hand as I held my arms aloft. My shoulder muscles were screaming.

"A life of laboring in the fields has made you strong and fit."

"Despite my recent weight gain?" I retorted. Sweat slid between my breasts. That had happened plenty of times when I'd been tending the fields, but now my breasts had grown large enough that they nearly touched.

"Your weight gain was needed, and considering you made this happen in the past month,"—he held his arms wide,

nodding toward the thriving plants and trees in the courtyard—
"You weren't exactly sitting on your arse. No, Lady Seary,
you're toned and strong, and now that you're a healthy weight,
your body is truly ready to start training in earnest."

I swayed a bit until righting my balance again. Screaming,
seriously, my muscles were *screaming* in agony despite
Sandus's claim that I was in shape. "I thought I was . . . to learn
weapons . . . not whatever this is," I said in between breaths.

He smiled ruefully. "Weapons come later. Balance,
strength, and technique come first." He circled me, tapping
areas of my body to correct my form. "Straighten here. Tighten
here." He did another two circles around me, nodding in
approval every time I made adjustments.

"Good. Very good. You're already further along than I'd
expected you to be. Your strength is good, your balance is excellent, and you seem to have a natural inclination for technique.
Every time I've corrected one of your positions, you were able
to make the subtle changes with my guidance. Most fae aren't
able to do that without months to full seasons of mind-body
training first." He scratched his chin. "Have you ever trained
before?"

I shook my head. "The only training I've ever done is to
tend fields."

Sandus clucked his tongue, then stood in front of me.
"Whatever the case, I think you're ready for the basic warmups
each warrior does before sparring. I thought it would be weeks
until we got into this, but I'm rather impressed by what I'm
seeing and think you can do it."

He finally let me relax my position, and I nearly fell to the
ground in relief.

"None of that," he said with a smile. "Now, watch and learn."

He demonstrated first, going through a series of movements that involved dipping, swaying, bending, and straightening. His entire body moved with effortless grace, even when he stood only on his hands or bent so low that his chest brushed the cobblestones. It looked like a dance unto itself, filled with positions that, at times, seemed to defy gravity.

"Follow me through each movement," he said when he finished. "I'll show the routine to you first, and we'll go through it until you have it memorized. Then I'll have you do it with me watching you, and I'll adjust you as needed."

For the next hour, we dipped and flowed through a series of connecting steps. I mimicked each and every bend of his knees, twist of his arms, and arch of his back. By the third time through, I caught on enough not to need his guidance, even though I couldn't fully execute the more advanced moves yet.

He stood back. Arms crossed, he watched me carefully, stepping in when needed to instruct how I should alter my position.

"Very good, Ilara." A grin split his features. "Are you certain you haven't had a warrior affinity manifest?"

I laughed, then sobered when I realized his question wasn't a cheeky one. "Are you serious?"

"I am actually. I've never seen a fairy move as you just did with such little training. Only warriors move like that or fae who've spent full seasons honing their bodies."

My heart beat harder when I remembered what Matron Olsander had said yesterday, about sensing something still inside me that had not yet awoken. Something that was still slumbering. And while I'd never been a fighter, there was something about what Sandus had just taught me that spoke to me. As though a connection had just been forged inside me that had always been there but had only needed a guiding hand to make the path.

"I don't know," I finally said. "How would I—"

A sneeze cut me off, and I twirled toward the courtyard's doors. My jaw dropped when I beheld Daiseeum, the crown prince, Cailis, and Nuwin.

From the looks of it, they'd all been standing there for a while.

Daiseeum sneezed again, then dabbed at her nose with her handkerchief. "Excuse me, Ilara. The marigold blossoms always get to me, but I just couldn't look away. What you were just doing . . . It was beautiful. Absolutely beautiful. I had no idea you were capable of such . . ." Her voice trailed off, as if she were at a loss for words.

"Art?" the crown prince supplied.

"I was going to say *exotic dance*," Nuwin replied, which got a glare from his brother.

I cocked my head at them, and the crown prince's sapphire gaze bore into mine. His expression was blank, yet his eyes burned with fire.

"'Tis how you appeared," Prince Norivun added. "Like a beautiful piece of artwork come to life, not like a sultry dancer as my brother so eloquently implied."

"Well, her breasts were straining quite regularly against her—"

"Enough, Nuwin," the prince growled.

Nuwin just grinned and gave me a cheeky wink. I knew he

meant nothing disrespectful by his comments, but a blush still tinged my cheeks.

Clearing her throat, Cailis glared at Nuwin too before adding, "What the crown prince was saying is true, Lara. I've never seen you move like that either, even when we danced or pretended to battle as children. You were truly—"

"Magnificent," Prince Norivun finished for her.

Cailis gave him a begrudging nod. "What he said."

"Oh, all right." Nuwin sighed. "It truly did look more like art than an exotic dance."

Wiping the sweat from my brow, I gave an embarrassed smile. "Well, thanks." Turning to Sandus, I said, "Tomorrow then, we'll do this again?"

"You can count on it, love."

I eyed the crown prince, knowing that if he was here, it was only for one reason. "Are we going to another field this morning?"

He dipped his head. He hadn't stopped watching me, not once, since I'd realized he was there, and the urge to pick at my fingernails grew. "We are. As soon as you're ready, we're going to Isalee Territory before your training with Matron Olsander. There's a new field I need you to revive—the very first field that died on our continent."

CHAPTER 6

After Daiseeum cleansed me with her magic and I consumed a quick breakfast, I was ready to depart with the crown prince.

But before I could join him in the main room of the Exorbiant Chamber, Daiseeum called, "Ilara, one more thing. Sir Featherton stopped by while you were training with Sandus. He plans to pop in again tonight after your training with Matron Olsander, to explain the rest of the Trial. Since your first date is in three nights' time, he would like you prepared."

My jaw dropped. "The courtship dates start that soon?"

"Indeed. Did you not know?"

All I managed was a shake of my head.

How are so many things that are completely out of my control happening so quickly?

THE PRINCE MISTPHASED us to a field on our continent's northernmost territory. Cold, icy wind bit into my cheeks the second the realm reappeared around us. Snow blew across a field in a raging whiteout.

The prince wore thick leggings today, which hugged his strong quadriceps. A long cloak hung around his shoulders, but the hood was down. Snow flew around his hair, which hung loose in silver waves. His dazzling blue eyes cut through the whiteout, as alluring as sapphire gems.

Like yesterday, I put distance between us immediately, not liking how his hands lingered on my hips or how a soft growl of discontent worked up his throat when I pulled away, but I didn't move far. In this blinding snow, I would likely become lost.

"Really?" I asked, peering up at him. "You had to bring me here today? Couldn't you at least have checked the weather first?"

I was practically yelling at him since the wind was so fierce.

He stepped closer, then leaned down until his lips brushed my ear. "It's always like this at this time of the season. The laborers here are used to it. They commonly tie themselves together while working so no one becomes lost."

"They work in this?" I yelled, refusing to speak into his ear as he'd done to me.

"Withstanding the fiercest weather on our continent is a source of pride for the Isalee Territory's fae. It's only going to get worse as winter sets in. I figured it was better to tackle this area now versus waiting until it sits under ten feet of snow. Unless you disagree?" He straightened and quirked a silver eyebrow.

Since my feet were already pushing through two feet of snow, I glared at him but surmised that he was right. If I needed to touch the soil and try once again to replenish life in this field, it was probably best to do it when I didn't need a shovel.

I yanked a lock of hair from my face that the wind whipped into my line of sight. "Fine, although I'm likely to freeze to death first."

"Allow me to assist." A wash of the prince's magic hummed along my skin.

The wind stopped.

My eyes rounded at the bubble of protective air suddenly surrounding us. Not one snowflake or breeze penetrated it. It was as though we'd become encased within a glass dome. "Why didn't you do that sooner?"

"Maybe I like whispering in your ear."

My stomach flipped as a memory his erection pressed against my most intimate area surfaced. I cleared my throat and hastily took another step away. "Do you think I could do that with my air element?"

He inhaled, and his lips curved before he said, "I don't see why not."

"How'd you do it?" I snapped, because dammit, he'd scented my arousal again.

"I called upon my air affinity and wished for an encapsulated area around us. My magic did the rest."

I nibbled on my lip. "Is it like what Matron Olsander was telling me? How if I visualize it, my magic should follow suit?"

"It's exactly like that, but with practice it becomes near instantaneous and only requires a single thought."

I knew we had work to do, that there were likely thousands

of fields like this throughout the continent that I needed to save, but it would be so much easier if I wasn't so dependent on the prince for everything. Perhaps then I could work without him and these insufferable reactions to him would cease. "Can I try?"

In a blink, his protective Shield was gone, and the icy gale bit into my skin again.

Closing my eyes, I felt for my magic inside me, that pulsing hum of power in my gut. All of my affinities were tangled together. My tutor had ensured me that eventually I'd be able to differentiate what was what and be able to feel their subtle differences, but I wasn't able to yet.

My magic throbbed as it had yesterday, and I remembered how I was supposed to be practicing my Outlets, but I still didn't know how to open them while also calling forth my magic simultaneously.

The prince's heat fluttered against my body when he stepped closer. I didn't have to open my eyes to know he was there. His sheer size broke the wind, allowing me a moment's reprieve from it.

"Picture a dome in your mind." His mouth caressed my ear as his breath tickled my neck. "Let your magic rise inside you as you imagine creating a protective bubble around us."

My stomach clenched at his nearness, but I scrunched my eyes closed and forced myself to concentrate. A flash of heat hit my skin. My eyes flew open to see a dome of fire around us. It melted the snow falling upon it, but it didn't stop the wind.

"Oops."

The prince chuckled. "Close, but not quite."

Closing my eyes, I tried again. *A dome. A shield. Allow my magic to rise. Create a bubble around us.*

The wind slowed, and some of the cold abated.

"Good, *very* good."

I opened my eyes and grinned when a similar dome appeared around us, but it wasn't quite as strong as the prince's. A few snowflakes still penetrated it, and a light breeze caressed my cheeks.

My grin turned into a frown. "It's not as strong as yours."

"But it's still very good, Ilara. Impressive actually."

"Really? But . . ." I held out my hand and caught a snowflake. "It's not a sealed dome."

"Only because this is new to you. Give yourself time. Your power rivals mine." He sounded so certain of that, so convinced that he was right. "But you should conserve your strength right now. You need to replenish this field's *orem*, and then you have training. It's important that you're resting thoroughly each night and consuming high amounts of sustenance. Learning new affinities demands much of a fairy."

"So no late-night dates?" I replied hopefully. "Sandus told me the king has ordered that the Trial continue as planned, and that the Olirum Accords still stand, meaning that I *have* to date the other males."

The prince's jaw flexed. "That's correct . . . for the moment."

My heart pattered as that fierce light grew in his eyes. That strange need for him followed, as though my body craved for me to step into his embrace and bring my lips to his.

What in all the realms, Ilara?

I turned away from him, my breaths coming faster as I forced myself to rest my magic. My dome disappeared.

In a blink, another formed, stronger and larger, thanks to the crown prince. A flush of warmth blew over my face, and I raised my eyebrows at him. "How did you do that?"

"Increasing the air's particle activity produces heat."

I sighed. "However that's done."

"You'll learn."

"But obviously not today." I sank into the snow and pushed the powder to the side until I found gray dirt beneath it. A tangle of thorny stalks encrusted in ice lay on top of the soil.

My lips tugged down. "How long has it been like this?" This field looked even sicker than Harrivee's.

The prince sat beside me. "Over a full season. It was the first to fully die, the fields around it dying next, as though the *orem's* death started here."

Digging my fingers into the cold ground, I felt for a hum of life. Unsurprisingly, I found none. "It's the same as the field by Barvilum. Nothing's here."

"At the moment no, but that's why I brought you." He leaned back, lying on the snow as though it were a bed.

I snorted. "Making yourself comfortable?"

"Considering we'll be here for hours, I don't see why not."

Sighing, I set to work. Similar to last week at Harrivee, I sank my fingers into the dirt as I would have if I were laboring back in Mervalee. Not even sure what I was doing, I simply did what I'd done before—poured my concentration into the soil and imagined that I connected with it as though it were my garden back home, and a part of me wondered if that was why my affinity had worked. I did a lot of visual imagining while I worked the fields, and perhaps I'd unconsciously called my budding affinity to the surface without even knowing it.

I worked quietly, and the prince remained silent. Outside of his bubble, the wind raged, the sound loud enough that its faint scream slipped through his Shield on occasion.

I loosened more dirt between my fingers. "You seemed to enjoy Lady Endalaver's company yesterday." As soon as the comment left my mouth, I wanted to kick myself.

Why did I just say that?

The prince pushed himself up on his elbows. His lips curved as he regarded me with unveiled interest. "She's certainly not shy, is she?"

I glared at him. "It doesn't matter to me if she is."

"Really? Is that why you asked about her?"

"I don't know why I asked. Forget I said anything."

"I don't think I will." He pushed up more, his smile growing, and now I wanted to strangle myself. "Lady Endalaver is powerful, but she's not as strong as you."

I rolled my eyes. "Considering I can barely call forth my magic, that's debatable."

"Don't mistake practice for strength. She's had several decades of training on you."

"Yet I'm supposed to catch up in a matter of months."

"It's imperative that you do."

"Why? You don't fancy marrying Lady Endalaver?" Just the thought made bitterness coat my tongue, but I swallowed it down.

"Not particularly."

"She seemed to have you wrapped in her affinity yesterday, so you could have fooled me."

"Her affinity." He scratched his chin. "Yes, that manipulation affinity she possesses is quite dangerous."

It wasn't lost on me that he didn't deny being enthralled by her. Not wanting to continue any talk of Georgyanna Endalaver, I sank my fingers more into the soil, relishing its coldness as that old anger began to simmer inside me again. The fact that he hadn't denied enjoying Lady Endalaver's company only strengthened it.

It heated my blood, roaring through me even more at the reminder of what my future held.

Ignoring him, I let my anger stew and threw my energy into the field, letting it take me away to a place far, far from here where there was no starvation or strife or potential war. Just soil, plants, and life. I hummed, caressed, and coaxed the dead roots and plants toward me as I found one after another. I moved along, clearing snow as I went.

Black roots. Chipped thorns. Dry stalks.

The prince's protective bubble expanded every time I moved even though he stayed where he was, but his bubble grew larger and larger.

I put as much distance between us as I could and pictured this field growing to life once more, kissed by the gods and teaming with crops.

I got so lost in what I was doing that I barely noticed when the prince suddenly crouched right beside me. "We need to leave soon. You should eat before training."

My stomach growled as though in agreement. "Let me do one more thing." I dug my fingers into the dirt. I'd felt the touch of a large root, one that traversed most of the field. If I could just reach it, I was certain it could perhaps speed the process up here. "I think I've almost—"

A wicked-sounding roar cut through the blizzard, the sound like razors down glass, and the dome around the prince and I shuddered from something large and heavy slamming into it.

I was on my feet in an instant, just as the prince cursed beneath his breath, and his Shield shattered.

"Snowgum!" The prince threw himself over me as a rush of air brushed my cheek.

Something *huge* flew over us, and then four massive paw prints appeared in the snow only feet away.

That was it.

Paw prints only.

Because the snowgum's magic had made it invisible.

"Oh Mother, save us!" I whispered.

"We're getting out of here. Now." The prince's arms wrapped around me as his mistphasing magic rose.

But just as fast, the snowgum slammed into us, tearing me from the prince's arms as the prince rolled to the side.

"My prince!" I called.

He yelled in pain as blood suddenly soaked through his tunic.

"Oh Blessed Mother! Oh Mother!" I scrambled to my feet as the invisible predator sank its fangs into the prince.

A blast of the prince's affinity had the creature shooting off him even though I couldn't see it. But I *felt* it. Power. Air. The rush of something massive being thrown through the howling wind.

The whiteout still raged around us. I could barely see the

prince through the swirling snow, but I leaped toward him, using his black tunic to guide me.

I landed at his side, and with a sickening sense, realized it wasn't only black surrounding him but red. Blood seeped through his tunic, and it was pooling beneath him at an alarming rate.

"Where did it bite you?" I clawed frantically at his clothing.

He groaned and slowly sat up.

"Can you mistphase us?" I tried to help him straighten, but he winced.

"Yes, come here," he rasped and pulled me close again, but his magic didn't rush to the surface as quickly as it had the first time.

"My prince?"

He groaned again, and his face grew paler. Muscles quivered in his neck, and his aura grew more and more diminished. A huge gush of blood appeared on the snow beneath him, then a shudder ran through his entire body.

"Prince Norivun!"

His eyelids dropped, and his limbs went slack as he fell in a heap. His full weight hit me like a huge stone.

Breaths coming faster, I struggled to hold him, but he weighed too much and collapsed back onto the snow.

Panic consumed me. "Prince Norivun!" I screamed again and began to shake him.

Nothing.

Frantically, my gaze shot over him as I tried to assess what was wrong.

Clawing at him again, I whipped the tunic out of his belt

and lifted the material to his chin. All of my fear collided into epic proportions of terror and despair when I saw his true injury.

A *huge* laceration slid along the length of the prince's abdomen. Blood poured out of it as intestines shone beneath. It was so deep and undoubtedly lethal.

"Dear gods," I cried.

The creature's claws had *torn him open*, and all because he'd been trying to save me from the snowgum's jaws.

"My prince!" I yelled again. My heart exploded in fear just as a vibration of magic rippled through the air.

It was the only warning I got before the snowgum pounced.

CHAPTER 7

The force of the predator hitting me knocked the wind from my lungs. Its hot breath came next, wafting over my skin like smoke. The snowgum's invisible body pinned me to the ground, my ribs screaming in agony under the feline's immense weight.

All the while, the prince continued to lie beside me. Unmoving. Possibly not breathing. Perhaps even dead.

My heart threatened to burst, and I only had a second to glance at the prince before the creature shifted its weight and nearly crushed my chest.

I wheezed as my body sank more into the snow. Coldness seeped into my back. And the snowgum . . . I could feel its mouth opening. It was going to eat me even though I saw nothing.

Blessed Mother, I'm going to die. Prince Norivun's going to die. Cailis will be alone.

Those last two thoughts had panic rising from me like an inferno. *No!*

Magic erupted in my gut.

I screamed. And then the realm tilted, as though everything were moving in slow motion. A rush of magic blazed out of me. Fire. Air. An inferno of power.

The snowgum roared as my magic burst free in a whip of blazing heat. It ripped beyond my control as one thought and one thought only seared my mind.

We can't die.

My head whipped toward the prince. I needed to save him. *Now.*

The snowgum's hide caught fire. The creature screamed again as its massive body erupted into flames.

My eyes widened at its monstrous size as I scrambled to Prince Norivun.

The snowgum continued to thrash like a demon from the underworld. Fire raged around it, lighting up its nine-foot-tall body with paws like small tables. It rolled in the snow, still roaring, as it slowly doused the flames.

The damage my fire had done cut off its magic, making it visible again, but even though I'd burned it, it was anything but down.

My fingers closed around the prince as an enraged snarl tore from the snowgum. Its massive body lowered on its haunches as it prepared to leap again.

"Prince Norivun! Wake up, now!" I shook the prince, grabbing him by the shoulders so hard that his blood seeped through my fingers.

But he didn't move.

The snowgum lunged, leaping from its position.

This was it.

We would both die.

Agony like I'd never felt before cut through me, slicing me open as my arms enclosed the prince. *Not today. Please not today. I don't want to die.*

My eyes squeezed shut as I pictured my sister. My parents. Tormesh. My village. All of it blended in a kaleidoscope of color.

My sister would be alone.

I can't leave you.

I pictured the castle. Safety. Healers. Help.

The snowgum's large body slammed into me, nearly tearing me from the prince as the reek of its burned flesh singed my nose. But I didn't let go of the prince. I kept my eyes squeezed shut as I imagined the castle again. Murl. Safety.

The realm suddenly flashed out of existence, and then we were torn through mist and shadows, air and wind.

The next thing I knew, the prince and I were crashing onto the ground at the castle's outer courtyard. Guards were only feet away.

Their shocked faces beheld me as my mind began to spin. The last thing I remembered was collapsing to the ground with the prince at my side.

A WARM HAND HELD MINE. It was soft, smooth, and thin. Fingers brushed over my skin, back and forth, and I frowned when I detected the scent of roses, then the feel of smooth cream rolling across my palm. *Someone was putting lotion that smelled of flowers on my hand?*

My eyes fluttered open.

I blinked, then blinked again. Surely, I was dreaming, or dead and dreaming if dreams were possible for the deceased, because Queen Lissandra sat at my side in the Exorbiant Chamber. A beautiful scarf covered her head. The rich blue silk reminded me of the shawls I'd often worn back home to hide my hair.

She smiled faintly and picked up my other hand before slathering it with the rose-scented lotion. "I figured you would wake soon."

She moved with sure purpose over my palms, coating my fingers. Her warm hands felt soft and comforting. The way my mother's hands had once felt.

This couldn't be happening. The last memory I had was of Isalee, the field, the prince, the snowgum—

"Where's Prince Norivun?" Alarm skated through me as I snapped out of her gentle touch.

"In the healer's infirmary. It's thanks to you that he's alive."

A heartbeat passed before that reassurance hit me. I sagged back against the bed, only then realizing that my heart was pounding, and a tender ache seared my ribs. I'd thought for certain he was dead. That the snowgum—

But wait, how did we get back?

"The guards tell me that you mistphased him here," she added in her serene tone.

I smoothed my confused expression as a blurry memory of slamming into the ground by the castle's outer wall filled my mind. Frowning, I sat up more. "There must be a mistake. I don't know how to mistphase."

"Perhaps you don't consciously, but your magic did."

I swallowed, realizing my mouth felt dry. As though sensing it, the queen lifted a cup from the table near my bed and held it out to me. "It contains a tonic that will help soothe aches and pains."

I glanced down at myself. "Am I injured?"

"You bear no cuts or abrasions, but a large bruise has formed on your chest and back. I expect you'll be tender for several days unless you drink this." She nodded toward the glass, her voice soft.

Bringing the cup to my lips, I sniffed. I scented nothing. I took a drink, and a burst of bubbles coated my tongue, then the hint of fruit. Tilting my head back, I finished the entire glass in three gulps.

"Murl said you would be thirsty."

I frowned. "He did?"

She nodded. "You've been asleep nearly a day."

My eyes popped. "I have been?"

"You've been sleeping since you returned, most likely because you completely drained your magic and needed to replenish it."

"But my training—" I was supposed to have met Matron Olsander. She'd been expecting me. And then Sir Featherton had planned to stop by to finish explaining the Trial.

The queen returned to slathering lotion on me, unperturbed. "King Novakin has excused you from your Trial duties until tomorrow, unless you choose to return earlier." Her lips pressed together, and a flash of what almost looked like anger scoured her face before her expression smoothed, making me wonder if I'd imagined that intense moment of rage.

"And Prince Norivun, how is he?"

"Awake and flaming mad." She smiled, as though not the least bit surprised at her son's behavior. "He's insisted that he be discharged from the infirmary and brought to see you, but Murl won't let him leave. The cut on his belly went too deep, and he's likely to tear open the healing Murl has done if he leaves too soon."

"But he'll heal completely?" I held my breath.

"He will. By tonight, Murl believes his healing affinity will have soaked in enough for Norivun to only bear a thin scar."

I sagged against the covers once more, relieved yet still confused about why the queen was at my bedside. I didn't know how to politely ask, so I settled with, "Are Daiseeum and my sister preoccupied with something, Your Majesty?"

The queen's eyebrows lifted. "I'm unsure. Shall I ring for them?"

"No, it's okay. I just wondered why—" My cheeks burned. Mother Below, I never was taught how to properly address royalty.

A knowing smile curved her lips. "You're wondering why I'm here."

"I'm sorry." I twisted my fingers together, the lotion making them slippery.

"Don't be." Her gaze drifted to my hair. Black locks fell around my shoulders.

She pulled the scarf from her hair, and I swallowed a gasp when the female staring back at me suddenly looked uncannily similar to my own image. It took me a second to realize that she wasn't wearing her customary illusion spell. She must have removed it before she donned her scarf.

Raven-dark hair fell in a waterfall down her back. Her hair

was as straight as an arrow, long and thick. And it was the exact shade as mine.

"I wanted to acquaint myself more with the female who bears hair like mine and to also see who my son has become so invested in."

My earlier blush returned with a vengeance. "Do you know why our hair looks like this, Your Majesty?" I asked, desperate to keep our conversation away from the prince.

She capped the lotion and set it on my bedside table. "I do not, and I've spent a fair amount of time trying to discover an answer."

"Oh." Any hope I'd once had of explaining my strange genetics vanished. If the queen of the Solis continent was unable to secure an explanation, the Mother only knew that I would never be able to. "Do you know anyone else who looks like us, my queen?"

She shook her head. "There have been Solis in the past with hair the shade of night—I've found that much in my studies, but other than a fluke of genetics, I've found no reason to explain it. Every other Solis who's had it had no family history of ebony hair, and it's a rare trait. I've met no others like us in my lifetime. You're the first."

"Truly?"

She nodded.

I frowned. A fluke of genetics—what an unsatisfying reason for the lifetime of torment I'd suffered from thanks to my black hair. I played with the bedsheets, wanting to ask her more questions as I mulled that over, but I was unsure if propriety allowed it. I tangled my fingers in the bedsheets more.

She laid her hand over mine. "There is no need to be

anxious. I'm here of my own making and am happy to speak freely." She leaned closer and whispered, "Nobody even knows I'm here." She winked, and the gesture was so ordinary, so *normal*, that it felt as though I was speaking with Birnee.

I laughed.

Her smile grew, and she patted my hand. A hum of her magic washed over me, vibrating beneath the surface of her skin, and in that prolonged contact, I felt it. The queen held power. *Immense* power. "Would you like to speak more?"

"I mean, I would. I just—" I twisted my fingers again, but instead of seeing annoyance wash over her features, she simply folded her hands in her lap.

"You may ask me anything, Lady Seary."

My eyes widened. "Truly?"

She smiled again. "Now, what is your first question?"

"Did your affinities also bloom late?"

An understanding lit her eyes. "Ah, yes, they did. Mine bloomed quite similar to yours in fact. My family was convinced that I was a defective—probably as your family also labeled you—but when my first affinity manifested, they were proven wrong."

"Nuwin mentioned that you have five affinities."

"That I do."

"And did they all manifest around the same time?"

She settled into her seated position more. "They did not. When the first one manifested, my illusion affinity, I thought it was to be my only one. But my second and third came several weeks later. A fourth a few months after that, and my final affinity, not until a full season had passed."

"They were that spread out?"

"Indeed." Her look turned serene. "I wouldn't be surprised if you're similar. The crown prince tells me that to date, you've had three affinities manifest. Is that correct?"

"Yes." I debated telling her what Matron Olsander had told me. That she sensed something slumbering within me, but I decided against it. If I truly was to manifest more affinities, the less fae that knew, the better. If having three affinities put a target on my back for the Olirum Accords, I didn't even want to fathom what more would do. "And in your family, did others have affinities like yours?"

"My mother shares my illusion affinity, but other than that, no, not in the slightest. Like you, I come from a non-noble family of average affinities. However, my mother's affinity was strong enough that she could hide my black hair from an early age as a way to protect me from hateful comments and gawking. Consequently, I grew up as any defective does and was able to lead a relatively normal life on the shores of Osaravee. My father was a merchant, and my mother was our store's bookkeeper. My four brothers still live there."

My eyes widened even more. I'd known the queen hadn't been born of noble blood, but I hadn't realized her beginnings were so humble.

"How did the king find you?"

Her expression took on a faraway look, as though morphing into a void that only she could see. "In the same manner that the three other females were found. Sir Featherton has proven quite useful in sniffing out fae with multiple affinities."

Her comment reminded me that I was supposed to have met with the noble last night, but I imagined Daiseeum would have shooed him away if Sir Featherton had made an appearance while I was sleeping. I also surmised that I would be seeing him soon, perhaps even this afternoon, so I could learn the rest of the Trial's requirements.

"Did you also partake in a Rising Queen Trial, Your Majesty?"

Her lips thinned. They sealed so hard they were practically white. "I did not. That is something the king has created for my son. The king has many beliefs that I do not share."

Her angry comment smoldered between us, but her aura didn't grow. Not like the prince's did when his emotions ran high. I figured she had mastered complete control of her Outlets, perhaps even discovering a way to release her powerful magic in a way that didn't affect others. I'd yet to detect any aura from her.

She took a deep breath and then another. Slowly, her thinned lips softened, and that faraway look entered her eyes again. After a few more breaths, she patted my hand, then replaced her scarf, covering her hair once more. "I must go now. I shall have your lady's servant notified that you've awoken."

I sat up more, wondering if I'd done something to offend her and sorely hoped I hadn't. "Thank you for coming to see me, Your Majesty. And thank you for . . . answering my questions."

She nodded swiftly, still breathing deeply. "The pleasure was mine. Goodbye, Lady Seary."

She walked quickly from the room, her head high, her shoulders stiff. Her deep rhythmic breaths continued, and I wondered anew if I'd done something wrong.

But I had a feeling I would never know.

CHAPTER 8

"**T**he necessary courting during the Trial will occur once per week, which means that you will have approximately one date with each potential male . . ."

I tried to pay attention as Sir Featherton reviewed the rules of the Trial. He hadn't bothered to sit down. A part of me thought the archon liked standing over me as I sat on the couch in my familiar tunic and leggings. At least this time, I was dressed.

"You do not have a choice in what order the males court you. You are expected to engage in polite conversation. Any discourse between you and another male may be reported to me."

The Trial archon had arrived not long after the queen left, and he didn't waste any time jumping into what was expected. He held a scroll in front of him, reading it off like he was a magistrate in the supernatural courts, as though this were an actual trial being held in a criminal case.

Several times I had to stop myself from rolling my eyes.

Cailis's hands were on her hips, a scowl painted on her features, as Daiseeum stood quietly in the corner. My sister had arrived just before the Trial archon and had been looking vexed ever since Sir Featherton had begun reciting the rules.

He continued reading, and my stomach turned into a ball of worry the more and more he revealed.

If anything, it was becoming entirely apparent that I no longer had any rights at all. None. And when he got to the tests, I learned that they could be won by using any means necessary. No outside interference was allowed in any way, even if a female's life was at stake, and none of the females would be given any information about what the tests entailed. All of us would be walking into them blind.

A flash of horror filled me. I could literally die in the tests.

My sister and I shared a veiled look. *Escape. We will escape.* Her silent look nearly screamed the reassurance.

"Thank you, Sir Featherton," I said when he finally finished.

He dipped his head. "My pleasure, and might I add that I'm pleased to see that you and the crown prince are both well after that terrible incident in Isalee Territory yesterday."

I inclined my head in thanks, and he bowed and left the room, leaving me alone with Cailis and Daiseeum.

"Have you seen the prince?" I asked Daiseeum tentatively. The only news I'd heard of Prince Norivun was that he was mending, and that had been from the queen.

Daiseeum pursed her lips. "No, but I'm sure he'll be right as rain. The prince has never let any injury keep him down for long."

I frowned, wondering how many injuries the prince had suffered that would create that kind of reputation. My frown increased when I recalled the scar I'd seen previously along his abdomen. And the way he'd confronted the fairy in High Liss who had the ice bear affinity without any hesitation . . .

I shuddered. Death and violence seemed to walk hand in hand with the crown prince.

"Are you feeling well again?" my lady's servant asked. "As energized as normal?"

I nodded. I'd finished an entire tray of food before Sir Featherton had arrived, and the magic in my gut was finally feeling replenished.

Daiseeum whisked the empty tray away. "In that case, Matron Olsander has asked for you to join her in the training rooms if you feel up to it. Sandus will accompany you. Of course, only if you're up for it. The king has excused you from duties today if you would prefer rest."

"All right. Thank you, Daiseeum."

The lady's servant bobbed her head before gliding from the room.

When it was just me and Cailis again, I lowered my voice even though nobody could hear us. "We need to get out of here."

"I know." She paced a few times by the window. "I couldn't believe it when Sir Featherbrain said you had to *engage in polite conversation,* and *any discord could be reported to him.* Not to mention you could die! I mean, *seriously?* This is such nonsense." Disgust pulled at her lips.

"I know, but, Cailis, I need you to figure out a way to get into the courtship dinner tomorrow night so you can help me figure out who's a friend and who's an enemy. The more I know about the fae here, the better off we'll be."

"I can do that," she replied.

I nibbled on my lip. "Any ideas yet on how we'll escape?"

She sat beside me. "No, but you mistphased yesterday. Can you learn to do it with control? That would be the easiest way out of here, especially if you can mistphase me with you."

I sat upright, my jaw slackening. I'd completely forgotten that I'd inadvertently mistphased me and the prince back to the castle. Like my life-giving affinity, I had no idea how I'd done it, but when death had loomed, my magic had come running.

"You're right," I breathed.

She nodded. "You need to learn that skill above all others."

"Okay, so we'll plan for mistphasing as our escape, but we still need a backup plan just in case I can't master it."

Cailis ruffled her wings. "Consider it done."

I squeezed her hand. "I'm so glad you're here."

She threaded her fingers through mine. "We'll always have each other, Lara."

Since Sir Featherton's talk of the Trial had left me anxious, I decided to take Matron Olsander up on her offer to train.

Consequently, the matron wore a shrewd expression as she gazed at me with arms crossed. Sandus stood in the corner of the training room, listening to everything we said. The only silver lining was that none of the other females in the Trial were in the training room about to watch me fumble through another lesson.

"Tell me again what happened," Matron Olsander demanded.

"I don't know exactly." I shrugged. "I was panicked, and the snowgum was nearly on top of me. All I could think about was that the prince and I would die if I didn't get us back to the castle."

"And then your magic mistphased you of its own accord?"

"I guess so. The prince was unconscious, so I don't think he did it."

She nodded and *hmmed*. "Interesting. Very interesting. Mistphasing is an advanced magical tactic that requires an immense amount of power. Most are never able to master the skill due to the amount of magic it requires. It would seem you have the capability, not surprising given that you have three affinities, yet consciously you don't know how to access that part of your magic."

"But I could learn, right?" I tried to keep the hope from my voice and did my best to keep my tone casually interested, as though my request wasn't at all from the calculated plan Cailis and I had contrived.

Matron Olsander harrumphed and rapped her knuckles on the wall. "Of course you'll learn! That's top of my list. Without wings, how else are you to travel throughout the realm?" Her expression told me everything about what she thought of my stupid question.

A grin threatened to spread across my face, but I managed to suppress it. "So you'll help me learn to mistphase and have that be part of my daily training?"

She swatted at my backside. "I don't like repeating myself, Lady Seary. Yes, you'll learn to mistphase. Now, climb the ladder. The balance beam is waiting. If you're fully healed from the snowgum's attack, we haven't a moment to lose. The day is squandering!"

DESPITE THE FACT that I'd nearly died and had depleted all of my magic the previous day, Matron Olsander wasn't dissuaded in the least. I could barely walk by the time we finished, but I felt marginally better about controlling my Outlets and Shields, sensing my magic and calling it forth, becoming educated on the mental aspects of mistphasing, and I had learned one cool trick. I knew how to self-cleanse now.

Matron Olsander might be strict and have a penchant for smacking me upside the head and rear, but I was grateful she was such an excellent tutor.

"You're doing quite well." Sandus smiled pleasantly as we strolled back to my chambers.

"Do you think so?" I rolled my shoulders. My entire body felt stiff, and it wasn't from the snowgum's attack. Matron Olsander had made me do chin-ups at one point when I'd accidentally started a training mat on fire.

He nodded and scratched his beard. "You're an anomaly for certain, love. You've had no magic until very recently, yet you've managed to replenish life to one of Harrivee's fields, outwit a snowgum, and then learn to self-cleanse. All within a week's time. I'd say that's something to be immensely proud of."

My chest tightened, and my aching arms didn't feel quite so

sore after hearing his prideful comment. "This is a bit of a change from how I've always been."

"A good change, though, eh?"

I managed a nod, but a part of me wasn't sure. While my life had been small in Mervalee, and Vorl hadn't exactly made it pleasant, I'd still been free. Now, my power was growing, but I was no longer the maker of my own destiny. I was a slave to the court.

I wasn't sure which fate was worse.

"I'm sure the crown prince would enjoy a visit from you," the guard said when we reached one of the convening areas between wings. To the right led back to my chambers, to the left led to the healing infirmary. "He's been asking for you."

My heart tripped, nearly falling from my chest. While I was immensely relieved the prince was mending and I wouldn't be the reason for his demise, I still didn't know how I felt around him. I had a hard time controlling my reactions to him. This ridiculous attraction overtook me at times, and I didn't like that. Therefore, the easiest way to pretend that I was indifferent was to avoid the prince.

"Well?" Sandus asked. "Should we stop by to say hello?"

"Um . . ." I twisted my hands.

"He's asked for you." Sandus raised his eyebrows, his meaning clear. The prince wanted to see me, and what the prince wanted, the prince got.

Sighing, I replied, "As you wish. Lead the way."

CHAPTER 9

"These are the most ludicrous demands I've ever heard." Prince Norivun's growly comment fluttered into the hallway. "I'm *fine*."

"If you try to return to duty now," Murl replied in a painstakingly patient tone, "you risk the chance of tearing your wound. By nighttime, you shall be fully healed. Please, my prince, allow yourself to rest for another few hours. That's all I'm asking."

"These inane, insufferable rules—" Prince Norivun's griping cut off when Sandus strode into the room with me in tow.

The crown prince, not surprisingly, had his own suite in the healing infirmary. Calming scents of lavender filled the air. The setting sunlight streamed into the windows, and a crackling fire filled the hearth.

The prince sat propped up in bed, his chest bare. A nasty-looking cut ran the entire width of his abdomen.

I stared at his laceration, my throat going dry. A flash of that wound pierced my thoughts. It was freshly sliced open, blood flowing freely, intestines showing . . .

I worked a swallow. The snowgum had come so close to killing him—*so* close. The infallible crown prince, the one who always caused pain versus receiving it, the fairy feared above all in our land, had nearly died from the lethal predator.

Sandus gave a mocking bow when we reached the prince's bedside. "Prince Norivun, I bring the dearest Ilara Seary, daughter of Mervalee Territory, to your bedside to keep you company whilst you mend." The guard's eyes glittered with amusement, making me think that perhaps such a wound wasn't that uncommon after all for the prince.

I studied the other long scar on his abdomen, the one running up his side. I wondered how many other scars the prince had that I was unaware of or how many previous injuries Murl had healed that'd left no scar.

The Bringer of Darkness glared at Sandus before looking me up and down. My bruises from the snowgum's pounce were hidden, but the prince's masterful aura surrounded me as though he were a great seeing eye, able to detect every malady and ailment that had ever occurred to me in my fleeting life.

I crossed my arms and resisted the urge to fidget. Magic hummed in my gut. Despite training vigorously with Matron Olsander all afternoon, my strength had returned and was far from depleted.

"Leave us." The prince flicked a finger at Murl and Sandus just as voices came from the hallway. Before either of them could depart, Lord Crimsonale and his son Michas flounced into the room.

Well, Lord Crimsonale flounced. Michas simply followed him.

A glacial expression descended over the prince's face, and Murl bowed before departing. Sandus merely smirked and strolled leisurely after the healer. The guard winked at me before closing the door but barely veiled a sneer in the Crimsonale's direction.

"Lord Crimsonale, what brings you here?" The authority in the prince's tone was back. One would never have guessed he'd uttered it from his deathbed.

The older lord glided toward us, giving me a long, lingering appraisal before reaching the prince. "We've only come to ensure your well-being."

Michas also cut me a look that while tense, didn't hold the derision his father's did. I remembered our conversation again on the balcony at the Betrothed Ball. Michas had a history with Prince Norivun. It'd made him accuse the prince of lying to me and sneaking into the castle to kill the fae that had gone missing. While I'd believed the prince in the end about not conducting those horrific acts, I didn't actually know the truth.

But perhaps Cailis could help me with that.

"How kind of you," the prince replied sarcastically. "But while I'm sure you were hoping to find me in a much dire state, I can assure you I'll be back to my princely duties by the morn."

The elder lord's eyes shuttered. "How fortunate."

Prince Norivun smirked before he addressed Michas dryly. "And what of you? Any words of affection or well wishes?"

Michas ground his jaw and balled his fists. Bowing, he replied, "Best of wishes for a swift recovery."

Prince Norivun's eyes only darkened further as Lord Crimsonale added, "Your father asked me to remind you that you have council meetings this week that you must attend." He gave another look in my direction. "Your time away of late is no longer acceptable."

"I see," the prince replied easily, but I still caught the tension in his jaw. "Please remind my father that I know exactly what my duties are."

"Of course." Lord Crimsonale bowed. "Have a blessed evening, my prince."

With that, they both strode from the room.

Once they were gone, I just stood there. The crown prince's aura threatened to swallow me—it was running so high. Crackling from the fire filled the room, but other than that, it was silent save for the blood thundering through my ears.

"Come here," the prince finally said.

I inched closer to his side but didn't sit down. I had no idea how to interpret the Crimsonale's visit, so I opted for a generic, "How do you feel?" since the prince seemed intent on studying me, yet his expression gave away nothing.

He cocked an eyebrow. "Why does everyone keep asking me that?"

I waved at his stomach. "Perhaps it's that claw that nearly ripped you in two. Just a theory."

Amusement twinkled in his eyes. "Ah, that sharp tongue of yours is making an appearance again."

I played with my tunic's hem. "Well, perhaps you shouldn't ask such *asinine questions* then, and my tongue would stay still."

His lips curved up more, and I wanted to kick myself that we actually had a private joke now, and I'd just used it.

Smoothing his expression, he patted his bedside. "Sit."

"Is that an order?"

"Isn't everything I say an order?"

Rolling my eyes, I did as he said but made sure to keep a respectable amount of distance between us.

He frowned, a low growl rumbling in his chest, but he stopped it, and his face returned to a mask of stone. His fingers fluttered, and his pointer finger brushed momentarily against my thigh.

Shivers danced up my side, and my entire body seized. His touch had been fleeting, if it could even be called a touch since it'd been more like a brush of contact, yet all of my attention zeroed in with razor-sharp precision to his hand. Those very fingers had nearly swept my underthings to the side just a few nights ago.

And I'd loved every second of it.

I swallowed sharply as my heart thrummed painfully hard.

"I owe you a life debt," the prince said at last.

"Because I saved you?"

"Yes, but you more than saved me. You saved yourself too."

I plucked at a thread on the bedspread as lavender scents from the candle billowed around me. I inched farther away from him. I needed him not to touch me again. If he didn't touch me, my head remained clear. "Perhaps. Does that mean that I can ask anything of you if you owe me a debt?"

"Do I want to know what you're going to ask?" A sly smile lifted his lips.

My lips curved in return, since I was unable to help it. "Probably not."

"You can't break our bargain. That's non-negotiable."

"I know."

"Then what is it you want?"

"To not partake in the Trial."

The arrogant tilt to his lips disappeared. "Does the thought of marrying me repulse you that much?"

I picked at the thread more. My heart beat harder, so hard I was certain he could hear it. "I wish to be free, not to be told who I have to marry and when."

"So it's not the thought of marrying *me*. It's the thought of being told you must marry me." His smug smirk returned.

I rolled my eyes. "I have no desire to have a debate over semantics, my prince. I believe I've made my wishes clear regarding marriage to you or anyone else."

His hand encircled my wrist, the pad of his thumb brushing lightly along my skin. The feel of his grip seized my lungs. Tingles shot up my arm, an explosive array of fireworks zinging along my nerves. I wanted to pull free of him, knew I should, yet . . . his touch felt incredibly addictive, almost hypnotic.

His voice dipped, quieter yet filled with meaning. "I cannot stop the Olirum Accords. Not even for you. I tried again today to ensure you'll never have to marry another, but the king refuses. I'm sorry."

Stunned, I didn't move. He'd apologized to me *again*. At one point in my life, I'd been convinced I would never receive any apologies at all from the prince.

Shaking my head, I brushed that realization off.

"But I meant it when I said I'll find a way to keep you from the other males."

I stilled. "How?"

"I don't know yet." He growled. "My father already knows

I have an undue interest in you. If he were to know the extent of what I . . ."

"Extent of what you . . . *what*?" I asked, brow furrowing.

"Nothing."

But his hesitance to answer my question reminded me of what he'd said on the night of the ball, that it was important for his father not to know what I was to him. Whatever that meant, especially considering all I knew was that the prince believed me a valuable commodity who he desired to own.

But why would he hide those desires from his father?

I frowned. "What aren't you telling me, my prince?"

His gaze searched mine, his look veiled yet . . . intense. "When the time comes that you *know*, your question will be answered."

"Riddles? Seriously?"

"It only sounds like a riddle to you because you're female."

I whipped my wrist from him. "Really? Is that where this conversation is going? That because I'm *female*, I couldn't possibly comprehend your cryptic words?"

He reached for me, but I rose from the bed and took a step back.

"You misunderstand me."

"As seems to be a common occurrence, my prince." I turned and strode toward the door and called over my shoulder. "You know, all of this would be so much easier if you simply spoke plainly to me."

But when he didn't explain what he'd meant, his expression only darkening, I made a sound of disgust. "Goodnight, my prince. I shall see you in the morning when you no doubt fetch me, your loyal slave, for another session of *saving the continent.*"

A rumble of his power vibrated the stone flooring, but it didn't deter me. Storming away from him, I slammed the door behind me.

CHAPTER 10

Sandus and I trained again the next morning, and the prince came for me promptly when we finished.

Despite still being angry with him, I couldn't stop from looking the prince up and down as anxiety pulsed through me. He stood tall and strong, his aura potent, yet only two days ago his belly had been torn wide open.

"Are you—" I forced myself to swallow. "Fully healed?"

Norivun's nostrils flared as a knowing smile spread his lips. "Why, Lady Seary, are you concerned for my well-being?"

I ran an agitated hand through my hair. "No, of course not, but I just wondered if you're . . ." I made a disgusted sound. "Can't I just ask how you are without it meaning more or you inhaling to detect every emotion I feel?"

His smile grew, and his nostrils kept flaring. "Very well, yes, I'm indeed fine and back to normal, thanks to Murl and you. And sorry, but no, I plan to devour every emotional scent you reveal. I can't help it. Your scents are mouthwatering."

Flustered, I put more distance between us. Staying away

from the prince was the only way I was going to survive my time at the castle given my innate attraction to him.

Behind him, Haxil, Nish, and Ryder waited. Given the dangers we'd experienced, I wasn't surprised that all four of his personal guards were accompanying us back to Isalee. I had a feeling they'd be joining us for the foreseeable future.

We spent another day very similar to the first. I kept as much distance from Prince Norivun as I could while I healed another field before returning to the castle for another grueling session with Matron Olsander.

By the time evening rolled around, my eyes were dripping with exhaustion, but I couldn't rest. It was the night of the first Trial dinner, followed by my first official date—with the prince nonetheless.

I sat on the couch in my living area, freshly bathed, my hair dry thanks to Daiseeum's magic, as she held up a floor-length dress.

"I thought this one would be perfect." Firelight caught on the gems woven through the midnight-blue material as Daiseeum twirled it about. The gown sparkled like a thousand moons. "It's so beautiful. Exquisite really. What I wouldn't give to have a figure like yours and don such a breathtaking item." Daiseeum smiled, her expression wistful.

"Do you want to try it on?" I offered. "You can borrow it if you want."

Daiseeum's jaw dropped. "Borrow a lady's gown? Have you lost your mind, Ilara?"

"I don't think so, although that could be debatable. Cailis certainly thinks I have."

The lady's servant's lips pursed as she shooed me to my

feet. "Up, up. We don't have much time since you trained so late. Come. We must prepare you."

I followed her into the bathing chamber, where she proceeded to doll me up using her affinity magic. Daiseeum's affinity was the ability to conjure beauty. It was considered a superficial one, a lesser affinity among our kind, but I once again marveled at the female's capabilities.

When she finished, even I was stunned at my appearance. My ebony hair cascaded around my shoulders in a silken waterfall. Large curls made it weave and bob as a ringed circlet of jewels crowned my forehead in a dazzling display of wealth. The dress's jeweled belt hugged my waist, and the gown's V-cut design plunged so deeply that the slit dropped to my navel, revealing more flesh than I felt comfortable showing. My arms were also bare, but that only drew attention to the gown's sparkling and twinkling gems woven into its material.

Daiseeum lifted my wrist and clasped a dozen small bracelets around it, either pure silver or plates filled with diamonds, sapphires, and amethysts. The finished display made me a vision of prestige, as though I were an actual princess.

"Where do all of these jewels come from?" I asked her as she finished with her final adjustments.

"The castle's vaults. The queen gave permission for her jewelry to be used freely by any lady staying in the castle on the king's behalf."

My eyes widened. "This all belongs to the queen?"

"It does, m'lady."

"That's very generous of her."

"Queen Lissandra is known for her kindness." Daiseeum

stepped back and gave a wistful sigh. "There. All done. You truly are a vision."

I thanked her again, then gathered my skirts for the long walk to the dining hall. I hadn't seen Cailis since returning from training, and I could only hope that she was devising a way to gain admittance to the Trial dinner so she could spy on everyone and report to me who was trustworthy.

Sandus's eyebrows lifted when I joined him outside my chamber. He looked me up and down, then shook his head.

"What?" I asked.

"Nothing. It's just that the prince . . ." He scratched his jaw. "I'm not sure if the prince will like other males seeing—"

"Seeing what?" I asked, my ire rising when he spoke of the prince.

His expression smoothed. "Nothing."

My nostrils flared as my slippers slid along the castle's stone floor. It felt like there was some kind of secret taking place that I wasn't in on.

We walked down the hall, and I debated asking the guard why the prince acted the way he did around me, then decided against it. The guards were loyal to their prince. I already knew he wouldn't tell me anything that the crown prince might be against my knowing.

"Enjoy the evening," Sandus said when we reached the dining hall. Inside, laughter and conversation flowed through the air. It sounded like everyone else had arrived. "I shall see you on the morrow."

I nodded tightly as my heart thrummed. *It's just a dinner. No need to be nervous.*

Surely, nothing terrible could happen at a dinner and single date with the prince.

Music filled the air in the dining hall as trays floated around the room, holding champagne flutes and little plates of bite-sized morsels. A long dining table spanned the room's length, and vases of turquoise and blue ice flowers dotted its center as fine porcelain plates ringed in silver sat at each place setting.

Similar to the Betrothed Ball, ice flowers were also suspended from the ceiling. They let out puffs of snow that melted before they came into contact with anyone. Snowflakes drifted everywhere, and the entire room swam with magic.

I didn't see the crown prince, but all three females from the Trial were present, a dozen other males as well, most of whom I'd never met before. Some turned to watch me as I entered the room. Others continued chatting in small groups, not looking twice in my direction. Anxiety twisted my stomach into knots while I searched for Cailis.

I finally caught sight of her on the balcony, hidden behind a draped curtain. My sister stood just outside of the room, on the terrace overlooking the large, snowy lawn. She was hidden enough that no one would easily see her.

I let out a sigh of relief. I had no idea how she managed to get onto the balcony without the guard the prince had assigned to keep her safe, but come tomorrow, I could pick her brain, and she would be able to tell me everything about the other participants.

"Ah, Ilara!" someone called.

I swirled around to see Nuwin waving from across the room, a smile lighting up his face before he glided toward me.

Nerves calming slightly, I snagged a flute of champagne off a passing tray and took a sip just as Nuwin reached my side. Like the crown prince, he was tall and broad, his face ruggedly handsome and his build thick. His black wings rose above his shoulders, not quite as high as the crown prince's, but the two brothers would make any female look twice.

The younger prince took my hand in his, then kissed me on the cheek, his lips coming dangerously close to my mouth. "You're a vision as always, Lady Seary."

I squeezed him in return, about to reply, but the prince entered the hall, and a wave of his aura pulsed toward me in the same breath. In a blink, he was at my side, moving so quickly on his air affinity it was as though he'd mistphased.

Nuwin snickered. "I wondered when you'd show up."

Prince Norivun's attire was similar to the night of the Betrothed Ball. Power rippled from him, and my stomach flipped, especially when a predatory light filled his eyes as he appraised me. A low growl rumbled in his chest, making my throat go dry. "I've got her, Nuwin. She's my date tonight."

Nuwin bowed and then winked at me. "Of course, brother. A thousand apologies for not relinquishing her to you immediately." He kissed the back of my hand, his eyes full of mischief when he added, "I look forward to the night when you'll be *my* date."

"Nuwin," the prince said, his tone low and warning.

Nuwin merely straightened. "You can't blame a male for trying." With that he sauntered off, leaving me in the crown prince's grip.

More eyes fell on us as the prince glided me across the room. "You're late," he murmured, his tone gruff when Michas Crimsonale lifted his champagne to me in a silent toast.

I nodded in acknowledgment, and out of the corner of my eye, I saw Cailis studying the Osaravee noble.

"I stayed to train a bit longer with Matron Olsander," I replied. "Besides, aren't *you* actually the one who's late since you arrived after me?"

He gave me a side-eye, then led me to the table. "That's because I left to retrieve you from your chambers, but it seems we missed one another in passing."

I shrugged and tried to ignore how wonderful the heat felt from his palm as he guided me to the table.

Even though nobody else was seated yet, he pulled out a chair for me, then took the seat at my side as everyone else proceeded to the table to join us.

Chairs were still being adjusted, skirts being swooshed out of the way, and champagne flutes being refilled when Sir Featherton entered the room, his chin high and proud.

When he reached the head of the table, he clasped his hands beneath his wings. "Good evening, fine fae of the Solis continent. Welcome to your first Trial dinner." He grinned, then held his arms wide. "In attendance tonight are some of the strongest fae of our mighty race."

There were a few murmurings and puffed chests following that comment. I still couldn't believe I was even considered a member of this group.

Continuing, Sir Featherton said, "As you all know, at these dinners each female will be paired with a male for a date following the meal, and in one weeks' time, they shall be paired with another male. The king and I hope you enjoy these evenings and use them as a way to better acquaint yourselves with one another." He straightened more, his wings ruffling slightly. "All we ask is that you keep an open mind and do your best to view each partner as a potential lifelong mate." He bowed slightly. "With that, I shall bid you a good evening and wish you all a wonderful time."

My stomach twisted at the reminder that this Trial would end in an arranged marriage no matter what. It didn't help that Prince Norivun's scent was clouding around me. I hastily took a sip of champagne.

Meegana smiled shyly at me from across the table. "You look beautiful, Ilara."

"Thank you, so do you." Like me, Meegana was dripping in jewels. Her gown was fuller than mine, holding layers of chiffon, and was a light teal color. "I love how your dress matches your eyes. It's stunning," I added.

Meegana's smile grew as her hand fluttered to her neckline. "Thank you."

Beside me, the prince adjusted how he sat in his chair, and his knee bumped me. I made a move to put more distance between us, but his large palm settled on my thigh, spanning the width of it.

My heart rate picked up when he didn't remove it, but his fidgeting calmed, as though touching me had some soothing effect on him, which was bizarre, but perhaps having his *property* within reach was calming since he was definitely a male who didn't like to share his things.

Heart still hammering, I tried to pretend I wasn't affected by the weight of his hand as servants appeared, bustling around the table. They served the first course—a delicate salad of greens, berries, and a tart dressing.

"Did you find the extra training helpful today, Lady Seary?" Georgyanna asked from down the table. She fluttered her hand, admiring the gleaming gems on her bracelet. "It looked like you needed it. Hopefully it was enlightening?" she asked with mock sincerity.

One of the males coughed, and another snickered at the Kroravee female.

Warmth bloomed across my chest since I'd struggled repeatedly that afternoon when trying to better control my fire element. I'd nearly burned Matron Olsander at one point, never mind the mat from the other day, but the tutor was quick on her feet despite her rotund figure. Of course, my training session hadn't stayed private, so everyone had witnessed my fumble.

Forcing my chin up, I replied lightly, "Indeed I did. I would offer to light the candles on this beautiful table, but I'd worry that I'd start the napkins on fire." I smiled sweetly at her and picked up my champagne flute.

The crown prince snorted, and Nuwin and a few of the other males outright laughed, not even trying to hide their amusement at my self-deprecating humor.

Georgyanna's lips thinned, and her eyes shot daggers my way.

I grinned, flashing my teeth, despite the fact that my heart was still beating a million times a minute and not just from the prince's claiming touch. Menace practically dripped from Georgyanna. But I wouldn't for a second let her think that my late blooming meant I was going to turn belly-up.

Glaring at me one last time, Georgyanna angled herself in her seat, giving me her back and slightly flexed wings as she laid a hand on the male's forearm beside her.

Trying to calm my racing heart, I took a deep breath just as Beatrice said pleasantly from across the table, "I heard your sister's joined you here at court." Her eyes were bright and open, carrying none of the malice that Georgyanna wielded. I cast a glance to where Cailis was watching on the balcony, but my sister had moved into the shadows. I still didn't think anyone knew she was there.

I took another sip of champagne as I nodded. "She has. She arrived a few days ago."

"Does she possess multiple affinities too?" Meegana asked as Georgyanna fell into conversation with all of the males surrounding her. I could practically feel the Kroravee female's manipulation affinity rising and wondered if that was how Georgyanna conversed with all fae—trying to bend their will to her own.

Gritting my teeth, I forced my attention away from her. Replying as lightly as I could to Meegana, I said, "She doesn't. Cailis only has one affinity. Truth."

Beatrice's eyes widened in delight. "How magnificent! I bet that affinity's come in handy a time or two."

My lips spread in a genuine smile as the two females and I quickly fell into easy conversation, sharing where we'd grown up, gone to school, and tidbits about our family. When it came to my turn to share details about my parents and siblings, I glossed over them, not revealing that the male at my side had ended their lives prematurely.

Prince Norivun tensed when I spoke of them, but when I

didn't cast him in a scathing light, the long fingers of his free hand, wrapped tightly around his drink, loosened. He even gave my thigh a small squeeze with his concealed hand, as though thanking me for not damning him for the entire realm to hear. I had to stop myself from jumping against that intimate touch.

The dinner carried on in relative peace for over two hours as dish after dish of succulent meats and an abundance of sides were served. Everyone drank, laughed, ate, and enjoyed one another's company for the most part, and nobody commented that I ate more food than half of the males in attendance, but such was needed for what was being demanded of me of late.

When the time came for each female to be whisked away by their date, I was more than a little tipsy after enjoying three flutes of champagne.

"Are you going to be able to walk for what I have planned tonight, or shall I carry you?" the prince whispered into my ear when he pulled my chair back.

I frowned, a fuzzy part of my mind telling me that there'd been another time when I'd had too much to drink around him, and perhaps less-than-desirable acts had taken place. Or had that been a dream?

"I can walk." I stood from my chair, and even though the damned floor swayed, I didn't fall.

He chuckled. "If you say so."

The other three females all cast envious glances toward the crown prince as he guided me away. Georgyanna was on a date with Michas Crimsonale, Beatrice with Nuwin, and Meegana with a male I hadn't met yet. It was crazy to think that this stupid Trial required me to date all of the males here.

I made a sound of disgust as the prince opened the balcony door for me, then my heart jumped into my throat when I remembered my sister had been hiding out here.

But she wasn't there when we stepped outside.

"Is everything all right?" he asked.

Flustered, I ran a hand through my hair and tried to calm my breathing. "Yes, I was just, um, thinking about this Trial and all of the males I have to date."

His shoulders tensed.

I eyed him, and maybe it was the champagne making me tipsy or the fresh air that breezed over my cheeks when he led me outside, but I found myself saying, "Do you really want to own me that badly? That you don't want any other male to have the chance to touch your things? But don't you already own me, my prince? Surely, that's enough."

His wings flared as a fierce light grew in his eyes. "I don't own you. Trust me, if you were *mine*, you would know."

His? My jaw slackened, and a memory slammed into my mind when I recalled that he'd claimed just that to Drachu and Vorl. The fierceness then and the fierceness now took my breath away all over again. I gulped in another lungful of air when Cailis's sudden hand on mine drew me up short.

"Cailis?" I yelped as my sister stepped to my side from the shadows. She was dressed in a woven top, pants, and a thick cape. Draped over her arm was my cloak.

"This is for you." She slung it over my shoulders, and the thick garment instantly warmed me in the chilled air.

"I don't understand," I said dumbly, then gave her a look as though to say *what are you doing revealing yourself?*

My sister cast a wary glance toward the prince. "Neither do

I," she replied, "but apparently, for your date tonight, instead of the crown prince taking you somewhere alone, he's decided to take you and *me* elsewhere."

"Elsewhere?" I raised my eyebrows at him, entirely confused why Cailis had been invited but thankful that it gave her an excuse to be on the balcony.

Prince Norivun's expression gave away nothing as he said, "I know you've given up a lot, and I know that I took you from your home when you least expected it, so I thought tonight that perhaps I would take you home. I've arranged for your sister, along with your village friends, to join us. I thought—" He paused, and I could have sworn that a flash of nervousness was upon his face. "I thought perhaps it would make you happy."

"Home?" My heart began to race as blood sped through my veins. *Home. Home. Home.* Mervalee Territory. My village. The humble abode my sister and I had grown up in. My garden. My kitchen. My *life*.

I'd dreamed of home since the prince had forced me from my village's barn weeks ago. Had dreamed of the moment I could once again lay my head on my own pillow, caress the tender stalks of my garden, hear the tinkling sound of Birnee's laughter while Finnley roared in happiness.

"Do you mean that?" I whispered. "Are you really taking me home for our date?"

"I am, if it's what you want?" His expression was still guarded. The usual suave look he wore had disappeared entirely.

It took everything in me not to fling my arms around him. Grinning, I replied, "Yes, I would like that very much."

CHAPTER 11

I hadn't known what to expect from my only official date with the crown prince of the Winter Court.

I certainly hadn't pictured it being the two of us sitting in the tiny living room of my family home while my sister, Birnee, and Finnley surrounded us and regaled us with funny stories and anecdotes from our childhood while we all drank too much leminai and laughed so hard that my ribs ached.

But the night was beyond memorable, the warmth endless, and some tiny part of my heart cracked open at the sheer thoughtfulness and generosity of the prince's gift.

Prince Norivun lounged in a chair near the door, leaving the area by the fire for me, my sister, and my friends. He watched me the entire night, content to listen rather than partake, the smile on his face growing broader every time I laughed or showed delight.

When the evening finally came to a close, Birnee and Finnley flew back to their homes, and the prince clasped ahold of both me and my sister. In a twist of mistphasing magic, he whisked us back to the castle, and we landed just outside of the eastern wing.

Cailis took one look at the prince and me, a slight frown marring her features, and I knew her wheels were turning.

"Thank you," she said, a hesitant tone to her voice. "For letting me come along tonight."

The prince inclined his head. "It was my pleasure."

That assessing look didn't leave her features, and if anything, her expression morphed into confusion.

"Walk with me?" the prince asked me.

"Of course," I replied, still reeling from the leminai and feeling of contentment that only home could bring. "See you, Cailis."

My sister squeezed my hand, and in that grip, I felt it—her warning, her unspoken words not to fall under the prince's spell.

I squeezed her in return, some of my head clearing.

Cailis reluctantly turned back to the castle, her guard opening the door for her.

The stars winked down on us, and a cold breeze swam through the night air. The prince tugged me along until we were strolling through the ice gardens.

"Our date continues?" I joked awkwardly.

"Until you tell me it's over."

My breath stuttered. I knew this was my one and only date with the prince. Since the Trial demanded weekly dates over the course of three months, it only left enough time for one private date with each male. One date in which each female was given the chance to learn what she could of the male. One night in which secrets could be laid bare and personality traits learned.

Just one.

I gulped when that realization hit me. Instead of using our one night to keep me to himself, the prince had instead given me a gift. He'd given me a chance to return home. He'd chosen something that would make *me* happy, not him.

I stopped in my tracks and faced him. "Thank you for letting me go home."

His eyes softened. "You seemed to enjoy it."

"I did. Immensely."

He gestured toward a bench near a frozen pond. "Shall we sit?"

Heart pounding, I wrapped my cape around me and sat on the frozen slats. Within seconds, shivers were striking me.

"Allow me." A whisper of the prince's magic misted around us, and then one of his encapsulating domes from his air affinity created a Shield. The air warmed. The frosty puffs from our breath disappeared. Yet the sky still twinkled above us. His magic was so powerful, able to create so much destruction but controlled enough to do something this gentle.

"You have a nice home," he said, breaking the quiet and pulling my thoughts from his power.

I arched an eyebrow. "That's polite of you to say."

"I'm not being polite. I mean it."

I angled to face him more. "My entire home can fit within the Exorbiant Chamber."

His lips curved, and my attention snagged to how perfectly they were shaped. "It's not the size I'm referring to. It's the *feel* of your home. Your friends. Your sister. It's obvious you all care for each other, that you'd all do anything for one another."

A small smile parted my lips. "We would."

"You're lucky to have that."

I frowned at the slight catch in his tone. "But what about you? You have this—" I waved toward the castle. "And your family. You all have power and rulibs. You have everything you could ever ask for, and if there's something you want that you don't have, you can just demand it."

He gave a rueful shrug. "It does appear that way, doesn't it?"

I frowned. "Are you saying it isn't?"

He sighed, and his wings draped more when he leaned into the bench's slats. "Appearances can be deceiving. Yes, I live in a castle. Yes, I have a family. Yes, I have rulibs and power."

"But . . ." I raised my eyebrows.

"But we don't have what you have. We don't have the freedom of anonymity. We don't have the luxury of nobody watching us. We don't have the easy warmth that so effortlessly flows through your family's home. We have—" He cut himself off and shook his head.

"What? Tell me?"

"Nothing. I'm speaking too freely."

"You're not. I want to know."

He turned to face me again, his gaze penetrating in the moonlight. "My family might have rulibs, power, and endless food, but we don't have the love that your family does, and I don't have the luxury of doing whatever I want, despite what some think."

I paused, not sure where to begin after hearing that. I

started with, "But what about Nuwin? You love him, don't you?"

He chuckled. "Yes, I suppose I do, even though he enjoys driving me mad."

"And your mother?"

His expression turned guarded before he said softly, "I love her very much."

"And . . . your father?" I probed.

All expression left his face before he said, "With royalty comes demands. With demands come chains."

His statement made me pause, not just because he'd refused to speak of the king but also because, for the first time, understanding hit me. "You're no more free than I currently am."

He gave another shrug. "Perhaps a bit freer than you, since I can command your servants, but in some ways, I'm not free at all."

His tone held a lightness to it that hadn't been there previously, but I still detected the underlying despair. And not for the first time, I saw again the deep-seated emotion that resided within the prince. He not only had empathy, but he felt things deeply, felt things so viscerally that I once again wondered what being Death Master of our continent did to him.

Breaths coming faster, I turned away. It was happening again, exactly what Cailis had warned me of. I was falling under his spell anew, feeling things for him that I shouldn't.

I abruptly stood from the bench. "I think I would like to return to my room now."

His expression closed off as he gazed up at me, but only a heartbeat passed before he stood. "Of course."

We walked silently back to my chambers, ambling through the outer paths until we ducked through a door into his private wing.

We passed a door I'd never seen before, and the prince angled his head toward it. "That leads to my private chambers."

"It does?"

He smiled, and some of the heaviness from our earlier conversation lifted in that one movement. "I could show it to you if you want." He waggled his eyebrows playfully.

I suppressed a laugh. "Are you asking me back to your chambers?"

"Would you if I asked?"

His tone suddenly turned serious, and my step faltered. "I can't bed you. You're to date other females while I date other males."

"I won't be inviting any of them back to my chambers."

"How do you know? You may." I quickened my pace, finally recognizing where we were in his wing.

"I won't."

I frowned as my stomach flipped. "Even if you don't, you still killed my parents. I could never bed you despite what happened at the ball." It was the closest either of us had come to discussing our kiss on the balcony again, that soul-searing tangle of lips and tongue.

His footsteps continued quietly beside me before he said hesitantly, "What if I didn't kill your parents, what then?"

My heart stopped. Just when I'd started to truly think that maybe, just *maybe*, the crown prince wasn't a monster and that he did harbor true kindness in his black soul, he had to go and throw that in my face.

"Don't be cruel." Ice formed around my heart, and I swallowed the tears that wanted to come as I walked even faster.

"Ilara, can I trust you?"

My brow furrowed as I abruptly stopped and faced him, my chest heaving. "Why are you asking me that again?"

He glanced over my shoulder, down the hall. The faint sound of servants reached my ears. "Perhaps I'll explain another time."

"Explain *what*?" I demanded as I rounded the final turn, and Jovin appeared. "What are you hiding now?"

But his mask had descended. Any hint of what his cryptic words would reveal had vanished.

I brought a hand to my forehead. Fatigue hit me suddenly. The prince was hiding something again, perhaps many things. He was a male of shadows and darkness, death and destruction, and whenever a hint was revealed as to what truly lay within him, a veil always descended, blocking me out. The Bringer of Darkness always stared back at me.

And right now, following too much champagne and leminai, a grueling day of training, and the late hour . . . I couldn't process his riddles, and quite bluntly, I didn't want to.

I sighed heavily.

The prince stroked a finger across my cheek, featherlight and so fleeting that only the trail of goosebumps left in its wake told me I hadn't imagined it. "I'll see you tomorrow."

In a wink of mistphasing magic, just as I reached my bed chambers door that Jovin began to open, he disappeared.

❄

EVERY MORNING over the next three days, I trained with Sandus and returned religiously to the Isalee field to heal what I could, followed by grueling lessons with Matron Olsander in the afternoons, which always bled into the early evening.

Each day was similar, exhausting, draining, yet exhilarating. But there was one change to my new daily duties—the prince no longer stayed with me in Isalee.

Every morning after he mistphased me to the field, he would cast warded magic around my work area before disappearing. If any snowgums came prowling, the wards would alert his guards, giving them precious seconds to mistphase me out of there.

Luckily, the giant cat that I'd burned during the previous attack had yet to make an appearance, and I had a feeling it remembered my scent and chose to stay away. I had no idea how badly I'd burned it, but its skin had been charred in places. And luckily, considering they were territorial creatures, I had a feeling it was the only giant cat in the area for millees.

As though the prince had come to the same conclusion, he seemed to feel comfortable that my safety wasn't compromised, so each day he left me in Isalee with his magic in place, under his guards' care, and asked me to continue my work.

I couldn't help but wonder if he'd regretted our date, perhaps regretted many things regarding me, especially when stress lines marred his features, and his manner remained closed off and guarded.

I tried not to care that for the first time since he'd begun demanding that I use my affinity to heal our land that he wasn't at my side, and I firmly reminded myself that his absence was what I wanted. Yet his presence had become familiar in a way, and as much as I didn't want to admit it—I missed him.

"What is it you're doing every day?" I finally asked him on day three, no longer able to keep my curiosity at bay.

"Princely duties," he replied, annoyance in his tone.

"Oh . . . sorry I asked," I mumbled as I slipped off my gloves and plunged my hands through the snow toward the dirt. A bubble of the prince's magic surrounded me and his guards, so despite the howling wind and fierce cold, where I worked was relatively comfortable.

A low growl came from the prince, and then he knelt by my side. "I'm sorry. I didn't mean to snap at you."

Haxil glanced over his shoulder at us, but when the prince bared his teeth, the guard turned back around.

I shoved my hand more through the snow, my movement agitated. "It's fine. It's not my concern. You don't need to explain what you do to me or divulge how you spend your time." I broke through a layer of ice at ground level. Cold, dry soil greeted my searching fingers.

"Perhaps not, but I didn't mean to sound irritated with you. It's not you who's annoying me. Council meetings are what have been pulling me back to the castle. I've been missing them as of late, and my father isn't happy."

"Oh." My erratically beating heart slowed as I remembered Lord Crimsonale's visit to the healing infirmary, and it struck me anew that spending all morning at my side while I worked the fields was incredibly draining of the prince's time. It also reaffirmed that I literally had no idea what the crown prince normally did or what *his* daily duties were, which reminded me of what he'd said on our date. *With royalty comes demands. With demands come chains.*

"Do you normally attend all council meetings?" I asked hesitantly.

His irritated scowl didn't lessen. He tore a hand through his hair. It was unbound today, and silver locks hung loosely around his strong jaw. "I'm supposed to, although our meetings haven't been pleasant lately."

"Because of the diminishing *orem*?"

He nodded. "Tensions are running high. Lord Crimsonale and Lady Wormiful are insisting we move our race to the southern continent and abandon our land before it's too late. My father is resisting."

A wave of relief billowed through me. "Because the king doesn't want war?"

The prince snorted. "I think the real reason is because he's stubborn, and he doesn't think the *orem* is truly vanishing." I frowned and wanted to ask more, but the prince stood. "I really must go. I shouldn't be late, but that's why I haven't been very pleasant lately and why I haven't been accompanying you."

I sat back on my heels, realizing it was the most he'd ever revealed about his daily life. I knew he regularly visited the territories and was required to uphold the law using his death affinity, but I hadn't considered the more diplomatic sides of his life. Council meetings. Political discussions. Subduing territory squabbles.

For some reason, I couldn't picture the crown prince sitting in the council chambers each day, listening to angry territory archons fight and bicker over the direction of our great kingdom. It seemed too caged of an existence for the prince, like it clipped his wings. He had so much power and strength in him that it almost felt as though he needed to move and roam, and a stuffy council chamber certainly wasn't for that.

When the prince made to turn away, I grabbed his hand. He stopped, stilling completely as his gaze fell to where I'd touched him.

I hastily removed my hold. "But why is Lord Crimsonale still insisting on moving south when Harrivee's field is showing signs of life? Don't they know that whatever I'm doing is working?"

The prince's eyes darkened, those sapphire blue irises like a raging storm. "They don't know yet, Ilara. I was waiting to tell them. If this field also shows signs of life, then I'll reveal what we're trying to the council. Until then, I don't want anyone's eyes on you."

An ominous shiver ran through me, and not for the first time, I thought about what had occurred within the castle's walls—the fae who'd gone missing. The ones who'd disappeared without a trace. They'd all been actively involved in the diminishing *orem*, either talking about it or trying to raise the alarm. None of them had ever been found.

And now I had dove headfirst into that very problem, a problem that had put targets on the missing fae's backs.

"Up you go, now!" Matron Olsander said shrewdly as I balked at returning to the balance beam. It stood nearly twenty feet in the air, yet from the floor, it looked like an imposing cliff.

I swallowed the hesitation in my throat yet still didn't move.

"None of this dilly dallying. Your first test will be upon us before you know it." My tutor swatted my rump, getting a yelp out of me.

I rubbed my backside and glared at her, but she merely shooed me forward, so I reluctantly began to climb the ladder.

"You can do it, Lara!" Meegana called, an encouraging smile on her face as she watched from below.

I gave her a small nod. Cailis had confirmed following the first Trial dinner that Meegana always spoke truthfully when she addressed me. Beatrice usually did too. Because of the trust I was developing in them, both of them were becoming my friends despite the Trial requiring us to compete with one another.

As for Michas and Nuwin, Michas was surprisingly honest when he spoke, most of the time, but Cailis said at times he'd bleed gray, which was her affinity's way of telling her he wasn't outright lying, but he was skirting the truth.

And Nuwin . . . I nearly snorted thinking of him. He was a true trickster, oftentimes pulsing in lilac waves, indicating he was fabricating stories to elicit a response from those around him. I hadn't been astonished in the least to learn that.

Not surprisingly, Georgyanna lied regularly, but her manipulation affinity was strong enough that even Cailis had a hard time seeing which colors she bled whenever she spoke, so Cailis and I had decided that it was best I avoid the female as much as possible.

And as for the crown prince, she hadn't been able to get any reading on him at all. His affinities were too strong, his Shield like a stone wall. She wasn't strong enough to see past it, and since the prince never released his Shield, not even for a second, it meant Cailis would never be able to see if he was truthful or lying.

I gripped the ladder tightly as I began to ascend while that thought struck me again. Shaking it off, I tried to concentrate on what Matron Olsander wanted me to do.

Some of the males watching me crossed their arms, arrogant smirks on their faces, while Beatrice plucked her hands on her hips, seemingly content to observe. Of course, everyone was in the training room again today, other than the two princes—both of whom were apparently attending a council meeting that was an all-day event.

I climbed higher, and a shrill laugh came from Georgyanna. Her aura heightened. A wash of it prickled my skin. It felt slimy, reminding me of oil, but instead of coating my insides, it slid off of me when I tethered my magic around me and practiced my Shield.

Thankfully, my magic was strong enough that I was able to thwart Georgyanna's attempts at control, but the male standing next to Georgyanna must not have been as strong as her, or his Shield was down, because a cruel smile twisted his lips when her affinity hit him.

Georgyanna nudged his side. "She looks so terrified. Don't you think?"

The male stepped closer to her, his lips twisting more. "Indeed, she'll probably fall. I don't even know why she's in this Trial. She doesn't even have wings."

Georgyanna shrugged, the portrait of innocence despite the fact that the male she'd just manipulated had never been cruel to me before.

I continued climbing, and my heartbeat picked up as Georgyanna leaned over and whispered something into Meegana's ear. Meegana frowned and pulled away. Georgyanna rolled her eyes, then let out an irritated huff.

That at least got a smug smile from me. Georgyanna's manipulation affinity had yet to sway my friend.

My hands grew slick as I neared the top, and I stopped once to wipe them on my leggings.

"Don't fall, Ilara!" Georgyanna called. "You wouldn't want an injury during the Trial. Who knows, they could decide to disqualify you. We would hate for that to happen." Her words, dripped with honey, and had almost sounded sincere, but I knew better.

The urge to flick my pinky at her grew, but I knew that would only prove that she was getting under my skin, so I tamped it down.

Ignore her, Ilara. Just keep going. So what if your magic is a hundred times less practiced than theirs? It doesn't mean you're weak. You're not weak anymore.

I gritted my teeth as my hands reached the last rung of the ladder. Carefully, I hoisted myself up and stepped onto the beam. Nothing but air surrounded me. Clear, crystal, barely perceptible air. Right. That was the purpose of these exercises, since it forced me to call upon my air elemental affinity and learn to control it.

"Close your eyes!" Matron Olsander barked from below. I did as she said, just as a plume of magic crackled around my skin. "I'm activating the tests. Call forth your air affinity to protect you. Remember, feel for the cushion of magic in your gut, the lightest one." Her affinity probed within me, guiding me toward that sensation. "*This* is your air affinity."

I nodded and her affinity withdrew.

All week Matron Olsander had been helping me differentiate what each affinity felt like inside me. All of them had their own triggers, and all of them required their own Outlets. It was mind-numbing at times, trying to figure out what was what. Half the time, I couldn't differentiate anything, and it all felt like a big swirling mess in my gut.

Rain abruptly pelted my skin, hitting my head like tiny needles, and I grabbed a hold of the sensation my tutor had led me toward.

"Call upon your affinity, Ilara!" Matron Olsander yelled again. "Form an air Shield around yourself. Nothing should be able to penetrate it."

A gust of wind nearly knocked me off the balance beam, and I shrieked, my concentration vanishing.

The rain and wind stopped. Matron Olsander sighed. "Again. Back to the beginning."

Georgyanna sniggered, and my cheeks flamed in embarrassment that I'd so easily been distracted. Taking a deep breath, I reminded myself what the prince had said.

I was worthy.

I was strong.

I could do this.

Nostrils flaring, I closed my eyes again when Matron Olsander instructed me to draw up my magic. That light, pulsing, feathery feeling rose within my gut, like a cloud of wind. It breathed through me, rising up, up, up.

A rain droplet hit my forehead, but I took a deep breath and focused more on each step along the narrow beam as I felt the air around me, called to it, and asked it to help me.

The chatter below vanished. Warmth kissed my skin. Not one raindrop touched my scalp. A smile of satisfaction spread across my lips as I opened my eyes, feeling the air around me as though it were a living, breathing entity that pulled at my senses and ignited my magic.

"Excellent, Ilara!" my teacher called.

I was almost to the end of the beam, despite water pelting my air Shield from every angle as gusts of wind pushed against it. But the air that I controlled was one with me. I didn't know where I ended and it began.

Another step took me closer to the safety of the platform. Five more steps, and I would be there and off the beam.

Almost there. Almost. Keep going.

An electric jolt pulsed faintly under my heel. Frowning, I tried to ignore it, but the jolt grew stronger. A zap of what felt like a hundred watts of electricity zinged up my calf. The pain of it made me yelp, but I gritted my teeth. I had no idea what this latest test was, but I was steps away from finishing. It did seem a bit sadistic of Matron Olsander, though. The electrical zaps stung painfully.

I took another step, and a surge of electricity bolted up both of my feet so strongly that my entire body seized. Eyes widening, I tried to take a step, tried to reach the end as my mind tumbled and spun with what was happening.

Where? Where is this coming from?

My bubble was around me, protecting me, encasing me. Yet electricity surged so strongly from the beam that I couldn't move. My body's synapses had frozen, my nerves going haywire from the strength of the beam's circuit.

"No!" I whispered, barely getting the word out as a violent

bolt of electricity scorched my nerves, burning the soles of my feet as I yelped in pain.

And then air was surrounding me. Nothing but air as my balance was lost, my legs buckling, my body tumbling from the beam. I was spinning, twisting, falling.

Screams filled the room. A shout from my instructor. A yell from Meegana. A cry of surprise from Michas. Panic seized my chest.

I squeezed my eyes shut only seconds before I hit the floor.

CHAPTER 12

"W"hat in the realm!" a male yelled.

My body stopped two inches from the floor. Only *two* inches.

Blessed Mother. I'd thought I was going to hit it.

Blood pounded through my veins. I hung there. Suspended. Someone had used their air affinity to stop me from breaking my neck. Someone who had actually *mastered* their affinity.

The mat lay a hair's breadth beneath my nose. Black rubber stared back at me. Tiny granules of the material were made up in a crisscross pattern. I was so close to it that I could almost differentiate the tiny fibers.

"Is this how students are taught now, Matron Olsander?" Nuwin asked, then laughed lightly as he sauntered into the room.

A rush of his magic had my body turning in midair. *Blessed Mother*. Prince Nuwin was like his brother. He held an air elemental affinity as well.

When I was vertical again, he set me down. My feet touched the floor so lightly it was as though I was weightless. He was that strong. That powerful. But I winced when my burned soles met the hard mat.

"All right then?" the prince asked me, giving me a wink for good measure.

I bit back a cringe, determined not to let anyone see that I was in pain. "Yes. Thanks."

It was all I could manage. I'd just been burned and had almost fallen to my death. My air elemental affinity had failed me when those electric jolts had skittered through my veins. It was as if the electricity that had been coursing through me was so strong that my magic was condensed.

"What in all the realm happened?" Matron Olsander gave me a shrewd scowl, her cheeks ruddy.

"Um, you tell me." My hands were still shaking. That plummet through the air had been terrifying. I'd truly thought I was going to die.

"You don't know?" she demanded.

I shook my head. "I thought I was controlling my air affinity and magical Shield well, but then those electrical sparks began running up my—"

I stopped short when Georgyanna coughed and covered her mouth. Her palm hid her face, but I could have sworn she was concealing a triumphant smile.

I frowned. *Did she . . . ? No, she wouldn't have.*

I tilted my head up to the beam. It soared above me, looking like nothing other than a plank of wood. But my magical Shield had been strong. Nothing should have gotten through it, so if

Georgyanna had used her electrical affinity to cause those jolts, how had it gotten through my Shield?

It would if she's stronger than you. That whispered comment drifted through my mind.

I curled my fingers into my palms, not liking at all where my thoughts were tumbling or what they implied.

"Well, explain yourself!" my tutor demanded, and I realized she had no idea what Georgyanna had done.

Georgyanna arched a silver eyebrow at me. She stood solemnly now, but she'd dropped her hand, and her expression was dripping with challenge. *Come and get me*, it seemed to say.

Nostrils flaring, I inhaled sharply. No. I wouldn't buy into her petty games and accuse her of something I couldn't prove. That would only make me look weak and defensive, as though I was looking to blame someone for my failure.

I reminded myself that I was new to my magic. Prince Norivun had told me repeatedly not to mistake strength for winters of practice. I simply didn't know my magic well enough yet to have controlled my descent as Prince Nuwin had done, and I lacked the expertise to fend off Georgyanna's attack.

"Well?" Matron Olsander demanded again when I remained silent.

"I can't explain it. I must have slipped when I felt those . . . sensations," I finally said.

Matron Olsander sighed. "I didn't command this room's magic to do anything electrical." She tapped her chin. "I shall have to call in one of our casters to recalibrate the room's offensive magic. It's been several winters since it's been properly utilized. Perhaps it's in need of a few adjustments."

Huffing, she waved her hand toward the door. "That's all for today. This shall take me the rest of the afternoon to fix."

I smiled tightly and gave Georgyanna one last look.

A grin split her delicate features.

Squaring my shoulders, I turned carefully as the males around Georgyanna snickered. Considering the female's aura was plentiful, I knew she was using her manipulation affinity again, and she apparently didn't have any problems with playing dirty.

Blessed Mother, she's truly like Vorl.

My lip curled as I walked toward the door, trying not to limp. It took me a second to realize someone walked right behind me.

I swung around, wincing at the movement, but I was ready to confront whoever followed.

Nuwin held up his hands in surrender. "I come in peace. On the Mother's honor."

It was only then I realized I was snarling, and I smoothed whatever feral expression I wore. "Sorry," I muttered.

"Don't be. I quite enjoy seeing you look like an angry kitten."

"A kitten?" When I made a disgruntled face, he laughed. "What are you doing here anyway, my prince?"

We resumed walking toward the door. I could feel the rest of the Trial's participants watching us, but I didn't glance back at any of them, not even at Meegana, who'd looked horrified when I'd nearly become splattered brains on the mat. I couldn't. My heart was still pounding, and I was two seconds away from losing it completely. I'd nearly *died*.

"Aren't you supposed to be in the council meeting?" I

added distractedly as pain sliced through my soles. I had no idea how badly Georgyanna had burned me, but I prayed my skin wasn't sloughing off.

"Indeed, but we're on a break, so I decided to visit the kitchens for a meat pie, but then I heard a shriek so came to investigate. And it's a good thing I did. You were moments away from landing headfirst on the floor."

I shuddered. The shriek had come from Meegana. Everything had happened too quickly for me to make a sound.

"Thank you for saving me," I said quietly when we stepped into the hall. I winced when the nerve endings in my feet prickled.

Nuwin glanced down. "Oh my. You're injured."

"It's all right. I'll be—"

"Nonsense." He swept me up in his arms before I could protest. "I consider it a great honor to assist a damsel in distress."

"But I'm not that in distress. I'm just burned."

He smiled cheekily. "Play along with it, darling. It does stroke my ego." His lips split into a grin, and for a moment, his likeness to the crown prince took my breath away.

Shaking myself, I smothered a smile. "Oh, all right, if it pleases you."

"It does, especially when Nori learns that I got my hands on you."

I began to snort, but then the hall vanished in a blur of mist and shadows, air and wind.

Nuwin, who could apparently also mistphase, took me to the healing infirmary and promptly asked Murl to assist me.

One potion, two cast spells, and a healing tonic later, I was no longer in pain, and my burned feet were mending. The skin was pink and new, but Murl insisted that by morning I would be fully healed.

"Thank you," I told Nuwin once we were back in the hall.

He gave a small bow. "Always happy to assist a lady in need."

My lips twitched as Sandus strode toward us, coming from around the corner. Considering the irritated expression my guard wore, I didn't think he appreciated our mistphasing within the castle without him.

"Where are you off to now?" I asked the young prince.

He sighed dramatically. "Back to the council meeting. Lord Thisslewater from the Dresher Islands has arrived, which means the next few hours will be sly diplomatic discussions, acting as though we don't need the Dresher Islands' help to replenish our food stores while my father grumbles, Lord Crimsonale and Lady Wormiful further their argument for leaving our continent, and other council members share their fears and gripes about the state of our nation."

"Sounds lovely."

"As lovely as a stinging nettles' nest."

Forehead furrowing, I said, "Despite your harrowing description, do you think that perhaps I could join you? Since my entire reason for being at the castle is to restore our crops, it would be good to know what's truly going on, and now that my training's been canceled for the afternoon . . ."

Nuwin cocked his head. "Well, I suppose that's logical, and if my father has a problem with it, he'll surely let you know."

And with that, we disappeared in another burst of Nuwin's mistphasing magic as Sandus let out a loud groan of frustration.

CHAPTER 13

Arched windows, a stone floor and walls, and a high domed ceiling brimming with fairy lights made up the council's chambers. The room was bright and grand with a hum of magic flowing through the air. The tingle of it caressed my skin, warming me.

"That's Lord Thisslewater of the Dresher Islands," Nuwin whispered under his breath as we stood beneath the door's alcove, not visible to anyone in the chamber. He nodded toward a pale-pink-haired fairy. "He occasionally attends council meetings, but his voice doesn't carry much weight since the Dresher Islands aren't a territory anymore."

"How often does he attend?" I asked.

Nuwin shrugged. "Maybe once a winter. He's only here now because of the crops' current state. Lord Crimsonale is calling for help from any Solis-friendly land that may provide it and asked him to attend."

I nibbled on my lower lip. "How have the crops faired on the Dresher Islands?"

"At the moment, they still grow normally, as do some of the crops in Mervalee Territory. Perhaps the sea that separates us will keep the islands safe, but whatever plagues our land has moved west to east and north to south. Thankfully, the entire continent is not yet affected, or we'd be in a much more dire state."

Snow flew outside as Lord Woodsbury, the archon of Isalee Territory, stood with Lord Thisslewater. They discussed something quietly as they surveyed a map of the northern continent on the wall overlooking the large central table.

The Dresher Islands, sitting off the eastern coast of our continent, were now considered an independent province. While the Dresher Islands were once a part of the Solis continent, hundreds of winters ago, they'd broken away, forming their own state that was able to maintain its independent autonomy through lucrative trade deals. Since the Dresher volcanoes erupted regularly, imbuing the islands with rare magic, the islands had a plethora of precious metals. The rich concentration of such a commodity was the only reason they had enough wealth to maintain their independence. That, and they were one of the few nations to actually engage in trade with every continent that chose to partake. Most of the larger continents preferred to maintain an air of self-sufficiency, not relying on trade with anyone. Our continent was no different, but occasionally trade deals would occur with Dresher, even though no one liked to admit it. Like all of the fae in our realm, the Solis were prideful, even though some of our race still conducted sly trade deals with the Nolus fae near our border. Of course, all of that was conducted through the ostracized markets.

Old habits, however, died hard even from the fae calling Dresher Islands home. The islands still had an archon, a remnant of their Solis roots, even though the inhabitants of the Dresher Islands were a mix of fae races.

The fairy lights glinted off Lord Thisslewater's pale-pink hair as he studied the map, but despite his Nolus coloring, he also had wings, hinting at his mixed heritage.

Other council members were sprinkled throughout the chambers as a table of refreshments stood by the far wall. My gaze swept over the room, and I stiffened the minute I spotted the Kroravee Territory archon, Taberitha Wormiful. She stood near the window, holding a cup of tea.

She brought the cup to her lips, and on her finger a silver inked eternal mark flickered subtly in the light, sparkling for the briefest moment—a circle with an array of connecting swirls and stars.

My brow furrowed. "Lady Wormiful has an eternal mark?"

Nuwin chuckled. "Surprising, isn't it?"

I couldn't help but wonder who her eternal mate was, especially since Lady Wormiful had always reminded me of a deadly serpent, but somebody loved her fiercely.

She spoke in low tones to Lord Crimsonale. Her height, pointy chin, lithe figure, and thin wings made for an intimidating picture. She gave the Osaravee Territory archon a nod, then glanced toward the table as she signaled the others to join her.

"Your Majesty?" Taberitha said as she glided toward the large round table placed in the center of the room. "If you're ready to resume, shall we be seated again?"

King Novakin plucked a sweet from the refreshment table and inclined his head. "Very well."

All of the council members returned to their seats. Prince Norivun sat beside his father, his expression like steel, but the second Nuwin and I stepped away from the alcove, Prince Norivun's nostrils flared, and he scanned the chamber's perimeter.

Mother Below. He'd detected my scent.

As if realizing the same, Nuwin placed my hand through the crook of his arm and smiled pleasantly before sauntering toward the table. I did my best to match his stride and appear at ease, but my smile was tight.

"Good afternoon." Nuwin inclined his head to everyone before pulling out a chair for me, then his own.

The crown prince's lips thinned. Prince Norivun's barely controlled glare slid to Nuwin, but the younger prince was either choosing to ignore him or oblivious.

"What's *she* doing here?" Taberitha Wormiful sneered from her seat two places down.

Lord Crimsonale leaned back in his chair, his wings tightening. Displeasure was written all over his face.

But the king merely waved dismissively toward the youngest prince. "Explain yourself, Nuwin. This is a closed meeting."

Like his sons, the king was tall, broad, and powerfully built. But at nearly eight hundred winters, gray streaks lined his white hair.

Nuwin's smile widened. "Considering Lady Seary has been using her new affinity to restore life to our continent's crops, and the dying crops are the entire reason for this day-long meeting, I thought it was only prudent she attend."

The king waved his hand again, looking more bored than interested, while Lord Crimsonale and Lady Wormiful shared a veiled look as their eyes narrowed.

My chest tightened. Nuwin had just revealed my purpose so casually after Prince Norivun had worked painstakingly to keep my reason for living in the castle a secret from this very council. *Blessed Mother, I should have warned Nuwin.*

I snuck a glance toward the crown prince. Sure enough, he was fuming. Straightening in my seat, I tried to calm my breathing, but my heart beat faster.

The other council members and archons from all of the territories, along with Lord Thisslewater, whispered to one another.

The crown prince's wings tightened behind him, his tone low as he said through clenched teeth, "It would have been nice if you'd thought to inform us of her attendance sooner, brother."

I kept my mouth shut since the crown prince's aura was rising.

Nuwin's smile faltered. "I apologize if I've caught anyone unawares, but I'm sure no one objects, considering the vast catastrophe we're facing. Surely, if Lady Seary can correct such a problem, it will stave much diplomatic discussion."

Lord Crimsonale's expression turned glacial as he subtly leaned toward Lady Wormiful and whispered something behind his hand.

Straightening, Lady Wormiful eyed me coolly. "Have you managed to restore life to multiple fields, Lady Seary?"

I cleared my throat. I could lie, say I hadn't, but I had no idea what affinities lay in this room. Since they were archons, I knew they were some of the strongest fae in our realm, and if one of them had a truth affinity, it would no doubt cast me in a scathing light.

Deciding honesty was the best option, I replied, "No, my lady. Only one so far in Harrivee, but I'm currently working on several fields in Isalee."

Again, Lord Crimsonale and Lady Wormiful shared an unspoken exchange, but before anyone could comment, the king spoke.

"Very well. You may stay, Lady Seary."

Sniveling, Lord Crimsonale turned his attention to the other council members. "Lord Thisslewater, thank you for joining us today. As I'm sure you're aware, our continent has been struggling as of late."

Lord Thisslewater nodded. "I've been told as much. It is a pleasure to attend this meeting with you all." He brought a fist to his chest in traditional Solis greeting and bowed slightly in his chair. "If the Dresher Islands can assist in any way, we would be glad to do so."

The rest of the table murmured pleasantries, before Lord Crimsonale said, "Would you be so kind as to inform us of the state of your crops?"

Lord Thisslewater launched into a rundown of facts and figures, his voice animated. When he finished, the scribe at the end of the table looked up from his parchment, ready to record whatever was said next.

Everyone watched Lord Thisslewater with rapt attention.

All except for Prince Norivun, who drummed his fingers on the table, his deadly glare still focused on his brother.

King Novakin leaned on the arm of his chair, looking unimpressed. "Thank you for sharing that information, Lord Thisslewater. Now, as you might have surmised, you've been invited here today to discuss possible trade negotiations, in favor of your island's export of food staples. I know the Dresher Islands don't produce anywhere near what our territories do, but while we wait for the next celestial event to replenish our *orem*, several of my archons feel it's necessary to secure further grain stores." He gave Wormiful and Crimsonale a disdainful glance. "For a short time, of course," the king added. His eyes traveled around the table, and each archon fidgeted in their seat at the king's challenging glare.

The king's look said one thing and one thing alone—we would *not* indefinitely depend on the Dresher Islands.

"I see." Lord Thisslewater inclined his head. "And what export are you suggesting in exchange for the Dresher Islands to help feed the Solis?"

"Precious gems," Lady Wormiful replied, "from Kroravee Territory."

Lord Thisslewater leaned back in his seat. "Interesting, although I'm not inclined to believe that gems are something we covet. Our islands occasionally produce those as well, and the Nolus fae have an abundance of gems. Trade with them is more appealing in regards to jewels."

Lady Wormiful scowled as Lord Crimsonale rapped his knuckles on the table. "Another option would be to purchase an island," the Osaravee archon proposed.

The king's expression turned downright glacial, and Lord Thisslewater's eyebrows shot clear to his hairline.

"Purchase land? Are you that desperate for food?" Lord Thisslewater's pale-pink locks glinted in the light when he sat forward more, reminding me of my acorlis vines at sunset. "No island is for sale, Lord Crimsonale. Besides, if we ever deemed to give up such a priceless resource, I can assure you the cost would not be worth it."

"Agreed, we'll be doing no such thing," the king snapped, his eyes flashing daggers at Lord Crimsonale.

Lady Wormiful tapped her pointy chin. "But, Your Majesty, we must consider the possibility that our *orem* will never fully return, despite what Nuwin is claiming this *female* will do." She sneered in my direction. "So what are we to do if we're unable to feed our fae? If we cannot secure more food stores from the Dresher Islands, then I propose we consider trading with the Nolus."

I stiffened. "Lady Wormiful, we *will* be able to feed our fae. I'm sure of it."

The room grew silent. Everybody stared at me.

Recovering first, Taberitha gazed down her nose toward me, her lip curling. "How can you be so confident?"

I fidgeted in my seat since everyone was watching me. I didn't know where my outburst had come from, but the last thing I wanted was for this talk to progress to discussions of war. "Because the Harrivee field has returned to life, and the courtyard outside of my chambers is flourishing with life. That's two separate patches of land that I've healed. Prior to me, those parcels of land had been deemed entirely without *orem*. I can do this. I'm sure of it. We don't need to change our way of life while we wait for another celestial event."

The aura pounding from Prince Norivun was now so strong it reminded me of crashing waves on the Osaravee coastline. Too nervous to look at him, I turned my eyes on the king.

King Novakin studied me, and for the first time, I felt as though he really looked at me and saw me as a fairy who was worthy of his attention. "Do you truly believe you can create *orem*, Lady Seary?"

"No." I twisted my hands. "But my affinity does something similar. It creates life, which is exactly what *orem* does, so I suppose you could say it's equivalent to creating *orem*."

The king's stare turned penetrating. "What field are you working on now?"

"It's in Isalee, outside of Whimseal. The first field to fully die."

Prince Norivun's chest rose and fell sharply with each breath, but I refused to make eye contact with him.

"Interesting. I wasn't aware the first dead field was where you were working when you mentioned Isalee." The king shrugged, no longer seeming impressed with me. "Very well, Lady Seary, continue as you've been, but as for the rest of you . . ." He gave pointed looks to Lord Crimsonale and Lady Wormiful. "Such talk of relying on the Nolus fae for anything is forbidden. The Solis fae have maintained our independent great way of life for thousands of winters. That won't change now despite what's occurred of late. We will *not* be purchasing land nor asking the Nolus fae to provide help. We are due for another major celestial event in eight months' time. We simply need to sustain ourselves until then. Between our stores and possible help from the Dresher Islands, I'm confident we shall be fine."

"Although, you're assuming the next celestial event will restore our land's natural *orem*, even though the others haven't." Lady Wormiful sniffed. "If the last two haven't, something that has *never* occurred, why would the next?"

Rage darkened King Novakin's complexion, but before he could respond, the Harrivee Territory archon said, "Your Majesty, what of the concerns my villages' archons have reported?" He gave the king a pointed look. "They're seeing changes in the soil in the southeastern portion of Harrivee. Frost has embedded itself so deeply into most of their land that now nothing will grow. That's never happened before in the history of our great continent, and it's been a recent change, only occurring within the past month."

"We shall discuss that later, Lord Pinebeer," the king snapped.

More murmurs broke out in the room, and my territory's archon raised her hand. "Please keep in mind that Mervalee's crops are still producing." Lady Busselbee's tone was warm, as though trying to soothe everyone's frayed nerves.

"Perhaps, but not at the rate they were two winters ago," Lord Crimsonale challenged.

Lady Busselbee eyed him coolly. "It's true we produced seven tons less last quarter than we did at this time two seasons ago and that all of the village crops have reported losses. All except for Lady Seary's village." She gave me a smile. "Which, if anything, should provide hope that she *can* restore our land's production just as she's claiming."

"And as a thank you for what her village has supplied, we

locked up her village's archon who was in charge of such production," Lord Crimsonale said with a disgusted snort.

"He tried to murder Lady Seary," Prince Norivun replied, his eyes glittering as he finally broke his quiet. For the first time, he turned his attention away from his brother and me. "Or are you suggesting that Vorl shouldn't pay the price for such an act?"

Lord Crimsonale smoothed his lapels. "I'm merely saying that he was never rewarded properly for such a high production."

"Don't you think that Lady Seary should be the one rewarded? Not him?" Prince Norivun cocked an eyebrow. "If you want to properly thank anyone, you should thank her."

Lord Crimsonale flushed just as the king held up his hand. "We're getting off track. Lord Thisslewater is only here for a short time. Let's return our talk to his islands."

The discussions continued, volleying between archons as they debated ways to keep their fae fed while also relying on the Dresher Islands for as little as possible. By the time the talk ended, Lord Thisslewater had agreed to ship a ton of grain per month for the next full season in exchange for two ships full of ice from the Cliffs of Sarum. The grain, while not plentiful, would help, but it'd come at a cost.

Harvesting ice from the Cliffs of Sarum was deadly and dangerous work. Few fae were skilled enough to do so, but since the cliffs were naturally enchanted, its ice never melted no matter the climate, and it was sought after by rival continents as a way to keep their food perpetually chilled in hotter climates.

And since the Sarum ice cliffs were unique to our continent, it was a good bargaining chip since it couldn't be found anywhere else in the realm.

As the meeting came to a close, Lady Wormiful and Lord Crimsonale strode off together, their heads dipped toward one another. The king saw Lord Thisslewater out, and when it was only the remaining three territory archons left in the room with both of the princes, Prince Norivun rounded the table and came to my side.

"Are you a fool?" he hissed at his brother.

Nuwin straightened his jacket. "Last time I checked, no."

"Do you realize what you've done by bringing her here?"

Nuwin frowned, but I cut in. "I'm glad I was here. I know you were hesitant to reveal what I can do, but I think the time's come that we must. The king won't listen to reason or to what's staring at him right in the face, so perhaps it's time we revealed what I can do to stop further discussions of invasions while soothing the unrest. Besides, it's given me motivation to continue working as hard as I can to restore our land's crops. We need to be self-sufficient again. Truly, my prince, I don't think any harm came from me attending."

"Harm? You want to speak about harm?" The crown prince leaned over me. "There *is* harm. The harm is that we just revealed to every archon in here that you're our *only hope* to fixing our land. Unlike the king, all of the archons here know our land is dying."

Nuwin and I exchanged a confused look.

"So?" Nuwin finally said. "What does that matter? Ilara can prevent all of that."

"Only if she's alive," Norivun hissed. "You just put a target on her back."

Nuwin's eyes widened. "Surely, they wouldn't hurt her."

The aura around the crown prince rose. "I don't know if they would or not, but they keep pushing for the Solis to move south. They have their own agenda, and we still don't know who's behind the missing fae. Who's to say it's not an archon."

"Surely, they *wouldn't*," Nuwin said lightly. "An archon wouldn't abduct fae. And we've existed peacefully with the Nolus for centuries, and like Ilara said, she'll fix what's happening."

"You're forgetting that peace has existed only because we've been well fed for centuries, but that's not the case anymore." Norivun eyed the door. "Whether Father wants to admit it or not, unrest is growing more and more each day. A winter ago, only Crimsonale and Wormiful were concerned. Now, *all* of the archons are questioning their king in one way or another. When's the last time you remember that happening?"

Nuwin's brow furrowed, but he didn't respond.

The crown prince's scowl deepened. "Until Ilara can replenish the fields enough to stave off the concerns that we're going to starve, I want her kept away from these meetings. I want her kept away from all of them. We don't need any of them seeing her as a threat to whatever they're planning."

"Then I'll work faster," I offered. "I'll fix the continent before any of them can act. If the king would only allow me out of the Trial, I'd have more time. I could work day and night in the fields. Surely, *that* is more important than the Rising Queen Trial."

Prince Norivun's eyes shuttered. "If you're out of the Trial, then there's no possibility of us ever marrying. Besides, you need your training. You're not going to learn your affinities by working alone in the fields morning till night. Your magical capabilities won't progress swiftly without help. But if you learn your affinities better, you could work faster and restore more fields in a lesser amount of time. You need Matron Olsander for that, so we'll continue as we have been."

I ground my teeth under the authority ringing through his tone, my ire rising more and more. "You're failing to mention, my prince, that you could simply command Matron Olsander to keep working with me even if I was out of the Trial. She and I could work together in the fields to train my life-giving affinity exclusively. You have the authority to command that."

"You can't just train one affinity. You need to master all of them to reach your full potential."

I threw up my hands. "Then have her teach me all of them *out* of the Trial."

His nostrils flared. "My father won't allow it."

"But he might if you convince him that restoring the *orem* is more important than the Trial. Please, tell him to release me from it. Don't make me marry."

His jaw worked, and a muscle began ticking in it. "No."

"No?"

"Correct, no. You're to continue as we have been, working in the fields each morning, then training in the afternoons." Prince Norivun's lips thinned. "Understood?"

I pushed to a stand, the chair squeaking on the floor. "Perfectly, my prince. Once again, you've reminded me of what I am—a slave to the court and to you. I won't forget again." With that, I gave him my back and stormed from the room.

CHAPTER 14

The next week passed in a haze of healing fields, training with my tutor, and one Trial date. I was so angry with Prince Norivun following the council meeting that I avoided him as often as possible. It helped that the return of his princely duties kept him occupied. And since it only took him minutes to mistphase me to the fields each morning, our encounters were brief.

The times he'd tried to see me in the evenings had been easy to avoid if I kept myself plastered to Cailis, and at the one Trial dinner since the meeting, I made a point to seat myself by Meegana so Prince Norivun couldn't snag the chair my date wasn't occupying. Even though the crown prince had watched me the entire night, he'd been forced to sit farther down the table, which made ignoring him entirely feasible.

Consequently, when the night of the third Trial dinner arrived, it'd been over a week since I'd spent more than a few minutes in the crown prince's company. That should have made me happy, smug even, but every time I saw him, something deep inside me ached despite my resolve.

It was entirely insane, and I reminded myself of the promise I'd made to my sister, that I would never fall for the prince or allow him to charm me again.

Don't forget your promise, Ilara.

"This color looks positively divine on you." Lord Waterline's comment snapped me back to the present. My third suitor leaned closer to me, then trailed a finger down my arm.

"Um, thank you." I pulled away as he inched closer despite my dismissiveness.

"And you smell . . ." He inhaled deeply. "Mouthwatering."

I snatched my wine goblet off the table and took a long drink.

Lord Waterline was turning out to be quite annoying, but at least he wasn't as bad as Lord Arcane Woodsbury, the male I'd had my second date with. I shuddered just thinking about him and was glad the Trial only forced one date with each suitor because Lord Woodsbury, the third son of the Isalee Territory archon, had made my skin crawl, and not because he was interested in me. He'd spent the better part of the evening watching one of the young serving girls. She'd still been in the midst of maturing. Wing buds had sprouted through her shirt, but she couldn't have been more than fourteen winters. Despite that, Lord Woodsbury had watched her avidly, his interest rabid and uncouth considering she was still a child.

Shivering, I shoved that repulsive memory away.

At least Lord Waterline didn't give off that vibe. Still, I found it hard to listen to him as he droned on about his family's wealth in their estate vaults. I ended up plucking at the seam on my dress for lack of anything better to do.

Tonight, I wore a gown of deep red even though I wasn't from Osaravee. Its neckline was square, not as daring as the previous dresses Daiseeum had chosen for me, but it was very fitted, which meant my cleavage swelled. Now, I was wishing I'd worn a tent, as the lord's gaze fixed on my breasts repeatedly.

"Did I mention earlier that after my father secured our third estate in Harrivee, he decided to embellish each building with silver-tipped spires? One pure-silver spire is posted on every corner of every building. That silver was, of course, mined in one of *our* mines. We have several, you know."

"Of course, you do." I finished my wine and signaled the serving staff for another. There wasn't enough alcohol in the realm for me to keep up my partially interested charade.

"But enough of my family's substantial wealth. Tell me more about you, Lady Seary. You must come from an esteemed bloodline yourself." His gaze dipped to my cleavage for the millionth time. "One built such as you must herald from time-less beauties."

Somehow, I managed to keep from burning his eyeballs to dust. "Are you always this charming with females you've just met, Lord Waterline?"

He grinned as he cupped his face in his palm. "You think I'm charming? That's delightful to hear."

I rolled my eyes, unable to stop it. Lord Waterline was as conceited as Vorl. On top of that, he was so pompous about his family's wealth and estate ownership that I was surprised he didn't carry a mirror around everywhere just so he could continually look at himself while reaffirming his oversized ego.

"Your dress certainly has a lot of buttons." The noble's finger trailed along my shoulder to the first button at the nape of my neck. He flicked it, as though hoping to undo it. He leaned closer, his hot breath wafting against my skin. "If you need help unbuttoning this later, I would be more than happy to oblige."

I flinched away just as a huge push of heightened magic wafted through the air. I knew without looking who it came from.

On the opposite end of the table, the crown prince wore a ferocious snarl, and it was directed entirely at Lord Waterline. Prince Norivun had been looking as though he was seconds away from murder all night.

Not everyone was wishing the night was over, however. A soft laugh came from Meegana as she and Nuwin conversed. At least one of us was having a good time.

"Tell me, Lord Waterline," I said and angled in my seat so his hand was forced to drop. "Have you read any good books lately? I just finished the most amazing story, courtesy of the castle library, called *Of Fae and Might*. It was a compelling story about a princess from thousands of winters ago who rebelled against a force from an alien realm who'd come to conquer ours. It had romance, adventure, and the most epic battle scenes. A true delight. Have you read it?"

The young lord's gaze fixed on my cleavage once more. When my nostrils flared, and a pulse of magic rumbled in my belly, he looked up.

"I'm sorry, what?"

"I asked if you'd read *Of Fae and Might*?"

"Read? Oh no, I don't read. Reading is too boring for me. Too tedious, don't you agree?"

I picked up my fresh glass of wine that a servant had delivered. "Considering I asked you if you'd read a book I just finished, no, I don't agree." I took another sip and wondered how much longer this evening was going to be. If the day came when a forced marriage to Lord Waterline was upon me, I just might adopt a few tips from the heroine in *Of Fae and Might* and shave his balls off.

Lord Waterline again trailed a finger up my arm, and I was two seconds away from enacting Lady Furyful's wrath when a squeak of a chair came from the end of the table.

Prince Norivun stood, his wings extending. "I think that's enough of this dinner, don't all of you agree? Perhaps we should all rise and mingle for a bit."

Nuwin snorted, glancing between me and the crown prince as Lady Endalaver plastered herself to Norivun's side.

"I think that's a wonderful idea," she purred. "Shall we go out on the balcony?"

My stomach tightened when she tilted her lips up. Of course, tonight he'd been paired with *her*, but despite feeling Georgyanna's oily manipulation affinity in the air, I had yet to see the Winter Court heir so much as give her anything other than a fleeting smile or disinterested nod.

"Actually, I was thinking we could all mingle in here. It's more fun to speak in groups, don't you think, Lady Endalaver? In fact, I was thinking we should start doing that at these dinners more often." Prince Norivun didn't wait for her reply and instead stalked toward where Lord Waterline and I sat.

"Lady Seary, may I refresh your wine?" the prince asked, his tone biting as he glared at Lord Waterline.

"Oh, I can do that." Lord Waterline pushed his chair back, but the crown prince shoved his foot behind the chair's leg, halting his movement.

"Allow me, really. It's no bother." The crown prince pulled back my chair and extended his hand even though my wine glass had just been refilled.

Lady Endalaver fumed from her end of the table.

Crackling energy surrounded the prince. He watched me. Waiting. Storm clouds raged in his sapphire irises.

I eyed his hand. Enough time had passed since the council meeting that my anger wasn't as acute, but it didn't stop how he viewed me. I was still his servant to command. His object to own. Despite nearly begging him to ask his father to release me from the Trial, he hadn't.

Still . . .

I glanced at my date. Lord Waterline gave me a sultry smile.

Ock. I took the prince's outstretched hand. *The lesser of two evils.*

Once I was standing at the prince's side, he firmly hooked my hand through his elbow. A rush of awareness billowed through me at that simple touch. Side by side, he glided us toward the corner of the room where a selection of wine bottles waited.

"You've been avoiding me," he said under his breath as his aura rose.

"I have?" I replied innocently.

"You have, and you know it. I wish it to stop."

My teeth ground together. "And I wish not to be here having to suffer through these horrible dates. I suppose we all have wishes that will never come to pass, don't we?"

"What have I done that's so horrible to make you avoid me for a week?"

"Other than reminding me that I'm simply an object you own who you can command at your will? Nothing."

He stopped in his tracks, and his wings snapped in tight. "Ilara." My name on his lips caused a shiver to course up my spine. "I didn't mean—" He raked a hand through his hair. "Dammit, I knew I fucked up at the meeting." He growled. "What I'm trying to say is—" Fuming, he tore a hand through his hair again.

I raised my eyebrows. "Yes?"

His nostrils flared, and the aura around him grew so visceral that it felt as though his sheer power draped all over me. "I'm sorry. I know you wish to be released from this Trial."

"I do."

"But I can't stop it, Ilara. I'm not the king."

"Why not try, though?"

"I did. I tried several times to have you released from these dates before the Trial started, but the king refuses."

"But that was just the dates. I want out of the Trial entirely, and when you last asked the king, it was before the king knew what I was doing with the *orem*. If you would only try again—"

"I can't, Ilara," he growled. "I won't. Besides, my father won't be commanded. Even if I demanded it, he would refuse."

Any hope I'd held at being released from the Trial again withered and died. Anger rose in me, and I began to tap my foot. "What a shame. You certainly command *me* quite easily."

His eyes narrowed. "Is that what this is about? That I commanded you?"

I worked a swallow, then began to fidget. "I don't like it," I finally hissed. "My life is entirely out of my control, and then you only make it worse by reminding me that I'm powerless."

"I . . ." His mouth opened, then closed, and a scowl twisted his features. "I'm . . . *unfamiliar* with not commanding fae. It's been instilled into me from a young age. But . . ." His scowl turned into a frown. "I can see how that made you feel." He took a deep breath, then said quietly, "For what it's worth, I'm sorry, Ilara. I didn't intend to make you feel that way."

My chest rose and fell with each breath, and I suddenly wished I still held my wine glass simply so I had something to grip despite the prince.

"Do you mean that?" I replied.

"Yes," he all but growled. "I don't view you as an object I own. I never have. I simply . . . command fae. It's what I do, but I can understand that it made you feel insignificant and powerless, and for that I am sorry. That wasn't my intention."

I eyed him carefully, because my heart was suddenly beating much too fast. "But that is how I feel. Whenever you remind me that I'm powerless to resist your wishes, my anger toward you returns."

His nostrils flared. "Ilara," he said so gruffly that my breath stopped. He cupped my jaw, and the feel of his fingers on my skin made a thousand nerve endings come to life. "I'm *sorry*. I don't mean to do that. It's a habit, but I'll try to be better."

For a moment, I couldn't breathe, let alone reply. The crown prince of the Winter Court, the heir to the throne, the next *king* of the Solis continent, was apologizing for commanding me. On top of that, he was telling me he would try not to order me again. It was his birthright to command others, yet for me, he was saying he would give it up. Or try to.

"Please accept my apology." He ran his thumb lightly along my jaw, and a shiver worked up my spine. "Please let me try to make it up to you."

My heart beat harder and harder. It was now a galloping beast in my chest. The prince sounded sincere. He *looked* sincere, but why would he feel such remorse for something he was ultimately entitled to? Even if it made me hate him?

My thoughts were spinning again, and my insides were warming. This male held such power over me, and it wasn't all related to my imprisonment.

I took a step back, anything to break our intimate contact that was messing with my mind. "All right. I accept your apology."

His hand fell as he searched my expression. "You do?"

I took a deep, steadying breath. "Yes."

He smiled, and his sheer beauty threatened to overwhelm me. *Blessed Mother, what is it about this male?*

He stepped closer, and his snow and cedar scent hit me. Mother, he always smelled so good.

His lips curved more. "Now, I believe I promised you a drink."

I gripped his arm again as we resumed walking. The prince propelled me along until we reached the wine table.

The servant standing behind it straightened and began stuttering, "Sir, sorry, Your Highness. What can I get you? Is the wine at the table not to your liking? May I—"

"It's fine. All's well, but if you would please grab a bottle from Lumalisbee, specifically the eastern plain label, I would appreciate it."

The servant bowed. "Of course, my prince."

I tapped my foot as I scanned the room, my thoughts still reeling from the prince's apology. A hum of conversation drifted in the air as the servant pulled out a stepstool to reach the bottle on the top shelf. Most of the females and males in the Trial had heeded Prince Norivun's suggestion to stand and mingle.

Lady Leafton and her suitor for the night had already slipped outside to the topiary maze while Meegana and Nuwin had joined a group of six males. All of them were laughing intermittently as they spoke, and Meegana was practically beaming at the younger prince. But while Nuwin was a gracious date, as he always was, his actions toward Meegana seemed more polite than actually interested.

Of everyone present, only Lady Endalaver looked vexed. She'd moved to stand by Lord Waterline and was whispering to him. The young lord nodded, his smile turning dopey.

"Has your date been enjoyable this evening?" the prince asked, an edge to his tone, as the servant grabbed a bottle, then put it back when it wasn't the correct label.

I snorted. "Enjoyable? No, I wouldn't call it that."

"Has Lord Waterline touched you anywhere other than your arms and shoulders?" The edge in his tone turned razor-sharp. "Is anything happening under the table that I can't see?"

"No. Why do you ask?"

The prince's jaw flexed. "Because even though you've been doing an impressive job of ignoring me, I've been doing the opposite with you. I couldn't help but notice that Lord Waterline's been touching you all night. I wanted to ensure he hasn't been doing more under the table that you don't welcome."

I fluttered a hand nervously through my hair. "No, nothing is happening under the table."

"Good." Some of the aura pounding from him dimmed as the servant finally located the right bottle.

The servant poured generous portions of the southern wine for both of us.

The crown prince clinked his glass to mine. "Solls."

"Solls." I took a sip, and a burst of berry flavors and wood smoke nestled over my tongue.

Savoring it, I wandered back to the group standing near the dance floor and inched toward Meegana. Considering a very powerful and masterful aura beat into my back, I knew the crown prince was right behind me.

When I reached my friend's side, she smiled and made room for me, so I sidled up next to her as Nuwin began telling a story about his time at the Academy of Solisarium, when his tutor had accidentally ingested one of the potions he'd been instructing his students to make. The tutor had sprouted horns that lasted an entire week.

A tittering of laughter followed, then a female purred, "Prince Norivun, there you are."

I stiffened when Lady Endalaver bumped into my side, sloshing wine out of my goblet as she pushed me forward in the group. Taking my spot, she stopped beside the prince.

"For a moment, it almost looked as though you'd forgotten that you're *my* date tonight," she continued in that silky tone.

The prince brought his goblet to his lips and took another sip. "I haven't forgotten anything, Georgyanna."

My heartbeat kicked up a notch at hearing her name on his lips, and a flare of unwanted jealousy fired through me. Breathing harder, I tried to stem my ridiculous response, but a heavy dose of magic zinged out of Georgyanna, directed entirely at the crown prince.

That oily feeling slithered through the air, making me want to retch, and I clutched tightly to my magic, doing as Matron Olsander had instructed me so my Shield stayed up and didn't allow others' magic to affect me. After the debacle on the balance beam the other week, I'd spent hours learning to control my Shield better.

A soft growl worked up the crown prince's throat, and he said in a low tone, "Really, Georgyanna . . . such an amateur move. Are you unable to charm any male without forcing your affinity upon him?" He took a step away from her and brought his glass to his lips.

With a suck of power, that oily feeling vanished from the air. Meegana and Nuwin both laughed, along with the other males around us, as Georgyanna's lips parted. A fierce burst of color worked across her cheeks.

She glared at me, her expression so vicious that any relief I'd felt at the prince being too strong to fall prey to her antics vanished. The look she gave me indicated *I* was to blame for the prince's reaction as an uncoiling angry energy vibrated the air around her.

I set my wine glass down. "I think I'm going to step outside. Do you want to join me, Meegana?"

Meegana bobbed her head and held her glass out to Nuwin. "Do you mind holding this?"

Nuwin took it easily as he continued talking to another

male in the Trial, a tall and thin fairy who was also from Prinavee Territory.

Meegana looped her arm through mine. I smiled gratefully at her as Prince Norivun watched us over the rim of his glass.

Georgyanna's death glare finally left me when Meegana and I stepped outside.

A light dusting of snow fell from the sky as the warmth from the dining hall faded behind us. Below us, the icy topiary maze gleamed in the moonlight. Beatrice and her date were long gone, but a tittering of laughter came from the dark garden stretching in front of the balcony. I could only guess that was where they'd disappeared to.

Concentrating on what Matron Olsander had taught me, I called upon my fire magic to keep me warm. I pictured a small kernel of flame gliding through my limbs. A second later, the goosebumps that had erupted across my skin vanished.

Meegana wrapped her arms around herself and headed toward one of the fire pits on the balcony. When she reached it, she held out both hands. "How's your date been with Lord Waterline so far?"

I forced a smile and joined her, letting the natural fire call to my own. "Honestly? Awful. He keeps touching me and has no interest in actual conversation. Instead, he keeps staring at my breasts while telling me how magnificent he and his family are. What about you? How's Nuwin been?"

She laughed, the sound genuine. "He's quite funny, actually. I like him even though I know he charms all of the females."

I grinned. "I like him too. He's only been nice to me since we met."

She fanned her hands more in front of the fire. "Do you like him in *that* way?"

My eyes bugged out. "No, oh no, not at all. More like in a brotherly way."

She smiled, her shoulders relaxing.

"Does that mean *you* like him in that way?" I teased.

She laughed. "Maybe?"

I laughed with her, and the sound was so natural from both of us that I relaxed even more as the fire's heat warmed us.

"Prince Norivun seems to be quite protective of you," she said after a moment of easy silence.

"He is." I frowned and nibbled my lip. "He's been that way since we met. Apparently, I'm a valuable commodity that he enjoys owning." My response was so easy, so automatic, because until tonight, that was what I'd always thought, but the prince's comments earlier had given me pause.

"My mother warned me to be careful around him, even though she also said to do everything in my power to marry him."

My stomach clenched. "Oh? Why did she tell you to be careful of him?"

"Because of his reputation. He's not very forgiving, and he's so dangerous. You know, with how easily he's able to kill fae."

"Are you worried he would harm you?"

She cocked her head and rubbed her hands more in the fire's heat. "When I first arrived, I would have said yes, but now? I don't know. Sometimes I wonder what he's truly like. I mean, if he's as awful as everyone says he is, or if it's all a misunderstanding."

I nibbled on my bottom lip more. "I've wondered the same," I admitted.

"Some say he's the reason behind the disappearances in the castle, though. So maybe I'm being foolish to think he's anything but terrible."

My spine snapped upright. "Who did you hear that from?"

"Michas Crimsonale." She nodded her head to the balcony doors, to where Michas stood inside with the other nobles. "But others are saying it too. They're saying that the crown prince is silencing anyone who brings forth concerns about the crops." She shrugged. "But I don't think it's the prince. Michas hates him. Everyone knows that, so of course, he would spread rumors."

My eyebrows rose, and not from Meegana also thinking the prince was innocent, but because she'd just spoken so easily of the crop failures, as though it truly was becoming common-place knowledge among the Solis that the *orem* was dying.

I was just about to ask her what else she'd heard of the crops when the door at the end of the balcony opened.

Lord Waterline stepped out. "Lady Ockson? I think Nuwin is looking for you."

"Oh?" Excitement danced in Meegana's eyes, and she gave me an apologetic look.

"Go." I swished her away. "Enjoy the rest of your date with him."

She smiled and squeezed my hand before sashaying away.

Alone on the balcony with Lord Waterline, I tried to stop my skin from crawling as he neared.

"And what about you? Are you ready for *our* date?" He sidled closer, and his breath reeked of alcohol, but more than that made me wary. A foggy gleam coated his eyes, the expression almost dopey, as though he'd also partaken in some kind of illegal substance only sold in the ostracized markets.

"I suppose," I forced myself to say. "What did you want to do?"

He inched even closer, and a pulse of heat undulated from him. It hit my Shield, and the potency of it nearly took my breath away.

Carnal lust coated my Shield, and with a start, I realized the male who held the seduction affinity that I'd detected on my first training day was Lord Waterline.

Shivering, I flamed my magic inside me, concentrating on not letting my Shield slip, but my attention was so fixated on my Shield that I didn't realize he'd moved so close. A shriek of surprise released from me when his arm snaked around my waist, drawing me to him even though I tried to pull back.

"There's a nice view from my chamber. I was thinking I could show it to you."

I recoiled when his hot breath hit my neck, and his affinity rose even higher.

Hot, pulsing need coated every line of my Shield. *Concentrate. Don't let it down, not even for a second.*

"No, I don't think so." I tried to extract myself from his arms, but his hold tightened, and a flare of anger pulsed from him.

"Why are you fighting this?" He grinned, the expression looking unhinged.

"Because I don't want my mind fogged by a male forcing his affinity on me."

"Even if I could use my affinity to pleasure you like you've never been before? I could have you throbbing, *begging* for it, you'd be so hot." He moved like lightning. In a blink, he had me pinned to the balcony's railing.

I swallowed a yelp when he bent me backward, my spine arching painfully. I frantically pushed when he roughly grabbed my hips. Images of Vorl's attacks reared in my mind, and a moment of panic consumed me. *Not again. Not again.*

But just as that age-old feeling of helplessness threatened to swallow me, I forced myself to remember that I was no longer weak or magicless. My Shield was strong. I was resisting his affinity, and I had power now. Immense power.

If only I chose to use it.

A maneuver that Sandus had taught me barreled to the front of my thoughts, and just as Lord Waterline tried to force his mouth to mine, I ducked and hit out, wrapping my fingers around his forearm before shoving and spinning as a rush of fire erupted across my skin.

Lord Waterline yelped in pain when I bent his wrist back and burned him at the same time, but I didn't stick around to see what he would do next. I fled from the balcony and burst inside.

The door slammed closed behind me, and all eyes turned on me.

Only Georgyanna, the crown prince, and half a dozen of the males remained.

One glance in my direction, and the crown prince's easy smile vanished. He cut through the group, striding toward me as his affinity rose, his aura so strong that it threatened to swallow me.

"What happened?" he asked when he reached me.

The door to the balcony opened, and Lord Waterline stumbled in, that dopey expression still painting his features. A ring of ice surrounded his burned wrist, his second affinity—a water element—helping his wound.

The crown prince stilled, and the air around him seemed to freeze. "What did he do?"

Each word came out as though it took actual concentration for him to speak. All of his energy had fixated on Lord Waterline, who was now casually ambling back to the wine table while everyone else carried on behind us, entirely oblivious to the prince's rage.

"Nothing," I replied as I wrapped my arms around myself and rubbed my hands on my biceps. "I got away. He wasn't able to do anything thanks to a move Sandus taught me and a little help from my fire affinity and Shield."

A thundercloud converged on Prince Norivun's face, his eyes darkening until they looked like a raging storm. "Did he attack you?"

"Yes, and he tried to use his seduction affinity on me." I cast a glance toward the male. Strangely, Georgyanna had joined him at the table. She was whispering to him again, and I could have sworn that Lord Waterline physically responded, his body loosening.

When she spun away, the young lord shook his head, then brought a palm to his forehead before glancing behind him. Genuine confusion covered his face, and in that moment, I *knew*.

Despite him being an absolute annoyance at dinner, Lord Waterline hadn't purposefully attacked me on the balcony.

Lady Endalaver had manipulated him to do it, and from the looks of it, he didn't even realize what he'd just done.

Blessed Mother. She's truly evil.

But before I could tell the prince what I'd witnessed, a ferocious snarl tore from his mouth, and Prince Norivun was striding away.

"My prince?"

But he flew forward, not responding, as his entire demeanor shifted until he was death on wings.

His powerful affinity rose with each step he took, and with a horrifying understanding, I knew that the prince was going to kill my date.

CHAPTER 15

"Wait, it's not him!" I sprinted until I stood in front of the prince, then pushed him with everything I had before anyone could notice his response. "Stop!"

"I'm going to kill him." Norivun's chest rose and fell rapidly, and the aura around him crackled with malice.

I planted myself to the floor. "You *can't* kill him."

His eyes darkened to a frosty blue. "No? Then you don't know what I'm capable of." He tried to sidestep me, but I moved just as fast.

"Prince Norivun, please listen to me."

"Ilara. Move." Murder had painted itself upon his features, and I knew if I didn't think of something immediately, he was going to murder Lord Waterline. And even though the lord was slimy and a cad, he wasn't an abuser, and he wasn't to blame for what had happened on the balcony. Georgyanna was.

The prince's air affinity surged around me, lifting me from the ground and gusting me to the side.

"My prince!" I called upon my own magic and burst through his. Gritting my teeth, I wrenched a huge gust of air from my gut that propelled both of us through the doors and out onto the balcony just as the first fairy attending the dinner glanced in our direction.

Outside, the crown prince snarled his irritation as he fixated his attention on the dining room once more. Before I'd even caught my breath, he was swinging the door open and about to return inside.

I spun him toward me at the last second and wrapped a hand around his neck. I plastered myself to his frame and then did the only thing I could think of.

I slammed my lips to his.

The second our lips made contact, his entire body stopped. The prince just *stilled*, as though frozen in time.

My tongue darted out as his taste flooded my mouth. I curled my hands around his neck as my heart pounded with the feel of him against me.

A single groan came from the prince as he crushed me to him. His arms wrapped around my waist, his grip strong and powerful as his pounding aura coiled around me.

A rush of his air elemental affinity whooshed, and then we were on the other side of the balcony, flying on his wind until we were hidden in one of the deep alcoves as shadows embraced us.

I gasped at his absolute power.

Growling, the prince crushed his lips to mine again as his hands slid down to cup my backside. He hoisted me up, plastering me against his broad chest as a snarl worked through his lips.

I moaned, unable to help it as heat spiraled through me. The male was a sorcerer with his tongue. And his scent. His taste. Mother Below, but once again, I *wanted* him.

"Ilara," he groaned, the sound guttural and barely fae.

His hands were everywhere, up my body, in my hair, cupping my breasts, feeling the curve of my backside.

Desire pooled between my legs, and his nostrils flared as a satisfied-sounding purr came next.

"You're *mine*," he said on a low growl.

That possessive declaration left his lips, and for the first time, I wondered if it wasn't entirely about owning my power, but then my focus became the taste of his mouth and the strength of his hands. Lust consumed me so completely that all of my thoughts fled.

Chilled air kissed my skin as my nipples peaked in the frosty air. The prince had me against a wall, my dress entirely ridden up with both of my legs hooked around his waist, and he'd somehow freed one of my breasts and was feasting upon my nipple like a dying male.

And *Mother* . . . did the male know how to use his tongue.

He growled again when I hissed as a thousand nerve endings came to life under his masterful touch, but when he bit my nipple hard enough for my head to clear, I realized what we were doing, and Mother Below, I was once again practically fucking *the murderer of my family.*

"Prince Norivun!" I tried to wrench myself away from him even though my core throbbed. "Prince Norivun," I gasped again, then clawed at his chest.

But he only growled more, then cupped my rear with his other hand and squeezed my soft flesh.

"Oh gods." My head tilted back when one of his fingers curved forward to tickle my clit. A shockwave of rapture spiraled through me.

"So wet," he groaned as his finger pulled back just enough to find my damp entrance. He swept my underthings to the side, and when his thick finger began to enter me, my entire body seized.

Yes. Gods, yes.

My eyes flew open.

No, what am I doing?

"You must *stop*." I pounded on his back. Shadows dipped his expression into such vicious beauty that, for a moment, I couldn't speak. My chest rose and fell so rapidly as my legs quivered around him.

Absolute need etched his features into dark desperation, and I struggled to remember why I'd stopped him.

"Ilara?" he finally said, his breathing ragged as his hard erection bulged in his pants.

We both panted, clouds puffing around us, but I somehow managed to whisper, "Um, it's, ah . . ." I closed my eyes, trying to clear my thoughts. "It wasn't Lord Waterline!" *Yes, that's it. That's why we're here.* "Lord Waterline isn't to blame for attacking me. Lady Endalaver manipulated him."

He blinked, then blinked again.

I forced myself out of his grip, and he finally released me enough that I was able to stand. My core throbbed, but I made myself take a step away.

His gaze fell, his lip curling savagely when he beheld my bare breast.

He was already reaching for me again when I took another

teetering step to the side and straightened my clothing, covering myself again. *Mother Below, what's happening?* I could barely function.

He snarled, and the sound of it sent a tingle straight to my clit, but I made myself stay away from his touch. "I had to stop you. I couldn't let you kill him, and I couldn't think of anything better to do, so I kissed you."

Silence.

"Prince Norivun?" I gulped in another breath.

"You kissed me," he finally repeated. Another second passed. "*What?*" Genuine confusion painted his features.

"It's not Lord Waterline. It's Lady Endalaver. You weren't understanding, so I kissed you before you could kill him."

His chest heaved, but his expression cleared slightly. "You're saying Georgyanna manipulated Lord Waterline to attack you."

I nodded frantically, my heart still beating much too fast, but at least the cold air was helping to cool my heated flesh. "Yes, yes, that's exactly what I'm saying."

He stabbed a hand through his hair, his bicep bulging. Every line of his body still exuded such a fierce aura that it was a struggle to stand, but I made myself stay rigid and out of arm's reach.

"You can't kill Lord Waterline." I gulped in another breath. *Blessed Mother, when did it become so hard to breathe?* "Georgyanna's behind what just happened. Not him."

The prince's head snapped toward where Georgyanna stood inside. She was with the circle of fae still in the dining hall, acting as though she hadn't a care in the world as her head tilted back every time she laughed or smiled coyly at the males around her. Thankfully, we'd been far enough away that they hadn't seen our air elements collide before we'd flown out to the balcony.

The prince took another deep breath and raked a hand through his hair again. "How do you know?" he finally growled. "How do you know it was her and not that prick, Lord Waterline?"

"I . . . I don't have proof," I stammered, "but it's not the first time she's tried to make everything harder for me. Please trust me. It's her."

I had never told anyone about the balance beam incident, and I wasn't going to. Lady Endalaver played dirty, but I wasn't going to run to anybody for help. I'd figure out a way to deal with her on my own. I wasn't weak anymore, and I refused to become another bully's victim.

"And you're certain that Lord Waterline wasn't acting upon his own mind on the balcony?"

I thought of that strange gleam coating his eyes, as though he'd been influenced, then gave a curt nod. "I'm certain. She manipulated him."

Prince Norivun took another deep breath, the ardor in his eyes finally cooling. "In that case, Lady Endalaver is about to realize what happens when someone messes with my—" He cut himself off and raked a hand through his hair *again*.

I frowned. "Your what?"

His lips sealed, and he shook his head. "Nothing, but if she thought she was getting a private date with me tonight, she's wrong."

THE PRINCE STAYED true to his word. Despite Lady Endalaver trying to persuade the prince to leave on a private date, Prince Norivun refused, repeatedly telling her that this was all he planned for the evening, and that was that.

And each time she tried to manipulate him or pouted prettily, he brushed her off and reminded her that this date was still within the rules of the Trial.

I kept my distance from both of them, still in disbelief at how quickly things had heated between the prince and me on the balcony, but it didn't stop my satisfaction every time the prince refused her.

Once again, the prince's protectiveness and possessiveness stirred my thoughts. Never mind the way we reacted to each other physically.

All this time, I'd thought his protectiveness was because he saw me as an asset, someone he must keep safe at all costs because of what I could do with the *orem*. He needed to keep me protected so I could save the continent, but that hardly explained his fierce desire. Each time he'd kissed me, he'd nearly look possessed. As though a succubus had ensnared him and demanded that he claim me.

I nearly snorted at that thought as the music continued around me while those remaining in the dining hall danced or chatted. Such a thought was ridiculous. The only time something *that* extreme happened was when . . .

My eyes turned to saucers as my heart jolted.

A fae male had found his mate.

My lips parted, and my breath stopped.

It felt as though the realm tilted off its axis.

I reached a steadying hand for the wall and gripped my

wineglass tightly. The only time a fae male naturally acted with such extreme behavior was if he'd found *his mate*.

My heart pounded more as blood thundered through my veins.

Near the wine table, Prince Norivun spoke with several males beside him while Georgyanna pouted in the corner.

My heart beat even harder.

No, surely, *no*. That *couldn't* be the reason.

But . . .

Wide-eyed, I stared at the crown prince. My mind exploded as the epiphany I just had smashed all of my thoughts. Could *that* be the reason for the prince's behavior? To find one's mate, the perfect half to one's soul, would elicit such a reaction in any male fairy. Males were known for feeling the bond sooner than females. Often times, the females wouldn't feel the full effects of the mate bond until . . .

My throat bobbed in a swallow. Until the bond was sealed during the first bedding.

Oh Blessed Mother.

My heart pattered wildly as I thought back to all of my reactions to him. It wasn't unheard of for females to catch glimpses of the bond. Longing. Fierce attraction. Desire. Being soothed in his presence. Coveting his company.

And I'd felt *all* of those things. A mate bond would explain why I was able to feel that for the murderer of my family.

My gaze shot to Norivun again, but his attention stayed on the male he was speaking to.

Mother Below, it made sense, perfect *sense.* Because another reason the crown prince would refuse to truly court Georgyanna, despite her repulsive personality, was a mate bond. Males were fiercely devoted to their females once the mate bond reared.

I swirled away from the remaining fae in the dining hall and rushed toward the outdoor balcony. I needed air, fresh air to clear my head.

Outside, I gasped in the night wind, but it didn't stop memories from swirling through my mind. All of the things the prince had said, things alluding to how he felt before he cut his sentences short . . . How many times had he done that?

He'd done it just tonight when he'd spoken of Lady Endalaver. *"In that case, Lady Endalaver is about to realize what happens when someone messes with my—"*

The word he'd been about to say was *mate*, but he'd stopped himself, because he knew I'd still been ignorant of the bond, and he was waiting for me to feel it.

Or the time when he'd been in the healing infirmary. *"When the time comes that you* know, *your question will be answered."* He'd been speaking of the mate bond then too—the bond that I'd been still ignorant of.

It was said that mate bonds were strongest when both parties came to accept it within their own time. No pressure. No outward forces. No wonder he hadn't outright told me then, and it had sounded like riddles.

But now . . . I'd come to realize it existed.

"Mother, help me," I whispered. I squeezed the balcony harder, my grip so strong my knuckles turned as white as snow.

I need to get out of here.

I abruptly pushed away from the railing and rushed through the dining hall. I fled from the room as swiftly as the northern winds, not even stopping to find Sandus.

How? How, how, how has this happened?

The gods could be cruel when they wanted to be. Mate bonds were created by them. Their way of interacting with our fates.

"Insufferable tyrants. The lot of them," I whispered angrily as my footsteps flew down the hall toward the Exorbiant Chamber.

The more I thought about it, the more convinced I was that I was right. It felt as though I'd been punched in the gut. My sister would never be able to accept the prince even if he was my mate.

I rounded the final turn to the prince's wing, and the lights dimmed. My hurried movements continued until the lights flickered. Off then on. Off then . . . out.

I ground to a halt as my rapid-fire thoughts of the prince abruptly stopped.

Silence surrounded me as darkness prevailed. *What just happened?*

My breaths came in loud pants as I turned in a circle. The hairs on the back of my neck rose. Dear gods, I'd been so consumed with my epiphany that I was fleeing through the castle *alone*.

"Sandus?" I called hopefully. I reached out, feeling for the stone wall just as a sound came from behind me.

I whirled around but couldn't see anything. Then the sound came again.

"Hello?" My heart began to pound as I swirled slowly in place. Darkness everywhere.

A chilling sense of foreboding slid through my veins. I couldn't see anyone. Shadows dipped everything into darkness, and only the faint moonlight through a high window provided any light, yet I felt *something*.

"Hello?" I called louder.

The sound came again.

Dear gods, someone or something was here. My nose twitched as a faint, pungent scent tickled my senses just as the absolute conviction that I was about to be attacked slammed into me.

Instinctive magic erupted inside my gut, and a ring of fire burst to life around me, creating a protective barrier and providing light.

A scream of pain cut through the darkness, but when I whirled toward it, a flash of something appeared in the air, and then . . . nothing. Although—

I sniffed. The lingering scent of something rotten permeated the air.

Boot steps reached my ears, then Sandus careened around the corner. "Lady Seary!"

"Sandus!"

"You're not to venture through the castle without me!" My guard was seething when he reached me, his eyes wild as I released my fire, allowing my guard to come to my side.

"I know. I'm sorry! I was—" But I couldn't continue. I couldn't very well tell him that my thoughts had turned into a spiraling tornado, and all reasonable action had left me when I suspected the prince was my mate.

"I didn't mean to." I settled with. "I wasn't thinking."

My eyes darted back to where I'd seen that flash, back to where I'd been certain someone had been about to attack me. "There was someone here. They killed the lights and then started approaching me, but I flung fire out, and . . ." I couldn't continue. I was breathing too fast, and my heart felt as if it would explode. Too much was happening. *Too much.*

Sandus snarled. "The prince will have my head when he learns of this. Come. We must get within the prince's wing, behind his wards. Then I'll notify him."

SURE ENOUGH, the prince was livid when he discovered that I'd left the dinner on my own and had nearly been attacked.

Only minutes after Sandus had sealed me within the Exorbiant Chamber, the prince and his three other guards burst into my room, carrying the vengeance of the gods with them.

The prince made me recall every moment of the harrowing encounter in detail, and with every second that passed, the aura around him grew higher and higher.

"You are *not* to roam the halls without Sandus," he snarled as veins bulged in his neck.

"I know." I wrapped my arms around myself, rocking back and forth on my bed as Cailis sat beside me. "I didn't mean to. I just—"

But I couldn't bring myself to say it. How did I say *I think we're bonded to each other? I think you're my mate, and the thought of that terrifies me, so I stupidly ran through the castle at night even though I know I shouldn't since it isn't safe.*

I sealed my lips as Prince Norivun's gaze glittered with barely leashed violence. He rounded on his guards. "Alert the castle commander. I want the grounds searched for any intruders. I want whoever followed her tonight found."

They all dipped their heads and strode from the Exorbiant Chamber before the prince addressed Sandus in a savage, gravelly tone. "Guard her with your life."

Sandus's jaw tightened, a deadly light entering his eyes. "I will."

CHAPTER 16

The entire castle was searched. Every hall, alcove, cellar, room, chamber . . . all of it. The prince didn't leave one stone left unturned.

But nothing was found. No intruders. No ghostly phantoms. No hired mercenaries sent to terrorize the court. Whatever had doused the lights and prowled toward me had disappeared, as though whisked from this very realm.

It was enough of a reminder, though, that fae were going missing and that it was stupid of me to have run alone at night. It also wasn't lost on me, or the prince, that such an attack had occurred *after* it'd been revealed that I was trying to save the crops.

The only comfort I took was knowing that the prince hadn't lied about killing the missing fae. Whoever, or whatever, had been with me in the hall definitely hadn't been the crown prince.

Still, despite being alive and safe, knowing that the prince and I potentially shared a mate bond brought an entirely new level of stress to my life.

The next week passed in a blur of following all of the rules. Even though my fire had fended off whoever had come near me following that disastrous dinner, I wasn't going to risk an encounter like that again, so I healed fields, trained on schedule, and never went anywhere without Sandus.

Each day was similar to the one prior, and the days began to bleed together. However, I welcomed the monotony after my epiphany about the crown prince, then experiencing what I had in the dark castle.

"What's gotten into you?" my sister asked one night when my magic burst out of me in a turbid rush.

To blow off some steam, I was practicing my air affinity, making the doors open and close under my magic while Cailis reported her findings. It was something she'd started doing weekly as we prepared for our escape.

I made myself sit still and stop practicing. "Nothing. Sorry. I'm fine."

"Are you even listening to me?"

"Of course, I am."

"Then aren't you concerned that I'm being followed?"

I stilled. "What?"

"I knew you weren't listening, but you should because I'm pretty sure someone's following me when I'm walking around the castle. More and more it feels as though someone's watching me. My guard insists that I'm safe and no one's about, but I can *feel* it, Ilara."

My heart beat harder, and I grabbed her hands as fear

threatened to consume me. "Do you think whoever it is was the same one who tried to attack me?"

"No." She tugged her hands free, then pulled me into a hug and only let me go once my pulse calmed. "That's the weird thing. At first I thought that too, but unlike what happened with you, I've never actually felt that my safety's in jeopardy or that an attack is imminent. Whoever I'm sensing has never approached me, and my affinity doesn't sense maliciousness. I just feel someone *watching*, like they're curious."

My heartbeat slowed even more. Cailis's instincts were usually spot-on, thanks to her affinity, but her experience only reaffirmed that very strange things were happening within this castle. "So, you believe someone's following you to *watch you?*" Whatever I'd encountered in the darkened hall the week prior had intended more than watching. I was sure of that.

"Yes, so, there's that interesting development, but there's also the matter of possible exits I've found."

She went on to describe them, and even though I was happy she was finding options for a potential escape, I still knew that mistphasing was the best choice.

I sighed. "I'm glad your searches are proving resourceful, but if I could only learn how to reliably transport someone with me, none of this would be needed."

"Keep practicing."

"I will." And I would, because knowing that my sister was also experiencing strange encounters within this clandestine castle lit a fire within my gut to try harder, because I needed to keep my sister safe, and it was becoming more and more apparent that staying in this castle was entirely dangerous—especially if the crown prince was my mate.

"Again, Ilara!" Matron Olsander barked at me. "Imagine your fire needling through the wall. Your affinity should be like an extension of yourself. It's no different than poking your finger at the wall."

Brow furrowing, I concentrated harder on the mental images that allowed me to better control my elemental affinity, and slowly, my fire burned a precise hole through the steel wall in front of me.

Matron Olsander nodded and crossed her arms. "Very good. Very good indeed."

I panted, the exertion of maintaining such control harder than anything Sandus was training me to do, despite those trainings making my muscles quiver and burn.

"Now, again. You still have much to learn."

I forced myself to straighten and concentrate, but it was hard. It'd been weeks since the dinner in which I'd had my epiphany about the prince and then was nearly attacked in the hall. Since then, I'd returned to avoiding the prince, even more so since my conviction in our shared mate bond grew—as though avoiding the prince would make our mutual attraction disappear—but despite my frustrations at having such a bond, one blessing did manifest in my life.

All of the Isalee fields I'd been working on outside of Whimseal had bloomed to life.

Like the field in Harrivee, young plants emerged, budding signs of life despite the fierce weather and raging snow. The gray dirt was gone, healthy and moist black soil taking its place. And the vibrant colors of the immature, nurturing plants made any doubt over those fields' failing future vanish from my thoughts.

"Again, Ilara! No dilly-dallying."

I pulled up my fire affinity once more. Across the room, Meegana and Beatrice practiced their affinities too, while a group of males watched on. Georgyanna hadn't made an appearance yet today, which had at least allowed me to practice in peace.

Matron Olsander barked out another order, then activated the training room's magic to make my next drill even more challenging. She didn't let up. The female constantly pushed and coaxed me, yet her uncanny knack for helping others understand their affinities benefited me immensely, and I was so very grateful for that.

Hours later, I eyed the clock as my stomach let out a ferocious growl.

Matron Olsander must have heard it because she said, "I think that's enough for today, Ilara. Why don't you venture to the kitchens for something to eat? You've worked hard. Consume much nutrition and get plenty of sleep tonight."

I inclined my head in thanks. Since Beatrice and Meegana looked busy, I didn't ask them if they wanted to join me and instead slipped out of the room.

Servants bustled down the hall as scents from the kitchen wafted through the air. It smelled of roasted duck and baked fruit pies. My stomach let out another growl, and I peered down the hall to the statue of God Xerious. It was often Sandus's favorite waiting spot, but when my gaze landed on the giant sculpture, my eyes widened in surprise.

The guard waiting by the statue wasn't Sandus. It was Haxil.

A grin spread across my face as I approached the round-cheeked, jovial guard. Even though Haxil ventured with me to the fields each morning, I hadn't been able to speak with him much since he took his guard duties quite seriously and never let his attention drop, especially after that incident with the snowgum.

"What are you doing here?" I asked with a smile.

"Sandus got called home. His sister just gave birth to her first babe, and the proud uncle couldn't wait to meet the wee one."

"She did? Oh, I'm so pleased. He's been talking about her for weeks. Do you know how the birth went?"

Haxil pushed away from the statue and fell into step beside me. "It was long, but I'm told that's normal during first births."

"Do you know the babe's name?"

He shook his head. "I don't, but I'm sure we'll hear all about it when he returns."

We laughed, and the sound was so easy and natural. I'd always felt at ease with Haxil, ever since that first night in High Liss when he'd been nothing but understanding as I came to grips with my new life beside the crown prince.

"I'm surprised you came to guard me," I said, peering up at him curiously. "I figured Prince Norivun would have sent Nish instead of you."

Haxil scratched his jaw.

I raised my eyebrows. "Is that look because Nish *is* supposed to be here instead of you?"

Haxil shrugged guiltily. "When Sandus left, he told either

Nish or Ryder to accompany you, but it's Ryder's day off, and Nish—" He coughed.

"Nish what?" I bristled.

"Ock, you know how he can be. He had a few colorful words for *babysitting* you, as he called it, so I offered to go instead."

I rolled my eyes at Nish's pettiness. The guard hadn't liked me from the start, and despite me becoming a permanent fixture in the castle and him traveling with me daily to the fields, it didn't seem as if that feeling was going to disappear anytime soon.

"Why does he hate me so much?"

"He doesn't hate you. He's just . . ." Haxil sighed. "Nish is hard to win over. It's not just you he's like this with, but if you do win him over, he'll be loyal to you for life."

"Like he is to Prince Norivun." I recalled Nish's snarl all too well when I'd first met the crown prince and uttered my contempt of him.

"Exactly."

BACK IN MY CHAMBERS, I rang for food, then stripped out of my sweaty training clothes and took a quick bath to ease my muscles. Once dressed in loose pants and a warm sweater, I ventured back into my living area.

Fragrant scents from the delivered food filled the room. An entire tray, brimming with my requests, sat near the couch. And of course, as was per usual, there was far more than I could consume despite needing a plentiful amount to maintain my magic.

I opened my chamber's door and quirked an eyebrow at Haxil, who stood in the hallway. "You hungry?"

The guard's hands were clasped in front of him, wings tight to his back while his familiar swords poked out from beneath each wing. He gave a wolfish grin. "I'm always hungry."

I laughed. "Come and join me then. Cailis is still out, and I'm getting nervous about my upcoming Trial tests. I would love some company so I don't stew over them."

Haxil bowed. "I couldn't say no to that. It would be my pleasure to distract you whilst eating all of that wonderful food I smelled on its way in."

I laughed, and Haxil closed the door behind him before joining me on the couch.

The huge tray took up most of the table. Roasted duck sat on a bed of grilled acorlis. Beside it were fried greens, buttery buns, pasta in a rich cream sauce, apple dumplings, tender meat loins in gravy, figs and berries in flaky crepes, and a few other side dishes.

"A feast fit for a queen." Haxil pulled a napkin onto his lap and spread it over his thighs before grabbing a plate.

I swallowed a smile and gestured to his napkin. "Such lovely table manners you have, Haxil."

He grinned. "I may be seen as a brutish guard by some, but I can assure you that I don't eat from a trough each night."

"I never would have assumed you did." I smiled back and insisted he fill his plate first since he was my guest.

He grumbled. "Females are to go before males."

"If you buy into that sort of thing," I said with a shrug. "Go first. Please."

He reluctantly did as I asked. When he finished, I reached for a plate and speared a few servings of meat before taking portions of all of the sides.

Haxil's plate sat in front of him, untouched as he waited for me. "So do you not approve of chivalrous behavior, Ilara? 'Tis the way of the Solis, you know."

"Perhaps." I leaned forward more and scooped up a spoonful of greens. "But I keep thinking about Lady Furyful. She's the heroine in a book I read last month that I can't get out of my head. It was *Of Fae—*"

"*And Might*," he finished for me.

My eyes widened, and I stopped mid-movement from grabbing a bun. "You've read it?"

"Indeed. It's one of my favorite novels. 'Tis a most enjoyable adventure. I loved the battle scene in Kroravee. Ock, t'was epic, although the swoony romance in the book I could have done without."

I turned to face him better and tucked my legs beneath me. He didn't begin eating until I grabbed my fork. "Then you'll know that Lady Furyful's viewpoint on males and females doesn't align with traditional Solis beliefs either."

Haxil took a huge bite of his duck and nodded. "Lady Furyful is very convincing in her beliefs about equality amongst fae."

I popped a fig pastry into my mouth. "Do you disagree with that?"

He finished chewing and forked a bite of pasta. "It's not that I disagree. Females can be just as powerful as males in their magic, and just because you're generally of slighter build doesn't mean you're in any way weak."

A smile spread across my face. "I knew I liked you for a reason. So what was your favorite scene in the book? Mine was when she led the battle against the Borggish in the end, putting an end to their advancement into our realm. When she confronted their leader near the portal and sliced his head clean off . . ." I leaned back and closed my eyes briefly before sitting back upright and picking up my bun again. "Her bravery took my breath away."

Haxil laughed. "How very noble of a scene you chose. My favorite was when Lady Furyful shaved Sir Risserton's balls off. It was wonderfully gruesome."

I laughed, and Haxil joined in.

The meal passed quickly as we ate while volleying our opinions about *Of Fae and Might* back and forth, before launching into other books we'd read. I was delighted to find that the guard was extremely well educated, putting my poor learnings to shame, although I was valiantly trying to correct that by reading everything I could get my hands on.

I told him of my latest book while sipping wine from my goblet. I had no idea how much I'd consumed, but the warm fire and the feeling sweeping through me could have been from the alcohol, or perhaps it was from the stimulating conversation. I'd never had a male friend who'd also liked to read. Both Tormesh and Finnley hadn't found much enjoyment in it, both preferring to spend their free time outside versus sitting in a chair with a book.

"And then, just when she was about to—" Intent on re-enacting a battle scene from a history book I'd read about a female general, I leaned over Haxil but lost my footing and fell face-first onto him instead.

His arm whipped around me automatically to break my fall, but I'd put too much momentum into the scene, so he couldn't stop me completely.

A rush of air whooshed past my face, and then I was on the floor, right between the couch and table with the guard on top of me.

For a moment, we both stared at one another, and then I burst out laughing.

Haxil did the same. "Ock, that was quite the warrior move," he said with a twinkle in his eye.

I laughed again as hair fluttered in front of my face. "Apologies for being so clumsy."

He grinned and was about to lift himself off me when a knock came on my door.

"Ilara?" The door to my chambers opened as the crown prince let himself in. "Can we talk? I know you're avoiding me again, but—"

He took one step into my room before his gaze cut to me, as though his heightened magic told him exactly where I lay. The second he beheld me on the floor with Haxil on top of me, a storm unleased upon Prince Norivun's face. A split second later, a tsunami of power barreled out of him, the force of it nearly whipping the curtains off the windows.

"Nori . . ." Haxil's powerful frame bolted off me while I lay on the floor rosy-cheeked from the wine.

Scorching rage filled Prince Norivun's expression as something infinitely darker lit his eyes.

"Nori . . ." Haxil said again, his tone growing warier as he backed up.

Rage rippled across the prince's face, and he crossed the distance between us in blurred speed, a terrifying snarl ripping from his throat.

"Nori!" Haxil yelled, moving faster than the wind as he retreated. "Rein it in. I *didn't* touch her."

But the crown prince lunged for his guard, wrath written upon his features.

"I didn't touch her!" Haxil roared once more.

I shot to standing and darted to the couch, hoping to place myself between the two males, but one glance at the prince's face pierced fear into my heart and made any doubt that he *wasn't* my mate vanish like the setting sun.

Terrifying fury rippled across the prince's features, and with a sickening sense of dread, I realized what was happening.

The mate bond had once again gained control of him, just like it had after Lord Waterline's attack.

All Prince Norivun had seen was another male trying to lay claim to me, and his instincts had taken over.

Which meant that he was going to kill Haxil if I didn't stop him.

CHAPTER 17

"**N**ori! Stop!" Haxil yelled again, then again.

"Prince Norivun, please calm down!" I screamed.

It was no use.

Horror descended upon me when I felt his affinity rise. It rushed from the prince, spearing right for Haxil despite the guard being his servant, his *friend*, who the crown prince cared for like a brother.

"No!" I screamed and launched myself in front of Haxil. I plastered myself to the guard. Fear twisted my features as I desperately tried to shield him with everything I had.

But the prince's affinity barreled right around me, piercing Haxil from the side, and with a sickening sense of dread, I knew that I couldn't stop it. The prince latched onto his soul, his horrible death affinity pulling that wispy essence from his guard.

"My prince, no! He's your *friend*!" I shot my own affinity out of my body toward the prince's magic, grabbing a hold of the shimmering lifeform that was Haxil's inner soul being sliced away from his form.

The second my affinity made contact with Norivun's, the energy in the room changed. The seismic pulsing from the crown prince ground to a stop, as though water doused a fire, and for the first time, recognition of where we were, who lay before him, and what he was doing barreled over Norivun's features.

"Please stop," I pleaded.

The prince stumbled back. Terror glazed his eyes as his affinity sucked back into him so quickly his magic rushed over my skin.

"Thank the Mother," I whispered when Haxil's soul returned to him.

The guard slumped, falling to the floor. The prince moved faster than lightning and broke Haxil's fall before the guard's head could crash into the table.

"Haxil," the prince said urgently as he peered down at his friend. Guilt coiled Norivun's features. He pounded his fist on the floor. "Fuck, no, what have I done? Haxil!"

The guard blinked, then opened his eyes.

"Thank the gods," Norivun said, slumping forward and cradling the guard to him.

Groaning, Haxil frowned. "Is that the thanks I get for keeping your—" The guard cleared his throat, then rubbed his side. He massaged the area that the prince's magic had speared. "For keeping your ward safe?"

I stiffened. *Ward?* No, something told me he'd been about to say *mate*, which meant the prince's guards also knew what I was.

The blood drained from my face as any lingering doubt over what the prince and I truly were vanished from my thoughts. I *knew*. Prince Norivun was my mate, and there was no running from that even if he'd killed my family.

I sank onto the couch, breathing hard.

"I'm sorry," Norivun said gruffly. "Fuck, Haxil. I almost . . . almost . . ." Such torment was written across his face.

Haxil sat up, still rubbing his side, but he nudged Prince Norivun. "I know. It's okay. Instincts in a male can be—"

Haxil cast a wary glance my way before he grunted and stood. He smiled at me sheepishly.

"Thanks for—" He shrugged, as though not sure how to thank me for the fact that my affinity had stopped one of his closest friends from murdering him. "Thanks for *that* and for the dinner and conversation. We'll have to finish it another time."

I could only manage a nod as the guard limped toward the door, his movements still stiff, but with each step he took, he seemed to heal and grow stronger. By the time he reached the threshold, he'd stopped rubbing his side completely, and his wings didn't look like razors against his back anymore.

He eyed us over his shoulder. "I'll just give you two some time. I'll be in the hall."

"No," Norivun said sharply. "You're to go to the infirmary and have Murl check you over and ensure you're all right. After that, you're to take the rest of the evening off. I'll guard Ilara. That's an order."

"Yes, my prince." With that, Haxil closed the door, and I was alone with my mate.

I sat stiffly on the couch, staring at the crown prince as my heart raced and my breathing grew shallow.

The prince stayed on the floor, looking toward where his friend had lain, had almost *died*. He wouldn't look at me. Wouldn't answer the questions that my silence asked.

I realized he wasn't going to admit what happened, so finally I said, "How long have you known?"

His shoulders rose sharply, his wings lifting above his head.

Inch by inch, his chin tilted up until those piercing blue eyes speared right into me, right to the center of who I was.

"Known what?"

His question was weighted, his gaze intense. Everything he felt and knew was in his eyes, but he wanted me to go first. Tradition dictated that males wait for females to acknowledge the bond before acting.

I knew I could deny it, could continue pretending that I didn't know, but there was no running from fate. Inevitably, it caught you, and I would rather this moment be on my terms than his.

"That I'm your mate?" I whispered.

His breath stuttered, and his wings lifted more as his breathing grew faster. A moment passed and then another.

"My prince?" I demanded.

He met my gaze again, his eyes swimming with barely leashed wildness. It was a look I'd seen so many times in him over the past two months, so—

My breath caught.

Months? I'd been seeing that look on him for *months*.

"When did you know?" I repeated but louder. *Blessed Mother, had he been feeling the bond that long?*

❄ 199 ❄

His jaw grew tighter, the muscle flexing in the corner. "For a while."

"How long? When did you first know?"

He released a breath. "When I brought you here to the castle. That first day when I flew us through the wards, and those two guards were fighting." His voice turned raspy and low. "It was when the injured one began to die, and I felt your affinity rise. That was when I knew. That was the moment the bond clicked into place for me."

I collapsed back onto the sofa. *He'd known all this time?* That meant . . .

"You've known the *entire time I've been at this castle*? You knew I was your mate when you locked me in these chambers for weeks on end?"

"I did."

"Yet, you did it anyway?" I screeched, remembering that time when I'd felt so much anxiety and distress over what my future would hold.

He winced. "I had to. Your affinity was only beginning to manifest and—" He growled. "I've already explained all of this. Why must I do it again?"

I sprang from my seat and began to pace. "Because it changes *everything*. You did all of those things to me, all of those horrible things that made me feel . . . *ock*—" I paced faster. "You did all of that knowing that I was your mate?"

He pushed to a stand too, his hands fisting. "Yes, I did, and do you know what it did to me? It killed me to treat you like that, Ilara, but I had to for your sake and our continent's."

I spun to face him, planting my feet on the floor. My chest heaved as my heart pattered like a trapped bird. *Why? Why must he be my mate? The murderer of my family? The male who's tortured me so?*

I swung away. "Who else knows?"

"My guards and Nuwin too."

"How long have all of them known?"

He sighed. "I told my guards within a few days of realizing it, and I told Nuwin the same day. When I hauled him out into the hallway, the night you first met him, and he'd teased you as being my courtesan, I told him you were my mate. I only told him so he'd keep his hands off you in my absence."

I covered my face with my hands. They'd *all* known. All of them, while I'd remained entirely naïve.

The prince's footsteps thundered in my ears. "Ilara," he said gently.

Tears flooded my eyes, but I moved away from him before he could reach me. "No. Don't."

I fled from his sight, flying through the doors to my courtyard, needing to get away from him and this bond that stretched so tightly between us that it felt as though my chest was caving in.

Moonlight pierced the night sky, and the warmth of my courtyard's *orem* bathed my senses.

I leaned my head back, closed my eyes, and inhaled deeply. Scents from the juniper blossoms tickled my nose, and the thick, cloying potency of the roses came next. *Breathe in and out. Just breathe.*

It was a tactic I'd used to ground myself after Tormesh and my parents had died. On the days when it felt as though I would shatter and everything around me was an illusion, I would plant my feet on the ground and let the soil curl between my toes as I breathed in the crystalline air of our northern realm. Slowly, the pounding in my heart would ease, and my tears would stop threatening to fall.

It was an act I did again now. I didn't know what else to do.

I didn't hear the prince approach, but his aura pummeled into my wingless back, barreling into me like crashing waves on the Tala Sea.

"I'm sorry," he finally said. "I never wanted this news to upset you."

I took one last deep breath before I spun to face him. Blinking, I held back the tears that threatened to fall. I would not cry or show him how destroyed I felt. It wasn't his fault the gods had chosen us for one another, but it didn't make me any less angry. *Why did they make* him *for me?*

I couldn't be with the male who'd killed my parents and brother. Even if I found it in me to completely forgive him, that stain would forever mar our relationship and taint any love that bloomed between us in blood.

He stared at me, the seconds ticking past as he waited.

"I can't be with you," I finally said. "Not now. Not ever."

His throat worked a swallow, his entire body going rigid.

"You killed my family. How can I forgive you for that?"

He moved so fast it was like lightning struck. He suddenly towered over me, making my head tilt back so I could meet his stormy expression as my chest threatened to swell.

Go to him, a voice inside me seemed to say.

I didn't. I couldn't.

"What if I didn't kill them?"

I laughed, the sound as bitter as I felt. "Not this again."

He clasped my chin, his fingers cupping that one small part

of me. My toes curled when a blazing jolt shot through me. *My mate. Mine.*

The words echoed in my mind, reminding me that I would forever have to live with this torment, this anguish that the one fairy who was meant for me was the one I would never allow myself to have.

He lifted my face more, angling it so I had to look him directly in the eyes. "I'm not being cruel."

I whipped my chin from his grip, a sharp retort on the tip of my tongue.

"Ilara," he growled. "I'm not, and I can prove it." He took a deep breath, the sound encompassing the weight of the realm.

I frowned. "What are you talking about?"

"What I'm about to show you could get me killed." When my frown only deepened, he added, "I'm trusting you, Ilara Seary, daughter of Mervalee Territory. I'm entrusting my soul to you. What I'm about to reveal has the power to destroy me completely if you choose to do so."

I didn't have time to process those words before his arms whipped around me, and the realm disappeared in a twist of mist and shadows, air and wind.

My scream caught in my throat from how unexpected the sensation was. And when my feet once again touched solid ground, my breath sucked in as a fierce wind and a spray of stinging ice pelted my face.

The prince hooked his arm around my shoulders, his wing stretching out around me to block the violent weather.

Blinding snow flew everywhere, obscuring my vision. A second later, a pulse of his magic bathed my skin, and then the fierce storm stopped due to a solid wall of air surrounding us.

"Where are we?" I asked. The cold no longer bit into me as warmth filled his protective dome.

"We're on the Cliffs of Sarum."

My eyes widened, and my entire body began to tremble. "Blessed Mother."

The Cliffs of Sarum were deadly. Stories floated throughout the continent of the magic encased within these icy cliffs and glaciers. Many fae had lost their lives here, getting lost in the labyrinth of enchanted caves and crevices, sucked in by magic, or falling prey to their own stupidity.

"I don't understand," I finally said as a shiver coursed through me.

He took another deep breath. "I created a small village here, hidden by so much illusion magic that nobody knows of its existence. Not the locals. Not my father. Not Nuwin. None of the council members. The only fae that know of what I've done here are my guards. Them and now you."

"Why would you do that?"

"Because I may be the Death Master of the continent, but I'm not what everyone claims me to be. I bring fae here, fae I was supposed to execute, but they are fae that I cannot kill. I stopped murdering innocents a long time ago, but my father doesn't know that."

My heart beat harder. Faster and faster and faster. *Innocents. Innocents were my parents and Tormesh.* He couldn't be saying what I thought he was saying. He couldn't have brought me here to . . .

My legs wobbled, my knees threatening to give out as I grasped his forearms tightly, my nails digging into him.

"Are you saying that my parents—" My throat grew dry, my tongue nearly paralyzed. "That my brother—"

But I couldn't say it.

I couldn't even think it, because if I was wrong, and this was all one giant misunderstanding or some twisted game that he was doing for his amusement . . .

It would destroy me.

His eyes softened. "Yes. They're alive, Ilara. They've always been alive. I never killed them."

CHAPTER 18

I collapsed. I fell to the ground, wet snow sinking through my pants and soaking my legs. Ice lay underneath it. Cold, slippery, clear ice that threatened to sweep me down the cliffs under the weight of my disbelief.

I shook my head over and over. "Where? Please! I need to see them."

A gigantic swell of his power ripped through the realm. Just outside of his protective bubble, a shimmer manifested, like a veil. The crown prince worked his jaw as the tendons in his neck strained. I blinked, then blinked again as the raging storm around us fell away, and an opening in a wall of ice appeared.

And behind that opening...

Fae walked within a hidden dome, visible in splotchy images as the ice fragmented their forms.

I stood, stumbling toward them, but the prince got there first, whispering something, a spell perhaps, and the opening widened, as though unlocking from his masterful touch.

Warmth from inside rushed over my face, and when I

crossed the threshold, a layer of protective wards—so strong that it put the dome encasing the castle to shame—gripped me. For a moment, it held me as though analyzing my intent, and then in a rush I was released.

Houses and lanes, shops and fountains—every which way I looked were signs of life. Of a fairy's home.

I nearly fell forward in my haste to see them, find them, hug them, love them, greet them. Mother Below, I didn't know what I wanted or what I was going to do when I saw them, but if they were alive and here and—

"Ilara?"

I stopped in my tracks. The voice that had just called my name . . . I would know that voice anywhere.

"Mother?" I whispered. I turned, almost afraid to do so, terrified that this was all a cruel illusion, that the prince was really my mate from the underworld, come to wreak havoc on my soul while playing demented games with my mind.

But then I faced her.

She stood just behind me, her expression a slew of disbelief, happiness, and joy. Silvery white hair cascaded down her back. Blue eyes sparkled with growing tears. Wings with quivering muscles splayed out on either side of her as her hands balled into fists. Those gentle hands had curved hair behind my ears, swatted me playfully when I beat her at her favorite game of cards, rolled dough on the counters in our worn kitchen, and carefully tucked covers around me, Cailis, and Tormesh when we were children, before she kissed us on our noses and wished us dreams of traveling through the stars.

And then she was running.

I was running.

Tears spilled onto her cheeks, mine doing the same. We collided in a crash of limbs and chests, wrapping ourselves around each other as incomprehensible sounds and words tumbled from our lips.

And then my father was there. Tormesh was there. Their laughter, smiles, and hands were everywhere, and their touches, kisses, and embraces obliterated the sorrow that I'd been feeling for so very long.

And it was all real. *They* were real.

I didn't know how long we stood there in a tangle of love and hope, but all of us were talking and blubbering. My father's lips lifted in a grin, and Tormesh's wings rippled in the icy light.

"How?" I finally managed. "How are you all alive and unharmed? How come Cailis and I didn't know?"

My mother cupped my face before pressing a kiss to my forehead as my father wiped tears from his eyes.

"He put us here," Tormesh finally said and nodded toward the crown prince.

A heartbeat of silence passed before I realized that Norivun stood near the village's threshold. His arms were crossed over his chest as he leaned against the ice wall. A sad smile played upon his lips as the northern storm raged just outside of his protective barrier.

I stared at him, so many emotions tumbling through me that I didn't know where to begin. *Why? How? For how long? Why? WHY?*

He'd said something about creating this place because he wasn't what fae claimed him to be. That nobody knew about it, not even his father.

"Why?" I finally said, unable to align my thoughts to anything other than that one word.

He walked toward us, gliding like mist over the sea. "To keep them safe. To keep *all* of them safe." His throat bobbed in a swallow, but he waved a hand behind me, to the tiny village, to the other fae mingling about, some whom had stopped to watch my family and me as we dissolved into a mess in one another's arms. I counted them. *Five, fifteen, no twenty-five.* The list grew. So many.

"I still don't understand," I choked out.

Prince Norivun's smile grew, but the gesture was filled with a heaviness that made the expression look forced. "There's much you don't understand, Ilara, but I couldn't hide this from you, not any longer."

Mate.

The unspoken word hung between us. He'd shown me this because of what I was to him, what he was to me. He'd known that even though I felt the mate bond as viscerally as he did, that I would never allow myself to succumb to its pull, not after what I thought he'd done.

My mother pulled me close again, her arm wrapping around my shoulders as her wing spread protectively around my side.

"It was the only way," she whispered into my ear. "As much as it pained me, your father, and your brother to know that you and Cailis believed us dead, we knew it was the only way. The king had ordered us to be executed, but it didn't stop us from hoping and dreaming that this day would come. My girl." She pressed another kiss to my temple. "My baby girl. I've missed you so much."

Tears flooded my eyes again, and I looked to the prince for answers, for an explanation of this hidden city's existence. *The king had ordered their execution.* But I'd thought Norivun had made that decision. Not the king.

The crown prince extended his hand. "Come, Ilara. I have a lot to tell you, but first, visit with your family."

CHAPTER 19

My parents led me to a small house as the prince walked at my side. Norivun had let go of my hand, but he walked close enough that our fingers brushed on occasion. And every time we touched, a path of lightning shot along my nerves. Each touch was electric, like a current ran between us, and only one tiny spark was needed to ignite an inferno.

I tried not to be distracted by that. Tried not to dwell on the bond that stretched between us that felt so palpable that I wondered why it'd taken me so long to recognize it.

With each step, amazement filled me, not just because Prince Norivun was my mate, but at where we were. This place truly was a living, breathing city, even if it was small. It had everything that our village in Mervalee possessed. Shops, houses, streets, vendors, tiny gardens. All of it. It was like a small oasis hidden in the most destructive patch of nature. Somehow, someway, the prince had created this bubble of paradise. And apparently, he'd done it all to shield innocents from his father.

"How did you create this?" I whispered.

"Magic. A lot of it." His words came out slow, tired sounding.

"Come, my prince. I shall prepare a meal to help replenish your stores." My mother smiled gently.

My eyes widened. "Are you weakened?" I'd never seen him anything but invincible, other than the snowgum attack, but the prince had shown immense strain when he'd opened the veil to this town and allowed me entry.

"A bit." His offhanded comment made my heart thrum harder, even more so when my mother and Tormesh ushered him into their home.

I rushed in after them, still not understanding how any of this was possible. The king had always made it sound as though he pacified his son's murderous antics, but a killer wouldn't have created this.

The hatred I'd been feeling for Norivun ever since the moment we'd met cracked even more. Everything that I'd thought I'd known about the prince was proving to be wrong. He wasn't evil. He wasn't my enemy. If anything, he was my family's savior.

My father followed me into their small two-room house at the end of a narrow street. Above, a shield of ice, nearly two hundred feet tall at the ceiling, protected them from the cliff's deadly elements. The storm outside still raged, the ice as clear as glass, and with a start, I wondered if that clear ice allowed them to see the sun on peaceful days, or the stars, moons, and galaxy on a cloudless night.

"This is where you've been living?" I said thickly, my throat and tongue still not wanting to work properly.

My mother pulled out a chair for the prince, then went to the stove.

"It is." My father put his arm around me, hugging me again. "Until the prince can figure out how to return us to our normal lives, this is where we have to stay."

Hearing my father say that made a new knock of reality shake me. The prince was working to free them?

Blessed Mother. There was so much I didn't know.

"Come help." My father closed the front door behind us. "The prince is always fatigued whenever he ventures here, even if he tries to hide it."

My brother lit the candles and used his magic to ignite the fairy lights in their home as Norivun accepted a cup of hot broth from my mother without comment. The scent of wood and the tickling of dust motes hit my senses. Their home was tiny, just a main living area and one bedroom with two beds.

"So small," I whispered. The living area had a narrow fireplace, a single sofa, and a lone table. Just behind it waited the kitchen. It was just as small with a dining table so minuscule it barely sat four. The simplicity of the design reminded me of our actual home in Mervalee, but this was even more cramped.

"I couldn't make the homes bigger," Norivun said, his deep voice reverberating all the way to my bones. "The amount of magic it took to create this village and then the supplies needed to fill it with everything the occupants would need was difficult. That and I have to reinforce the wards every so often, and the larger the village, the more taxing that is, so it was either make fewer homes larger, or make more homes smaller. I chose the latter so I could accommodate more fae."

"I wasn't judging." My cheeks blazed that he was apologizing for not giving my family a larger house. "You truly kept them alive when the king wanted them killed, and you're sorry the house isn't bigger?"

His throat bobbed as my mother continued to fuss over him.

My entire body trembled with the emotions that were overtaking me, so I swung back to my father so I didn't embarrass myself. He was still looking at me as though I was a ghost, and Tormesh wasn't looking much different.

"Come, rest by the fire." My mother gestured for both the prince and I to sit on the single sofa, then proceeded to pull out fixings for dinner while my father caught a hen in the pen behind their house.

Even though I'd eaten not too long ago with Haxil, I found the tantalizing scents of my parents' home cooking and the feel of familiarity as my family surrounded us to make me hungry for the life we'd once led.

And as Tormesh began telling me how he filled most of his days, I sprang from the couch, no longer able to sit still as I grabbed plates from the single shelf on the wall and glasses for drinks. Every few minutes, I snuck glances at the prince. He sat rigidly, and he made no move to help, yet a part of me knew that wasn't from bad manners. His magic was that depleted.

My hands shook when I set each plate on the table until Tormesh elbowed me, a grin splitting his face.

"There's a well in the back." My brother inclined his head toward another door. "Water from the sea is pumped and filtered daily. Come, I'll show you."

Thankful for the distraction, I followed him out. A single pump stood at the corner of their property. We both spoke rapidly as he pumped the well, each of us trying to fill in the other as much as possible so we knew everything that was happening in each other's lives.

"You have three affinities?" He nearly dropped the bucket of water when I told him that. "And the king entered you into the Rising Queen Trial?"

I nodded. "My first affinity manifested a few months ago. It's why the prince took me." I explained my other two affinities as well, but neglected to mention Vorl's involvement. My brother hated Vorl for how he'd treated me. Even though I'd hidden most of the abuse from my family, they'd still seen enough to know that Vorl was anything but kind to me.

"You have a fire element too, just like mother and me?" Tormesh grinned.

"I do, and watch out, I can probably best you in a fire wielding competition."

He snorted. "Doubtful." A lasso of his fire whipped out of him and around me.

Laughing, I released my own affinity. I coiled my fire around his, shoving it off.

"I'm not that easily thwarted." He circled me, and we battled playfully, lobbing fireballs at each other, whipping strands of fire at one another's ankles, and creating walls of flames to halt the other's progress.

Tormesh soon began sweating, and the surprise on his face was priceless when my fire again cut through his.

"You truly are stronger than me." The teasing left his voice, awe taking its place.

I sucked my fire affinity back into me, shrugging.

Tormesh's smile broadened. "Who would have thought my sister would become so powerful." He shook his head in wonder, but then his lips downturned. "I wish I could have seen you manifest."

My chest tightened. The prince had brought my family here to keep them safe, but this tiny village was still a cage. Nobody could come and go willingly. It was too great of a risk that would expose them all. Basically, it was a prison, and that stirred memories of the time I'd been locked in the Exorbiant Chamber.

If it wasn't such a sad situation, I probably would have snorted in amusement. While the prince's intentions were noble, he also had a habit of locking fae up. Although life on the Cliffs of Sarum, with the hope of one day being free, was better than entering the afterlife.

Tormesh bumped me with his elbow again. "Don't look so sad. It's really not that bad here. We've gotten used to it, and honestly, it's not that much different from life back home. We just can't do trips to Firlim anymore, but how often did we leave our village anyway?" He shrugged. "Besides, I saw a lot of the continent when I marched with the Solis Guard. At least I got that."

"Oh, Tormesh." I pulled him into a hug. He'd always been an optimist.

He hugged me back just as fiercely, and then our father hollered from inside, asking where the drinks were.

We both laughed as tears pricked my eyes again before we joined everyone else.

The rest of the evening passed in a blur, and it was so

surreal it felt magical. We all crowded around the tiny kitchen table, catching up on all that had occurred in the past full season. My family had endless questions about me and Cailis, and the wistful sigh on my mother's face told me she wanted to see my sister as desperately as she had wanted to see me.

But I didn't know if the prince would allow it. He'd seemed cagey and concerned about bringing me here, and the secretiveness of the place told me that he'd taken a huge risk just by allowing my entry.

But I didn't let those concerns cloud my thoughts. Instead, I focused on the present and soaked up every second of my family's company while the prince remained quiet but ate a mountain of food.

By the time the sky darkened to the deepest night through the window-like ice above the tiny village, I knew it was time to go. We'd been gone for hours, and just because the bombshell of my family's survival had hit me like a ton of bricks, it didn't stop everything else that was occurring in my life.

I still needed to wake up early to heal another field, I still had to train, and I still had to prepare for my three Trial tests, which were only weeks away.

So when we stood to leave, I didn't fight it.

"I'll mistphase myself, and if you'd like, I can mistphase you too," I said to the prince, knowing his pride wouldn't allow him to admit that his magic was weakened.

Surprise filled his eyes. "You can mistphase others?"

I nodded. "I've been reliably able to for a few weeks now thanks to Matron Olsander, and mistphasing us from here will be good practice for me."

"You can *mistphase* too?" Tormesh's eyes bugged out as my parents gaped.

I laughed. "I can do a lot more than that now."

"Who would have thought that my daughter with her black hair and missing wings would grow to be so powerful." My mother wrapped me in a hug, then my father did the same.

My family walked us to the veil that shrouded their tiny village. Now that I knew my parents and brother were alive, a sense of peace settled over me. But more than that filled my soul. The male standing at my side with his great wings and masterful affinities was the reason they'd survived.

And suddenly, the thought of being the victor of the Rising Queen Trial, of becoming Norivun's wife . . .

For the first time since I'd learned of my fate, that thought didn't make me want to run.

It made me want to win.

CHAPTER 20

I mistphased us back to the castle just after midnight, landing precisely where the prince told me to go even though it wasn't an area of the castle I'd ever ventured to before.

When our feet touched a solid floor, I took in the dark and unfamiliar room surrounding us. A bed bigger than the one I slept in rested against the wall. Large windows allowed moonlight to stream in, highlighting the grand fireplace, couches and chairs surrounding it, along with a massive closet filled with garments of all cuts and colors.

"Where are we?" I asked.

"This is my private chambers." In the dark, the prince's wings rose behind him like horns, the talons at the tips like sharp claws.

"This is your bedroom chambers? But isn't it warded?"

"Of course it is, but it's never been warded to you."

That statement slammed into me. He'd never warded his

most private chambers to me because I was his mate, and he'd known I was his mate since the second I first entered this castle.

For a moment, I didn't know what to say. I'd never seen where he slept, had never even thought to ask since I'd been fighting the attraction that had so naturally born between us.

But now . . .

I wrapped my arms around myself. "I'm still in shock that they're alive."

His fingers immediately covered my lips, silencing me. A current ran through me at that light touch. He dropped his hand, his eyes gleaming in the moonlight, and the unspoken words that passed between us told me that he'd also felt that buzz of energy. But more importantly, my silence over that village in the Cliffs of Sarum was imperative. No one could know about it.

Magic rumbled inside me, and I called upon my air element and concentrated on forming a silencing Shield around us. My affinity flowed out of me, creating a wall of air until I knew nobody outside of my magic could hear us.

"I won't tell anyone," I said, my tone low in the dark room despite my Shield. "But I have to tell Cailis. I can't keep this secret from her." When he opened his mouth to argue, I added, "She won't tell a soul. Not if it puts our family's lives in jeopardy."

He frowned but gave a curt nod. "Cailis and Cailis only. If word were to ever get out, my father would destroy that place, kill everyone inside it, and my end would come just as swiftly."

I paled. We'd spoken of many things tonight, but it'd been mainly catching up with my lost family and learning how they'd been fairing. It hadn't been about the logistics of why the prince had created that tiny city and how I could have been so wrong about him.

"Sit with me?" He gestured to the sofa before stoking the kernel of flame that was suspended in the fireplace. A fire immediately roared to life, crackling in the hearth as the crown prince fed it wood while I sank onto the couch.

"Drink?" he asked once the fire was roaring.

"Please."

He ventured to the small bar in the corner. It wasn't as extravagant as the ice bar in my chambers, but it held numerous bottles and decanters.

He poured two glasses of amber liquid, not leminai, and the scent that drifted to me when he neared told me it was just as strong.

"Are you trying to get me drunk?" I asked with a small smile. My heart pattered more the closer he got. My fingers itched to move, to touch him, to feel him.

Blessed Mother, is this what he's been feeling for months?

I balled my hands in my lap until he held out my glass to me, then I grabbed it with shaky fingers.

The second I had it, I brought it to my lips. Bitterness hit my tongue, then a scorching fire cleaved down my throat. I coughed and made a face. "What is this?"

"It's called whiskey. I had it imported from that *other* realm."

"This could kill a domal."

His lips curved as he took a sip from his own glass. He winced slightly, but the liquid rolled down his throat in a swallow, and my gaze snagged to the muscles of his neck.

Nostrils flaring, he gave me a knowing smile as he inhaled my aroused scent.

I quickly looked away, back to the fire where the flames danced. It called to my own fire affinity since my Outlets were open. Slight, steady puffs of my magic were exuding from my pores. I *had* to keep them open. The turmoil of the night was ratcheting through me, heightening my magic even more.

Taking a deep breath, I faced the prince, determined to ignore the ripple of tension. Attraction might burn like a wildfire between our souls, but there were more important things to discuss. Things that were bigger than him being my mate.

"Why did you have to create that village? How often do you go there? How hard is it for you to maintain? Why did you lie about killing my family? And did you know when we met that they were my family?"

He settled onto the couch as an amused smirk curved his lips. "Should I answer those questions in order? Let's see. It was either create that village, or everyone in there died. And I don't go there often, only when I need to replenish their supplies or reinforce the wards, and—" His jaw clenched as his amusement vanished. "It takes a lot of magic to reinforce the wards. When I do, I usually make sure it's at a time when I'll be allowed at least a full day of rest afterward to replenish my magic. And no, when we first met, I didn't realize I held your parents and brother there. It was only when you told us your name at Liss Lodge that I made the connection."

I pulled my legs beneath me, turning on the sofa to face him. "Why didn't you tell me about that place once you knew you kept my family there?"

"Because I didn't know if I could trust you."

I frowned. "You thought I would report what you'd done after learning that you'd saved my family?"

His shoulders lifted. "I knew you would be happy beyond words to know they were still alive, but yes, I didn't know if you'd report me or not. You hated me, Ilara."

I nodded. "Yes, I did, but a lot of that hatred came from believing you'd killed them. I wouldn't have reported you if I'd known they were still alive and that you'd saved them."

"Even if it would disrupt the entire Trial and potentially stop you from being forced into an arranged marriage?"

My breaths grew faster. He knew how much I despised the thought of being forced to marry, but that accusation still stung. "Do you believe me that selfish? That ungrateful?"

"No, but I hardly knew you when I brought you here. I needed to see more of your character. I needed to learn if you could keep a secret."

"And you now believe I can?"

"I hope so, but if we're being truly honest, that's not the only reason I took you there tonight."

Mate.

The unspoken word hung between us again. That had been the deciding factor for the prince. He wanted me to accept him, so he'd made his decision to share that secret oasis with me because we were mates, because he knew I would never accept him despite the bond if I continued to believe he'd killed my family.

Breaths coming faster, I brought my glass to my lips and took another burning swallow. My heart was beating like a beast now. "But why would your father want to kill my family?

And why did he make it sound like *you* were the one deciding to deliver those executions?"

A rumble of the prince's magic vibrated the couch as he scowled heavily, and a moment of relief hit me that his power was swiftly returning. "My father knows of the unrest that's been growing as of late. He wanted it squashed, so when fae began arriving to the castle, voicing their concerns and worries, he wanted them silenced. He ordered me to execute all of them."

My jaw dropped as everything I'd believed of our king came into question. "Could *he* be behind the fae who've gone missing of late if it wasn't you?"

Norivun scratched his chin, drawing my attention to the cleft in its middle. "I've been starting to wonder the same. It doesn't make sense for Wormiful or Crimsonale to kill them. They want the unrest to grow, but my father . . ." He shrugged. "He wants talks of war banished."

"If it's him, that means he sent whoever tried to attack me in the hall that night. But why me?"

Another rumble of his power shivered beneath the sofa. "I don't know." His lips thinned into razors.

"If the king *is* behind it, how do you suppose he's killing the fae he's caught?"

"My guess is he's using his personal guards to discreetly remove and murder any fae speaking out. His guards are loyal to him and will do as he commands, but if the public were to learn of it, he'd have to deny any involvement and execute his guards for appearance's sake. It would explain why the disappearances have all been so clandestine."

"But how did his guard, or whoever tried to attack me,

disappear?" I paused, remembering that strange smell that had accompanied that night. It'd smelled like rot. I'd never smelled a fairy like that before.

"Perhaps they mistphased?" The prince's frown grew as I pondered the situation more.

"It's so extreme, to openly attack and kill innocent fae. And all to quiet an uproar? But I wasn't trying to create an uproar, so again, why me?"

His eyebrows drew together so tightly, a line formed. "You're right that it doesn't make sense, but to understand any of this, you have to know my father. He doesn't like his hands being dirtied. He likes that the fae of our land love and support him. It's part of the reason he's been able to stay in power for so long, which is why he's raised me to be the villain."

"He does that just to maintain the love of our fae?"

The prince nodded.

"So if he orders you to deliver all of the executions *he* wants, have you killed any fae who've attempted to cause dissent?"

Norivun's easy expression vanished. His look became haunted, as though a thousand ghosts tortured his soul. "Not those fae, no, but there were others in the past that I was forced to kill. Many winters ago, before I created that village in the Cliffs of Sarum, it was either kill them or—" He brought his drink to his lips again.

"Or what?"

"Watch my mother be tortured."

I gaped, my mouth falling open so completely that I had to force myself to snap it closed. "What in the realm are you talking about?"

The energy around him grew. "My father isn't who the public perceives him to be. He likes to control me. I've always been kept on a tight leash. He's used my mother to ensure I stay obedient."

A sick feeling grew in my stomach. "What do you mean?"

"From a young age, he knew of the power that lay within my veins, and he knew that once my affinities fully manifested, that he wouldn't be able to stop me if I truly unleashed them on him. He knew I could take control of his throne—something he will *never* willingly relinquish—so many winters ago, he taught me what the consequences would be if I didn't adhere to his rulings."

The sick feeling inside me doubled. "By using your *mother*?"

He nodded. "If I don't do as he commands, he forces her into isolation. If I refuse to kill fae that he wants disposed of, my mother is starved, and then there's the physical beatings. He's beaten her to within an inch of her life more times than I want to remember, and it was all because I hadn't done exactly what he'd commanded."

Nausea rolled through my stomach. A second passed and then another. I was so shocked that I couldn't speak, but I managed to choke out, "That's horrific."

"It is. He's a monster, Ilara, but our kingdom doesn't know that. He's used me as the scapegoat for so many seasons that our fae hate me, but they don't hate him."

I worked a swallow and then asked something that I couldn't *not* ask. "Why haven't you just killed him outright if he's that evil? If he's dead, he wouldn't be able to hurt your mother."

The prince took another sip of his whiskey, letting it roll across his tongue before he swallowed. "I've wanted to, so many times, but if I murdered the king in cold blood, regardless of my reasons, I would be held accountable. I would be brought to trial before the supernatural courts and found guilty. My execution would follow, and even if I managed to avoid that, even if I somehow managed to take the throne as my own, the Solis wouldn't forget what I'd done. I'd one day find a knife in my back or a poison in my wine. Our continent would ultimately have my head if I murdered the king in cold blood."

My breath came out in a rush. He was right. Of course, he was right. Murdering the king wouldn't solve anything. It would only lead to Norivun's downfall as well.

I sat back, trying to wrap my head around all of this. According to the prince, I was totally and completely wrong about everything. Prince Norivun wasn't a murderer—the king was. And Norivun had never used his magic unjustly, only when forced to by the king's hand.

I thought back to the fairy in High Liss, who the prince had killed with his affinity. I'd been so sickened by it then, thinking he'd done it without a second thought, but he'd given that male several chances to transform back into his fairy form. And the prince's guards had been so furious when I'd accused the prince of being a cruel monster. It was because they'd known what the prince had done to save others. They'd been aware of the village hidden away in the Cliffs of Sarum. They knew who Norivun truly was.

"Do all of your guards know the king's true nature?"

He took another drink and gave a curt nod. "They've been

with me since I fully manifested. They've seen my father behind closed doors. They know."

I shuddered. It felt as though insects crawled under my skin. Every interaction I'd had with the king had gone easily for the most part. I'd never once suspected that he could be one side of a two-faced coin. But things the prince had once said to me began to percolate in my conscience—things about his mother and my parents that had left me slightly confused at the time.

She lives in peace—when he'd been referring to his mother as we flew by her tower. She lived in peace, avoiding beatings and starvation, because of the sacrifices Norivun made to protect her.

I regret what taking your parents and brother from their lives did to them, you, and your sister. He'd removed my parents and brother from Mervalee and from my life, but he hadn't killed them. He'd simply relocated them, which explained that strange description. And the time he'd lied outright to me about their deaths had been because he hadn't known if he could trust me with his secret.

And what he'd said about the king. *It's important that my father doesn't know what you are to me. It's important that I act a certain way around you when he's near.*

My breath sucked in. Was that because he was afraid of his father learning I was his mate? That he knew the king could beat me, starve me, and torture me as he had his mother? Given what Norivun had revealed, it wouldn't be above his father to also use me as a weapon to ensure his son stayed obedient.

My heart pounded as all of those strange comments fell

into place. "Does all of this have anything to do with why your mother always looks so lonely?"

He nodded. "My father forbids her from interacting with other fae, and a long time ago, he built a magic-tethering chamber within this castle using spells I still don't fully understand that trapped my mother's affinities within her. I destroyed that chamber once I found out, but ever since that incident, she can't access her magic normally. Sometimes, she'll get glimpses of it, but no amount of effort on my part has found a way to counteract what he did and free her from the cage he's locked her in. Now, she has to practice deep breathing regularly to keep her affinities at bay, otherwise she'll implode without being able to properly utilize her Outlets."

I made a sound, a half-strangled sob at the thought of living like that, and then with a crashing realization, I remembered that I'd witnessed her struggles. The way the queen had acted when I'd woken following the snowgum's attack had been so bizarre. She'd looked rattled and had started taking strange, deep breaths.

It had to be true, everything the crown prince was saying. I'd seen firsthand the affects her locked magic had on her.

"But her hair's hidden beneath her illusion spell, right? So she must be able to use some magic."

He shook his head. "Her hair used to be hidden under one of her illusion spells, before my father suppressed her power. Now, I conceal it under *my* illusion spell at her request."

My eyes widened, and I thought back to the day she'd visited me wearing a scarf. "Did she ask you to remove the illusion the day the snowgum attacked you?"

He cocked his head. "She did when she came to the infirmary to see me."

Bitterness and anger rose in me simultaneously, making my lip curl. I'd suffered abuse in my life, but nothing as vicious as what Queen Lissandra had endured.

I took a moment to compose myself, but my voice still shook when I asked, "So even though you do as the king says, he still abuses your mother?"

The prince shrugged ruefully. "The abuse she suffers is the lesser of the two evils. He won't beat or starve her if I continue doing as he wants, but he knows that she's nearly as powerful as me. If my mother's magic was freed, either of us could kill him if we chose to, no matter how many guards he has surrounding him, so he controls me through her, and her by trapping her affinities." He took another sip of whiskey, his expression bitter. "My father is always thinking ahead. I can guarantee that he has other safeguards in place if the day ever comes that one of us decides to betray him. It's another reason I can't kill him outright or assassinate him covertly."

"But why? *Why* does he do that at all? You're his family. Family protects and loves one another."

"Not everyone's father is like yours, Ilara. My father has been ruling the northern continent for hundreds of winters, longer than any king. That reign hasn't come from kindness. He's brutal and ruthless, and above all, he relishes power. He's done whatever's been necessary to keep his throne and any threats to it at bay."

"And now it's being threatened."

He nodded. "My father refuses to admit there's a problem with the crops because he's lived for so long and has seen so many magical cycles of our continent that he's convinced it's merely a delay in the celestial events, and eventually, our land's *orem* will be replenished, but he's wrong even if he won't admit it. If the celestial events truly have stopped, he's powerless to fix that. I don't think he wants to accept that, because this would be the first time in his reign that he can't control the outcome of our continent."

"So he's buried his head in the sand because he doesn't like the consequences?"

"He has. I've tried to talk sense into him. It's no use. He's convinced the land will thrive again if we just wait it out."

"And meanwhile, fae will starve."

"Correct. They'll starve and grow bitter and angry that nothing's being done, but that's where I come in. If I control any wayward fae who takes it upon themselves to cause unrest, other fae will see that and stay quiet. It makes me the hated one, not him, so he continues his rule, and nothing threatens his power while he waits for the *orem* to reappear."

"Yet, there's been talk of war and if the king should stay in power."

"My father's been watching the council members who are stirring such talk. He hasn't outright told me to kill them, but I know if they step too far, he will."

"But . . . can you do that?"

He shook his head. "If I killed them, the uproar from the fae of our continent would be so great that even my father would have no choice but to kill me as payback."

"But he'd still risk that. Sacrificing his own son, silencing the council members who oppose him, and all for what? To stay in power?"

"He'll do anything to keep control. His brutality has no bounds."

"Norivun," I said sadly, achingly. I'd been so wrong about him, about everything.

He stilled.

Lips parting, I realized it was the very first time I'd ever called him by his given name.

His chest rose and fell swiftly with each breath as his hand inched across the sofa until it rested near mine. I looked at his long fingers, his large palm. He stayed rigid, waiting—waiting to see if I would accept him.

I slipped my palm beneath his and didn't resist when he tentatively threaded his fingers with mine.

A lightning bolt of longing coursed through me.

He loosed a breath, as if he'd felt the same, and that my acknowledgment, my touch, soothed some deep part of his soul.

But he wasn't the only one affected. Feeling him, touching him . . . it called to something within me too. Something that was unfurling and growing, some hidden part of me that had been dormant and was only now coming to light.

Mate.

"How do we stop the king?" I whispered. "And how do we permanently fix our land?"

His eyes darkened in the firelight, brimming with barely leashed desire. "We start by you winning the Rising Queen Trial."

CHAPTER 21

Thehose words hit me like a punch to my gut. Win the Trial. Marry the prince. Destroy the king.

"What if I can't?" I pulled my hand away and wrapped my arms around my waist.

"You *can*, Ilara. You're stronger than all of them. Just because your magic is new doesn't deter from its strength. You're powerful. You just need to believe in yourself and hone it."

"But if I win, we'll—" I licked my lips as my stomach coiled. Desire tingled within me, desire for *him*. "We'll marry."

"We will." That wild light entered his eyes again. "And then you'll be *mine*." Those instincts reared in his expression, the feral longing, the harsh desire.

Males always felt the mate bond more viscerally than females. It wasn't unheard of for males to kill another male who in any way threatened their female. There were laws in the courts that allowed such acts, simply because the instincts were so strong that they were at times uncontrollable.

And that fact hit me like a thunderbolt. No wonder he'd tried to kill Vorl and Lord Waterline when they'd attacked me. And no wonder he'd nearly killed his guard when he believed Haxil was trying to claim me.

"Is your interest in me solely because of the bond?" I asked.

"No."

I arched an eyebrow as I took in his broad shoulders and massive wings. He was as alluring as the underworld, dark and full of sin. I'd tried to fight my attraction to him, but I wanted him.

He inhaled, subtly, but I still caught it. "And is your interest in *me* only because of the bond?"

My chest rose faster, and I hastily took another drink. "No."

He inched closer, his gaze like a predator. "I know we haven't known each other long, but it's not just the bond that attracts me to you, Ilara. You're strong, brave, kind, and much more resilient than most give you credit for."

My gaze whipped to his. "How do you know that?"

"I've seen enough to know that much, and I've heard things too. The servants speak of you, of your kindness and willingness to always help. They've never met a lady like you. You don't see yourself as above them or them as merely there to serve you. You see them as fae, as individuals. It hasn't gone unnoticed."

"Because they are fae who deserve to be treated with kindness and are more than just servants. Since when do rulibs determine one's worth?" I said vehemently.

His eyes flickered, an emotion shining in them before he veiled it. "You're inherently good, Ilara, and I've committed more sins than Lucifer, but I'll spend the rest of my life proving that I'll be a worthy mate to you. I'll cherish you, and I'll show you that I'm not as evil as everyone believes—"

"I already know you're not."

He stilled.

"I've seen enough to know the same of you, my prince. You've sacrificed more than anyone in this kingdom knows, and you've done it all selflessly. You haven't looked for recognition or gratitude when you've helped fae who've demanded your affinities be used for their needs. You created an entire village to shield innocents from your father even though it could lead to your demise. You're not a monster, Norivun. I see that. I *see you.*"

His chest heaved, his mouth tightening, and then he squeezed my hand again, his fingers once more encircling mine. "I've waited so long to find you."

I squeezed him back just as tightly. Tears began to fill my eyes, because it wasn't fair. It wasn't fair that he was hated when he gave so much.

A moment passed as thick emotion tightened my throat. My heart thundered. Everything in me was swirling, colliding, igniting. Being here, with him . . . everything about it felt right. I felt complete.

Crackling from the fire filled the quiet. Shifting, the prince's wings splayed out more behind him. "I want you to be mine, Ilara. I never want to be parted from you. Let me claim you. Please."

My stomach flipped, and everything in me wanted to say yes, to throw caution to the wind.

But everything right now wasn't just about us.

I stood and took a deep breath before I faced the fire. Magic simmered inside me as energy in me began to build. I itched at my chest, trying to suppress the feeling that rose higher and higher, as a deep pulsing ache began in my core.

The prince's nostrils flared as he watched me, his expression carefully veiled.

"I can't accept you yet, only because of what lays ahead."

"Why?" he asked quietly before coming to his feet and prowling silently toward me.

I worked a swallow. "Because I can't be fully bonded to you. I have to concentrate on the Trial, on saving my family, on stopping your father, but it doesn't mean I don't want you."

He stopped only inches away, and his snow and cedar scent clouded around me as his broad shoulders and pounding aura commanded my attention. "You can still be bonded to me and do all of that."

I shook my head. "I can't. You're quite . . . distracting. I need to concentrate on healing fields and learning my magic better in the last few weeks that I have. And what if I lose the Trial? Then what? I'll be bonded to you while having to marry another."

His eyes narrowed as a deadly gleam filled them. "You will not marry another."

"I'll have to if the king orders it."

His hands pumped into fists as a muscle worked in his jaw.

"We can't, Norivun. Not yet." As much as I knew the prince detested to admit it, we both knew that we couldn't stop his father unless Norivun was willing to pay the price—the price being his mother's safety or his own execution for defying the king.

Such a choice would destroy him. His life or his mother's

well-being for my safety and happiness. Those were his choices if he defied his father. I would never put the prince in that position.

"Let me win the Trial first, and then I'll accept you as my mate." I laid a hand on his chest. His muscles jumped beneath my palm.

His chest lifted in a breath that was so deep it seemed to carry the weight of the realm when he released it. He covered my hand with his, then leaned down until his forehead touched mine. "I ache for you, Ilara."

My heart squeezed at that quietly pained statement. "I ache for you as well."

He trailed a finger softly along my cheek. "Are you sure I can't convince you otherwise?"

My entire body tingled, and a shudder ran through me.

He shifted, pressing a kiss to my throat before he inhaled my scent. "I could make you scream in pleasure." He kissed my neck again, so softly, so suggestively, that a swell of desire bloomed in my core.

A shiver danced down my spine as goosebumps broke out across my skin. He slipped an arm around my waist, slowly, questioningly. As if he didn't want to force anything on me and was waiting to see what I would do.

I knew I couldn't bed him, not yet, but that didn't mean we couldn't enjoy other things.

He seemed to sense my acceptance the moment it hit me.

A low growl rumbled his chest, and then he lifted me, sweeping me into his embrace before striding toward his bed. Wings rippling behind him, he cradled me to him as steady channels of power oozed from his pores.

My heart beat harder, painfully hard. But I didn't stop him, didn't voice any concern. Because *Blessed Mother,* I wanted this male, wanted him so badly that I burned, even if I couldn't fully have him yet.

When we reached the bed, Norivun lay me on it and paused as longing washed over his face. "I've wanted to see you in my bed for so many months."

His hands went to the hem of my pants before he removed them slowly, languidly, as if he were relishing every moment of undressing me now that the time had finally come. He removed my shirt next, his breath hissing when only my underthings covered me.

"So beautiful." He lifted my foot and brought the arch to his mouth. My toes curled when he pressed a kiss there, then he ran his fingers up my calf. "So soft. Your skin is like silk."

He trailed his fingertips up my thighs, and I nearly bucked off the bed when his fingers brushed fleetingly on my core.

He chuckled darkly as desire heated his gaze before he bent my knees, then wrapped both of my legs over his shoulders, hooking my feet behind him, right between his wings.

My attention snagged on those leathery appendages. They were spread slightly, as though he wasn't able to keep them locked in tight, and my toe inched toward his left wing before running slightly up the inside, where the bone met flesh.

Norivun hissed, and a shuddering groan left him. "Do that again."

My heart beat faster as I mimicked the same movement, first on his left wing and then on his right.

His entire face tightened as energy coiled around him. Squeezing his eyes shut, he took a deep breath and then another. And when he opened his eyes, such a fierce emotion shone in them that I couldn't breathe.

"I need you naked." In a clash of power, his magic tore through my underthings, and then I was bare, fully revealed.

His entire body just . . . *stopped* as the power around him soared.

My chest heaved as he drank me in, the aura around him rising higher as the pulse leaped in his neck.

"So beautiful. So exquisitely perfect." His gaze glided over my skin, traveling from my open thighs still cradling his head, to my stomach, then across my belly and up to my breasts. "I've been wanting to see you again. That brief glimpse at Liss Lodge wasn't nearly enough."

"I was skin and bones then."

"You were still beautiful. I'll always find you beautiful, Ilara." His breath sucked in. "And now, you're the most gorgeous thing I've ever seen. All curves and swells. I could spend eternity giving you pleasure, memorizing every dip and turn of your flesh."

His eyes were wild when he prowled upward and kissed my breast, first one and then the other, before rolling my nipple with his tongue and then sucking. I moaned, arching into his touch.

"I could spend all day here," he growled.

I moaned again when his fingers trailed up my sides, and then his clothes were flying from him, shredded completely under his magic before he stood naked above me.

My breath caught, snagging on the appendage between his legs that was so stiff and hard it curved upward. His cock was huge. So large and utterly beautiful with the twisting, throbbing veins and broad head that held a bead of dew on its tip.

"I want to taste you," I whispered.

I hadn't been with many males. Only two in my lifetime, and I'd never had a male in my mouth, but looking up at the prince now, at his utter power and ferocity, had my belly quivering and liquid longing flooding my core. I *needed* to taste him.

Norivun's nostrils flared, and he shook his head. "I'm tasting you first. I fear what I'll do if that pretty mouth of yours closes around me before you've found your pleasure."

I bit my lip, and the wildness in his eyes grew.

His head lowered. "You smell like the sweetest bud I've ever scented." And then his mouth was going to my core.

His lips and tongue met my sensitive flesh with a clash of heat and fire. I bowed off the bed when his mouth latched onto me, his tongue starting slow as he groaned with each lick. But with each flick of his tongue, the energy around him soared as I became frantic in his arms.

He was driving me wild, taking me toward the brink, and as his hands curled tighter around my thighs and a deep possessive growl worked up his throat, it went straight to my clit.

"Norivun, oh gods, Norivun!"

It was as though he was a starving male coming to his one and only feast. He devoured me with his mouth, sucking and pulling, licking and biting in the most intense way that made my legs lock around his head as my fingers turned into claws in his hair.

I rocked against his face, moaning and clawing as he devoured my flesh, demanding that I surrender to him completely.

"Oh gods!"

He flicked my clit again with his tongue, and then I was shattering all around him, coming so hard that I saw stars, but he didn't stop. He slipped two thick fingers inside me, hooking them at the end until he scraped against a spot deep within me, and—

Mother Below!

A second orgasm ripped through me, coming so fast on the heels of the first that I didn't know where that one ended and the second began.

I moaned and clawed more, coming so undone in his arms that my eyes rolled back in my head, and my entire body spasmed.

It was only when I lay panting and shuddering that he finally released me. Carnal light shone in his eyes, his mouth glistening with my essence.

He crawled up me, his body scraping against mine, and despite the fact that he'd just completely wrecked me, I shivered, and amazingly, I still wanted him.

He lay down on top of me, his lips curving. Satisfaction poured off of him so strongly that it bathed the room.

I bucked when his erection prodded my entrance, and he raised an eyebrow in silent question.

Somehow, I managed to reply, "Not yet."

A look so crestfallen fell over his expression that I laughed.

"When?" he asked, nipping at my neck. "When can I fully take you?"

I placed my hands on his shoulders, wiggling as he kissed me. "After I win the Trial." I rubbed my legs together, trapping and squeezing his cock.

He hissed.

"Lay back." I used a huge rush of my air affinity to spin him beneath me. His shocked expression was worth more than a million rulibs, and I grinned in delight. "I've never tasted a male before."

His eyes darkened. "It's best that I don't know of any males that you've been with, Ilara Seary."

My lips parted. "Are you jealous, my prince?"

He bared his teeth. "Quite. I can't stand the thought of any male being with you, and I'll kill them for seeing or touching what's mine."

That possessive look flared in his eyes, and my stomach dipped at how savage of a mate he would be. I had no doubt he'd follow through with that threat. Any male who looked at me twice could fall prey to the prince's affinity.

Lips curving, I eyed him hotly as the flame inside me grew. "Then it's good that the only male I want to taste is you."

"Careful, female. If you keep looking at me like that, I'll have you against that wall before you can speak as I plunge—"

I slipped his cock into my mouth, and his words vanished. He went utterly still, his entire body stiffening until he was as hard as Isalee steel. Wings jutting out behind him, his hips bucked.

Tentatively, I took more of him into my mouth. His length and girth were large, but he tasted pleasant, and I danced my tongue across his shaft, exploring and doing what I'd always been curious to try.

He hissed when I swallowed him deeper, and his breath sucked in so hard I feared he'd stopped breathing.

I released him from my mouth. "Are you all right, my prince?"

Veins bulged in his neck. "Yes," he rasped. "Fine. I'm fine. Fuck, Ilara. I'm more than fine. Do that again."

Smiling, I pulled him into my mouth once more, and then I didn't hold back. I sucked on him like my body sang for me to do and wrapped a hand around his shaft's base as an instinct drove me.

And then I was feasting on him as he'd done to me, tasting and devouring him until his thighs tightened so hard that his body bowed.

Picking up my tempo, I sucked and bobbed on top of him, swallowing and devouring.

"Ilara!" His hands gripped my hair tightly, his entire body stiffening to a board, and then a roar ripped from his throat.

His seed flooded my mouth as his hips bucked. He came as violently as I had, and I relished every second of it, savoring the power and control I had over this male, before I swallowed down his essence as greedily as he'd consumed mine.

When the pumping from his cock finally subsided, I climbed over the prince to lie on his chest.

He was breathing rapidly, his breaths coming so fast I feared he was hyperventilating. But he gathered me in his arms and turned until I was tucked into his chest. I listened to the powerful beat of his heart as his hands were everywhere, running up and down my body, through my hair, around my shoulders. Their march was like a possessive procession as he kissed my neck and seemed to stamp *mine* upon me wherever he touched.

A stirring began inside me again, and longing grew as the familiar ache in my core began anew.

His fingers drifted south, stroking along my thighs until he found my clit. Fire licked my insides, and I gasped and clung to him while his fingers began working me in earnest.

"You're mine, Ilara Seary," he growled softly in my ear. "Forever. You are my mate, and you belong with me. Anyone who tries to take you from me will suffer my wrath."

And then his mouth found mine as he pumped a finger inside me while kissing me deeply. All I could manage was to cling to his shoulders as his air affinity heated my skin and licked at my clit while his fingers wrung another climax from me again and then again.

CHAPTER 22

The prince was insatiable. All night he worshiped my body, making me come again and again. Even though I did the same to him just as often, he still wanted more. More. *More.*

We dozed intermittently. Each time we climaxed after a clash of teeth, tongue, or magical air affinities, he would pull me to him, touching me softly while murmuring promises into my ear. And then we'd fall asleep only for him to wake me again a short while later as his body hardened and his desire flamed.

I was completely exhausted by the time dawn arrived. Matron Olsander would be furious if she knew I hadn't heeded her instructions to sleep, but I didn't regret a second of it.

Norivun stroked my hair as I lay on his chest. "I don't want to, but I have to go."

His arms tightened when I tried to stand. "Stay. Just a little bit longer."

I leaned up and kissed him softly. He cupped my jaw, pulling me closer.

"I can't. I have to meet Sandus."

He growled when I dragged myself out of bed. I looked at my tattered clothes on the floor. The only thing intact was my pants. I pulled them on before glancing in dismay at the window. A fierce wind howled outside.

The prince stood, still naked. Everything about him was strong, big, and enticing. My pulse quickened when I took in the broadness of his chest and thick muscles. He was hard again, his erection begging me to forget my responsibilities, and just thinking about the grueling day ahead made me want to crawl back into his bed.

His arm curled around me, his movement tender despite his arousal. "Do you need a day off?" he asked quietly, gently, almost reverently. It was as if he'd known what I was thinking. His hand ran up my back, so softly. "Why don't you take today to yourself. No fields. No training. No Trial dinners. And no—" He swallowed, and a soft growl escaped him. "No *dates*."

"No dates, even with you?"

His lips lifted in a crooked smile. "Well . . . a date with *me* is another story."

I suppressed a smile and stepped away from him. "No. This is why we can't let things progress between us. Not yet. I have no idea what my future holds, and you're likely to be an insufferable territorial mated male any chance you get."

"Are you saying you would disapprove of me ripping any male to shreds who tries to touch you?"

A laugh slipped out of me despite trying to stop it. "That would be a tad . . . overkill."

He scratched his chin. "Really? It seems rather tame to me."

"How about you direct that aggression toward Vorl and leave the other innocent males alone?"

A dangerous light grew in his eyes. "Ah, yes, Vorl. I've been meaning to pay him another visit."

"Another visit? You've visited him? What have you done with him so far?" I almost didn't ask, not sure if I wanted to know, but curiosity got the better of me.

"A few threats. Several beatings, but nothing beyond that . . . yet. I'm taking my time with him. Savoring it."

"You've beaten him?"

A manic glow lit his eyes. "Twice now, and I enjoyed every second of it."

I blanched.

"But don't worry. I've decided to let him sweat for a few more months before I visit him again because my next visit won't be so tame."

I winced. "You're not actually going to torture him, are you?"

"Would it displease you if I did?"

I picked up my shredded shirt. "I don't relish the idea of anyone being tortured regardless of what they've done."

The manic light in his eyes didn't abate as he trailed a finger along my collarbone. I shivered. "And that's the difference between you and me. You're inherently good, and I'm—" He shrugged.

I placed a hand on his arm. Sinewy muscle jumped beneath my fingertips. "You're *not* a monster. We both know that even though your father's tried to turn you into one."

His look grew pensive. "Do you truly believe that?"

"I do. After seeing what you did—" I pointed toward the

window in the northern direction toward the Cliffs of Sarum. Since neither of us had created a silencing Shield around us, and since I didn't know if anyone was listening, I only said, "Yes, I do believe that."

"But if I did torture Vorl, and I enjoyed it, would that change your opinion of me?"

I frowned, trying to recall what I'd heard of mate bonds. It was quite common for the male to submit to his baser instincts. If those instincts demanded that Prince Norivun punish Vorl excessively, I wouldn't hold that against him.

Still, I shuddered. "I suppose I prefer that you don't, even though I despise my former archon, but if you're unable to control yourself, and you do torture him . . ." I wrapped my arms around him. "I won't think any differently of you, but I don't want to see it."

All amusement fled from his face as he caged me to him. He gripped my hips and leaned down before breathing in my scent. A low growl rumbled his chest. "When it comes to you, Ilara Seary, I'm *not* above torturing a male."

My breath sucked in at the wildness in his tone. "Did you feel that way about me before the bond clicked into place for you?"

His nose trailed up my neck, sparking a ripple of desire in me. "I did. I abhor violence against females, so when I saw those bruises on your throat back in your field barn, it took immense self-control not to rip Vorl to pieces right then and there."

I gripped his shoulders more tightly. "Do you hate violence against females because of your mother and the abuse she's suffered?"

A pained look entered his eyes when he lifted his head. He nodded. "While females can be much stronger than males magically, if that magic is stripped from them, physically they are at a disadvantage. My father has no qualms about using his superior strength and size against my mother. Any male despicable enough to submit to such weak depravations against a female—" His jaw tightened, the muscle pulsing. "There are times I relish being Death Master of the continent. So much so that you may change your mind about me not being a monster."

My jaw slackened. "Those actions are to protect fae who cannot protect themselves, and you still think I would view you differently? Never."

Some of the darkness around him lightened. "And that, Ilara darling, is why you're perfect for me."

This time, I couldn't stop my laugh. I swatted him playfully when the aura around him grew, and I pulled away before he could sway me to join him in bed again. "You're insatiable. I need to go, get dressed, and meet with Sandus for training before you whisk me away to another field."

I picked up a shirt on the floor, one belonging to the prince. Even though it was much too big for me, I would rather wear it than mistphase back to my chambers with my bare breasts on display. I slipped it on, and it settled to the tops of my knees.

"You know, as you saw last night, I'm getting quite good at mistphasing. Matron Olsander said I have a natural aptitude for it. Maybe I should start transporting myself to the fields each day. It would be one less task for you to do."

I waited for the prince to answer, but his attention was fixated on my breasts.

"Norivun?"

"Hmm?" He finally lifted his head.

"Did you hear anything I just said?"

He rubbed the back of his neck. "You in my shirt is rather distracting."

I bit my lip to hold back a laugh. "I was talking about mistphasing. If I mistphased myself, you wouldn't need to take me to the fields each day."

"True." He curved an arm around my waist before I could stop him, then nuzzled my neck. "But then I wouldn't have an excuse to see you every morning."

"Do you need an excuse now that I know you're my mate?" I asked breathlessly. *Blessed Mother, when he ran his tongue along me like that . . .*

He lifted his head, smiling devilishly. "Perhaps not, as long as you don't plan to avoid me again?"

"I won't. I have no reason to anymore."

"Very well, but I'll need to see that your mistphasing is reliable enough to transport you exactly where you need to be."

"Didn't I prove that last night when I mistphased us here?"

"Humor me."

"Are you doubting me?"

"No, but I wouldn't feel as restless if I was able to trust that it'll work every time."

"So what do you want? A demonstration?"

"Perhaps."

"Later this morning then? After my training with Sandus?"

He kissed me softly. "I may be a fool to admit this, but it's near impossible for me to deny you anything, so yes, later this morning is fine."

A tingle raced up my spine. "Good, then in that case, I'll see you soon, my prince."

I MISTPHASED BACK to my chambers, and the second I appeared, my sister spun toward me.

Her hair was in disarray, her eyes bloodshot. "Blessed Mother, where were you? I've been worried sick all night."

Her frantic expression made guilt bite me hard. "I'm sorry. I should have sent someone to tell you I was fine."

"But where were you?" She gripped my hands, her wings flexing.

Sighing, I cast a silencing Shield around us, then nodded toward the sofa. "Come. I'll tell you, but it's imperative that you don't breathe a word of this to anyone."

She cocked her head but followed, and once I was certain Cailis understood the gravity of the situation, I told her. Everything. About the way I'd been feeling toward the prince all this time, his secret oasis hidden within the Cliffs of Sarum, our family's faked deaths and that they were actually still alive and living on the tip of Isalee, the acknowledgment of the mate bond I shared with the prince, and the magical night I'd spent by his side.

When I finally finished, it was well past sunrise, and I knew Sandus would be growing impatient at my late start.

"They're alive?" she finally breathed as tears poured down her cheeks. "Mother? Father? Tormesh? They're all alive?"

I nodded, emotions bubbling up in me as we hugged and

clung to one another. "Alive and well. And they're happy, Cailis. Well, as happy as they can be given the circumstances."

"Can I see them?" she asked. "Can I visit them on the Cliffs?"

"Not now, but soon hopefully."

She pulled back, wiping her eyes. "And you and the prince, he's really your . . ."

"He is."

She shook her head, her look of disbelief turning to wonder. "How long have you known?"

"I've suspected it for a few weeks, but I didn't know for certain until yesterday."

She shook her head again, then laughed as another tear rolled down her cheek. "I had no idea."

"Neither did I for the longest time."

"Does this change our plans, then?"

I nodded vigorously. "It does. I don't want to escape anymore, Cailis. I want to win the Trial. I want to marry the prince."

She squeezed my hands. Shock, awe, and humbleness I rarely saw in her surfaced as she nodded. "If everything you've said is true, then yes, you need to win that Trial and marry the prince."

Several hours later, Sandus told me another story about his new niece, an adorable little female that his sister had named Harpelin, as we finished our training in the courtyard.

"She sounds like a true blessing," I said as I wiped the sweat from my brow.

The guard grinned, the portrait of a doting uncle, as he sheathed his swords. "She certainly is. She's already strong. Did you know that she can lift her arms all the way up? I think she's going to be very advanced."

I managed a serious nod while keeping my smile at bay. "I'm sure you're right."

"Shall we eat before heading to Isalee?" He gave me a wolfish grin. "You must be quite hungry after last night."

Eyes widening, I smacked his side. "How did you know?" I hissed.

He laughed. "There's not much that happens with Nori that Ryder, Nish, Haxil, and I don't know about. I'm just glad you finally know he's your mate. Have you bedded him then? Is the bond fully sealed?"

Blushing scarlet, I nodded toward my chambers. "We're eating now, and you're keeping all comments to yourself, and you're never to ask me anything like that again."

He barked out a laugh.

The prince showed up right after Sandus and I finished breakfast, and the second the prince's aura caressed mine, my blood hummed through my veins.

"Good morning, Ilara." The prince dipped his head, his eyes hooded.

Sandus grinned while Cailis assessed the prince curiously.

I quickly devoured the last of my food, then jumped from my seat before Sandus could embarrass me again or Cailis could launch into a thousand questions. At least Daiseeum and the other servants weren't around. Small blessings.

I dragged the prince out through the double doors and tried to ignore the zing of pleasure that bolted through me when we made contact. Once we were safely outside, I released my grip as his tantalizing scent of cedar and snow drifted around me.

He grinned. "Are you feeling all right? It's almost as though my presence *affects* you."

"Oh, you're going to be insufferable. I can already tell."

His grin only broadened.

I hastily took a step back. "Please stay where you are, my prince. You're here to ensure I know how to mistphase, remember?"

He crossed his arms, although his air affinity continued to caress me. "Very well. Let's start with the basics. As I'm sure Matron Olsander has taught you, half of mistphasing is picturing the area in the realm that you want to travel to, and if you've never been there before, you picture where it is on a map or focus on a location's name."

"Yes, my prince. I'm already aware of all of that."

"All right. Show me that you can mistphase to the corner of this courtyard."

I rolled my eyes and easily mistphased to where he wanted.

He stroked his chin. "You're fast."

"So I've been told by Matron Olsander," I replied sweetly.

The prince grinned.

Inside my chambers, both Cailis and Sandus watched us, and once again, Cailis was looking at the prince with awe, her usual scorn absent.

I sauntered back to Norivun, my hips swaying. "Now where would you like me to go, my prince?"

His eyes darkened as a carnal light entered them. "Perhaps

you could mistphase to my bedroom chamber? That's farther. Of course, I would have to escort you to ensure you reached the correct area."

A shiver of longing ran through me, but I made myself reply, "I think not, I have work to do today."

"Tonight?"

I managed to suppress a giggle. "Perhaps."

He grinned wildly.

"But I believe we're supposed to be practicing mistphasing right now."

He inclined his head. "Of course. In that case . . ."

The prince had me mistphase to several areas of his choosing, each one farther and farther away from the last, but when I landed in the exact spot each time, he finally relented and said that I could mistphase without him each morning.

It was ridiculously gratifying, as if I was the star pupil, and my instructor had just told me that I was head of the class.

But considering I now knew what was at stake, between my hidden family, the king's brutal personality, and our continent's dire state, I poured everything I had into healing the fields and continuing my training.

As before, the days began to bleed together. I trained. I visited fields. I concentrated on honing my magic at every lesson, and when necessary, I attended the stupid Trial dates and dinners.

Anytime I felt tired or dismayed, I would remember my parents' smiles and Tormesh's laugh. Everything became a tornado of swirling goals and needs. There was so much to do, but I wouldn't fail. I *would* win this Trial.

And somehow, even though I secretly joined the prince in

his bed each night, I managed to resist the need pulsing through my blood to seal our bond. As much as I relished his naked body beside mine, I knew I couldn't allow that final act just yet. It would be dangerous if we became fully bonded, and the king learned of it. We needed to keep it a secret, and I needed to keep my head clear. A fully sealed mate bond wouldn't allow me to do that.

So I kept my focus on the tasks at hand, and before I knew it, the last few weeks of my training passed, and the morning of my first test was upon me.

CHAPTER 23

It was hard to believe three months had passed since Vorl's attack, the birth of my three affinities, and my forced admittance to the Rising Queen Trial, but here I was. The day of my first test—the test that would ultimately choose the next queen of the Solis continent—had arrived.

Sweat lined my palms as I stood just outside of the castle's main entrance. Above, the wintery sky was visible through the warded dome. I stared at it, using the dome's sparkling beauty to ground me.

Meegana coughed beside me, making me jump. She covered her mouth sheepishly, then smiled apologetically in my direction. Beside her, Beatrice stood stoically, the epitome of glacial coolness. And Georgyanna . . .

I sighed. I didn't even want to look in her direction. The Kroravee native had been preening like an overinflated hen since we'd arrived at our first test. Her cockiness and confident swagger as she'd strolled out of the castle, along with her haughty demeanor, were as foreign to me as planet Titun in our realm's solar system.

I had no doubt her bravado was entirely genuine. Or maybe, that was her tactic. Maybe she faked that smugness so the rest of us would sweat.

Of course, if that was her grand plan, it was working . . . I wiped my damp palms again on my slacks.

A subtle kick from Matron Olsander, standing just behind me, had me quieting my nervous movements.

"You shall be fine, Ilara. Quit your fidgeting and keep those shoulders back." Matron Olsander slapped my backside.

I glared over my shoulder at her, rubbing my rump through my leggings. All of us wore training clothes for our first test.

"Was that necessary?" I hissed.

She crossed her arms and lifted her chin. "It stopped your jostling, didn't it?"

I swung back around, but my trainer's warmth pressed into my back when she leaned closer and whispered, "You're strong enough to be the next queen, Ilara. Don't forget that."

For a moment, I couldn't breathe. Matron Olsander wasn't one to give compliments lightly. I gave her a small grateful smile. She dipped her head, then looked pointedly toward the gathering crowd.

Subtle murmurings and conversations drifted in the air, drawing my attention back to the spacious courtyard. The huge expanse of grounds that stood bare between the castle's front gates and the distant perimeter wall were lined with hundreds of Solisarium citizens. Both nobles and commoners filled the crowd. It didn't seem as though the royals had discriminated today. All were welcome to watch the first test that would ultimately determine their next queen.

But I didn't study any of them too closely. Rising on a dais at the center of the crowd sat the queen and both princes. Queen Lissandra looked as she always did. Calm, poised, and regal. Her sons sat beside her while the king's throne lay empty, seeing as he wasn't here yet.

I'd felt Norivun watching me ever since he'd arrived to his throne. During the brief moment we'd made eye contact, he'd seemed to catch himself, as if it was too obvious that I'd captured his attention. In response, he'd sat back and relaxed his shoulders. Following that, he'd fallen into easy conversation with Nuwin. He was the portrait of a noble male used to having females compete for his hand.

Surrounding him and Nuwin were other males of the court —those who might be chosen to marry the three lowest-ranking females in our group. The dozen males wore eager, intrigued, or bored expressions. The one from Prinavee Territory even appeared drunk.

I balled my hands, then loosened them and wiped my palms on my pants again. Sir Featherton had promised that the remaining three males would be identified by the final test, but why the king hadn't declared them yet, I didn't know.

As if sensing me studying them, Michas Crimsonale shot his gaze to mine. His face remained expressionless, but then his lips quirked up in a mocking gesture before he nodded his head subtly. I wasn't sure if he was doing that to wish me luck, or if he was giving me a bow of farewell since he thought I would surely lose the first test.

Flustered even more, I began to tap my foot.

"Ilara!" Matron Olsander swatted me again. "Stand still. They're about to explain the test."

As if on cue, the door behind us opened with a flourish, and the Trial's archon sauntered out of the castle and dipped around us before dashing down the steps to make a show of his arrival.

The crowd went wild, hooting and hollering before they began thumping their feet in anticipation. Meegana and I shared a nervous look while Beatrice's lips thinned, and Georgyanna preened.

To the crowd, Sir Featherton raised his hands more, a grin on his face as he waved for them to quiet. It took almost a minute before the deafening roar finally abated, but once everyone was calm, the archon swirled toward us. "Dearest daughters of the Solis continent, welcome to your official first test in the Rising Queen Trial!"

Another wild cheer went up, even louder than before.

"And now . . ." Sir Featherton bowed deeply. "May I present our king."

A flow of air washed over my cheeks as the sound of marching footsteps reached my ears. Six of the king's guards appeared, surrounding a hovering enchanted carpet that the king stood upon. It rose above the shoulders of his guards as magic held it aloft.

The crowd worked into a frenzy when they saw King Novakin, cheers and roars filling the air, before they all dipped into low bows, following Sir Featherton's lead.

Blood rushed to my cheeks when I beheld the king. Everything Norivun had revealed to me swirled through my mind. This king was the reason behind Queen Lissandra's abuse. He was the instigator of the attacks on my family. And he was the male who raised his hand in vengeance against his own sons.

Somehow, I managed to bow like the females at my side, but my teeth grated.

When the king reached the courtyard, we all straightened, and the king deftly stepped from the carpet to be seated on his throne as the floating carpet lowered to the ground while his guards positioned themselves in front of him.

Queen Lissandra gave him a vacant smile as both Prince Norivun's and Nuwin's expressions went slack, their eyes glazed as they became portraits of his dutiful sons versus who they really were—children of an abused female who did everything in their power to keep her abuse to a minimum. They were the perfect puppets, and the puppet master sat before them.

The king raised his hands. "Rise, sons and daughters of the Solis continent, and let the first test begin!"

Another wild cheer rose from the crowd as everyone straightened. More than a few bounced on their toes as excited grins split their lips.

Sir Featherton gave a final bow to the king before waving an arm out in dramatic fashion. "I'm sure you're all wondering what test we have in store for our future queen?"

Cheers rose as fists pumped in the air.

Meegana and I shared another anxious look. I entwined my fingers through hers and squeezed. She squeezed me in return just as hard.

"The first test in the Rising Queen Trial will be conducted right here in the castle courtyard." Sir Featherton made a sweeping spin.

The crowd looked around, as though searching for contraptions or mazes or some obstacle course for us to survive.

Nothing presented itself.

Sir Featherton's grin broadened. "May I have all of you look toward the sky?"

All of us tilted our chins back. A gasp came from the crowd, then another. Some began pointing as whispered murmurs erupted through the gathered fae. Even the princes shared a concerned look before Norivun's gaze cut to mine.

My heart beat harder, but I still saw nothing.

"Mother Below, look!" Meegana pulled me to her side, and I followed her outstretched finger.

My eyes widened when I beheld a hovering flag high up in the atmosphere, and my stomach immediately plummeted.

An amused snicker came from Georgyanna, and she cast me a mockingly sympathetic look. "Looks like we'll need wings for our first test."

The stone in my stomach sank even more, and my fears were only amplified when Sir Featherton said, "The flag hovering in the sky is five millees above the ground. The first female to reach it and deliver it to the king will be the winner of our first test, and remember, no one is allowed to intervene or assist the females in any way. If anyone is found to be aiding our next queen, you shall suffer a lengthy stay in the dungeons or the Death Master's wrath."

My brow furrowed as confusion filled me. "So it's a *flying* test?"

Meegana squeezed me, her tone sorrowful. "It appears so."

Disappointment filled me. *Why have I been working my backside off if all they care about is how quickly we fly?*

The crowd seemed to share my sentiment since surprised murmurs erupted along with a few disgruntled snorts.

"You might be wondering why the test is so simple." Sir Featherton twirled toward the crowd again. "And that's because it's *not* that simple."

He spun toward us and spread his arms wide. "Daughters of the Solis continent, be sure to keep your wits about you. This isn't a test merely to engage your flying skills. It's also a test to determine the range of your skills along with your ability to see beyond what meets the eye."

Leaving us with those cryptic words, he dipped back to face the crowd and grinned wickedly. "May the strongest female win."

THE FOUR OF us were ushered to the center of the courtyard. I tried to wish Meegana and Beatrice good luck, but the guards positioned us away from each other so quickly that I didn't get a chance.

The entire time I felt Norivun's gaze, like a predator prowling against my back. His aura rose more and more, the sheer power of his affinities like a cloud around us. The intensity of his energy completely dwarfed the crowd's excitement. More than a few citizens drifted farther from the dais, giving the crown prince wary side-eyes before positioning themselves out of his sight.

King Novakin didn't reprimand his son, though, and the king's smug look made me wonder if he'd chosen this test intentionally to rile the crown prince because the king knew that the prince had taken an interest in me.

Despite Norivun trying to keep his obsession with me a secret, and despite no one knowing of our secret nights together, anyone with eyes could sense how he watched me.

And with a flag over twenty thousand feet above us hanging in midair by some unknown magical force, the king knew I would surely lose, because the other females would fly as fast as their wings could carry them, but I couldn't. I didn't have wings.

None of them had an air element, though. But even an air element couldn't assist me without wings. Not yet at least.

While Matron Olsander had been teaching me to under-stand the subtleties of my affinities, I hadn't mastered how to change air pressures. Once I did, I would be able to create pockets of higher pressure beneath my soles, allowing me to literally walk on air as my affinity lifted me, but I wasn't there yet. I couldn't rise higher than a few feet from the ground every time I'd tried, and the king probably knew that too.

Sweat lined my palms in earnest as the possibility of complete humiliation loomed. I cut Matron Olsander an anxious look. Her lips thinned as she stood atop the stairs leading to the castle's front gates. Eyes burning into me, she subtly made a fist before whipping her hand to the side and spreading her fingers.

My lips parted. She couldn't mean what I thought she meant . . .

I shook my head in disbelief as Sir Featherton began to issue orders to the guards, ensuring they kept the excited crowd at bay, but my trainer's attention held firm. Her lips moved, and

I strained to read them through the distance that separated us. On her third attempt, I finally understood.

You can do this. She made the same motion with her hand, and it took everything in me not to gape.

My trainer wanted me to mistphase to the flag.

"But that—" I didn't realize I'd said anything out loud until the guard at my side gave me a quizzical look.

I clamped my mouth closed. She was crazy. Completely without sense if she thought I could mistphase to the flag while it hovered in midair thousands of feet above the ground. The amount of concentration, skill, utter perfection at mistphasing magic that it would take to pull off such a feat . . .

You're mad, I mouthed back at her.

She arched an eyebrow and plopped her hands on her hips. *Do you have a better idea?*

I scowled. No, I didn't. Of course, I didn't. I didn't have any idea what to do to retrieve the flag because I couldn't fly.

The sense of my impending doom weighed even more upon my shoulders until I felt Matron Olsander's firm look.

I glanced her way again to see sheer determination etched upon her face. *You. Can. Do. This.*

That statement left little room for argument. It was either try or fail.

She was right.

I had to try.

Some of the fluttering in my stomach calmed as the prince's aura rose even higher. I didn't dare look at Norivun. I was worried enough as it was, and it would take all of my concentration to attempt what Matron Olsander suggested. If I saw even a hint of worry rolling across his features, it would no doubt break my resolve.

"On my mark!" Sir Featherton raised his hand.

A flurry of sparks erupted from the archon's fingertips as a spiral of his magic coasted upward. A number appeared suspended high in the air, like a glittering firework shaped in the number *three*.

"Two . . ." The shimmering number changed to the next in the countdown.

"One!"

The entire crowd went wild.

Meegana, Beatrice, and Georgyanna all took flight simultaneously. The crowd roared in approval as my hands balled into fists. Magic rumbled in my gut, heating and roiling within me. I closed my eyes and forced all of my concentration inward, but then a shriek rang through the air.

My eyes snapped open, and I gasped when Meegana tumbled midflight. Georgyanna had viciously cut into her path, knocking my friend off course, just as a gust of air hit all three of the females at once.

The crowd gasped as a dazzling display of fireworks abruptly exploded in the air, and all three females screamed in surprise as they were again knocked into tumultuous falls. Only their strong Shields had kept those explosives from killing them.

Meegana quickly regained control and began flapping her wings rhythmically again, but all three females kept getting thrown off course as explosions pummeled the air. Unseen air currents also seemed to be at work as the three spun and dipped for no apparent reason.

Somebody was weaving their air elemental affinity on purpose, and fireworks were purposefully being thrown in their paths. It must have all been a part of the test.

I didn't bother trying to understand more of it or wonder what other magical tricks were in store for us. If anything, the unseen attacks were buying me time.

Concentrate, Ilara. Concentrate!

Closing my eyes again, I poured everything I had into what I'd learned of mistphasing.

I pictured what I needed to do. I had to mistphase through the air, grab the flag, and transport it back to the ground all within seconds. I would need to time everything perfectly. The second I appeared in the air five millees above the ground and whisked the flag from the magic that held it, I would begin falling. My air affinity could slow my fall, but if I didn't keep my wits about me, I would inevitably plummet to my death.

Breathing more deeply, I let my magic build inside me. It rose and warmed my bones as I called upon everything in my reserves. My magic unfurled within my gut, like a flower in my garden that bloomed before the sun. Its petals curled open, one by one, until it practically burst to life.

I pictured the flag in my mind until it was the only thing that penetrated my thoughts. The crowd quieted to a distant roar in my ears. My breaths became steady rises and falls in my chest.

Breathe in. Breathe out. The flag. Only the flag.

My magic bore down on me, pressing upon me until it felt as though it was moving through me, liquefying my bones and igniting my senses. I gathered my power tightly inside me as I centered all of my thoughts with pinprick precision on that wavering piece of cloth fluttering high, high above.

And then . . .

I let go.

The world abruptly tilted beneath my feet. I disappeared in a blur of mist and shadows, air and wind. Magic roared through my blood, and then cold air slammed into my senses with a shock so sudden that I couldn't breathe. It felt as though I'd been submerged in a frigid pool, that ice floated through my veins. The air was so thin that I gasped.

My air affinity held me aloft, but already the high pressure bubble beneath me was dissipating. I opened my eyes to see the flag hovering right in front of me.

The three other females still raced upward. Georgyanna seemed to sense exactly what I'd done the second my hand reached out to clasp the flag. She screamed in fury as my fingers wrapped around the delicate silk material.

My bubble snapped.

Air abruptly tumbled around me as I fell through the atmosphere. A scream of fear spilled from my lips as I passed the other three on my way back to the ground.

Georgyanna's eyes narrowed into razors, and Beatrice and Meegana wore horrified expressions.

I closed my eyes, doing everything in my power to gather the concentration I'd had only moments before. I called upon my magic, begging it to do as I asked, and with every ounce of my being, I pictured the ground that I'd just been standing on.

My magic began to activate. My body started to disassemble as I enacted a mistphase once more, but then Georgyanna was right beside me. Her wings had turned into slits at her back as she free fell like an arrow until she'd caught up with me.

Somehow, she maneuvered herself in the air until she slammed right into me. The force of it punched my breath into my chest. A cackle of pure satisfaction exploded from her lips as she snatched the flag from my hands.

"No!" I screamed and clawed for the flag, but Georgyanna's wings were already spreading. Her descent slowed, but I was still plummeting down.

Furious rage scoured through me, and I called upon my air elemental affinity. I slammed a huge bubble of air into Georgyanna, crumpling her wings behind her like tissue paper.

She screamed in pain and began to fall too, but then a lasso of fire erupted from her. It moved so fast it was about to hit me in the chest until I ripped my own fire element from my gut.

Our powers collided in an explosion, her fire trying to burn through mine and mine hers. A ring of heat grew between us, sweat pouring from me due to her element, but I didn't let it deter me.

I sped up the air bubble behind her, and she screamed in terror as she barreled right toward our colliding fires.

She released her fire at the last possible moment, and I knew I could have kept mine ignited. I could have burned her to death right there, but I relinquished my fire and concentrated more on my air affinity. Her eyes widened in horror as she fell right toward me. Her wings spread. She tried to gain the upper hand again, but righteous anger at all she'd done to me narrowed my concentration until all I thought about was bringing that witch to my side.

The second she came within my grasp, I ripped the flag from her fingertips, and she flew right past me.

She plummeted toward the ground faster than I was, but I was still free falling. If I didn't mistphase *now*, I was seconds away from landing in a pile of broken bones and shredded skin for the entire capital to witness.

I dispersed my air affinity from behind Georgyanna, allowing her to fly once more as I gripped the flag tightly to my chest.

I pictured the top of the dais upon which Prince Norivun sat. I pictured his smile, his hooded eyes, and imagined his alluring scent. I called upon the bond that tethered us, the unbreakable cord that the gods had placed between our souls.

My magic unfurled within me again, as though wanting to join my magic to his. Wind screamed through my ears as the air around me grew warmer. Denser. The ground was fast approaching, but I didn't let my concentration wane. I pictured the prince, my *mate*.

And then the world disappeared again in a blur of mist and shadows, air and wind.

My feet came to a sudden stop on a solid surface. The crowd immediately erupted into shrieks of disbelief and wild furor.

I opened my eyes to see King Novakin swivel around on his throne as a look of complete bewilderment painted his face. I thrust the flag toward him, bowing low on instinct as my heart thundered in my ears.

The flag was still in my hand, the silky material balled so tightly in my fist that it took a moment before I released it to the king. But when my hands were free, I reached out and came in contact with warm fingers that wrapped around mine.

The crown prince squeezed my hand as a shocked grin split his face. Somehow, I'd mistphased just to the left of his throne.

"Well, hello there," he said with a crooked smile.

And with catlike grace, he rose to his feet as pride and wonder lifted his lips even more.

I straightened as he raised our hands, bringing them high in the air as the crowd's cheers rose even more before he declared, "Ilara Seary, daughter of Mervalee Territory, has won the first test!"

CHAPTER 24

I won? *I actually won?* I gazed in shock at the crown prince as Sir Featherton rushed to the top of the dais, all smiles and congratulations as the other three females flapped back to the ground.

Meegana beamed at me as Beatrice gave a nod of congratulations even though disappointment soured her expression.

Only Georgyanna gave me the death glare. Fury rippled through the Kroravee native's features, and the pure hatred that shone from her eyes made me look away as ice-cold dread slid through me.

But then I caught Matron Olsander's brimming smile and my sister jumping in the distance as she clapped her hands from the bottom of the stairs, and any concern I'd had over Georgyanna exacting revenge melted away.

I'd won the first test. And now, I was only two tests away from winning this competition, bonding with my mate, and righting all of the wrongs that his tyrant father had set out to do on his hundred-winters-long, power-infused reign.

Nuwin grinned and clapped my back as Prince Norivun lingered at my side. The crown prince had dropped my hand, his expression impossible to read, but I had a feeling that was because the king had also risen from his throne to face us.

Sir Featherton waved his arms to shush the crowd, and I forced my smile to widen as the cheers finally subsided, but the king's penetrating assessment of me, and then his son, grazed over my skin like hot razors.

I subtly took another step away from Norivun as the crown prince's wings rippled.

The king arched an eyebrow. "Norivun, aren't you going to properly congratulate our winner?" His booming voice resonated over the courtyard.

Eager energy buzzed through the crowd.

"Father?" Norivun cocked his head. A breeze ruffled the silver hair skimming his shoulders, sending a few strands to brush against his jaw.

"She's one step closer to becoming your wife," the king said, the portrait of a doting father. "Surely a congratulatory kiss is in order."

"Indeed!" Sir Featherton bobbed his head. "A kiss for the beautiful daughter of Mervalee Territory."

The trial archon swung back to the crowd, arms raising as he pumped his hands up and down. "And what say you, fine sons and daughters of Solisarium? Don't you think a kiss from the crown prince would be the perfect congratulations to the Trial winner of the first test?"

Fists raised in the air, screams of agreement following as the crowd once again went wild.

Nuwin leaned closer to me and whispered, "One would think they'd never seen a male kiss a female before."

His snicker and mischievous wink made some of the tension in my shoulders ease.

"Well?" The king crossed his arms, and something in his expression made me want to teeter farther away from Norivun. "Best not to keep the crowd waiting."

"As you wish." Norivun gave a stiff bow to his father, then swung toward me as the anticipation of the onlookers surged. Wings bobbing, the prince closed the distance between us with predatory grace.

Every particle of my body vibrated in awareness. The bond that tethered us surged and tightened. Now that I'd acknowledged it, I was amazed that I hadn't recognized it sooner. Every part of me yearned to touch him. Feel him. Kiss him.

I balled my hands at my sides, and the weight of the king's stare bore down on me as I endeavored to hide what I felt. I tried to keep my chest from rising too quickly. Tried not to let color bloom upon my cheeks like a budding rose in my garden.

But the prince's aura called to me. I was as helpless to resist the attraction between us as the oceans were to the moons' pulling tides.

The prince stopped only a hair's breadth away. Eyes like diamonds glittering in the sun drank me in. His mouth tightened as that wildness slipped past his mask. Savage need etched into every line of his face.

He slowly slid one large hand around my neck, his thumb grazing my jaw as he tilted my mouth up to his.

And as he leaned down, my attention focused on his lips. The air between us warmed as his affinity wove around me. A feathery, phantom touch trailed across my neck causing a shiver to skate up my spine.

I called upon my air element to do the same to him. It stretched from me, as though ghostly fingers trailed down his chest.

A low, throaty growl was his only response before his lips met mine.

My eyes closed as the taste and scent of him spiraled through me. Snow and cedar wrapped up in heat and fire penetrated my senses. Before I could stop myself, my arms were slipping around his shoulders, tangling in the hair at the nape of his neck as cheers and roars echoed from the crowd.

But those sounds fell into a void, like a vacuum sucked all of the sound from the air, as every fiber of my being centered on the male holding me and ravishing my mouth. His tongue entwined with mine. A growl of pure possession rumbled in his chest as I moaned softly in answer.

The crown prince deepened our kiss, answering a call that fate demanded we heed, until fire raged between us. I clung to him, my entire body weakening as he bent me backward, his kiss feverish and claiming.

A desperate ache formed low in my belly as the prince's wings snapped around us, hiding me from view. I knew my desire was so heightened that other males could scent it, but I couldn't help my response. Norivun was my mate, and my body sang for him as though the stars had aligned our souls.

I had no idea how long we kissed. How long we hid beneath his wings. The realm had disappeared into nothing. My focus was on him and him only.

But then he was pulling back, his wings were retracting,

and I whimpered softly in protest. His thumb caressed my jaw as lust coated his expression, but eventually he broke our contact and stepped back.

The other males around us murmured to one another, but my head was still so fogged with my mate that I couldn't decipher their comments, but some were wickedly grinning. Others wore shocked expressions.

Prince Norivun's nostrils flared, and one thunderous glare at the snickering males had them quietening.

Nuwin cleared his throat from behind me, and when the spell finally dissipated completely, I saw the tight smile plastered across the younger prince's face.

My heart pounded as I became more aware of my surroundings. Everyone was watching us, which in itself was to be expected, but their looks and whispering told me that what had just transpired between me and the crown prince had been witnessed and understood by all.

"Interesting." The king's single comment had my entire body seizing.

Prince Norivun snarled quietly before Nuwin subtly kicked him from behind. The crown prince snapped upright, but even I could see that he was visibly struggling to suppress his mating instincts. Males were surrounding me. My heady scent swam through the air, and the king had just flagrantly commented on what had transpired between us.

Dread slid through my veins. King Novakin was smiling, no *grinning*, as he looked between me and his son. He mockingly inclined his head before a dark flash ghosted across his expression. The crowd was still cheering, although it was more jeers now than joy, and the males were loudest of all as the females tittered behind cupped hands.

But despite the chaos, it didn't stop me from hearing what the king said next. Words like a whisper floated to me through the air, and with a start, I realized who the crown prince and Nuwin had inherited their air affinities from.

The king's comment siphoned to me on a magical breeze meant for my ears and my ears only. "It seems as though we have more to celebrate than just your victory, Ilara Seary, daughter of Mervalee Territory. Or should I call you *mate* to the crown prince?"

I TRIED NOT to let the king's comment derail me as Daiseeum dressed me for my last date of the Trial. But all day I'd been picking at my nails and biting my lip. It was impossible not to heed the king's statement that had been subtly laced in a threat filled with deadly promise.

This was a male, after all, who had ordered the execution of dozens of Solis fae simply for voicing their concerns and causing unrest.

I hadn't told anyone about what the king had whispered to me. Not even Norivun. I couldn't. The mating instincts flaring from the prince every time someone threatened me would no doubt end in bloodshed with his own father if the crown prince knew of the king's veiled threat.

And while Nuwin would probably be understanding of my worry, I couldn't drag him into this mess. I still didn't know if he was aware of his brother's secret agenda.

The one fairy I wanted to confide in above all others, my sister, was nowhere to be found. After the king had witnessed my and Norivun's mate bond, Cailis had fled with her guard. Knowing her, she was seeking more exit points in case a crisis unfolded, and the king demanded my head.

So I'd tried to distract myself by visiting another field following the first test. I was already on my tenth large field in Isalee, and the crops were slowly coming back to life. Following that, I'd spent the remainder of the day training with Matron Olsander. My magic had grown so immense that even my intense mistphasing that morning hadn't depleted it.

Matron Olsander had gone easy on me, though. A first. But she'd been so proud of me that even her iron-willed heart had softened and allowed me a moment to relax and enjoy my victory. It was the only time today that I'd actually smiled in earnest following the king's comment.

"This color looks lovely on you," Daiseeum said, drawing my attention back to the present.

My lady's servant stood just behind me, her magic brimming as she made me look more beautiful than I ought to. Jewels hung from my neck and dripped from my ears as she buttoned a deep-blue gown up my back. "And I have to say that was quite the kiss you shared with the crown prince earlier today."

The warm memory of my trainer's approval doused when I beheld Daiseeum's barely suppressed smile in the mirror.

"Oh? Was it . . ." I raised a hand self-consciously to my neck. Cool metal from the jewelry met my fingertips. "Was it easy to see our kiss from the castle?"

Daiseeum lowered her head as her fingers continued

moving deftly from button to button. "One didn't need to see it, my lady. One could *feel* it."

Oh Blessed Mother. I'd known as much, but hearing it confirmed only made my stomach drop even more.

"We were caught up in the moment," I said, a tad defensively.

"Is that what you call it?" She resumed her primping, smoothing the voluptuous tulle down my legs before draping the silky azure material over top. Beads and lace had been sewn into the top layer, adding texture and sparkle to the gown. "I suppose the prince won't take kindly to your date with Lord Michas Crimsonale tonight?"

She helped me slip into dancing slippers and then straightened before giving me a wink.

I forced myself to respond lightly. "We are all required to court one another. I'm sure the prince will be fine with it."

Her cheeks lifted in a knowing smile. "Something tells me he won't be."

"Goodness, Daiseeum. You might as well just come out and say what you really think—" A knock on my door stopped my outburst.

Sandus poked his head in. "All ready, love? You've been summoned."

My nostrils flared at Daiseeum. At least she had the decency to look contrite.

"Enjoy the evening, my lady." She bobbed a curtsy.

Calming, I replied, "Thank you. You as well." I squeezed her hand, just so she would know I wasn't angry at her. I enjoyed the camaraderie that had bloomed between us. I truly did, but sometimes, the lady's servant enjoyed riling me. And today, I was too on edge to handle it.

Of course, I couldn't actually fault her teasing. Daiseeum was only speaking out loud what everyone else was thinking. The true fault fell on me and the prince for not being able to control our reactions to one another. And now, it seemed the entire capital was aware of the magnetic attraction between me and Prince Norivun.

Sighing, I gathered my skirt and followed Sandus down the hall.

The guard cocked an eyebrow at me. "Everything all right, love? For someone who just showed the entire capital how powerful she is, you're looking quite glum."

I forced a smile. "Really? Oh no, I'm just tired."

"Is that the ruse we're going with?"

I sighed again and resisted the urge to hang my head as I cast a silencing Shield around us. "I just wish everyone knew about him, and I wish everyone knew the truth about the king."

"Wishes will get us nowhere, dear Ilara. It's best to accept that."

"I know, but how do you do it? How do you stand by while the entire realm thinks Norivun's a monster when really it's the king who's the demon?"

The guard glanced over his shoulder, but no one was around. We were still in the prince's private wing, which was usually empty save for a few scurrying servants, but I wasn't stupid.

"I cast a silencing Shield around us, Sandus. Nobody can hear us. You may speak freely."

His eyebrows rose. "You did? I didn't even feel it."

"My air affinity has grown quite strong, and subtle, but back to the matter at hand. How do you stand it when everyone detests him?"

"It's hard." The guard shrugged. "All four of us struggle with it, as you saw in High Liss when Nish wanted to ram his sword down your throat, but I imagine that it's probably even harder for you to stomach since the crown prince is your mate."

I wrung my hands. "Do you think the entire realm knows we're mates now?"

His lips quirked. "You two practically set that dais on fire, so yes, I think it's safe to assume most know. That kind of explosive attraction is only seen between mates."

"Will the king do anything about it now that he knows?" A shiver ran down my spine. Just thinking of the king's comment made me want to run.

Sandus's mouth tightened. "That, Ilara, is a very good question."

MICHAS SWEPT toward me the second I stepped into the dining hall. The Osaravee noble slipped my hand around his forearm, getting a glower from Sandus that Michas merely brushed off.

Across the room, the rest of the Trial occupants watched as the young lord made a show of escorting me.

"Someone's been keeping a secret," Michas said quietly as he leaned down to whisper in my ear. "And here I thought I was potentially in the running for winning your heart."

A pounding aura suddenly pressed into my side, and I

knew that the crown prince had just entered the room. I tried to dip farther away from Michas, but he followed and stayed plastered to my side.

"I shall marry whomever the king deems me suitable for," I said carefully.

Michas's lips kicked up in a smile. "Are you sure the crown prince would allow it?"

"I don't think he'd have a choice."

Energy continued to pulse from Norivun. Veins swelled in his neck, and his eyes glued to Michas.

"You're playing a very dangerous game," I said quietly to my date.

"I like to live dangerously. I've never courted a mated female before."

"We're not mated yet."

"Oh? You're saying he hasn't bedded you?"

I squirmed and wondered why I'd blurted that out. "Who I bed is none of your concern."

He scratched his chin as music drifted through the air, and a floating tray glided by us. He snatched two flutes of champagne off of it, then held one out to me.

"I suppose this does explain the prince's attraction to you, *and* since you're not bonded to him, but he's fully bonded to you, it would explain his absolute rage and inability to control his reactions where you're concerned." Michas grinned. "Do you know this is the first time in my life that I haven't seen the crown prince under perfect control? Usually, he's so cool. Nothing ruffles him. But three months of you in the court, and he looks set to explode like the volcanoes on the Dresher Islands."

The knots in my stomach tightened more. It was exactly as I feared. Everyone knew. And if Norivun was truly incapable of controlling his instincts right now, then it fell to me to keep the wolves at bay.

"He'll kill you if you prove too bold," I said casually and sipped my champagne.

A fleeting flash of fear shone in Michas's eyes before he hid it behind a grin. "Then I suppose I'll have to balance very carefully on that edge."

I took a sip of champagne, letting the bubbles burst in my mouth as every muscle in my body coiled. Courtly politics and devious scheming weren't for me, but I was quickly learning that Michas thrived on them, which meant I needed to learn to play the game, or I would end up a discarded pawn.

"Shall we sit for dinner?" The Osaravee lord waved toward the table. "I'm quite excited for the evening ahead and would love to get it started."

CHAPTER 25

I picked up my butter knife and leaned closer to Meegana.
"Do you think this is sharp enough to stab through my
eye and put me out of this misery?"

She snorted, nearly blowing her champagne through her
nose. "Not likely, Lara." She dabbed at her mouth and said in a
lower tone, "But it's kind of cute how much your ma—" She
coughed. "I mean, the crown prince, is protective of you."

I gave her a strained smile as Michas leaned closer to me
and trailed a finger up my arm. At the head of the table,
Norivun flashed his teeth as a rumble of his magic shook the
dinnerware.

I sighed. The entire dinner Michas had done everything in
his power to provoke Norivun. It was male dominance on full
display, and unfortunately, I was the female caught in the
middle.

The only saving grace was that Georgyanna left me alone.
She sat three places down from me, and I thought for certain
she'd utter snide comments, say that I'd cheated to win the test,

or stare daggers my way, but instead, she'd grown entirely quiet. Almost frighteningly so. A cunning look had entered her eyes that was as cold as ice. She still watched me. Still studied me, but her petty remarks remained at bay. Instead, I could have sworn that she was planning something, and that gave me pause more than any other interaction we'd had.

By the time the final course was cleared away, I stood warily. Norivun was already striding toward me as Michas crowded my space.

I held my breath as I waited for the fireworks to truly start between them, but just as the prince was about to round the table, Sir Featherton stopped him and murmured something into his ear.

The prince glared at Michas, then narrowed his eyes at the Trial archon. Norivun raised his hands, arguing, but Sir Featherton lifted his shoulders and gestured to the door.

Fuming, the prince finally gave a curt nod and followed him out of the dining hall.

I straightened. The prince was gone, and Michas was my date. Now could be my one and only time to truly learn what Michas knew of the king, the unrest, and the missing fae.

"Did you have any particular plans for us tonight?" I asked him and prodded him toward the balcony doors.

"I did actually, but I'm afraid they didn't pan out." He cast an aggrieved look toward where the prince had departed.

I gave him a sly smile. "Did they have anything to do with Prince Norivun?"

Michas grinned wickedly. "I was too apparent, wasn't I?"

"I expected more from you," I replied, forcing my tone to sound playful. "You seem like the type who manipulates others well, but what you were doing at dinner was anything but subtle."

"Indeed, but I couldn't help myself. It was too easy. If only I had Georgyanna's manipulation affinity. Dinner would have been immensely more interesting then."

"Those who are true masters at the art of manipulation don't need magic to do their bidding."

He cocked an eyebrow. "You sound as though you speak from experience." He held the balcony door open for me as music from the dining hall carried outside into the night. I stepped onto the balcony's smooth stone floor as a gust of wind grazed my skin.

Shivering, I pulled my shawl up. "Your father would know better than me."

Michas joined me by the railing. "Are we really going to speak of my father on our date?"

"I can't help it. He intrigues me."

"Why?"

I propped an elbow on the railing and faced him. "He's so bold. It's obvious he wants to take the king's throne. I'm surprised King Novakin hasn't executed him."

Michas sneered. "As if the king could do that. If he started executing territory archons, anarchy would ensue."

"So your father acts the way he does because he feels his position keeps him safe?"

Michas frowned and scratched his chin. "Let's not talk about him."

"Then what would you have us talk about? The Trial? The test today? My wonderful performance?"

He laughed when I batted my eyelashes. "You blew the

other three away. I had no idea you'd mastered such control of mistphasing."

"I had to. Without wings . . ." I shrugged. "I needed to learn how to travel, and mistphasing was the only solution."

He eyed my bare back. "It is peculiar that you lack wings. I've never met another Solis without them."

"Be careful, Lord Crimsonale, or you may offend me."

He chuckled. "Something tells me you're not easily offended."

I sighed. "You may be right. Many fae have singled me out because I'm different. I've grown used to it."

"I wasn't singling you out, and I certainly wouldn't whisper about you like the commoners were at the test." He took another sip of his champagne, a genuine frown knitting his features.

A moment of doubt hit me at his sympathetic response. It looked . . . sincere.

Months ago, my initial impression of Michas had been mostly positive at the Betrothal Ball, even though I hadn't been sure if I could trust him. But Cailis's truth affinity had warned me to be careful. Michas was too gray to fully trust . . .

I shook my head. Everything had always been convoluted with the young Crimsonale.

Stepping closer to him, I studied his expression. "You know, I've been wondering if you're kinder than your father. He would no doubt gloat if he saw the Solisarium citizens ridiculing me."

Michas studied me over the rim of his glass. "Back to my father, I see."

"Can you blame me?"

"Why do you want to speak of him?"

I scrunched my eyebrows together. "Can I be as frank with you as we were the night of the Betrothal Ball?"

His lips quirked up. "I don't see why not. There's something about you that just begs me to be honest."

Hopefully, that's true. "In that case, what does your father have against the king?"

"Back to this . . ."

"In all fairness, you're the one who started this conversation when we first met. You can't be annoyed now just because I'm curious."

His wings ruffled slightly. "But that was before."

"Before what?"

"Before I knew you were the prince's mate."

I arched an eyebrow as a cold breeze drew goosebumps from my skin. "So you believe since he's my mate that you can't speak freely with me anymore?"

"I believe that the prince is loyal to his father, and since you're the prince's mate, I'm assuming by default that you will also be loyal to the king."

I sucked in a breath. Michas Crimsonale, for all of his tactile maneuvers, didn't seem truly evil like his father, even if he did have a competitive history with the crown prince, so I decided to throw caution to the wind.

"What if neither of us was loyal to the king?" I said quietly.

Michas's drink paused halfway to his lips. "What game are you playing now?"

"No game. I simply gave you a statement, and I'm curious what your response will be."

He brought his glass to his lips and sipped slowly, his gaze locked in scrutiny. "If neither of you were loyal to the king, I would ask why not."

"What about you? Are you loyal to your father?"

"Of course."

I cocked my head. "That was a quick response."

"Because it's true."

"So you would support your father attempting to overthrow the king?"

Michas glanced over his shoulder to the empty balcony behind us, then to the open courtyard. But no one was around. Still, he hissed quietly, "Lower your voice."

I took another step closer to him and said in a softer tone, "Are you afraid of being executed if such treasonous talk gets out?"

He gripped my elbow and pulled me to the corner of the balcony, but his movements were filled with fear, not aggression. "The king would execute *anyone* who planned treason as would be his right."

"Yet you still take that risk. You and your father. Why?"

"Because—" He paused, then eyed me warily. "Never mind. We don't support any treasonous movements. Long live King Novakin."

I rolled my eyes. "Who do you think you're fooling, Michas? I saw enough on the first night we met to know you're actively seeking willing participants to join your father. And you saw me as someone new to the court with potential for rising to some kind of power. You saw me as a valuable ally. And now, as the potential future queen, surely your outlook on my value hasn't changed?"

His chest rose faster, but in the cool night with lights from inside the dining hall spilling out onto the balcony, his face was dipped in shadows. Yet I felt him studying me, weighing . . . something.

"I've been nothing but truthful with you so far," I pressed. "Don't shut me out. Tell me what your father is planning. Tell me what you know."

He studied me for a long moment. Seconds passed, but I waited.

Finally, after letting out a deep sigh, he said, "My father is concerned that—"

The door on the other end of the balcony whipped open, and Georgyanna and her date stumbled out. Michas immediately stiffened, his hand wrapping around my elbow as the two drew up short when they spotted us.

"Are you two still out here?" the male asked. He was a noble from Isalee territory who I'd had a date with last week.

"It would appear they are, and they're lingering in a dark corner from the looks of it." Georgyanna grinned as her affinity puffed in wafts from her. That slimy feeling tried to coat me, but my Shield repelled it. "What would the crown prince have to say about that, I wonder?"

"He wouldn't have anything to say as I was just leaving." Michas gave a formal bow in my direction and refused to meet my gaze. "Good night, Lady Seary. Thank you for a pleasant evening."

And with that, he turned away and took my chance with him at learning what really drove his father.

CHAPTER 26

They gave us two days to rest before our next test. Two days to stew over what was to come. And when the day finally arrived, I was more than ready to get it over with.

"Are you nervous?" Cailis asked as Daiseeum braided my black hair in a long line down my back.

"Yes," I replied, tapping my foot on the stone floor as nerves tumbled my stomach. "I have no idea what this next test involves. All I know is that we're meeting in the courtyard before mistphasing somewhere." My anxiety was heightened even more because of what else had happened in the past day.

Three more fae had been reported missing. They'd all disappeared without a trace. And what was most concerning about that was the sheer number. *Three.* Before it had always been one.

Cailis frowned. "I don't understand why I can't come to watch and why no other fae are invited."

"They say the area is too small for spectators at this one.

And something about it being far away, so it would be difficult for those who can't mistphase to attend." The knotting twists in my stomach resumed. Not even Matron Olsander was allowed at the second test. I was on my own.

"Did they say why it's so far away? Or where it is?" my sister pressed.

"No." My fingers trembled as I smoothed a few strands of hair behind my ears.

Daiseeum used her magic to tame the wisps. "There. All done." She patted my shoulder. "You shall exceed today like you did at the first test. I just know it."

A knock came on my bedchamber's door.

"That must be Sandus." I gave Daiseeum a smile of thanks, then hugged my sister, but when I opened the door, my breath stopped when I beheld the crown prince. A smile parted my lips as my stomach coiled. "What are you doing here?"

"Is that how you greet your prince?" he asked in a teasing, husky tone.

I tried to ignore the flutter in my heart that had nothing to do with the test. Prince Norivun's wings rose high above his shoulders, his cut jawline also demanding my attention. He wore a rich blue tunic. The fitted material clearly defined his powerful chest muscles hidden beneath.

Blessed Mother, he's a beautiful male.

Somehow, I managed to bob a curtsy, but my voice came out breathy when I replied, "Sorry, good morning, my prince."

He took a step closer to me, crowding my space as his aura wrapped around me. His air affinity kissed the skin on my neck, sending a shiver of goosebumps cascading down my spine.

"To answer your question, I'm here because there's something you need to see."

I straightened, and some of the curling motions disappeared in my belly at his grim tone. "Now?"

"It's important."

"What's happened?"

"The fields in Isalee—" His brow furrowed, and the worry that etched into his features was deeper than anything I'd seen of late. Dread filled me.

"What's happened?"

"Come."

I didn't have time to ask what he intended to do before his hand wrapped around my forearm. The realm disappeared in a blur of mist and shadows, air and wind.

We reappeared in a blinding snowstorm, and the gusts were so strong I was nearly knocked off my feet. Shielding my eyes, I called upon my air affinity to create a warm bubble around us.

My magic responded immediately, easily ten times faster than it'd been three months ago.

Norivun's lips kicked up, and some of the tension that had knotted his expression lightened. "You're nearly as fast as me with your air affinity now."

I arched an eyebrow. "Nearly?"

He chuckled. "You can't expect to be as strong as the Death Master of the continent."

Despite the fact that I was in a snowstorm right before my second test, I laughed. "Did you really just whisk me from my chambers, minutes from the beginning of my second test, just for a jaunt in the snow, my prince?"

The fleeting lightness on his face vanished. "Do you recognize where we are?"

I peered through my air bubble and frowned when memories surfaced of the familiar brutal winds and raging storms. "Is this the Isalee field where the snowgum attacked you? Where the crops first began to die?"

He nodded. "And look at it." He waved his arm toward the field, toward where growing crops had been.

My lips parted, a stone settling in my stomach as I took in withered black stalks lying limp on the snow. They dotted the entire landscape, barely visible through the blinding storm.

My mood plummeted. "How? What happened?"

The prince scowled. "I don't know. Truthfully, I have no idea."

"But . . . only days ago, this field was thriving. Lord Woodsbury proclaimed it at the last council meeting." Bending down, I frantically dug through the snow, having to push several feet aside until I came to the hard, cold dirt. It was dry and gray—exactly as it'd been before I'd restored this land's *orem*.

A mewling sound escaped me. *No, no, no.* Sitting back on my haunches, I stared at the dead ground before me.

"Are the gods working against us? Do they want us all to starve? Is saving the Solis continent truly beyond anything we can fix?" Because if my magic only restored life to these crops temporarily, then we were all doomed.

Norivun crouched at my side. I leaned into him, and his hand pressed into the small of my back, steadying me and drawing me close.

But it wasn't until my side met the firm warmth of his thigh that I realized I was allowing the bond to soothe me when I should be anything but calm right now. I snapped upright. "What's happened here since we left?"

The prince's eyes glittered. "The villagers say the crops had been thriving since you used your affinity, but then this morning, they woke up to this."

My jaw dropped. "The plants died *overnight*?"

His single nod had my heart clenching. Leaning forward, I shoved my hand into the soil. *Where? Where are you?*

When I'd left this field two months ago, pulsing *orem* had beat through it. But now . . .

My breath stopped.

Nothing. *Nothing* rippled beneath my palm.

I moved my hand, frantically searching the soil for something, *anything*. I called upon my life-giving affinity and willed a heartbeat of life to tingle back into this land, but the second my magic surged forward, it collided with something that bit back at me. The shock of it was so sudden I nearly fell to the side.

I yanked my hand back. "What in the realm was that?"

The prince frowned. "What's wrong?"

"There's something here."

Norivun's brows drew together. "What do you mean?"

Tentatively, I laid my hand back on the ground and closed my eyes, then searched for that *zap* I'd just sensed, that strange barrier, but . . . it didn't respond. Shaking my head, I opened my eyes.

"I don't know. I could have sworn I just sensed something, something that punched back at me, but maybe I didn't. Maybe my magic is all tangled up right now. I'm nervous about the second test, but Mother Below, how can this field be dead again?"

He raked a hand through his hair and let out a frustrated sigh. "I wish I knew."

My braid settled on my shoulder as I stared at him with pleading eyes. "Is everything we're doing hopeless? Have all of these weeks that I've spent visiting fields been for naught?"

Outside of my bubble, the wind raged. A moment of help-lessness hit me when the absolute bleakness of our climate met me with full force. Life here on the northern continent would *never* grow without the aid of magic. This land was too cold, too frozen to ever foster plants naturally.

My mouth twisted with concern. "Will I never fulfill our bargain? Will our fae ultimately starve no matter what I do?"

Norivun loosed a breath and drew me close. His aura thrummed beside mine, but when he met my gaze, I saw the answer in his expression before he said, "I'm starting to wonder if we can be saved."

Norivun mistphased us back to the castle, and we re-emerged in the castle's main courtyard. The other three Trial females were already present, along with Sir Featherton, the queen, and the king. Standing just behind them were all of the territory archons, but there weren't any other spectators today or guards. Not even Nuwin was present.

"Ah, there she is!" Sir Featherton said dramatically. "We feared we would have to disqualify you from the second test if you didn't appear soon."

Everyone glanced between the prince and me, some not bothering to hide their snickers. My cheeks heated at the conclusion they'd obviously reached that explained my tardiness. *If only . . .*

"Norivun, what is the meaning of this?" the king asked, his tone amused, but his expression hard.

The prince's shoulders tightened. "I escorted Ilara briefly to Isalee. A troubling event has occurred."

"Oh?" Taberitha Wormiful pushed to the front of the group as her pointy chin jutted up. "What's amiss?"

"Indeed," Lord Crimsonale chimed in, "if something is causing you concern, surely the council should be made aware."

Lord Woodsbury, the Isalee Territory archon, cleared his throat loudly. "Excuse me, fine fae, but if something is problematic within Isalee, then I believe *I'm* the one who should be consulted." He stared down at me with narrowed eyes. "Report if you would, Lady Seary."

Prince Norivun growled. "Speak to her with more respect, Lord Woodsbury."

The Isalee archon sniffed but said in a less spiteful tone, "Well? Report if you will."

I clenched my hands into fists. "The field I restored to life two months ago outside of Whimseal has died again."

Everyone gasped.

"It's as I've been saying," Lord Crimsonale said, his expression thunderous. "The fields are dying. When will the council take this seriously?" He gave the king a pointed look.

The king waved his hand. "The fields will be restored at the next celestial event as they inevitably always are. And if the

Isalee field has truly died again, then I think all that proves is that Lady Seary's affinity isn't as powerful as my son had hoped." He looked me up and down. "Perhaps none of your affinities are as strong as I've been told."

The crown prince leveled his father with a glacial glare. "She's more magical than any female here."

Georgyanna bristled as Beatrice and Meegana remained quiet but shared anxious glances.

Lady Wormiful straightened to her full height and said icily, "Shall we begin the second test? Perhaps we'll know more about the strength of each female after its victor emerges."

Sir Featherton explained where we were to mistphase, and everyone disappeared one by one. Those who excelled at the magical means of transporting disappeared faster than others. But this time, when my magic transported me instantaneously across the realm, I didn't land with confidence. My legs shook when I materialized on the Bay of Nim.

Crashing waves reached my ears as soaring hills rose alongside the body of water that cut deep into the northern land of Mervalee Territory. I was the first to arrive at the bay, first to step foot back on my home soil, and a moment of relief hit me. My magic had transported me here before all of the others, even Norivun, but that consolation was short-lived.

Because all I could think about was what if the king was right. Perhaps my affinities weren't that strong. I'd worked extensively at mistphasing in my training with Matron Olsander, so it made sense that I'd become so proficient at it, but it was possible that was where my superior capabilities ended.

Maybe I couldn't fulfill the bargain I'd made with the prince. Maybe I'd never be able to restore our land's crops because I lacked the inherent capabilities to do so.

The age-old feeling that had plagued me my entire life, the knowledge that I was magicless and weak, reared its ugly head. I thought I'd finally squashed that insecurity, but the Isalee field was dead. That was a fact. My affinity hadn't saved it, so that meant all of the other fields I thought I'd been healing could fall sickly once more too.

"Stop." The crown prince's quiet voice brushed against my ear.

I jumped at the feel of him, not even realizing he'd just reappeared only inches behind me. His large hands gripped my hips as he leaned down more to whisper in my ear. "Don't let him play his mind games with you. This is what he does. Stop second-guessing yourself."

I nearly choked on the tears that threatened to fill my eyes. "How did you know that's what I was thinking?"

"Worry is coating your scent." His grip tightened. "But look at how strong you are. You arrived here first, even before me, and no one else is here yet. Their magic isn't as powerful as yours. Your mistphasing is nearly instantaneous."

My shoulders sagged, some of the tension oozing from me. He pulled me back against his chest, and I melted into him, my form aligning perfectly against his hard abdomen. A low, satisfied-sounding purr rumbled in his chest as his nose drifted down to inhale along my neck.

He placed a soft kiss right beneath my ear, and that lulling feeling of safety cocooned around me once more.

"Come here." He spun me in his embrace, his arms closing around my waist as his lips met mine.

I clung to him, desperately molding myself to him as our tongues danced together while I chased away all of my old fears and anxieties. I soaked in his belief in me. He'd *always* believed in me, and I used that to align my thoughts with his own.

Snow and cedar wrapped around me as a smile parted his lips. "Your scent's changing." He nipped at my lips again, and I moaned.

"In what way?"

"You smell more confident and—" His breath sucked in. "And *fuck*, your arousal is giving off the most delicious aroma. I need to taste you again tonight."

My pulse pounded as my core throbbed. *Mother Below, I wanted this male.*

"When?" he asked as he kissed down my neck. "When can I fully claim you?"

"Soon." My breath hitched just as he pulled back.

Magic rippled in the air around us, alerting us to the others arriving.

With lips pressed to my ear, the prince said, "You're strong. You're powerful. And you're *mine*. Don't forget any of that."

With that, he released his grip on me, moving two feet away just as the king appeared, followed by the rest of the group as they arrived one by one.

The last to appear was Lord Pinebeer, the archon of Harrivee Territory. He gave a sheepish smile when Lady Busselbee, my territory's archon, smirked. Nobody commented that the queen wasn't present, and I couldn't help but wonder if they'd made the connection that the queen never mistphased anymore. She couldn't with her magic suppressed.

The king stood stoically, watching me, but I made myself step closer to Meegana and concentrate on the test and not the soothing words from the powerful prince or the way desire pounded through me.

The mate bond that tethered us was clouding my vision again, and right now, I needed my head to be clear.

"Daughters of the Solis continent!" Sir Featherton clapped his hands in delight. "Welcome to the second test in your Trial. Today we shall see just how strong *all* of your affinities are, because the test we've created for you cannot be completed by any fairy who holds only one affinity. Oh no, today's test will truly push you to your limits." His smile turned razor-sharp. "Within the Bay of Nim, the treacherous waters known for sucking fae to its depths and never letting go, waits a trinket. It's lying at the deepest part of the bay, over a thousand feet below sea level. The first female to find it, retrieve it, and arrive safely back to shore and present it to the king will win the Trial."

He clasped his hands behind his back, and a moment of fear stole over me. With life-giving, air, and fire affinities, I had no idea how I would ever reach it.

The Trial archon's smile grew even broader. "Good luck."

CHAPTER 27

"Finally, a test that my affinity will excel at," Meegana whispered under her breath. As a female who harbored a water elemental affinity, along with shapeshifting and sound sensory, Meegana's gifts hadn't allowed her to excel in the first test, but here in the bay, she undoubtedly would.

I squeezed her hand. "You'll do great."

She nodded, her expression relieved, but when she faced me, worry etched into her features. "What are you going to do?"

I racked my brain for a response and came up short. "I don't know yet."

Because here, in the open ocean, I had no idea how my life-giving, air, or fire affinities would help me. It was possible I could create a mask of air around my face so I could breathe underwater, but to swim a thousand feet below the surface . . . Dangerous creatures lurked within the depths of the Brashier Sea, predators that also swam into the Bay of Nim.

I shuddered.

It didn't seem I was alone in my concerns, though. Both Georgyanna and Beatrice also wore masks of worry. Georgyanna held four affinities—fire, electric, constructo, and emotional manipulation. Of the four of us, she seemed even worse off than me.

Beatrice would also have to get creative. With her earth element, sight sensory, and telekinesis, she was also at a disadvantage without a water element, but I supposed that was the point of these tests. Only the most ruthless, cunning, and strongest female would win.

I gave a wary glance toward Georgyanna. A small smile had formed on her face.

Taking a deep breath, I stirred the magic inside me. It rumbled in my belly, rising and waking as I pulled on it. I still had to concentrate when I blended my affinities together, but Matron Olsander assured me that with more practice it would become second nature.

"On my count!" Sir Featherton raised a hand as the king and council members watched on. "Three . . ."

Norivun stood apart from the crowd, his expression impossible to read. He crossed his arms, and I could have sworn that a flutter of worry rolled from him, but when he saw me watching him, he only nodded curtly.

The mate bond inside me unfurled, threatening to overpower my concentration on my magic, so I quickly averted my attention and focused on the water.

I would have to create an air bubble around my face, perhaps even my entire body. Maybe I could create bubbles behind me to push me down into the bay's depths. Perhaps my fire could light the way. Worry rose higher inside me, because I couldn't think of any way to use my life-giving affinity, which meant I was down to two affinities—air and fire only.

"Two . . . " Sir Featherton's arm rose higher. "One!"

Meegana shot into the water like an arrow, diving effortlessly into the bay and disappearing into its depths in a single stroke. My eyes widened when the ground rumbled, my knees wobbling as the entire realm shifted. Rocks and boulders abruptly shot from the hillside, cascading down the mountain in a rolling sweep of jagged stone.

The boulders tumbled down the incline, moving faster with every second that passed. I thought for sure we were about to be swept away in a rockslide, but then the stones lifted in the air.

I gaped when I realized what was happening. Beatrice's forehead furrowed as she wove her hands through the air.

The rocks abruptly pulverized into tiny pebbles as they hovered above us. Several council members clapped and nodded in delight. Beatrice's rock creation spiraled toward the water and then shot into it like a magical drill as she used her earth elemental and telekinetic affinities.

Beatrice pointed her hands downward, and the hundreds of tons of rock burrowed into the water. I knew she'd hit the seafloor's bed when a breath of relief escaped her.

The spiraling path of pebbles she'd created widened until it formed a perfect tunnel in the water. All of the water was contained on the outside of it while the inside stayed dry.

A grin split her face as she jumped into her magically made, fully enclosed slide. With a squeal of glee, she slid down her earthen creation, going down, down, down so fast that her squeal turned into a laugh of pure fun that echoed back to those of us at the surface.

I had no doubt if Meegana wasn't already at the bottom of the seafloor, Beatrice would be there before all of us could blink.

Only Georgyanna and I still stood on the water's edge, and for some reason, the Kroravee native seemed in no hurry to join the other two.

Not wanting to know what she was up to, I plunged into the water. My lungs seized when its frigid embrace took hold of me, but I ignited my fire inside me to heat my limbs. Calling upon more magic, I formed a bubble of air around my head, and then I swam under the surface. I kicked as quickly as I could, but I wasn't moving fast enough.

Calling upon more magic, I created bubbles around me. Defying gravity, my magical bubbles shoved me through the water, propelling me at impossible speed until I was rocketing toward the seafloor.

In the back of my mind, I wondered again what Georgyanna was doing, but that thought fled when a flash of movement shot past my peripheral vision. A dark shadow. An open mouth.

Fear raced through me as a huge predator cut through my path. Its mouth was over five feet wide. Fins like knives sliced through the water. It could swallow me in a single bite, and it probably could propel itself faster through the water than my magic.

Another shadow cut through the water to my left. They were circling me. A burst of panic shot through me, and I closed my eyes as I flew toward the bottom of the sea. I concentrated on what Matron Olsander had taught me. I expanded the air around me until it formed a diameter of over ten feet. Magic pulsed in my gut as I ignited my ringed bubble in fire.

A scream tore through the water, and I knew that one of the predators had been burned by my flame. But as long as I kept my fire encased within my air bubble, the water wouldn't douse it.

Sweat beaded down my back as I wove my affinities together, needing to use both as the bubbles propelling me down increased. *More.* I needed more magic to get me there.

Another flash of movement to my left had me shifting my attention to my fire magic. At the last moment, I reined it in when I realized it was Meegana beside me.

She grinned as the tunnel Beatrice had built appeared to my right. The three of us were racing for the bottom, nearly neck and neck.

It felt so strange to compete like this against my friends, but then I remembered what was at stake. I needed to win this Trial. I could only hope that my friends understood that I couldn't let them beat me.

I coaxed more magic from my belly and put everything I had into increasing my speed. Even though Meegana's element was water, I shot ahead, moving faster than her. The crown prince was right. I was stronger than her. And for the first time since Norivun had taken me from my village four months ago, I truly felt like a queen ascending to her destined throne.

I was the strongest female here.

A grin split my face as my confidence at another victory reared, but just when I thought for certain I would reach the bottom, the water disappeared, and I screamed.

I tumbled through a huge pocket of air resting in the water above the sea floor.

Meegana's scream came next as her water elemental affinity proved useless as the magic around me grew.

But it wasn't my magic. It was the test's magic. The test creators must have planted this pocket of air here, forcing someone with a water elemental affinity to use another power.

But Meegana continued to fall. With a shapeshifting and sensory affinity, she had nothing.

"Meegana!" I screamed just as she was about to hit the bottom of the air pocket.

I shot a stream of air magic out, catching her before her body could break.

It all happened so fast that she only had a second to recover before I released her, and she dove back into the water at the bottom of the air pocket.

To my right, Beatrice hadn't slowed. Her earthen tunnel had cleaved right through the air pocket as her telekinetic magic threw every predator that threatened to ram it far away from her.

Still, despite how strong both of them were, I reached the bottom of the sea before either of them.

The glowing trinket waited, beckoning me with its light. It was a golden crown studded with jewels and precious gems that had been enchanted with radiance, making it glow like a beacon.

My hand burst through my fire-encrusted bubble, my flames not burning my fingers. I snatched the crown from the sand and reversed course.

Beatrice let out a wail of fury when she reached the bottom

and the trinket was gone, but Meegana only grinned. Her smile was so bright when I flew toward the surface of the bay.

My magic shot me upward. Power sang in my blood and heated my heart.

I would win this Trial.

I would become the next queen.

And I would marry the prince and claim him as my mate.

When I exploded through the surface of the Bay of Nim, the archons' eyes went wide, and a grin spread across Prince Norivun's face. Out of the water, my air affinity excelled. A gust of wind blew me toward the shore, and a new victory was within my grasp.

Georgyanna still stood where I'd left her. When I realized she hadn't moved at all, shock flitted through me. It was as though she was trying to lose.

Frowning, I calmed my magic and let my air release me as I dropped to the sand.

The second I came in contact with land, a jolt of pure electricity zinged along my soles. I screamed in pain as my entire body seized. Electric currents coursed through me, burning me from the inside out.

Oh gods!

A roar of fury came from Prince Norivun as his wings flexed, and a cruel smile spread across Georgyanna's lips.

No, no, no.

I'd relaxed my magic too much. I'd let my protective Shield down just enough for Georgyanna's magic to take hold.

Before I could react, the Kroravee native plucked the crown from my electrified fingertips as her lips widened in a gleeful smile.

She gave me her back and flounced toward the king.

I burst through her magic and lunged toward her, but I was too late.

Bowing low, she lifted the crown to King Novakin.

"Your Majesty, may I present you with the trinket that was waiting at the bottom of the sea. I do believe this makes me the winner of test two."

CHAPTER 28

Taberitha Wormiful grinned as I sputtered, "But, she can't . . . I mean, how can she do that!" Water dripped from my clothes, and hair stuck to my cheeks while my chest heaved.

Norivun leveled a deadly scowl at Georgyanna just as Beatrice appeared at the top of her earthen tunnel, and Meegana shot out of the water and landed on the beach only feet from me.

But King Novakin only gave a low laugh and accepted the crown from Georgyanna's outstretched hand as the other two females and I stood with gaping mouths.

Beatrice and Meegana gave me a bewildered look as the king eyed Georgyanna thoughtfully. "Cunning and cruel. Two traits that would make a fine queen indeed."

My denial that Georgyanna would actually be declared the winner withered and died when I saw the king's approval. He *applauded* what Georgyanna had done. Of course he did. The male was a monster. The true monster here. And then there were the rules of the Trial. These tests could be won by any means necessary.

My entire body slumped as the absolute devastation of losing test two hit me. Georgyanna had no doubt felt similar when I'd won the first test by outsmarting her, and now I'd lost test two because Georgyanna had outsmarted me.

It was cruelly ironic.

Sir Featherton clapped his hands. "What a delight! A true competition! We now have two females in the running for our future queen. Since Lady Seary won the first test and Lady Endalaver won the second test, they will compete in the final test tomorrow. Ladies Ockson and Leafton, you have my deepest condolences on your losses, but seeing as neither of you has won a test yet, you shall be removed from the Trial. The king will ultimately decide who your betrothals will be and will let you know following the final test." Sir Featherton bowed at them as my heart beat even harder.

Meegana and I shared a fearful look. She was out of the competition? Just because she hadn't won a test yet, she was no longer in the Trial?

I squeezed Meegana's hand as worry etched her features. I knew she was thinking of Nuwin.

"He might still be your husband," I said quietly. "This could still work out in your favor."

Tears brimmed in her eyes. "But he's the king's second son. How can he possibly be given to the third or fourth winner? Surely, he'll be betrothed to the runner-up of the Trial."

I frowned, my eyebrows pulling together. Something told me the king didn't favor anyone, even his own son, if another was stronger.

Enraged pulses of power beat from Norivun's aura. His jaw locked tightly as his murderous gaze stayed latched to Georgyanna.

But he must have felt me looking at him, must have felt my plea.

Prince Norivun and I exchanged a weighted look. His brow grew heavy, as though the entire realm rested upon it. Neither of us had expected that the final test would come down to only two. Which meant I *had to win* the final test.

Otherwise, the prince would be forced to marry Georgyanna.

Everyone mistphased back to the castle and arrived in the courtyard we'd initially departed from. Since the king was watching, Prince Norivun didn't approach me, but the look he continually gave Georgyanna could have melted glass.

"I believe celebrations are in order, don't you think?" Taberitha Wormiful said to test two's winner.

The tall and lithe Kroravee archon stood as regal as a royal. One would think she was the reason Georgyanna had won, given her proud aura.

Georgyanna preened and adjusted the crown on her head. "Why, Lady Wormiful, I would be delighted."

The crown shone from Georgyanna's silver hair, the gold flashing in the sun as the jewels sparkled. She wore the crown so easily, as though she truly believed she was born to rule.

Anger stirred in me again, and I took a deep breath. The crown that I'd retrieved from the bottom of the bay had been given to Georgyanna by the king. It was a gift for winning the second test—the test that should have been *my* victory.

A sick feeling twisted my stomach as they ambled away, loudly discussing their territory's clever win.

"Norivun?" the king said, a guileless smile on his face. "Let your mother know the outcome of the second test, if you will."

Prince Norivun's nostrils flared, but he gave his father a stiff nod and strode back to the castle.

Still shaking from what happened, I approached Meegana. "Do you want company?"

Beatrice had already left, stalking back to the castle as soon as we'd arrived in the courtyard, but Meegana had stayed. A cool breeze ruffled our clothing. I'd dried us with my air affinity before we'd mistphased, but the wind was still biting.

She shook her head. "Even though I would rather spend the day with you, I need to find my mother and tell her what happened." Worry lines appeared around Meegana's eyes as she wrung her hands. "She's going to be so angry that I won't be queen."

I bared my teeth. "Just because you won't be the next queen doesn't mean that you're not strong or worthy, and if your mother doesn't see that, then the fault lies with her."

Meegana laughed humorlessly. "I think I might have said something like that to you when we first met."

"You did, and you were right. Just remember that when you speak with her."

"I'll try."

I squeezed her hand.

Behind us, the king was speaking with Sir Featherton. The

two were in deep discussions but they were behind a silencing Shield so nobody could hear them.

"I'll send a prayer to the Blessed Mother for you that you'll marry Nuwin," I whispered to her.

A smile parted Meegana's lips, a true smile. "Thank you."

We headed opposite ways, and I hurried back into the castle. Not surprisingly, Sandus was waiting for me at the gate. He didn't say anything as he fell in step beside me, which made me think Norivun had found him and told him already what had happened.

I was glad he didn't bring up my loss because the last thing I wanted to do was discuss it.

"Have you seen Cailis?" I asked instead as we rounded the corner toward the prince's private wing.

"She's waiting in the Exorbiant Chamber for you."

When we arrived back at my chambers, Cailis was pacing by the courtyard doors. The second I closed the door behind me, she ran to me with wide eyes and grabbed both of my hands. "How did you do?"

I shook my head.

"You lost?"

I nodded. "Second place. Meegana and Beatrice have been removed from the Trial. The final test will be between Georgyanna and me." I briefly explained what had happened and how Georgyanna had tricked me.

"What a cunning witch." Cailis seethed, and the look was so protective and reminiscent of our childhood that I couldn't help but laugh.

"This is one fight you can't shield me from, Cailis."

"But you're stronger than her. You can beat her."

I forced a smile, then rubbed my temples as I tried to stave off the headache that was brewing because it wasn't just the final test I had looming over me. "Have you heard about the Isalee field?"

She cocked her head. "No, is something wrong?"

I told her about the black crops. "That's what the prince came to tell me about, before my test." Sighing, I sat on my bed and hung my head. I'd been so consumed with the second test that I hadn't properly considered what the dead crops in Isalee meant. "Do you think everything I've been doing is for naught? If all of the crops are eventually going to lose their *orem* once more, what's the point of me trying?"

She sat at my side. "You're certain the field is truly dead again?"

"It is. When I touched the soil, it felt just as devoid of life as it had the first time I visited it." I stood and went to the courtyard door.

Outside, my private garden shone brightly. Vivid colors burst from every plant and flower. Scented blossoms perfumed the air. Warmth kissed my skin when I opened the door, and the breeze flowed in.

"I just don't understand it, Cailis. How can this courtyard still be alive but that field dead? I did the exact same thing there as I did here. My affinity, if anything, is stronger now, so I don't understand why the crops died."

My sister came up behind me and wrapped me in a hug. She shrugged. "I wish I knew the answer."

I encircled her forearms with my hands, gripping her tightly as fear dashed through me. "If it's true that my affinity can't save the fields, and if the celestial bodies don't replenish our continent's *orem* at the next major event, then our entire race—"

I couldn't say it.

Cailis squeezed me harder. "We'll all starve," she finished. "Unless everyone leaves this continent, and we abandon our frozen home."

"Just like some of the council members want us to do." I pulled from her embrace and frowned as I turned to face her. "*Just like some of the council members want us to do,*" I repeated as my frown deepened.

A flash of what I'd felt in the field this morning hit me like a thunderclap. That feeling that something had been . . .

I spun toward the door, my mind racing. "Cailis, I need to go. I need to find the crown prince and visit that field again."

Sandus led me to the training room, telling me along the way, "The prince needed to blow off some steam after telling the queen what happened at the second Trial."

I frowned. "What do you mean? What's he doing?"

"You'll see."

Scents from food baking in the nearby kitchens wafted in the air when we stopped just outside of one of the large training rooms. My eyes popped open when I spotted the prince, Haxil, Nish, and Ryder sparring.

The urgency I'd felt at returning to Isalee came to a sudden halt. All four males were shirtless, their wings tucked tightly to their backs as they rolled, struck one another, and fought. Their sparring made a tingle grow deep in my belly, and it wasn't just from the glistening sweat beaded on the prince's chest or the way his muscles bunched and moved every time he dodged a blow. It was more because something about their dance called to me.

I brought a hand to my stomach, to where my magic resided. It pulsed stronger and more fervently than it normally did, and a memory of what Queen Lissandra had revealed surfaced, about how her affinities had manifested slowly over time. I couldn't help but wonder if a warrior affinity truly was still sleeping within me. Matron Olsander had sensed more in me, but nothing had yet shown itself.

Grinning, Sandus called out, "Don't look now, Nori, but a beautiful young female is watching you."

Norivun's head whipped in my direction, allowing Haxil to land an easy uppercut to his jaw.

The prince's head snapped back, and my eyes widened when his lip split, but the prince only grinned and let loose a huge gust of his air element.

Haxil flew from his feet, his wings spreading wide as he tried to stop the wind magic from pinning him to the wall.

Nish laughed and tackled Norivun from behind, but the prince spun and landed a kick to his guard's stomach. Ryder howled in amusement when he joined Nish, and the two of them wrestled the prince to the mat.

All of them were panting, and victorious howls came from Nish and Ryder as Haxil finally broke through the prince's air affinity. He joined the guards and piled on top of the prince.

Norivun sputtered a breath when Haxil knocked the wind from him with an easy punch.

"Cheating bastards!" the crown prince choked out as he wheezed and laughed.

The guards chortled.

A devilish grin split Norivun's face. "Don't say you didn't deserve this."

In a flash of magic so strong that I felt it in my bones, the prince's form abruptly vanished. A second later, a roaring dragon stood in his place. My eyes turned into saucers, and I blinked, then blinked again.

The dragon was still there.

"That is the most realistic looking illusion I've ever seen," I breathed.

Sandus crossed his arms, smirking. "It's not an illusion."

"*What?*" I backed up, but Sandus stopped me.

"Just watch. He'll want you to see."

"He? *That's* Norivun?"

Sandus grinned.

Black scales covered the dragon's . . . no, *Norivun's* entire body as puffs of smoke blew from his nostrils. Huge, leathery wings tipped in talons lay against his body as a long tail swung along the floor, knocking all of the guards from their feet.

"Oh, fuck," Sandus said from beside me as he huffed a laugh. "He hasn't pulled that stunt in a while."

The guard leaned against the door, an amused smile on his face as we watched the chaos that was being unleashed.

My eyes widened more as I took in the sheer size of Norivun, who apparently had a dragon shapeshifting affinity—an extremely *rare* affinity that the prince never told me about because he liked seeing me curious. Since dragons were only normally found in the underworld, guarding the gates to

Lucifer's kingdom, it was unheard of for a Solis fairy to acquire their form when a shapeshifting affinity manifested. I'd read in a history book that it'd only happened once and that had been centuries ago.

"He's truly unique, isn't he?" I said in amazement.

Sandus nodded. "That he is."

In his dragon form, Norivun rose twenty feet tall. At his full height, his lips split into a grin as long, razor-sharp teeth hung from his gums. The guards had completely given up on besting him in their sparring, and I could have sworn that Norivun was grinning at me.

"Very nice, Nori. She's thoroughly impressed." Sandus waved toward the prince's shredded clothes on the floor. "Would you like me to grab you a new pair of pants and a tunic?" He headed toward a chest against the wall.

In a second brilliant flash of magic, so strong it nearly knocked me off my feet, Norivun shifted back to his fae form. His huge leathery wings, tipped with talons, appeared at his back again, and my eyes widened.

"*That's* why you have talons on your wings?" I blurted as the crown prince pulled on a fresh pair of pants that Sandus had thrown to him. "It's your dragon affinity that caused that?"

He gave me a crooked grin. "I wondered how long it would take you to figure out."

Haxil, Ryder, and Nish all laughed or smirked, and I resisted the urge to smack the crown prince on his chest.

Norivun's grin increased as his nostrils flared. "Is that scent I'm detecting from you anger or admiration?"

I crossed my arms. "You could have just told me about that affinity and saved me the shock. I thought it was an illusion."

He laughed. "And miss seeing the disbelief you're still wearing? No way."

Haxil chuckled while Nish laughed so loud that he had to prop himself against Ryder to keep from tipping over.

"If it makes you feel better," the prince said, stepping closer to me, "I don't often shift. It's my weakest affinity, and I can't hold my dragon form for more than a few days."

Glowering, I tightened my arms over my chest. "What's your last affinity? Now that I know of five of the six, surely, you can just tell me what the last one is."

He grinned. "Nope."

I shook my head, but I couldn't stop my smile. "Well, if you're done showing off and using me for your amusement, I was hoping you could join me on an outing."

The crown prince cocked an eyebrow as a wolfish grin streaked across his face. "To my bed chambers?"

His guards snickered.

I rolled my eyes but had to smother a laugh. "No, you filthy-minded prince . . . to Isalee."

The energy in the room sobered as the prince frowned. "Back to Isalee? Why? What's wrong?"

"I want to study that field again. Something tells me that it's possible the lack of *orem* isn't what's killing the crops."

CHAPTER 29

The prince and his four guards accompanied me as we mistphased to Isalee. When we arrived at the same field, a clear pale-green sky and a stunningly bright sun blazed down on us. It was the exact opposite from the weather this morning.

"A clear winter day in my home territory." Haxil whistled. "Count yourself lucky. These days only happen a few times a season."

Taking that as a good omen, I created a dome of fire around the five of us, spreading it wide enough that it didn't burn anyone in the interior, but it was hot enough at the perimeter that it would keep any wayward predators from thinking twice about attacking.

Ryder cocked an eyebrow as his long braid trailed down his back. He did a slow circle, admiring my handiwork. "You've become pretty proficient with your affinities, Lady Seary."

"I was just thinking the same thing," Haxil said with a grin.

Nish frowned, but a new light entered his eyes as he

crossed his arms, studying me. "I have to say it is rather . . . impressive."

"Thank you," I said, suppressing a smile. "Anyway, the reason I wanted to return here was because of what I sensed earlier. It got me thinking." I leaned down to the snow and pushed at least four feet to the side before kneeling on the frozen ground.

Norivun joined me, inching closer to me until we touched. "What did you sense?"

I leaned more into him, that soothing feeling rushing through me as I laid my palm flat against the ground and closed my eyes. "I'm not sure, but . . ."

Magic swirled in my belly, and I drew upon it, calling my life-giving affinity to the surface before pushing it out of me. My power spiraled into the land as I searched for a hint of *orem*. Once again, nothing was there. I pushed deeper, trying to find that *off* sensation I'd detected only hours ago.

My magic dove through the ground, hunting and searching. Despair began to plague me, but then I hit something. It was so very deep in the land. Deeper than I'd ever tried to push my affinity before.

Forehead furrowing, I concentrated on assessing it, letting my magic spread out like probing fingers. It took so much concentration that I had to call upon everything Matron Olsander had taught me.

"How strange," I murmured. "It almost feels like a veil or some kind of net is deep within the land." I paused and glanced up at the prince as my mind raced. "Do you think our crops are dying from an unnatural occurrence that has nothing to do with the gods? That perhaps whatever I'm feeling in the land is encapsulating the *orem*?"

The prince's lips parted. "Does it feel like that?"

"I don't know, but I wasn't strong enough before to dive my affinity this deep. It makes me suspect that what I'm feeling now has spread throughout the continent."

He scowled, the expression making him look downright scary. "If that's the case, my guess is that Wormiful and Crimsonale are behind whatever you're feeling."

"That's what I'm thinking too, and if they've found a way to douse our land's *orem* and starve our fae, then we'd be forced to move south. It plays into exactly what they're pushing for."

His hand pressed against my back. "But how are they doing it? How are they creating whatever you're feeling?"

I shook my head. "I have no idea, but if we don't figure it out, my affinity can't save us."

I closed my eyes and returned my attention to the soil. Brows scrunching together, I dug deep into my reserves to force my affinity to dive farther.

Whatever was in the land zapped me again, its responses growing stronger the farther down I went, almost as if it was trying to deter me. But I pushed my affinity through it anyway, burrowing my magic as deep as it would go. The netting heated in response, growing hotter and hotter and hotter as I drilled through it.

ZAP!

I was flying.

Arms and legs extended upward as a clear sky shone above me.

Pain ricocheted through me as something followed me from the soil.

I landed on the ground so hard that I couldn't breathe.

"Ilara!" the prince yelled.

My head lolled. My sight blurred. Everything went black.

"ILARA!" Hands gripped my shoulders as anxiety filled the male's voice. It sounded as though he called out from far away, as though the male was underwater. "Ilara!"

My entire body was convulsing. Vibrating. No, that wasn't right. The male was shaking me as he tried to rouse me.

I opened my eyes to see the crown prince bending over me, his eyes blazing as intense fear lined his expression. His hands gripped my shoulders as power ratcheted off him, radiating around him in an aura so strong that I flinched.

I blinked as an aching pain in my gut made me wince. Groaning, I tried to sit up. "What happened?"

"Don't move." His hands traveled rapidly over me as he felt for injuries, but there was no blood. No broken bones. Not even bruises as far as I could tell. Just . . . pain.

I brought a hand to my forehead. Hair flew around my head as a slight throb twisted my stomach. "Norivun, what happened?"

His face twisted in worry. "I don't know. You were feeling the soil, using your affinity, and you said something about it being strange, and then—"

I hissed as pain slid through my gut, strengthening with every second that passed.

"Ilara?" His voice grew quiet, his hands gentled. "Talk to me. What's wrong?"

"I don't know. Nothing? Everything? But I'm okay. I think." But I didn't know for sure. Whatever I'd just felt in the soil had done something to me. It was internal if the roiling in my stomach was any indication.

Taking a deep breath, I tried to sit up more. "Let's go back to the castle."

The aura off Prince Norivun throbbed even more. "Yes, I want Murl to check you over."

Before I could respond, the prince's arms were around me, and he was gently lifting me as he stood. Around us, his four guards had their backs to us. They'd formed a protective circle, as though guarding us from any unseen attacks.

My ring of fire that had been encasing us was gone.

I froze. "When did my fire stop?"

"When you flew from the ground onto your back." Norivun tucked a lock of hair behind my ear. Tightness lined his expression. Even his wings had closed around me, as though every fiber of his body had gone into hyper-protective mode.

I nibbled my lip and felt for my magic. Pain accompanied that attempt, but my magic still swirled in my gut. It was still there, but it didn't rise readily.

"My magic is . . ." I shook my head. "I don't know what's going on."

Norivun's eyes shuttered. "We're going back to the castle. Now."

❄

THE PRINCE MISTPHASED US BACK, insisting that I conserve my strength. I didn't argue. Whatever had resisted my affinity in the Isalee field had left a lasting scar. My magic felt drained and weak. It'd already been low since I'd used so much during test two, but I hadn't realized that searching that field for life would have such a detrimental effect.

We reappeared just outside of the healing infirmary, the prince's guards only seconds behind us.

"Murl!" Norivun barked.

The castle healer appeared in a rush through the door, his hair tousled. He took one look at us and gestured us inside. "Lay her on that bed."

Norivun did as he said, moving on a gust of air that transported us across the room in a blink. The prince set me gently down, and then Murl was there, hovering and assessing.

The healer's brow furrowed as his affinity dipped into my body. Warmth spread through me, a tranquil feeling following.

I sighed.

Murl's frown grew. "You were in pain."

I nodded, which got a scowl from the prince.

Haxil, Nish, Sandus, and Ryder all moved to areas in the room to stand watch. Even here, they didn't let their guard down.

"Tell me what happened. Tell me what prompted this visit." Murl's hands continued to flutter over me as I told him about the deeply buried veil I'd sensed in Isalee's soil.

He frowned. "So something in the land pushed back at you?"

"I think so."

"Do you have any idea what it could be?"

I shook my head. "No, I don't. I've never felt anything like it."

Murl's frown increased, but he continued working, quietly probing and evaluating. When he finally finished, he settled back on his stool. "I don't know what to make of it, Lady Seary." He tapped his chin, his expression remaining perplexed. "Something feels strange within you, but I don't know what."

I sat up straighter as the aura off Norivun rose.

"What do you mean?" the prince demanded.

"It's almost as if something is encapsulating her magic, like it's suppressing it. It's as though something in the Isalee field attacked her."

A snarl tore from the prince's throat. "Attacked her? What would do that?"

Murl shook his head. "That's a very good question, my prince. At the moment, I'm unsure."

I brought a hand to my gut, to where I always sensed my magic. "Is that why it hurt here before you doused the pain?"

"My guess would be yes."

"Your guess?" The prince's scowl turned ferocious.

Murl ran a hand through his white hair. "I'm sorry, Your Highness, but I have no further ideas at this time. Let me consult a few texts and see if I can find anything. In the meantime, I suggest that Lady Seary eats a large meal to replenish her magic, and then she rests. With any luck, this will be a temporary malady and will have passed by tomorrow."

My eyes widened. "Is that possible? Could this correct itself?"

Murl patted my hand. "When it comes to magic, anything is possible. But rest and nourishment are always the best to help replenish our stores. I shall give you a potion to help you sleep well tonight."

"But I have my final test tomorrow. What if the potion leaves me groggy or ill-affected?"

"It shan't. My best potions leave no lasting side effects."

The prince growled. "See that she gets it."

Murl stood and bowed. "Of course, my prince."

Once the healer had retrieved the potion, Norivun lifted me from the bed.

I suppressed a smile. "I can walk, you know." Especially since the pain was now gone.

But his frown only deepened. "Let me do this. It . . . soothes something in me."

My eyes softened. I knew there was no point trying to fight his mating instincts, so I nodded.

The prince dismissed his guards, and after all of them said their goodbyes and wished me well, Norivun mistphased us out.

We reappeared in his chambers. The familiar huge room and gigantic bed waited in the dark. "You want me to sleep here?"

"Yes." His frown grew. "I want you close tonight."

He set me on his bed, then went to start the fire. Crackling flames soon filled the hearth.

"What would you like for supper?"

I shrugged. "Surprise me."

He rang for food, and Balbus answered the call. The portly servant's eyes widened when he saw me. Usually, the prince and I kept our encounters a secret, even from his servants, but since the prince didn't try to shield me from Balbus, I knew his worry had surpassed his concern over our relationship leaking.

At least Balbus was trustworthy. He'd never been anything but loyal to the prince.

The prince gave him a laundry list of food to bring.

Balbus bowed. "Of course, my prince. I shall endeavor to have all of it delivered swiftly." He gave me a bow as well. "Lady Seary, a pleasure to see you again as always."

"You too, Balbus," I replied. "I've missed our chats. Tell me, how's Marcina?"

Surprise flitted across his face, then he beamed. "She's fine and has recovered completely from her ailment. I shall tell her you asked of her."

Still beaming, the servant swirled from the room, and when it was just me and the prince, Norivun sat beside me on the bed as his wings draped behind him. "You know his wife?"

I shook my head. "I've never met her, but he's told me about her and his family. She got sick a few months ago. I'm glad she's better."

Raw emotion filled his eyes as he grasped my hand. "You amaze me more and more every day." His finger stroked the back of my hand as his frown returned. "How are you feeling?"

"Tired." My cheeks warmed as the bond between us billowed, as though an invisible tether connected us, and each of us was tugging at the other.

"Come here." He pulled me to his side, tucking me into him. Unlike our usual time spent in his bed, he didn't try to seduce me or drive me to distraction with his mouth.

He just held me.

I laid my head against his chest, and his steady heartbeat was like a soothing balm on my nerves. With each of his breaths, my head lifted slightly, and soon, my eyes were closing as sleep pulled at me.

He stroked my hair, his hand moving up and down my back and arms. They were soft, lulling motions that made me shiver with need while wanting to sleep simultaneously.

A soft knock came on the door, and then Balbus bustled through with an enormous tray.

"My prince and lady." He bowed. "Where shall I set this, Your Highness?"

"By the fire is fine, Balbus."

The servant did as asked, moving around the room on ghostly steps until everything was ready for our meal before departing just as quickly.

Once we were alone again, my mate lifted me and carried me to the couch, and I let him since I knew keeping me close and feeling that he was doing something to protect and care for me were what his instincts demanded.

"Are you warm enough?" His brow furrowed, worry lining his eyes as he settled me on the sofa.

I sat back more and tucked my legs beneath me. "Yes, I'm fine."

He proceeded to dish up a plate for me, and I ate everything on it. He joined in, eating his fill, but his eyes never left mine as he watched me carefully, as though he was afraid I would pass out again or the pain in my gut would resurface.

When I finally finished, he whisked my plate away and cleaned everything up before returning to my side. The couch sank under his heavy weight.

I nestled against him and trailed a finger up his chest. Even though the aura around him began to rise as desire tingled in my belly, neither of us acted on it. It seemed both of us were content to enjoy the quiet, the feel of our arms wrapped around the other, while we enjoyed our solitude. It was all oddly peaceful despite what had happened, and the bond deep inside me hummed.

It was crazy that in all of the months I'd been in this castle, we'd had so little down time with just the two of us. We were always working, training, learning, or trying to save the fields. Hardly any of our time had been devoted to just us, and since I'd only recently discovered that he was my mate, it felt like I'd been living in a fog the entire time I'd been here.

"I'm sorry for how I treated you when we first met," I said quietly.

His wandering hands, gliding along my back and arms, stopped. He tilted my chin up, forcing me to meet his gaze. "Why? You have nothing to be sorry for."

"I do. I thought you were a monster, and I treated you horribly. I have everything to be sorry for."

His breath stuttered, and then he pulled me up his chest, draping me across his body.

Instinctively, I straddled him. Our lips met as his hands settled on my hips, gripping me to him as my hands splayed across his shoulders.

He kissed me softly, reverently at first, but then heat between us began to build. In a sweep of power, the prince had me in his arms and was striding toward his bed. We fell onto it in a tangle of limbs as his wings stretched around us.

"I want to make you mine so badly," he said, kissing along my throat.

I arched into his touch, breathless as he trailed kisses down my neck. "Tomorrow, after the final test."

He stopped, his head lifting. "Truly?"

"Yes, I just need my mind clear until then and not gripped in the haze of a newly sealed mate bond."

With a growl, he stripped me of my clothing, and then devoured me in earnest.

I arched against him as a low, pulsing ache uncurled deep in my belly. He soon had me writhing against him, feral in my desire as my naked body was his to attend.

I was clinging to his shoulders, my lips swollen from his demanding kisses and my fingers like claws as aching lust burned through me.

The prince picked up the potion from Murl. Before I could ask what he was doing, he brought the vial to my mouth and tipped it between my lips.

I swallowed it hastily, my grip questioning as his large hands moved down my sides to spread my legs.

"Let me make you come," he said huskily. "After you climax, the potion will kick in, and you'll fall into a deep sleep."

A smile curved my lips. "You sound quite confident in your ability to pleasure me."

His look turned reverent as he dipped lower in the bed, positioning himself over the edge as his mouth came to my core. "I was born to pleasure you, Ilara Seary."

"But what about you?" I asked before he could make good on that promise. "If the potion makes me sleep right after, what about your pleasure?"

He shook his head, his eyes like blue diamonds as he

regarded me in the firelight. "Tonight is about you. My mate. My queen."

My breath sucked in when his tongue ran up my center, and then my head was tipping back, my hands clawing the sheets as he laved me with his tongue.

His mouth had the waves building inside me so quickly, so easily. He licked and sucked, eating me out in a way that was nearly feral.

"I could suck your pussy all night," he murmured as he paused only long enough to slide a finger inside me. He hooked it at the end, scraping against me as though he knew exactly where my body would respond most.

I bucked against him, and the satisfied expression on his face was overpowering.

"You'll always be *my* female." He licked me again, the motion teasing as he began pumping his finger into me. His gaze darkened into a carnal and savage expression that made me almost come just looking at him. "You are mine, Ilara Seary. Tell me you are. Tell me that only I will ever be the one to touch you, fuck you, love you from this moment forward."

My breath caught. *Love.*

I nodded and was unable to speak as my head tilted back when he licked, then sucked my clit into his mouth, biting it to the point that my breath stopped completely.

I forced myself to gasp in air as my legs trembled with the uncoiling climax that kept building and building.

"Say it, Ilara."

"Yes, I'm yours, Norivun Deema Melustral Achul, from now until the end of time."

A ferocious and victorious snarl emerged from him, and

then he gave me what I wanted, latching his mouth and tongue to me as he relentlessly used his fingers to heighten the experience.

And when my orgasm ripped through me, I saw stars. My body spasmed as if lightning had struck me, and a scream caught in my throat. I could barely breathe, let alone think as my body pulsed around him.

And afterward, as I was coming down from the high, with my hands still entwined in his hair, he crawled up my body, his heavy cock throbbing against my stomach. But he didn't push for anything more. He demanded nothing of me as the blissful aftereffects of my pleasure wrapped around me as the potion began to take hold.

"Sleep, my love," he said softly as he trailed kisses up my neck before coming to my mouth.

I had just enough energy to kiss him back, and my touch was a promise that next time, the pleasure would be his.

As though understanding, he chuckled deeply. "Oh, my sexy mate, you have no idea what I'm going to do to you tomorrow night."

It was the last thing I heard before sleep claimed me, and the darkness pulled me under.

CHAPTER 30

I awoke feeling as though I'd slept for a thousand nights. Sunlight pierced my closed eyes. I stretched languidly and reached for Norivun. My searching fingers encountered his supple wings.

I opened my eyes to find him on his elbow, his face cupped in his hand as early morning sunshine shone on his silvery locks. I cocked my head. "Have you been watching me?"

He leaned down and kissed me softly. "I have."

My cheeks warmed as I stretched again. "For how long?"

He tenderly brushed a lock of hair from my face. "For most of the night."

"You didn't sleep?"

He kissed me again, and a flutter began in my stomach. "I slept enough. But I wanted to watch you. Last night was the last time in which you won't be fully bonded to me. Tonight, you will be entirely mine."

My toes curled, and I wrapped a leg around his waist. He growled, and when he shifted closer, I realized both of us were still naked. His hard shaft pressed against my abdomen, and I wanted so badly to spread my thighs and have him sink inside me, but today was my final test.

I needed to prepare.

"I should go back to my chambers and get ready."

He kissed me again, nodding regretfully. "I know. How does your magic feel today?"

I felt inside my gut for it, and a pulse of worry strummed through me when I sensed that whatever had encapsulated it was still there. "It's the same."

His hopeful smile vanished, and then he was off the bed and striding across his chambers. His huge wings and taut backside snagged my attention, until he said, "I'm going to find Murl, then talk to my father and Sir Featherton. If your magic is compromised, they need to postpone the final test."

My eyes widened. I hadn't even considered that being a possibility. "Do you think they will?"

"They must."

I MISTPHASED BACK to my chambers, relieved that my magic worked enough to do that, although the amount of effort it took was worrisome.

Cailis was snoring quietly and still in bed when I appeared in the Exorbiant Chamber, but as soon as I made a sound, she sat up and rubbed her eyes. "Ilara? What time did you get in?"

"Just now."

"You were with the prince again?"

"I was. Sorry to wake you."

She shook her head. "Don't be. I'm glad I get to see you before your final test."

She scrambled up, and since nervous energy was already buzzing around her, I didn't tell her about what had happened in Isalee.

"Hungry?" she asked.

"Always."

She rang for food, and within minutes, Patrice, Balbus, and Haisley were at the door. All three of the prince's personal servants arrived with jubilant expressions and hands clapping in glee.

"Can you believe that at this time tomorrow we shall be addressing you as, *Your Highness*?" Patrice bowed deeply.

"I knew from the moment I saw you that you were destined for great things," Haisley said in a nasally tone, then matched Patrice's bow.

Balbus merely looked down his nose at the two of them. "Leave the lady be. She needs to get ready and eat a hearty breakfast. We shall be transporting to the stadium in two hours' time."

"Stadium?" I cocked my head.

"Oh my, she doesn't know!" Patrice brought an aghast hand to his mouth.

"Know what?" But before anyone could answer, Daiseeum bustled into the room.

Tense energy vibrated around her as she shooed the prince's servants away. "Out! All of you! Ilara needs to concentrate and ready herself for what's to come today."

My mouth fell open. "But . . . hasn't the final test been postponed?"

All of the servants froze as Cailis gave me a quizzical look.

"Postponed?" Haisley replied. "No, Lady Seary, the entire castle is readying for the test at this very moment."

I gave a tight-lipped smile. *Of course.* Norivun must not have reached his father or Sir Featherton yet. Things were still on schedule.

The servants turned into a flurry of activity again, so I grabbed Balbus's hand. "Balbus, please find the prince. He was going to speak with Murl, Sir Featherton, and his father. Will you please ask him to come see me when he finishes?"

Balbus frowned. "I shall try, Lady Seary, but the king has already begun issuing orders. I'm unsure if I'll be able to do as you request."

A stone formed in my stomach. The tension building within me grew more and more with every second that passed.

"Please try," I begged of him.

Balbus bowed. "Of course, my lady."

He hurried off as Daiseeum's lips pursed. "Sit and eat. We shall dress you as soon as you finish."

I did as she said even though anxiety was threatening to swallow me. *Balbus will find the prince. Norivun is probably talking to Sir Featherton and his father at this very second. Everything will be fine.*

I forced food into my mouth as I reassured myself again and again.

But the minutes ticked past, and neither Balbus nor Norivun appeared.

"This was made for today. The king insisted that each female be dressed in her Territory's colors." Daiseeum held up a beautiful green tunic.

I fingered the soft, supple fabric. It stretched easily yet felt warm and sturdy.

"What's it made of?" I asked distractedly and eyed the door again as my sister cast me another anxious glance.

"A magically synthetic fabric. The tailor has been working on it ever since the Trial began. It's warm, lightweight, bends and flows with every flex of your body, and shall whisk away any perspiration. It truly is the work of a master craftsman, if I do say myself."

"Okay," I said hesitantly.

More minutes ticked by without a word from Balbus or the prince, and my stomach roiled. My magic still rumbled in my belly—that constant feeling that I'd grown so used to in the past few months that I hardly noticed it anymore—but whenever I dipped into it or tried to access it, it felt as though I was tugging a heavy blanket through a tiny hole.

Thankfully, my magic responded if I pulled hard enough— like I'd had to when I'd mistphased back to my room—but it was resisting me. As if something tried to stop it.

"Ilara, what's wrong?" my sister asked me quietly.

"It's my magic. It's not responding normally."

The worry in her eyes grew just as my door flew open, and Balbus rushed into the chamber.

His hair was in disarray, his cloak fluttering behind him. "Lady Seary, I offer a thousand apologies, but the prince is unable to come. The king has summoned him and is refusing to let him leave the throne room as the royal party prepares to depart for the stadium."

All of the blood drained from my face. "So the final test will continue?"

"Yes, my lady. But the prince did send for Murl, who shall arrive shortly."

I twisted my hands but took some comfort in that. Maybe, just maybe, the healer had been able to find something to fix my magic in the texts he'd consulted last night.

EVERYTHING BECAME a blur as I was whisked from my chambers by two guards I didn't know. Cailis was forced to stay behind, and when I asked them if I could talk to Matron Olsander, that was denied too.

Before I could blink, I was on my way to the stadium in a jostling carriage pulled by four domals. The one blessing was that Murl had arrived just in time to jump into the carriage before it departed.

I grabbed his hands. "Did you find anything in your books last night?"

The carriage passed through the castle's wards, and the streets of Solisarium appeared around us.

Murl shook his head, his expression grave. "I'm sorry, my lady. I did not. Perhaps if I had more time, I would have been able to."

I let out a breath, the reality of what was happening falling upon me. "So I have to partake in this test even though my magic is weakened."

His eyes dimmed, and he squeezed me tightly. "I'm so sorry, my lady. I tried to bring you several potions that would give you temporary strength and speed, but the guards took them off me, stating that no potions of any kind are allowed before the final test."

I sat back as distant cheers flowed through the carriage's windows. With each creak and jostle, we were getting closer to the stadium. Closer to where I would battle Georgyanna with diminished magic. Closer to where my fate would be decided.

When we arrived at the stadium, I didn't have time to ask Murl anything else, let alone thank him for everything that he'd done and had tried to do.

I was escorted out of the carriage as spectators cheered and went wild. Fae were everywhere. Not only flying in the air, but lining the streets, and the cheers coming from inside the stadium told me that thousands of citizens were present.

Four guards ushered me inside as the crowd threatened to swallow me.

My heart beat harder and harder and harder. I still hadn't seen Norivun, and I searched frantically for him in the crowd. But he was nowhere to be seen, and then I was inside the stadium and being led down a stone stairwell. I asked repeatedly what was happening but didn't get a response.

Anger began to swirl inside me, but I pushed it down. Nobody would tell me anything, but I knew the guards were only following orders. Either the king or Sir Featherton had silenced them.

When we reached the bottom of the stairwell, the guards led me through a narrow tunnel underneath the stadium. Footsteps and hollering came from above, echoing through the stone walls.

We stopped at a room underneath the large complex, and one of the guards shoved me inside. "Wait here."

He closed and locked the door, and my breaths were coming so fast now that I felt lightheaded. Nothing but cool stone and shimmering candles surrounded me. There weren't even fairy lights to illuminate the space.

I closed my eyes while trying to steady myself and prepare for what was to come. I had no idea what lay above me or what the final test would entail, but I couldn't lose even if my magic was impaired.

No matter what, I had to win this test and marry the crown prince.

IT FELT like much too soon, but not long enough, before the door to the tiny room opened, and I was ushered out and taken up another set of stone stairs.

Guards surrounded me, as if I was a prisoner. The irony of it made my stomach twist into knots because if I won this Trial, I would be the continent's queen. All of these guards would bow to me and do as I commanded with Prince Norivun at my side. We wouldn't have a marriage like his parents. I knew my mate would treat me as an equal and seat me beside him on my own throne.

When we reached the top of the stairs, the sun shone down brightly into the open stadium. Frigid air swirled about as the pale-green sky was clear and cloudless, as if the gods were smiling down on us and the capital's celebration.

"You're to wait here until the test begins." One of the guards pointed to an area on the arena's floor. A small X had been placed there.

I took the position as instructed and waited for whatever was to begin, but the second the crowd became aware of my presence, they went wild.

Screams and yells cascaded through the stadium. A flash of purple across the arena caught my attention. Georgyanna stood opposite me, coming from a tunnel on the other side of the open arena, emerging from it just like I had.

At least a quarter of a millee separated us. The stadium was so huge that it could easily seat thousands upon thousands of the capital's residents.

And not one of those seats was empty.

Ignoring Georgyanna, I searched the crowd, trying to find the prince. My eyes fell on the dais in the middle of the stadium, hovering directly over the arena and undoubtedly with the best view. Now that I'd spotted it, I didn't know how I hadn't immediately zeroed in on it.

King Novakin sat on his throne, his sons at his side. My breath sucked in. I could practically feel the power emanating from Norivun. He sat rigidly in full-black attire, royal embellishments on his chest and shoulders, and the shining silver crown on his head made him look every inch a royal. It was the first time I'd ever seen him wear a crown. But it was a prince's crown, small and simple, nothing like the crown perched atop his father's head.

Despite his resplendent attire, it was the look on Norivun's face that truly captured my attention. His features were a mask of fury encased in ice, and the way he stared at the king with murder in his gaze made my heart beat even harder. He looked as though he wanted to kill the king.

Behind them, Queen Lissandra sat on a smaller throne, and the king's throne blocked her view.

I didn't have time to assess anything further since Sir Featherton bustled out to the center of the arena and used a magical device to project his voice. "Good morning, sons and daughters of the Solis continent! I welcome you to this fine day in which we welcome our rising queen to the royal family."

The crowd went wild as Sir Featherton dipped in a low bow toward the king and queen.

"Queen Lissandra has ruled by our blessed king's side for many centuries, and she will continue to do so until our king is ready to step down. When that day comes, we shall always hold her dear in our hearts, and she shall remain a beckoning light in our memories. Her beauty and kindness have surpassed all of our great continent's presiding queens, and I know that she is beloved among all of us."

Everyone stood in their seats and angled to face the dais. Each and every citizen brought a fist to their chest and bowed deeply toward their queen.

Queen Lissandra rose from her throne and brought a fist to her chest in return, nodding her head in quiet acceptance of their love and praise.

The crowd cheered again, their love for their queen obvious, but the second Sir Featherton turned his attention to the king, their cheers rose even higher.

"And our great king, King Novakin, is why we're here today on the Eve of Olirum. It is his great foresight and strong leadership that has created this Trial that shall once again prove to our realm the strength and might of the powerful Solis race!"

The roar became deafening.

I bristled from where I stood. Sand shifted beneath my feet. My hands clenched into fists as the king, oblivious to the daggers I was mentally shooting at him, seemed to relish the cheers and roars of the fae around him.

It made me want to scream in fury.

After the crowd finally quieted, Sir Featherton spoke of the affinities Georgyanna and I held as the crowd oohed and awed under his theatrical performance. The entire time I felt Norivun watching me, but I couldn't look at him. This was happening. There was no way out of it, and I couldn't let anything distract me.

"And now, without further ado. May I present your rising queens." Sir Featherton spread his arms wide, his right arm going toward me and his left toward Georgyanna. He beckoned us closer as the wild cheers rose again.

Georgyanna and I walked toward him. I took in the expanse of the arena and the thousands upon thousands of Solis citizens who had arrived for today's final test.

"I'm sure you're all wondering how the victor will be decided today," Sir Featherton said, stopping Georgyanna and me with his hand motions when we were halfway to reaching him. He halted in a dramatic pause as everyone seemed to hold their breath. "There shall be many perils and challenges presented to our future queen today. The winner . . . will be the first to reach the crown."

As if on cue, a pillar abruptly rose from beneath the sand just behind Sir Featherton. It shot from the ground to rise high above and wait fifty feet in the air. Seated atop it was a crown worthy of a queen.

The crowd sucked in a collective sound of breaths as the glittering gems and jewels upon it sparkled in the sunlight.

Sir Featherton beamed. "This crown shall one day be worn by one of you as you sit atop the queen's throne."

I eyed Georgyanna from the distance that spanned us. Her gaze had fixated upon the crown as a dark snarl twisted her features. I knew she would do whatever was needed to reach that crown.

But I would too.

CHAPTER 31

S ir Featherton raised his arms. "On my mark." His finger pointed upward as familiar sparks and fireworks of magic exploded from his hand. A dazzling three appeared in the sky.

"Two." Another firework of magic shot up as the three disappeared. A flaming two appeared in the sky, hovering where the three had been only a second prior.

My muscles tensed and coiled. I felt again for my magic. It was still there, but crap, something still covered it.

"One."

The second he uttered the final word, he was whisked off the arena's floor, and a blast of magic rocketed into me. The ground moved, shifting and vibrating, and then chasms split open in the sand as a flood of insects lifted from beneath the stadium.

Georgyanna leaped back as the ground split before her as well.

My eyes widened when a swarm of stinging nettles suddenly clouded the air in front of me.

Terror slid through my veins. The deadly insects were only found on the southernmost tip of our continent, but the potency of their venom was legendary. One prick from a single stinger would paralyze a fairy until their lungs seized completely, and their heart stopped. To have a swarm of them buzzing toward me at this very second . . .

"Blessed Mother, help me," I prayed.

Georgyanna seemed in a similar state of panic as she staggered back. She raised her hands, and a huge gust of her electric affinity flew from her. The buzzing creatures seized midair but didn't fall as electricity spiraled through them.

I called upon my magic, trying to do the same, but to my horror it was once again sluggish to respond.

I ran backward, stumbling away from the nettles, as Prince Norivun shot to standing.

I tripped when a dozen rocks suddenly appeared behind me. The arena's floor was shifting and moving with every breath I took—just another trick of the final test.

I screamed in fury that my magic wasn't responding, and perhaps it was the panic in my call, but a flash of my fire element abruptly blazed around me.

The swarm of nettles incinerated in midair, but it had been so close. One of the insects had only been feet away from me before my magic finally responded.

Georgyanna was already through her cloud of deadly insects and sprinting toward the crown. She tried to spread her wings and fly toward it, but a zap of magic appeared from the air and stifled her flight.

I called upon my mistphasing magic, but whatever was zinging through the air, zapped that out of me too.

As if sensing that magic was working against our powers, Georgyanna began to run. I pushed to my feet and did the same, legs pumping beneath me as our eyes met across the arena.

The crowd continued to cheer and roar, as a look of feral victory glowed in the Kroravee native's eyes.

But before either of us could reach the pillar, the ground shook again, and a new cavern opened, but instead of deadly insects, a gush of water rose and flooded the arena.

The crowd screamed in surprise as Georgyanna and I did the same.

The water rose swiftly, first to my ankles, then my knees, then my waist. Before I knew it, I was swimming through powerful currents, trying to reach the pillar as the water rose like a torrential flood.

I called upon my magic again. If I could just create a buoy of air beneath me, I could rise above the water.

But my magic didn't respond. Once again, I was begging it to heed my command.

Beneath the swirling, dark water, something tugged on my foot. I barely had time to suck in a lungful of air before a tentacle curled around my ankle and pulled.

I went under.

Panic reared in me. I fought the currents.

It was no use.

Dark, gushing water flooded my sight as the creature tugged me into the depths.

Down.

Down.

Down, I went.

My lungs burned. I thrashed beneath the surface and tried to work myself free. Something squealed when my free leg connected with a fleshy mass.

My ankle released.

I kicked and swam upward, but then a dark shape swam past my line of vision. Panic consumed me again when I recognized one of the deadly predators of the Brashier Sea. It was the same creature that had swum in the Bay of Nim.

I surfaced and gasped for air, just as a huge fin cut through the water. Across from me, about a hundred yards away, Georgyanna sat on a boat as the crowd continued to scream and yell.

I blinked. A boat. She sat on a *boat*. She'd obviously created it using her constructo affinity while I'd been underwater.

Victory shown in her vicious grin as she paddled toward the pillar, just as the predator with the tall fin began to circle me, creating a whirlpool effect.

Prince Norivun pumped his fists, his wings fully extending as veins protruded in his neck. But he couldn't interfere. If he did, I would be disqualified, and Georgyanna would automatically be declared the winner.

Closing my eyes, I tried to find the calmness within me. I needed to get out of this turbid water.

Breathing deeply, I latched onto my magic through the thin veil and siphoned it slowly through the netting. Cold winter wind continued to flow over my face, but sweat beaded on my forehead despite the frigid water.

The predator's whirlpool began to suck me down.

Around and around.

Faster and faster I spun through the water.

Slowly, my magic responded.

A cushion of air formed beneath me and pushed me up. I called upon more of it, and I rocketed above the swirling currents just as the predator's jaws closed over the water where I'd been swimming only seconds prior.

My air element shot me up, moving me into the sky. The crowd clapped and cheered as the water began to recede beneath me.

Just as quickly as the huge pool had been formed on the arena's floor, it vanished, sucked away as it moved through pipes or magical siphons.

Georgyanna howled in fury as the water and predators disappeared, and her boat suddenly landed on wet sand.

I called upon my affinity more. With enough magic, I could use the wind to blow me toward the top of the pillar where I could snatch the crown and place it atop my head, but just when I tried to wrench more from my gut, a whip of magic burst through the arena, and I plummeted to the ground.

I landed on all fours, panting as the ground shifted beneath me. Georgyanna's arms went wide to steady herself just as vines shot up from beneath the sand, coiling and growing at an unnatural rate. They wrapped around my wrists, ankles, and torso, doing the same to Georgyanna.

Fire immediately cleaved from her, burning the plants as quickly as they ensnared her, but my fire was sluggish to respond, and my air was tapped out from my weakened state.

Thick roots encircled me again and again, trapping me in their embrace as Georgyanna effectively cut through hers using a combination of her fire and constructo affinities. Blades conjured from the sand cleaved the plants at their roots, freeing her quickly.

I closed my eyes, gasping for breath as the vines tightened their hold. Panic began to consume me anew, but then I remembered what Sandus had taught me—the warrior moves used to burst free of restraints when one's magic was doused.

Snarling with the effort, I released my hold on my trapped magic, letting it fall back into my gut. With a bend of my knees and a twist of my elbows, I reverted to the months of daily training the warrior guard had instilled in me.

The vines twisted and writhed, but I swung and tore, dipping and maneuvering out of their suffocating embrace as I used the skills and movements the guard had taught me.

Sweat poured from my brow as the winter wind blew over my wet clothing. My muscles strained, but slowly, I made my way toward the column, fighting and straining for every step that I won.

But just when the column was within my grasp, Georgyanna reached the other side. A burst of electricity shot into me as the vines disappeared back into the ground, and the sand beneath me suddenly rose higher and higher, hardening into bricks at my sides.

My breath stuttered. Pain sliced through me as the burn from the electricity set my nerves on fire. Through the haze of my sizzling essence, I glanced toward the other female. I thought for certain Georgyanna would be in a similar state, but the twisted smile on her face made my heart nearly stop.

This new challenge wasn't the test's magic. Georgyanna was using *her* affinities against me. Again. Just as she had during the second test and when she'd tried to kill me on the balance beam.

She seemed to sense the second I did that I was weaker than her. A maniacal cackle split her lips as her constructo affinity stacked the sand, solidifying it into bricks around me. The bricks rose higher, then higher. She was burying me alive.

"No!"

An oily tendril suddenly curled around my mind, and then—

I'm going to die.

She's going to kill me.

I screamed when thousands of tiny bugs appeared everywhere upon my skin.

I'm being buried alive.

Eaten alive.

Blessed Mother, save me!

The insects crawled along my skin and burrowed into my flesh. I thrashed and swatted at them, but they remained. Eating. Digging. Skittering.

Get them off me! Oh Mother Below!

Brick after brick continued stacking. I kicked at the solid sand, but it was too solid to crumble.

Georgyanna's wicked grin spread wider.

My vision grew hazy.

Another electric burn skated over my skin. I screamed again.

Burning alive.

Buried alive.

Eaten alive.

Someone. Anyone. Save me!

Something rumbled in my gut. *Magic.* For a brief second my mind cleared. I glimpsed my magic, reached for it, *begged* for it—

Georgyanna's magic increased.

A fresh electric sting seized me as a thousand more insects appeared.

Oh gods! They're eating me again!

No.

No.

NO!

I'm going to die. I'm going to die.

A small, aching part of me knew that I was losing. Georgyanna was defeating me because something in the Isalee field had caged my power.

And then the crowd was cheering. Through the echo of pain in my mind came the jeers and roars.

A commanding voice spoke over the wildness of the citizens as the brick cage around me abruptly stopped. The bugs halted their burrowing. The knives cleaving my mind pulled away.

And then the sandy bricks burying me alive just . . . melted.

The oily sheen coating my mind finally, *blessedly*, receded.

I sucked in a deep breath of air as my entire body shook.

The last to go was Georgyanna's electrical affinity. It felt as if my skin had peeled off my body, but when I glanced down, nothing but smooth intact flesh stared back at me.

I blinked, my chest heaving, as the remnants of Georgyanna's power fully disappeared.

And then I was staring at what lay before me, shivering in

the brutal winter wind as reality refused to penetrate the dissipating fog from my brain.

Standing above me, Georgyanna was wearing the crown.

She dipped low into a curtsy, her fist to her chest as the crowd cheered around us.

King Novakin grinned from his dais as the crown prince yelled with so much fury that eight guards forced him away under the king's command.

And when I finally accepted that what I was seeing wasn't a trick of the mind and was actual reality, my heart shattered into a million pieces.

Georgyanna wore the queen's crown.

Georgyanna had won the final test.

Georgyanna would marry the prince.

I failed.

Sir Featherton beamed as he spun in a circle on the arena's floor. All of the magical tricks and illusions had vanished. Once more, I was lying on the dry, sandy ground as the citizens of our great continent welcomed their next queen.

King Novakin stood from his throne, and with amplifying magic addressed the crowd. "May I present the next queen to grace the Solis continent, the female who will lead with my son, the crown prince Norivun Deema Melustral Achul. In one month's time, he shall wed Lady Georgyanna Endalaver, daughter of Kroravee Territory!"

CHAPTER 32

I stood frozen in time. Couldn't move. Couldn't think. Couldn't speak. *How? How has this happened?*

I didn't have time to process any of it before the door opened from the arena's side, and guards ushered out Meegana and Beatrice. They were both wide-eyed, their faces ashen, and I had a feeling they'd been spectators in the crowd and had just witnessed my downfall.

How has this happened?

The king's grin grew as he waved toward the two new females that had joined us.

"As you know, I've enacted the Olirum Accords, an ancient Solis tradition that once served a great purpose on our mighty continent. Our strength and power shall grow again with each union that blesses our court with a new babe, so without further ado, I would like to announce the additional betrotheds for you all to welcome. Lady Meegana Ockson, daughter of Harrivee Territory, shall marry Lord William Waterline, son of Osaravee Territory."

Meegana blanched as the crowd cheered more.

The king waved toward Beatrice. "And Lady Beatrice Leafton, daughter of Prinavee Territory, shall marry Lord Dameel Brusher, son of Mervalee Territory."

Cheers rose higher and higher.

The king's grin grew. "And of course, our runner-up shall not be left empty-handed." King Novakin turned his malicious smile on me, and all of the sadistic pleasure he wore shone in that horrifying grin. "Ilara Seary, daughter of Mervalee Territory, shall marry Lord Arcane Woodsbury, the third son of Isalee Territory."

I nearly doubled over and vomited right there. Lord Arcane Woodsbury. The pedophile who enjoyed hurting animals. I wanted to wither and die.

I shivered anew in the frigid wind. I could *never* marry a male like that, let alone have his children.

"And without further ado," Sir Featherton said with a beaming smile, "let us begin the celebrations. Lady Endalaver, please join us as we return to the castle and the festivities begin."

Georgyanna preened and nodded, blowing the king a kiss, which made the monarch chuckle.

The Kroravee winner gave me an evil glare before she said under her breath, "I knew I would beat you, but it doesn't end here, Ilara. I will remember how you humiliated me in this Trial. Your time will come in which I'll make you pay. Once I'm queen, you'll wish that you were never born."

And with that, she sauntered off with the guards as I was left with Meegana and Beatrice, both of whom looked as though they were about to burst into tears.

❄

I WAS FORCED to attend the festivities. Forced to sit in the suffocating dining hall as the king sat at the head of the table with Georgyanna on one side of him and Prince Norivun on the other. The crown prince looked as though he was about to enact his death affinity. Every time he glanced at his father, hatred burned in his gaze. But the king must have known of the potential wrath he would face. Queen Lissandra sat right beside Norivun, and with one order from the king, Norivun's mother would be removed from the hall to wait in her chambers for whatever horrific abuse the king chose to inflict on her.

Don't, I mouthed over and over to the prince, every chance I got.

The warring in his expression told me he was close to losing control. Close to throwing away his entire family to take me and flee from the capital, but even if the crown prince killed his father and every single council member who could take his stead, the Solis citizens would never forget the prince's horrific acts. They would hunt us down, thousands no doubt dying in the process when they faced the Death Master's affinity, but eventually they would win by sheer numbers. We couldn't guard ourselves in sleep, and we couldn't run forever.

Inevitably, Norivun would fall, then I would fall, and then anarchy would undoubtedly ensue as our great continent fell to pieces.

Don't, I mouthed again.

Norivun gripped his chair tightly, his knuckles white as King Novakin and Lady Endalaver danced and ate, sipped wine, and laughed.

Meegana, Beatrice, and I sat at the other end of the table with our newly declared fiancés sitting across from us. I couldn't look at any of them. All three of them were despicable males, and I could've sworn the king chose them for us merely to torment us.

Nuwin sat at the queen's other side, but his normal cheer and teasing mood were absent. A somber and distant aura had taken its place. He kept glancing toward his older brother, then down the table at me. The troubled expression on his face grew.

I didn't know why the king hadn't assigned Nuwin to marry one of the females. I could only imagine that he had other plans in store for his second son. And I knew that like us, Nuwin was powerless to stop it.

Hours upon hours passed in that dining hall. All I wanted to do was sink through my chair and pretend that this was all a bad dream and would go away.

But it wasn't a dream. I had lost the Trial. Norivun would marry Georgyanna, and I was to marry a sick pedophile.

My stomach was a tumultuous twist of nerves and anxiety, and for the first time since I'd learned the outcome of the Trial, I knew I couldn't stay.

I couldn't marry the creep across for me, and I certainly couldn't stand by and watch as the prince married the vile leech that sat beside the king.

My eyes flew to my sister's from across the room. Cailis was seated at one of the lesser tables, where family members of the more powerful fae were allowed.

She and I exchanged weighted looks. Her eyes softened, as

though she understood the desperation weighing upon my soul. *Tonight*, she mouthed.

I gave a subtle nod in return, and it felt as though my heart was shattering all over again.

I glanced down the table, toward my mate, my love, the male I'd wanted to claim tonight as my own, and I knew with an aching realization that such a bond was never to exist between us.

Even though the gods had made us for one another, the king had decided otherwise. He knew that Norivun was my mate and me his, yet I had no doubt King Novakin took perverse delight in the fact that we would both be wed to others.

So when the time came that we were finally dismissed from the table, I flew from the room with my sister at my side. I could feel the crown prince searching for me, striding toward me, but I couldn't see him again. I couldn't look upon his face and lie to him about what we planned to do. Every part of me was shattering into a thousand pieces over and over again, and one look or touch from him, and I would break beyond repair.

So we flew to my chambers, gathered the supplies that my sister had so carefully acquired yet we'd never thought we'd actually use, and then we stood gasping as the weight of what we were doing fell upon us.

"This will be seen as treason," I said quietly to her, giving her a chance to back out. She didn't need to go down with me.

She grabbed my hands. "I know."

A sob threatened to overtake me, but I swallowed it down and rubbed the tears from my eyes.

"Can you mistphase us?" she asked worriedly.

I felt for my magic. It was still trapped, still slow. I'd barely been able to mistphase myself from Norivun's room to here this morning, let alone a long distance with my sister at my side. "I don't think so."

"Then we'll use the escape tunnel near the training room."

I was about to agree when the door to my chambers abruptly opened. My heart locked in my throat.

"My queen?" I breathed.

"Ilara!" Queen Lissandra rushed to my side, her hair unbound, her expression frantic. "I know what's happened today. I know about your magic. Norivun told me."

"But—"

"Please listen. You must hurry. Guards are on their way here right now to remove you from the prince's wing." I blanched, but she carried on. "I know you've been planning to escape. I know what your sister's been doing."

Cailis and I shared a wild look, and then it struck me, what Cailis had said only weeks prior, that someone had been watching her in the castle. Following her.

It'd been the queen.

"Take this." The queen shoved two vials into my hand. "The orange one is a very rare potion that allows a fairy with minimal magic to mistphase anywhere in the realm. The other is a potion that will hide your whereabouts. I brought one for each of you. Nobody will be able to find you. Not a seer, not someone with the ability to scry. No one."

"What? But how—"

"Listen to me!" the queen said firmly, her eyes ablaze. "I know you're aware of what's been done to my magic—what the *king's* done to me. I've had these potions for full seasons in case I ever needed to escape and take the princes with me, but you need it more. You're stronger than me, Ilara. Our continent needs you. Use these potions now and escape to one of the other continents. You can't stay here. The king will find you. Escape to somewhere safe, to wherever you and your sister have planned. You need to regain your magic and return so you can fight the Solis king."

My blood ran cold that she was giving me the only potions she possessed with such rare capabilities.

"Don't argue." She pressed the vials more firmly into my grip. "Do as I say. *Please*."

"Yes, my queen." I gave a swift nod as distant boot steps sounded down the hall.

"I must go. May the Blessed Mother be with you." She kissed me on the cheek, and then she was gone.

Cailis turned wild eyes on me, and in a flurry, I grabbed a sheet of paper and a quill from my old writing supplies on the desk.

I hastily scribbled a note, then tucked it beneath my pillow as the footsteps grew louder. I knew that when Daiseeum found it, she would deliver it. The lady servant had been nothing but loyal, and I knew she would honor my one last wish.

Cailis's movements grew frantic as she collected our hidden bags. "Where should we go? We can't go to the Cliffs of Sarum, not if Norivun isn't with us and isn't able to grant us entry."

"I know, but I wouldn't go there anyway. We would be imprisoned, and right now is the time to act. Not hide."

"So where?"

"The Glassen Barrier Islands. It's the only option since I

don't know if anyone on the Nolus continent will allow us entry, but I'll need you to tell me immediately if Drachu can be trusted."

She nodded gravely as I uncapped the vials and drank the contents from both in a single gulp. Cailis uncorked hers and did the same. The potions burned through me, heating my blood, and in a blink, immense magic surged through me.

I grabbed my sister's hands just as the boot steps sounded outside my door. "Ready?"

She gave a terse nod and a shaky smile. "Ready as I'll ever be."

The mistphasing potion's magic surged forth just as the first guard appeared in the doorway. The guard shouted, rushing toward us, but the world was already disappearing in a blur of mist and shadows, air and wind, as I put all of my concentration on the one area of our realm I wanted us to go.

We moved through the realm like wraiths on the wind, and when our feet reappeared again, a glittery night sky bore down on us as pounding waves from a dark sea crashed against foreign shores.

My heart pounded. My chest threatened to cave in. We were gone. Our home was behind us. My love, my life, my friends, *all* of it was behind us now.

Cailis and I stood exactly where I'd been the night that I'd visited these islands with the crown prince all of those months ago. I didn't know if the Lochen king knew I was here or how long it would take for me to find him, but just when I thought for certain we would have to go in search, a presence came into existence behind me.

Drachu's power wafted over me, the sheer strength of it so strong.

Cailis's breath sucked in as I turned to face the ruler of the Lochen Fae. I squeezed her hand tightly, trying to communicate that *he* was the one I needed her to assess.

I wasn't surprised to see the familiar glowing orb that hung from around his neck shining bright green against his brown skin.

His lips curved in a knowing smile, as though he and I shared a secret.

I lifted my chin higher. "You told me once if I ever needed to escape the Death Warlord, that your shores were open to me. Does that offer still stand?"

Drachu's grin widened, revealing white teeth and sharp canines. "It does." His gaze didn't flick to my sister, not once.

"Will you keep us safe?" I asked.

His lips curved more. "The Lochen will guard you with our lives."

Cailis squeezed my hand once. *Truth.*

"And you won't keep us as prisoners or use us for your personal gain?" I pushed.

His eyebrows drew together. "Don't insult me. You are a queen, and you will be treated as such."

Cailis's lips tightened, and her brow furrowed. Her hand still held mine, but it took a moment before she squeezed once, but it wasn't a confident gesture. Under her breath, she said, "I think."

Confusion filled me. I wasn't a queen. I was a farm girl from Mervalee, but Drachu had always looked at me as if I was so much more.

I studied the necklace he wore again, wondering what it did. "Thank you," I finally replied. "For giving us safe haven."

Drachu grinned, the smile transforming his face into one of savage beauty. "Of course, *Krelahala*. I've been waiting for you to join my clan and for you to learn who you really are."

And with those cryptic words hanging between us, he prowled softly toward me, the sea lapping at his ankles, until he stood only inches away. His sheer size dwarfed my frame, forcing me to tilt my head back.

That smile stayed on his face, and even though nerves fluttered through me, I could only hope that I was making the right decision.

EPILOGUE

NORIVUN

My fingers shook as I took the paper from Daiseeum's outstretched hand. All night I'd been searching for her, hunting for my mate who'd fled from this castle and disappeared from my existence in a whisper of wind. I was in hell. My soul was in shreds. It felt as though Lucifer had captured my mind.

My mother had tried to console me, tried to tell me that right now, this was for the best. But my soul howled for Ilara. My dragon roared. My death affinity simmered beneath my skin, just waiting to be unleashed on the tyrant who sat atop the throne.

With shaking movements, Daiseeum bobbed a curtsy and fled from my chambers as my aura pounded into her back and into anyone that dared come near.

My stomach dropped when I recognized Ilara's hastily written scrawl across the paper, *Nori*.

Holding my breath, I peeled the paper open, and my gaze flew over the words as my power rose like a storm inside me.

My prince, my love, my mate,

Please forgive me for running. I want to be at your side just as you want to be at mine. But right now, I must go and find a way to fight what your father is trying to force upon us. Please know that just because I'm running from the court, does not mean that I'm running from you.

I will return. Somehow, someway, I will find my way back to you. I vow to keep my bargain with you to heal our land, and I vow to one day be the mate at your side.

Fight for me, Prince Norivun. Fight for us until we can find a way to defeat him.

I love you,

Ilara

My hands were shaking when I finished reading it, and then I read it again and again. Fire raged in my soul. Violence pounded through my blood. Darkness rose within me as revenge coated my senses and demanded that I claim vengeance for what had been done to my mate. My *love*.

A roaring wind spiraled through my veins as power rumbled the floor beneath my feet. I slid her letter into my tunic, keeping it close to my heart. I would read it each night. Read those words and scent her alluring essence that clung to the single page. Every time I felt my hope slipping, I would read it and remember.

Ilara would return. She would fight to stop the tyrant on the throne, and she asked that I fight in her absence.

Because one day we would be reunited, and I would be ready for her.

My mate.

My *queen*.

BOOK THREE IN FAE OF SNOW & ICE

I should have won the Rising Queen Trial. The crown that was destined to be placed upon my head now rests atop the vindictive witch who sought to steal my throne.

Left with no choice, I flee from the Solis continent even though my heart is shattering at leaving my love behind. But I can't return to Solisarium until I've reclaimed my affinities and am able to fight with the crown prince at my side.

Yet enemies lie everywhere, and those I thought I could trust prove to be the biggest traitors of them all.

Trapped far from the icy north, I struggle to survive while learning who I'm destined to become.

One thing I know—victory comes to those who are worthy—if only I can achieve the destiny the gods have created for me.

ABOUT THE AUTHOR

Krista Street loves writing in multiple genres: fantasy, sci-fi, romance, and dystopian. Her books are cross-genre and often feature complex characters, plenty of supernatural twists, and romance in every story. She loves writing about coming-of-age characters who fight to find their place in this world while also finding their one true mate.

Krista Street is a Minnesota native but has lived throughout the U.S. and in another country or two. She loves to travel, read, and spend time in the great outdoors. When not writing, Krista is either chasing her children, spending time with her husband and friends, sipping a cup of tea, or enjoying the hidden gems of beauty that Minnesota has to offer.

THANK YOU

Thank you for reading *Thorns of Frost* book two in the *Fae of Snow & Ice* series.

If you would like to know what Norivun was thinking when he first met Ilara, sign up for Krista's new release text alerts, and you'll receive a FREE digital copy of Chapter 3 from *Court of Winter*, told from Norivun's point of view.

Simply text the word NORI to 888-403-4316 on your mobile phone.

Message and data rates may apply, you'll only receive a text when Krista releases a new book, and you can opt out at any time. Visit Krista's website to learn more.

www.kristastreet.com/contact

Last, if you enjoyed reading *Thorns of Frost*, please consider logging onto the retailer you purchased this book from to post a review. Authors rely heavily on readers reviewing their work. Even one sentence helps a lot. Thank you so much if you do!

To learn more about Krista's other books and series, visit her website. Links to all of her books, along with links to her social media platforms, are available on every page.

Made in the USA
Monee, IL
23 December 2024

75224847R00224